Land of Monsters

USA TODAY BESTSELLING AUTHOR
STACEY MARIE BROWN

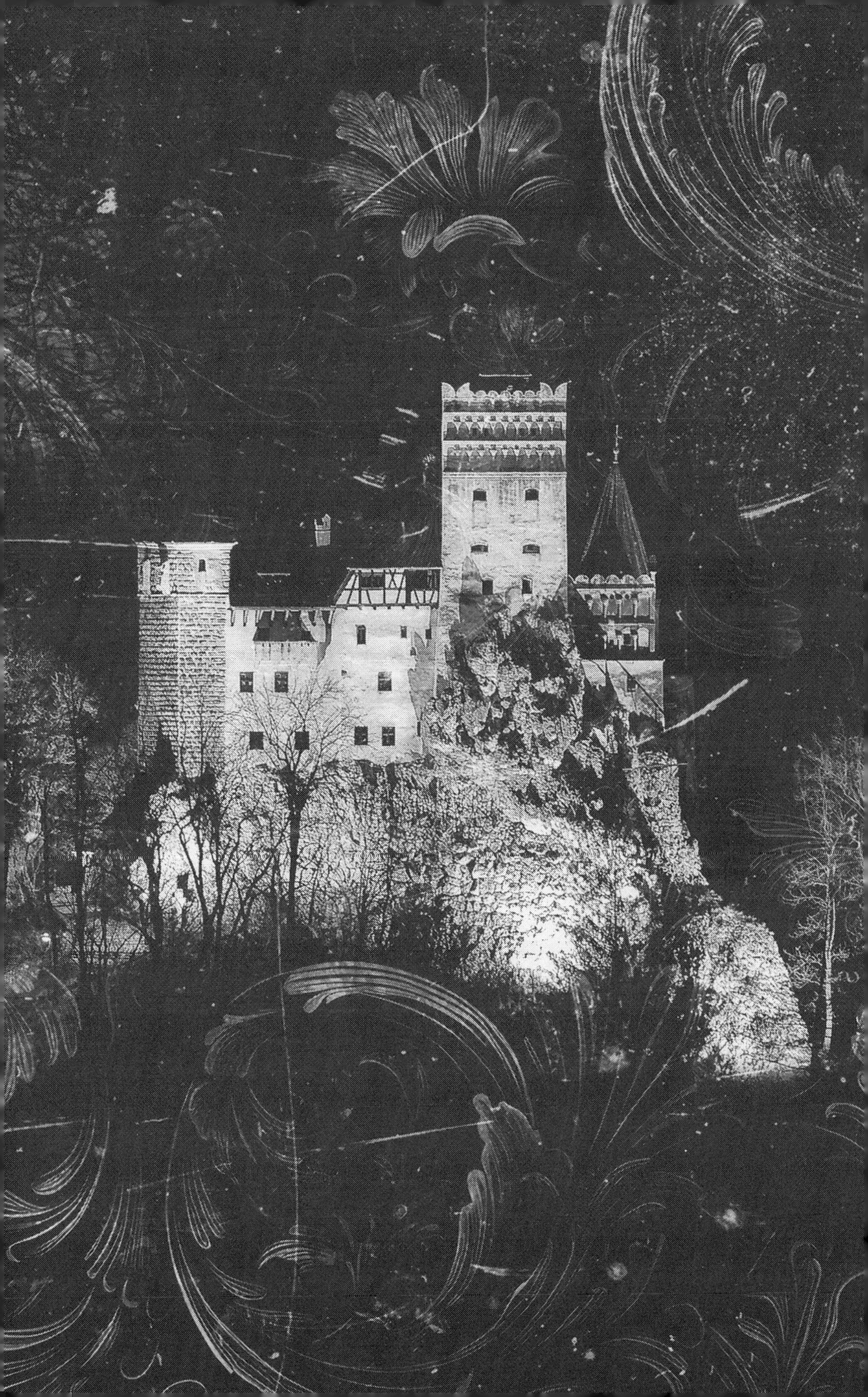

Land of Monsters, Copyright © 2024

This is a work of fiction. Any references to historical events, real people, or real locales are used fictitiously. Other names, characters, places and incidents are the product of the author's imagination and her crazy friends. Any resemblance to actual events, locales or persons, living or dead, is entirely coincidental.

This book is licensed for your personal enjoyment only. It cannot be re-sold, reproduced, scanned or distributed in any manner whatsoever without written permission from the author.

All rights reserved.

Published by: Twisted Fairy Publishing Inc.
Layout by Judi Fennell (www.formatting4U.com)
Cover by: Jay Aheer (www.simplydefinedart.com)
Edited by Mo at Comma Sutra Editorial (thescarletsiren.com) and Wendy Higgins (www.wendyhiggins.com)

ALSO BY STACEY MARIE BROWN

Paranormal Romance

Darkness Series
Darkness of Light (#1)
Fire in the Darkness (#2)
Beast in the Darkness (An Elighan Dragen Novelette)
Dwellers of Darkness (#3)
Blood Beyond Darkness (#4)
West (#5)

Collector Series
City in Embers (#1)
The Barrier Between (#2)
Across the Divide (#3)
From Burning Ashes (#4)

Lightness Saga
The Crown of Light (#1)
Lightness Falling (#2)
The Fall of the King (#3)
Rise from the Embers (#4)

Savage Lands Series
Savage Lands (#1)
Wild Lands (#2)
Dead Lands (#3)
Bad Lands (#4)
Blood Lands (#5)
Shadow Lands (#6)
Land of Ashes (#7)

Devil in the Deep Blue Sea
Silver Tongue Devil (#1)
Devil in Boots (#2)

FAIRYTALE RETELLINGS

Winterland Tales
Descending into Madness (#1)
Ascending from Madness (#2)
Beauty in Her Madness (#3)
Beast in His Madness (#4)

The Monster Ball Anthology
The Red Huntress

**See end of book for
Contemporary Romance
and
Foreign Translations**

Dedicated to the monsters waiting inside us.

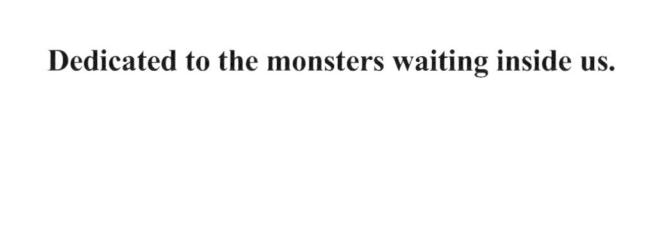

Chapter 1

Ash

Raven Haley Scarlet Dragen... I am the daughter of Queen Kennedy and Lorcan Dragen."

I trudged through the snow, my breath resounding in my ears as the freezing night sheared my lungs. Deadweight dangled in my arms, my own energy hanging by a thread. It was her heartbeat, her warmth, that pushed me to keep going, to get us to safety.

Snapping my gaze from side to side, I tried to see through the encroaching darkness, plucking out the danger that could still be looming around, lying in wait for us.

Or maybe what I was carrying was the most dangerous thing of all.

"I'm a dark dweller... and a Druid. Not just a Druid but a natural obscurer."

Alarm pricked up my neck at the rustling of brush behind me. I waited for men to step out of the forest, their bullets finding us in the night, the Russian Mafia coming to finish the job. Instead, a chilling chorus of howls from hungry wolves sang. Fear thumped a pulse in my neck. They could smell the blood covering us, wetting their palates.

Drained of magic, Raven curled into my chest. After her confession, whatever strength she had left gave out. Her system shut down and she fell to the rocky earth, her body going into healing mode. My body was close to blacking out, working hard to try and heal the bullet wound in my gut, but holding Raven ripped it open, causing fresh blood to trickle out, draining me of more energy than I was taking in from nature.

A low growl carried on the wind, chilling my blood and shoving out any thought except survival. I came to a stumbling stop, fear gripping my heart, when a deep snarl came from the darkness in front of us. More sounded from each side, the wolves circling their prey. In the dead of a cold, harsh winter, in an unforgiving land, food was scarce. And we were wounded and weak.

Over a dozen eyes reflected in the night, moving closer and closer. Various threatening sounds vibrated through the air, the wolves communicating with each other, ready for the alpha to give the attack call. Breath caught in my throat, my muscles locking as more of them inched closer. If I moved suddenly, they would strike.

Peering down at Raven's pallid face, I swallowed back my trepidation. Black blood was dried under her eyes, nose, and mouth, making her appear more threatening than the things hunting us. Yet there was something delicate about her as well, so vulnerable, creating a frantic need to protect her. My gun was empty, my energy waning, but I would at least die trying to fight, trying to save her.

Going against my instincts, I slowly lowered her down onto the snow, my hand sliding back to the pickaxe on my backpack, anger curling my lips.

Twelve massive gray wolves surrounded us like a noose, teeth bared and snarling. When the Otherworld and Earth meshed, the magic had transformed native animals. It had made them bigger. Stronger.

And they were hungry.

Stepping over Raven, I spun around, trying to keep eyes on each of them, but there were too many to keep in my sight. My back was always turned to a few. The moment I turned to one side, leaving myself unguarded, I presented them with an opening.

A growl shuddered up the back of my neck as I veered around, swinging the pick, the tip colliding with the wolf's paws. It tumbled back into the snow, a yip echoing in the air like a cry of war, summoning the troops.

They came at me with relentless precision, eager to take down their prey. Swinging the pick and scattering a few back, I kicked out, my boot cracking against a wolf's ribs while two more leaped for me, their teeth bared, saliva dripping from their mouths.

My howl of pain rang out when incisors sank into my arm. Swinging my weapon again, I nicked the one digging into my arm, prying it from me like a crowbar.

My attention was contained to one, leaving me wide open to the rest. Teeth snapped down on my calf, pain exploding into my nerves as the alpha shook his head, tearing through the muscle. My leg gave out, my body dropping to the ground. Once I was down, I knew it was over.

Another one went for my side when I tried to push back up, sinking its mouth into the open wound in my gut. A cry ripped from my throat as I tried to shove it off, pain causing me to tumble fully to the ground. I was dead. It was only minutes before they would tear into me, feasting on my flesh.

Raven would die here too, her family never knowing what happened to her. She would never have a full life… all because she followed me.

Get up. Get up now! Protect her! my brain ordered. My head lifted, my eyes squinting through the flakes of snow, spotting her body barely inches from mine. "Raven…" Her name was a rough whisper.

A wolf darted in for her, nipping at her arm, investigating the life left under the skin.

"No!" My voice was hoarse. Digging my fingers into the ground, I crawled to her. "Stay away from her!" I tried to cover her with my body as another one moved in. A growl vibrated the ground. Wrapping around her as much as I could, I waited for the end. I no longer felt teeth sink into me, my mind numbing the pain.

The air crackled with another threatening snarl. It was so deep I felt it wrap around my spine, boring into my gut. It took me a moment to realize the vibration was coming from under me.

Raven shoved herself up, her throat rumbling with a deadly threat. Black fur pushed out from her skin, the structure of her face changing slightly, her teeth pointed daggers. Deep crimson eyes flamed through the darkness.

"No." Raven's growl danced over the snow, razors bursting from her vertebra, her claws sharpening.

The pack stopped, one of them whining as it sniffed the air, sensing the danger. A change in prey and hunter. The alpha pranced, looking like it wanted to move in again, but wary of her. It understood she was the true alpha here. The one they should fear.

"Mine!" A roar rattled the air like an earthquake, her body lunging forward, her clawed fingers swiping out, nicking the muzzle of one.

Yips squealed in the air, the pack baying as if they had all been wounded before retreating into the forest. Their cries continued as they fled, growing fainter in the distance.

Her back to me, Raven heaved a heavy breath, the dark dweller retreating, leaving the petite girl standing there. Her clothes torn, her back curved over, her long hair tumbling in her face.

"Raven…" Her name was little more than a wheeze as I tried to sit up.

It was another few beats before she turned her head to me, blood trickling from her nose, the fire in her eyes draining back to green, revealing the girl underneath the beast.

"Ash." She mouthed my name before she dropped, landing hard on the icy ground.

Painful grunts spit through my lips as I shoved myself up onto my feet. With a groan, I grabbed the pick from the snowbank and hobbled over to her, my blood marking the ice like a connect-the-dots puzzle. Her knotted strands fanned out over the snow, her body arched like a Michelangelo painting, dying the landscape a rich red and black with her own blood.

My body screamed in agony, but I turned off my brain. Running off sheer will, I scooped her up in my arms.

Fresh black blood dampened the crusted stuff under her nose and eyes. Her skin was so pale I leaned my head against her chest to make sure her heart was still beating.

"Don't die on me," I demanded. "Not now, not after all this."

I was struggling to stay upright, dizzy from the pain and loss of blood. I had to get us out of the elements, away from the threat of more animals, the Russians, or even hypothermia. Raven was already trembling, her lips turning bluish.

Shuffling forward, I staggered toward the boarded-up stone ticket booth. The woodshed next to it was long depleted of kindling. The snow began falling heavier, freezing on my eyelashes, my breath billowing in front of my face. Placing Raven down again, my numb hands struggled to grip the handle of the pick. It weighed heavily in my palm as I hacked off the lock, clenching my teeth against the vibration as metal hit metal. The door swung open to a small hut that was dark and freezing, not much better than outside. At least it was some protection.

Zeroing all my energy into lifting her, I stumbled into the space. The only things left inside were a stool, an old calendar from before the Fae War, some maps of the cave and surrounding area, an outdated ticket machine, and a ratty rug in the middle. Placing Raven down on the carpet, I slammed the door behind us, putting us in almost complete darkness.

Fatigue was taking over, and I knew I couldn't stay up and guard. We were protected from the wolves but couldn't stop the Russians from finding us. Hoping they wouldn't notice the busted lock if they came by, I collapsed next to Raven as throbbing bile bubbled up my throat. I needed to rest. Heal.

The moment I laid down next to her, Raven's body jerked and trembled violently against mine.

"Raven?" I reached over, my fingers brushing over her skin. I was freezing, but her skin was ice. "Raven!" I gripped onto her, her body shaking so badly it was like she was convulsing. I couldn't make her out clearly in the darkness, but I knew hypothermia was setting in. She was already weak and vulnerable, but protecting me, saving my life, tipped her over. She had no immunity against the cold, not while her system was fighting to regain any strength from what happened in the caves. Shifting again when her shields were down was like setting a newborn in a snowbank for hours. She couldn't fight that too.

Small, pained cries gurgled in her throat.

"Fuck." She needed heat. And there was only one way to achieve it in a freezing hut with no source of outside warmth.

After ripping off my jacket and sweater, I fumbled with my pants, kicking off my boots at the same time. My bones cracked as I stripped in the arctic room. "Fuck!" I hissed again. Turning to her, I didn't hesitate, tugging off her ripped sweater. I rolled her over, undoing her cargo pants. They were damp from the snow, so I struggled to get them down her legs, finally peeling them off along with her boots. Leaving her in just tiny knickers and a sports bra, I lay next to her.

"I need to get you warm." I spoke more to myself than her, lying behind her and pulling her into my chest, using our discarded clothes as blankets.

Her body jackknifed and shivered, and I tucked in tighter around her, using my body to fully cover hers, pinning her in place. My legs and torso were her blanket.

My backside was freezing, but where my skin touched hers, it started to unthaw, the heat between us melting me into her. It took a while, but slowly, her muscles relaxed under me. Her breath evened out, and her heartbeat returned to normal.

The ground was painfully cold and hard as the wind outside rattled the door, but all I felt was her. Curling around her until there was no separation between us, I dug my head into her hair, letting sleep snatch me from consciousness. Raven's heartbeat was steady against mine, rocking me like a lullaby into oblivion.

Pale light stirred me from a deep slumber. Warmth ignited the front of my body, and I curled into it, wanting to drown in it. A deep-seated comfort I didn't want to wake from dragged my head deeper into darkness, trying to ignore my body stirring.

But reality flooded in swiftly, reminding me of everything that had happened yesterday. And why my backside was an ice cube while everything else was nestled in heat, my face hiding in her hair, my mouth against the curve of her neck.

Awareness slammed into me when I realized that not only was my dick hard and tucked in Raven's ass, but my arm was wrapped around her, my hand inside her panties, my fingers cupping her pussy like it was mine. My index finger pushed between her folds, curling inside her.

Holy. Fuck.

Jerking my hand away, I rolled over on my back, feeling her shiver the moment I moved. Scouring my hand over my face and through my hair, I could smell her on my fingers. As if they had been tucked inside her all night, saturated in her juices.

"*Szar*," I groaned, squeezing my lids together. I needed the icy air to cool me down, to take away this constant need thrumming through me. What was wrong with me? Every time I fell asleep with her, I woke up nuzzled in, touching her, about a hair away from fucking her.

It took just a minute for the temperature to prickle at my skin, forcing my lids open again. I seized another huge inhale and sat up, peering down at my healing wounds. Still red and tender to the touch, they at least had stopped bleeding. They were a touchstone, a reality check to everything that had happened last night. The truth of who she really was.

My gaze flew over to the curled-up figure, her torn jacket and sweater laying over her delicate frame. It was hard to liken this petite, stunning girl to the deadly creature I saw last night.

She saved my life… twice. However, I couldn't fight the betrayal I felt from her not telling me. From feeling like I was being deceived since day one.

Now I understood it was never the Russians who put the cuff on her wrist to lock away her powers. She had done it herself. To keep her powers in check, hiding them from the world.

There were so many things I missed, not putting the pieces together. Her elegant mannerisms and refined etiquette. The diamond earrings she wore and didn't even think about them being ostentatious, yet at the same time being so meticulously trained in fighting.

She was a dark dweller—a bloody *princess*. Her mother was the queen of the entire Unified Nations, a Druid, and could have my head on a spike. Her father was one of the most feared "retired" assassins from the Otherworld and was rumored to still do shady shit for the king.

In a sick twist, I had met her father, Lorcan, already. The year before, when they helped us fight Istvan, though I barely remembered any of them. That night was a haze for me, except for one moment. I didn't recall much outside of watching Lukas and Kek die.

Sighing, I shoved out my thoughts from burrowing deeper. Exhaustion already sagged my shoulders, my body wanting to go right back to sleep and continue to heal. But we couldn't. It wouldn't be long before the Russians came back searching for us. And they would come prepared.

Climbing to my feet, I pulled on my pants, watching her as if she'd rise like some horror movie. The fragile girl was only the shell of what lay inside.

A Natural Obscurer.

"Spread out. Search everywhere." A thick, muffled voice from outside broke through the silence, seeping through the wood door and jerking me around in terror.

Holy shit.

Snagging the pick from the spot where it laid next to me all night, I snuck to the door. Built into a mountain, the old ticket booth had two small boarded-up windows on either side of the entrance and one cut out of the door for dealing with customers. The wood covering the ticket window was weathered and warped, allowing me to peek through the gap.

Expecting the Russian Mafia, I caught my breath when I noticed figures dressed in light camouflage tracking down the path, blending in with the snowy terrain, carrying automatic rifles.

Their arms bore a royal insignia patch.

Sonya's.

My pulse thudded against my neck, and I gripped the handle, like the axe had any chance against their guns. One round would tear through our flesh, cutting our bodies in half in mere seconds.

With everything going on, it hadn't occurred to me that Iain was still out there hunting us. Stupid. Of course he wouldn't just let me slip away like that, but the fact they tracked us here? Not good.

My attention jumped over to Raven, out cold, oblivious to the danger lurking up to us. Fae might have a lot more strength, speed, and infinite life compared to humans, but we still had our weaknesses. Those times when we were vulnerable. When we had to shut down and knit ourselves back together, we were at our most defenseless.

At least a dozen various-sized figures crept by the sloped stone incline up to the booth. The heavy snow and years of nature taking over concealed it slightly from the main path. Though I knew it was only a matter of minutes before someone came up here to investigate, finding the door lock busted.

And we had nowhere to go.

One way in and one way out.

Sweat dotted my hairline, and the axe handle was damp under my grip. Holding my breath, I waited. It would just take one to point at the booth and we were dead.

A dozen soldiers slunk by their target on the way to the caves, probably thinking that was where we hid. And in any other circumstances, it would've been. Safe from the elements and a lot warmer than out here, it would be a natural place to make camp for the night.

The crack of branches heavy with snow murmured that nature was waking up to an overcast day. I watched the group creep by, still ready to hear one shout out. Every thud of my heart was like a bomb ticking down. Waiting felt like years as I tried to keep my anxiety in check.

Warwick was always the cool one in situations like this, the one who never seemed fazed in life-and-death situations. Maybe because he had died. Brutally. Brexley dragged his soul from the depths and brought him back.

Death was his comrade, not his enemy.

Normally I was collected and calm as well, while Kitty was the one who would be listing all the things that could go wrong.

In the last year, I had lost all fear of death. If anything, I begged for it. Demanded it come and get me. Take me into its dark embrace because nothing could be worse than the hell I was living. But somewhere, something had changed.

The pure, unfiltered fear of them finding us made me dizzy, except I knew it wasn't in fear of my own death. My gaze was caught by the figure tucked into a tight ball, her body shivering again.

Peering out of the gap, the hum of nature the only thing I could hear, I pushed away from the door, hustling to Raven.

"Hey." I crouched down, shaking her shoulder. "Wake up."

She didn't move.

"Come on." I jiggled her harder, my nerves still jerking my head back to the door like someone was going to plow through it at any moment. "We have to go."

A small noise came up her throat, her forehead wrinkling, but she didn't wake.

"Raven!" I whisper-shouted. Dropping the axe, I slid my hand around her back, trying to sit her up. "Wake up."

Her lashes fluttered, the crease in her forehead deepening, sleep possessively trying to keep her.

"Wake the hell up, *princess*," I snapped, more anger threading through my tone than I expected.

Land of Monsters

It was a name Warwick always called Brexley because of the privilege she grew up in, but here, the term wasn't just a pet name. It was Raven's actual title. She was an actual princess. Royalty.

Her lids cracked open like the moniker was how she was woken up every day. A frown cut over her features.

"Don't call me that." Her voice was barely a whisper, her lids starting to fall again.

"Why? It's who you are, right? *Princess* Raven Haley Scarlet Dragen, right?" I snapped out her full name like it was an insult. "And wake up. Sonya's men are here. We need to leave."

Her eyes bolted open, and she shot up to sitting. The few damp pieces of clothes covering her fell to her lap, showing she was only in a thin sports bra and knickers. She stared down at herself like she was still trying to figure out where she was and why the hell she was almost naked.

"You were going into hypothermia," I defensively spit out, standing and stepping into my boots. "I had to get you warm." I reached down for my sweater, tugging it back on, anger bristling over my shoulders. "Get dressed. We have to leave *now*!"

My tone impelled her into action, but she struggled to put on her icy clothes, her movements sluggish. I still couldn't feel much magic from her, fatigue and cold slowing her progress.

Impatience had me stomping to her. Leaning over, I took the shredded sweater from her hands and shoved it over her head, my knuckles dragging down the sides of her breasts to her ribs, tugging it in place.

"I can dress myself."

"Then do it," I growled and moved away from her.

A shout pierced the air, sending me back to the door, peering through the slight crack in the wood. My breath stuck in my throat. More muffled voices came from up the passage.

They found where the wolves attacked, the signs of struggle, the blood coating the snow. They would realize we either never made it to the caves or were no longer in there and head back this way. The snow overnight might have hidden some of our footsteps up to the ticket booth, but someone would take notice of the disturbance of pristine snow.

I swore under my breath, hearing Raven scrambling behind me, trying to get on her boots, her actions far slower than normal.

"We have to go," I barked hoarsely, glancing back at her.

A frown marred her expression as she finished tying her bootlaces, fatigue sagging her frame. But she hardened her shoulders and shuffled to me, her skin drawn and pale.

For a second, I could feel a crack in my wall—a need to touch her, pull her into me, make sure she was all right. But I was halted by the memory of how she tore out that man's throat, her words bursting another man's brains, her mere existence scaring off a hungry pack of wild wolves.

If anything, *I* needed protection, and it wasn't the dark dweller part I was afraid of.

"Stay close," I uttered, gripping the pick in my hand. Taking a breath, I pulled open the door, peeking out. White robbed the forest of color, leaving only the brown bark of the trees to bleed through the snow. I strained to hear anything but the drips of water dropping from the leaves, the powder buffering the voices from down the road. "Come on." I trampled down the incline to the path, making sure Raven was behind me before I took off.

Using the footprints in the snow from the soldiers, we retreated down the footpath, passing the sign announcing the closure of the Valea Cetatii Caves, which we crossed less than twelve hours ago. How much had changed since then. The Ash who ran up this hill toward the caves had no idea what was ahead. What he would unshackle.

Ash. She muttered my name with a warning.

"Wha—" I heard the rumbling of a motorcar coming up the hill, my gaze snapping back to the road. The deep vibrations conjured the image of an MTV—Medium Tactical Vehicle—in my brain.

More soldiers were coming.

"Az istenfáját!" Oh, the God's tree! I mumbled under my breath, my attention zipping around, catching shouts from down the cave path. By the pitch, I knew they had discovered our hideout, the broken lock and muddy footprints on the stone floor. They would beeline this way, hoping we were still within reach.

The frame of the MTV dotted through the line of trees, only a dozen yards away from arriving here. We were trapped on both sides, and going down the hill meant heading right into enemy territory.

We needed a place to hide. Somewhere no one could find us.

Seizing Raven's hand, I tugged her into the woods behind us. Navigating the steep, rough terrain, deep with untouched snow, felt like slogging through thick tar. "Come on!" I pulled Raven's arm so hard I was practically dragging her, needing to get us safely away from view.

"Gaseste-i!" Find them! *"Trebuie să fie aproape."* *They must be close.* The order ricocheted off the canopy of trees, slamming right into my spine, and my nerves buzzed with terror. We were both too fatigued to run fast, to think as clearly as we needed to. Survival was our only goal.

Land of Monsters

Raven tripped and stumbled, trying to keep up with me. Desperation was bitter on my tongue, and adrenaline pumped through my veins, moving my legs over the terrain, leading us away from peril.

"Where are we going?" Raven finally asked when we were far out of earshot, surrounded only by the sounds of birds and wood creaking under the weight of the snow.

"To the only place I know we'll be safe." I turned to look at her.

Raven's eyes met mine, her throat swallowing as she nodded, lethargy already shaking her muscles. She understood the trek there would be difficult, treacherous, and bone-aching.

Her hand stayed clasped in mine and without the bracelet blocking her powers, blocking me, I realized for the first time how much I could feel her. Like the snow seeping into my clothes, she soaked into my system. Not her emotions or anything, but her presence. Even without her power and magic, I could feel her force. Her aura. The same as I felt the earth and the life around me.

Wildness under a royal mask.

The beast behind the woman.

Chapter 2

Raven

Sweat dripped down the back of my neck at the same time my body shook with cold and fatigue. My legs ached, each step getting harder to take while wrestling through the rugged terrain. The gluttonous clouds eagerly dropped more snow on us. The endless patter on my face and head never seemed to stop. Another thing tapping at an exposed nerve.

My whole body was raw and tender, my strength waning as we silently hiked over the mountains. The snow clung to my lashes, and I took in the back of Ash's physique. His shoulders rolled forward, his body tense, trekking forward without pause.

He had barely looked at me. Not in the eyes, anyway. My throat tightened, tears pricking at the frozen ducts.

It was exactly what I feared. What I knew would happen. It was how most who learned what I was responded. Fear. Horror. Disgust. It was why my parents kept quiet about me and my brother after we were born. Only close family and personal royal guards knew what we were capable of.

The world, of course, knew my brother and I came from a dark dweller and a Druid, but most didn't know my mother was a natural obscurer. That *I* could inherit it from her. Be all the "evil" parts of my parents' union.

My brother was far luckier.

Fear rose when my brother and I were born. Rumors swirled about what my parents could produce, but as the years went by and we grew, the talk died away. It was purposeful. An image we had to maintain. Little did they know the very thing they were so afraid of was even worse than they thought. Or at least for me.

My brother, Rook, was the perfect one. I was the problem.

"Just over that range." Ash flicked his chin at the mountains ahead of us, his attention gliding over me clinically, no emotion escaping him. When he held my hand, I swear I could feel him, the blood in his system, the beat of his heart, his aura giving me strength.

Now he let nothing show, while I felt exposed and thin as parchment.

I nodded, my fingers searching for the cuff like a security blanket. To despise and miss something equally left me more unsettled in my body. Like a convict who escaped jail but realized they enjoyed the security of the cage.

My powers were empty, a side effect of my glitch, but I still wanted to run back to the protected pen of my cuff, scared of what I could do. It had been almost a year since I put it on, the spelled metal containing my magic, and I had grown accustomed to it. To being without my powers.

Part of me had wanted it off, to feel the wildness roar back in, to be free. The other wished I had walked away from the cave, telling Ash the truth.

I might be half of myself, but nobody would die.

The taste of the man's blood still coated my tongue, the sound of my teeth tearing into his flesh echoing in my ears. Maybe it horrified me, but the beast enjoyed it, and the obscurer craved it. Natural obscurers were banished for a reason among Druids. We weren't the healers and protectors; we were the killers and the darkness. We were born of black magic and went against everything of the Druids' white magic.

My obscurer got off on the power of controlling people, seeing their brains leak from their noses and ears.

I was born to be a murderer.

Ash turned from me, trudging through the snowdrift, his demeanor colder than the ice around us.

Much of last night was a blur after the Russians found us. Only a few moments stuck out amongst the high of blood and power bringing my monster back to life. Except my mind kept rolling back to the tiny hut. Waking up buzzing with heat and lust, the dweller needing to fuck, while Ash barked at me to get up and move. Ordering me around.

I expected my dweller to lash back; she didn't even obey our alpha at home. But with every demand, wetness seeped into my panties, and I was compelled to strip what was left of my clothes.

Sometime last night, he had undressed me, used his body to keep me warm, saved me from hypothermia… even after knowing what I was. What I was capable of.

My blood heated at the memory of the hut, but I didn't know why I'd awoken so needy. Like I had sex dreams about him but couldn't remember. Not that horny wasn't a natural state for a dark dweller, especially after a kill.

A few yards ahead of me, Ash changed our trek sharply and stopped, pinching his nose like his head hurt.

"What's wron—" A wave of magic slammed into me. A thick, knotty spell, smelling of earth, layering over my skin, tapping at my most basic instincts, telling me to walk away.

The last time we neared the pagan temple, the spell around my cuff had blocked it, but now I felt it speak to every fiber of my being. Without my bracelet, the Druid spell blasted through my system with recognition and annoyance. Familiarity and challenge. As if we were still set back in the days of warring tribes, a Druid's signature laid a subtle threat to all who neared from other clans.

Pushing on, I knew Dubthach (*Dew-aach*) would feel me enter his spell, the metal no longer disguising what I was. Like a fly hitting a cobweb, even in my weakened state, he'd feel power ripple over his, engulfing his own. I could lose my magic forever, but I was still a Cathbad, coming from one of the most powerful lineages of high Druids. And most of all, I was a Dragen. That alone usually sent people fleeing.

None of my senses were up to par, yet I could feel and smell people creeping up to us, hear the soft clink of a gun's safety being taken off.

"They know we're here," I spoke to Ash, lifting my hands in peace, my gaze roaming the brush in front of us.

"Don't move or we will kill you." The voice came from the forest.

"It's us." Ash's hand went up.

"Exactly." Vlad stepped from behind a tree, his weapon pointed at us. Viorica and Codrin shuffled out from other angles. "You think I trust you anymore? Especially after what happened at Râșnov?" he snarled, stepping closer.

"We told you we needed sanctuary from Sonya," Ash replied.

"It was more than that." Vlad scoffed, his head shaking. "Iain came *solely* to the fortress *for you*. People were beaten and taken prisoner yesterday, all because you two got away." He progressed even closer, his voice tight. "I helped you escape, now help us by leaving. You are a threat to this place. To us. Leave now."

Over his shoulder, my eye caught movement. Dubthach's dark skin stood out against the white snow, his rich black, brown, and orange dashiki popping life into the colorless terrain. His expression was stern, his back stiff, his defensive gaze locked on me.

"I knew something was not right with you," Dubthach sneered, though his eyes held fear. "You are dark. Unnatural." He came up behind Vlad. "You hold *black magic*." Every insult was crammed into those two words, coated in abhorrence and righteousness.

It was how my mother and I were treated when they found out. With repulsion.

My mother's throne was still threatened by those who continued to hold prejudices about Druids. Death threats and revolts were daily events. Whispers of her past circled about her being "evil," but most chalked those up to rumors. She worked hard at hiding the darkness inside. Something she and Aunt Fionna tried to teach me… and failed.

"You are a traitor to our kind." Dubthach peered down at me. "A disgrace!"

"I'd watch your fucking mouth," Ash growled, his hands rolling up.

"She should not exist." Dubthach's nose flared, more confusion and fear registering in his eyes. He sensed something else was wrong with me. Another element in there besides the dark Druid. "What are you?" he whispered before his fear won out. His mouth started moving with an incantation, his hands rising to inflict his magic upon me.

I was empty, with no claws or spells to guard myself, but I held my ground, my chin up. Dragens didn't run.

"Stop!" A man called out, stepping up behind his group, turning everyone to his stout form. "This is not who we are!" Iacob, dressed in a thin cotton robe and unbuckled snow boots, tramped through the snow. His hair and beard were mussed, like he just woke up and threw on what was near and came running.

"But—"

"She has black magic—"

Both Vlad and Dubthach rebutted, turning to their leader.

"No." Iacob's voice barked like a command. "We do not turn away anyone asking for help."

"Sir—" The Druid tried to speak again.

"I said that is not who we are." Iacob cut him off. "Too many claim they are open for *all* in need and are not. I will not be a hypocrite. I saw it too much growing up." He stepped up to Vlad, putting his hand on the muzzle of the gun and pushing it down until it pointed at the snowy ground. "We help those who need it." He nodded at Viorica and Codrin, getting them to lower their weapons too.

Iacob's gaze came to us, his stout frame taking a few steps in the snow to us. With a heavy exhale, he crossed his arms over his chest, his expression growing more serious.

"Though I think you owe us the full truth." His dark eyes darted between us, landing on me, his tone sharp. "Tell us who you *really* are."

Minuscule pinpricks jabbed at my thawing skin inside the warm dome, causing my nose to run and my bones to ache. The spell around the encampment buzzed overhead, making me realize how much the bracelet had dulled my senses before. How little I was living, yet the onslaught of it had me longing for the buffer. It was as if I was standing naked—raw and exposed. And way overstimulated.

The herb and mushroom tea in my hands did very little to soothe my nerves. Eyes from all around the dome sliced into me, especially from Dubthach, though the insignificance they had addressed me with the first time was gone. I was depleted and weak, yet they still detected the unusual power that lay within my bones because I was too exhausted to wall myself up.

Dubthach examined me like he was trying to peel back all my layers and ascertain what threat I posed, what powers were lingering just out of his grasp.

I had learned from a very early age to guard myself. I was always around powerful figures and international leaders, people who would feel threatened by the truth. Most already feared my father just from his name alone, knowing my uncles and aunts also stood behind him as well. They knew what my twin and I were, but after years of showing no sign of any particular threat, they relaxed.

The press cooed over my brother, the media fawning, finding no flaw within his six-foot frame. Rook was engaging with everyone from heads of state to maids and even the tabloids, his charm winning people over instantly. I learned to smile, flatter, pretend I was the same. That I didn't come out fucked up and resenting the cage of royal life.

"Are you ready to explain?" Iacob sat on a bench near us, his robe opening across his bare torso, displaying his hairy chest. Celeste cuddled up next to him like she was a little girl visiting Santa; they all were so free with touch and displaying affection with each other.

One side of me grew up going to the dark dweller ranch with a huge, physically affectionate family. The other side lived in a castle, curtsied, and addressed leaders formally. I couldn't step out of place because the press seemed desperate to find something wrong with me. From my lunches with friends, shopping sprees, or helping with Aunt Zoey's orphanage, they found ways to tear me down and make me always seem frivolous and shallow.

Little did they know the depths I kept hidden.

Ash cleared his throat, sipping his tea. He still wouldn't fully look at me, and I couldn't deny the ache in my chest. It shouldn't matter. He made it clear we were nothing. This partnership would end if we made it out of here alive. And now that he knew the truth, the end was coming sooner than later.

Exhaling, I started first. "My name is Raven, and I am a dar—"

"*I'm* the reason we are hiding here." Ash cut me off, his eyes sliding over to me so quickly I almost missed it, but I could sense his body stiffening, telling me to shut up. "She was dragged into my mess like you have been."

I blinked at him, knowing he was lying. Or at least not telling the whole story. I was just as much the problem. The Russians were here for me. I was the one who brought even more weight down on us.

"My real name is Ash." He set down his mug, looking at Iacob. "I have come here to seek revenge for people I loved who were taken from me." His voice stayed steady. "Sonya and Iain are not hunting me. I'm hunting them."

"Ash?" Vlad muttered his name, his eyes widening. "The same Ash who is said to run with the legend Warwick Farkas? *The Wolf?*"

That name had some sucking in breath, as if saying it would conjure whoever this man was.

"One and the same." Ash dipped his head.

"*Futu-ți gura măti!*" *Fuck your mother's mouth!* Vlad stood up, hissing out a curse.

"Many did," Ash replied.

A laugh snorted from me, my hand clasping over my mouth.

"So wrong," I mumbled.

He shrugged one shoulder at me. "But true."

"The Wolf? The man who the legend says came back from the dead? That not even death would have him, spitting him back out? Who can slaughter hundreds in mere seconds?"

"Whoa." Ash held up his hand. "That's a total exaggeration. He can kill maybe a dozen, two dozen at most in seconds."

The entire group stared at Ash in silent horror.

"That kind of violence," Iacob finally spoke. "Doesn't it go against a tree fairy's constitution?"

"I'm not the conventional tree fairy," Ash said matter-of-factly. "I tried for a bit. Didn't really stick." Ash clasped his hands, taking a breath. "I am here to kill the queen and her son, so I understand if you do not want us here. We bring a lot of danger to you. But if you would be so kind to let us have a night to regroup and heal." He gestured to me. I could see Iacob really noting the blood covering us, the ripped clothing and healing wounds. "We'd be so grateful. We will leave early tomorrow."

Iacob leaned back, folding his arms over his chest, watching us for a moment. "You do bring a lot of trouble to our door. I'm convinced it's why my brother dropped you here." He huffed. "But I keep to my word. Helping people shouldn't be conditional."

Vlad and Dubthach whipped to him, "Iacob…"

He held up his hand again. "We are a democracy here. So we will vote on it." He stood up. "Nays?"

Twenty or more hands went up, including the Druid and Vlad.

"Yeas?"

Only half went up right away, but slowly, a few more hesitantly put their hand up.

I counted. It was an exact tie.

Celeste sat up, her hungry eyes on Ash, a salacious grin turning up her mouth as she lifted her hand, like her vote came with obligations. Ones he'd owe her later.

Deep within, my dark dweller crawled up to the surface. I didn't even know a low growl came from me until Ash's head jerked over, an eyebrow curving up.

Embarrassment flooded my face. I hated the feeling of being out of control. I wanted the bracelet back.

"You can stay." Iacob turned to us. "The beds in the healing room are still open for you."

"Sir." Dubthach stood, his expression pinched, his head shaking. "You don't understand what she is."

"I don't want to hear it." Iacob shook his head. "We voted. It's done." He padded away, rubbing at his messy hair. "Now I'm gonna go back to bed. Don't wake me unless it's an emergency."

Some people followed him out, heading for their own bedrooms or to the food tent, while others stayed, lounging by the fire.

Ash rose, giving me a signal with his chin to follow. We made it five steps before Celeste put herself right in front of Ash, her shirt so thin it didn't cover the fact she wasn't wearing anything under it.

"I'm happy you came back." She reached out and rubbed his arm, her teeth nipping at her bottom lip.

"Didn't have a lot of options." No emotion came from him, making me curious if he really felt nothing about this stunning, practically naked woman or if he was pretending he didn't. I mean, how could he not be into her? She was a nature fairy like him. Gorgeous, sensual, and offering him uncomplicated sex.

Unlike you. A voice said in my brain, and I shook it out instantly.

"You know the best way to heal?" She nodded to the dried bullet wound in his stomach, brushing her nipples into him as she rose to his ear. "Sex." She didn't bother whispering. "You can just lay back and take all my energy. Heal while I ride you back to health."

Fury climbed up the back of my neck, another low growl humming up my throat. I was seized by the need to kill. To taste blood. Watch her brain melt from her ears.

Ash's head jerked to me, his eyes widening.

"Maybe another time." He grabbed my hand, pulling me with him toward the healing tent, looking back at a stunned Celeste. "Fuck, Raven," he hissed, dragging me through the door. The dome was exactly the way we left it, even the messed-up sheets from when we slept on the floor together the night before last. "I'm trying to keep what you are hidden while you're about to tear out her throat, exposing yourself. For what? Jealousy?"

"Jealousy!?" My tone pitched in response, the allegation hitting dead center. "Over you? Are you kidding me?"

"Then why do you care if she hits on me?"

"I don't!" I sputtered, my arms going out.

"Right." He huffed, neither one of us believing me. "We aren't doing this again." He rubbed at the back of his neck. "You need to be careful. Your eyes turned red."

"I can't control it!" Shame bubbled up inside me, along with more anger and defensiveness. I never really could. My brother was a master, while I was a broken mess. "It's why I wore the bracelet."

His attention went to my empty wrist, the absence of it screaming through the room. It highlighted all the things we had yet to discuss. No moment to understand what happened last night.

"Tell me." His voice dragged across the ground, his green eyes looking directly into mine. It made me feel vulnerable. Bare.

"What do you want to know?" I shuffled my feet, folding my arms around me.

"Everything."

I scoffed, my head tipping back, staring up at the cloudy sky above as flakes flittered down but never touched the glass dome.

"You probably know who my parents are…" I started.

"Yeah." He laughed. "I actually met your father once."

"What?" My focus snapped to him, my mouth falling open.

"They came to help us with the battle last year against Istvan."

"Oh." My head wagged. "That was the mission Uncle Lars sent them on. Mom only told me Uncle Lars had sent them somewhere."

"*Szar*." Ash's hand went back to his head, and he started to pace, a crazed laugh billowing out. "Uncle Lars…"

"Yeah?"

"Your *uncle* is the fucking *king*!" He exclaimed, his arms out wide in bewilderment. "Your mother is *the* queen… and your whole family are deadly killers!"

He wasn't wrong. Druids to dark dwellers, I came from *very* powerful roots, not to mention my extended family of pirates, wanderers, incubi, sirens, pixies, and a monkey-sprite.

"How could you not tell me?" Ash's voice rose. "You are a princess! You should not be here. I thought you needed to go home when I thought you were an average rich girl! I'm shocked they haven't tracked you down and killed me yet!"

"The bracelet cut off any connection to me."

His eyes widened. "So now it's off?"

"It's not like I have a beacon on me or anything." I flapped my arms. "And only my brother would have any connection to find me."

"Your *twin,* you mean?"

"Yes, but we don't have some supernatural twin psychic connection where he can find me out of thin air. We're normal twins. Well, he came out normal. I did not."

"Normal?" Ash huffed. "You think being half Druid and half dark dweller is normal?"

"No. Rook and I are the first of our kind. But at least he isn't fucked up like me."

Ash stilled, his brows lowering. "What do you mean?"

"He's just a regular Druid and a regular dark dweller."

"You mean he's not a natural obscurer?"

"No." I shook my head. "I was the only one who inherited that gene from my mom."

"Inherited? I thought the mother had to practice black magic during pregnancy for her child to become one. And even that is very rare."

"Yeah, so we thought." I rubbed my cheek on my shoulder, feeling prickles behind my eyes. My mother held vast amounts of guilt, though it wasn't her fault. "My grandmother did black magic when she was pregnant with my mom. It was during the time Queen Aneira was slaughtering Druids by the thousands. My mother didn't know she carried this power until her twenties. She found out with me it was something that could be passed down."

"But not to your brother?"

"No. Rook, of course, came out perfect."

"You keep saying that." Ash frowned, like he was mad at me for being so hard on myself.

"Because it's true." I started to move around, hating the envy I carried when it came to my twin. "Rook is seamlessly split. He can turn into a full dark dweller and hunts and fights with the pack. Or he can work his Druid magic. He's one or the other. Never together."

Ash's head tipped back in understanding. "You can't."

"No." The burning started behind my eyes again. "My powers were never separate. They came out jumbled and flawed. I get stuck in this in-between state, where I can never fully be a dark dweller, and I have never been a high Druid with white magic like my brother. My mother is a natural obscurer, of course, from her mother, and Aunt Fionna can do black magic, but they both mainly stick to white magic now." Aunt Fionna still loved to dabble a bit in black magic every once in a while; she still had the choice to do either. I didn't. Before she reunited with my mom and her own daughter, Piper, she practiced heavily in black magic. She was part of the alliance to take down the fae, but her life took a huge turn when she fell in love with Uncle Lars.

Aunt Fionna was the one who helped lace my cuff with the Druid protection, spelling it to hold back my obscurer and buffer the goblin metal from trying to drain me of all my powers. She saw my heartbreak and knew I needed to be protected from myself, and her daughter was part of the reason for my downfall.

My older cousin Piper was my idol growing up. From the moment I was born, I had been in awe of her talent, intelligence, beauty, and her seer powers. I trailed after her, copying everything she did, said, and wore. I worshipped her, happily sitting by her side on days she was absent from our world, lost in visions, and flighty to reality.

Then she became my foe. Taking the only person I ever loved.

"You could never control them?" Ash's voice pulled me back to him.

"Well, no. I was okay with dealing with them... before."

"Before what?"

A tear finally slipped out.

"Before Wyatt left me." His name was a dagger to the gut, instantly putting the image of him in my mind. His rare smiles and cheeky winks.

A carbon copy of his father Ryker, Wyatt was six-two, broad, blond, and had the prettiest white/blue eyes I'd ever seen. A wanderer like his mother and father, he had his mother's dimples, which I think I fell in love with the moment I was old enough to understand their power.

"Wyatt is the ex?" Ash's jaw gritted.

"Yes." I nodded. "He was my best friend, my first love, and I thought my last. We lost our virginity together. He was my whole world."

"But…?"

"But he was secretly in love with my cousin."

"Ouch." Ash flinched.

"Yeah. She was older than us, and for a long time, thought of us as annoying kids. I don't know if Wyatt ever really thought she'd see him as more, especially being raised like family together. We dated, and I think he fell in love with me too, at least for a moment there. But we grew up, and things shifted between them. Between us. They began hanging out more."

I couldn't go on, remembering how I found them kissing. My heart had shattered into pieces because I could tell it was more than a simple kiss. I couldn't deny how they looked at each other.

They were fated mates.

And my whole world combusted.

"I was so heartbroken, so lost… I went on a work trip to Russia with my mom and Uncle Lars to get away." I swallowed, memories of that night flickering in my head. "Another boy was there, saying all the right things, telling me how pretty I was. How much he desired me and always had. I wanted the hurt to stop…" I wiped at my cheek. "No, I wanted to punish Wyatt. I think deep down I was hoping he'd find out and realize what a mistake he made."

Ash's head bobbed like he perfectly understood.

"We got really drunk and took some fairy dust." I closed my lids, more snippets from that night coming through. "We were so high." I recalled how rough I had been riding Alexsei, how desperate I was for pain, to taste blood, to lose myself, like I could bleed myself of the agony rotting my core. The drugs twisted my mind, making me see Wyatt and Piper next to me, watching him fuck her, grinning wickedly at me, telling me I had never been good enough, that it had always been her pussy he imagined when he had been with me.

The dweller and obscurer lashed out, wanting everything to feel the anguish we did. I had heard his bellows of pain, his distress, even when I felt him come inside me, but I didn't stop. Nothing felt real, like it was all a faraway dream.

"I snapped." I swiped faster as a few more tears fell. "I woke up laying in his blood, his throat and heart torn out, blood pooling from his eyes and ears." A sob racked my body, and I quickly curbed it. There was no image sharper than when I had stood up, his blood dripping from my mouth and hands, while his cum dripped down my legs, and I stood over his dead body.

"The boy…" I lifted my head, looking directly at Ash. "Was Alexsei Kozlov."

Ash's mouth fell open, his eyes widening. *"Faszom!"* he barked, his hand going through his hair. He paced in a circle, understanding the significance of my declaration.

"The son of Dimitri Kozlov," I continued anyway. "The leader of Russia."

Ash let out a strangled laugh. "And head of the fucking Mafia!" Dimitri denied his involvement in the Mafia, though it was the worst kept secret. Even Lars was unnerved around them, and if you knew my uncle, that said *a lot*.

"These people will torture and murder your whole family for looking at them wrong," he exclaimed.

"But you knew Nikolay was after me."

"Yes, but I didn't realize how severe the connection was! This isn't a little insult. You slaughtered his *only* son."

"Yes. I know." I struggled enough to come to terms with what I did.

"Ó, hogy bassza meg egy talicska apró majom!"

"Did you just tell me to fuck a wheelbarrow of small monkeys?"

"It's a Birdie expression." Ash walked the floor.

"Who's Birdie?"

"Someone who'd be kicking my ass for getting myself into this shit." He swung to me. "So let me get this right, we most likely have the king and queen of the Unified Nations looking for you with a pack of killer dark dwellers at the same time the Russian leader has his Mafia out hunting for you, while I have the entire Romanian army searching for me?"

"Yes." I dipped my head, feeling overwhelmed. "Plus, I think the Druid here really hates me and wants to see me dead too."

"Szar." Ash rubbed at his face. "I think the wheelbarrow of monkeys just fucked *me*."

Chapter 3

Ash

The strong *țuică* burned down my throat, my head buzzing from the alcohol. Tipping back in the chair, I continued to stare at the curled-up figure sleeping soundly on the mattress just a few feet from me.

Her silky brown hair, knotted and tipped in dried blood, had slipped over her eyes like a shield. The urge to lean over and brush it out of her face was strong, making me wrap my fingers tighter around my cup.

Fatigue finally took her down, the need to sleep overpowering everything else, including jumping in the shower. I should've been sleeping too. Healing. I couldn't.

I scoured my head, a small grunt forming in my chest. The last twenty-four hours were slowly sinking in, my brain acknowledging everything that came to light. And how utterly fucked I was.

Of all people in the world, my path had to cross with the princess of the Unified Nations at the bar a month ago. If I had only known, I would've run from that place so fast. Or I would have handed her over to the UFN without hesitation. Her family was far scarier than any Mafia out there.

Looking at her, I struggled to see the rich co-ed I first assumed she was, running off with me for shits and giggles. I'd thought her life boring and sheltered, figured she needed a thrill.

Fuck.

She might be young, but she'd already gone through so much. It was a lot to take in.

There was stress enough with her being with me before I knew the

Land of Monsters

truth; now it was like carrying a fragile bomb, and with any bump, it might go off. My mission was to deliver the bomb back to the parents before they arrested me for kidnapping the niece of the Unseelie demon king and the only daughter of the queen and her consort, the hired assassin, Lorcan Dragen.

And with Lorcan came his brother Eli and all her other uncles and aunts, who could string my guts up before I could even make a sound.

I was so fucked.

My eyes trailed over the shape of her face, the way she tucked in on herself, looking so vulnerable. I couldn't deny she was stunning. That had never been the issue, but now I could so clearly see the resemblance to her mother and father. Lorcan had the same color eyes and a similar mouth, but most everything else was her mother. Raven was a blend of both with her own uniqueness.

Uniqueness… yeah, this girl had it in spades. Never in my wildest dreams did I think I'd ever come across a Druid and a dark dweller. The rarity of her and her twin was up there with dragons still existing. Yet, here she was, all five foot three of her, teeming with powers no one could fathom or understand. And when people don't understand something, they fear it, hate it, want it *destroyed or controlled.*

I downed my last swig on that thought, rising from the chair, my body and mind restless. I needed air. I needed to think without her in my face, making me doubt everything I knew I had to do.

Stepping outside, I fell against the side of the dome. Snow darkened the sky, the day already winding down. As I took a deep breath, the sudden craving for fairy dust sprang up, causing my lids to shut with agony. *Just a little, just enough to take the edge off.* The weak-willed part of me nibbled at my thoughts. I had been so good, but the craving would always be there—the need to forget, to not feel.

But this time, it wasn't from the raw pain of losing Kek and Lukas. It was the thought of losing *her.* Either to one of the many groups after us or… myself.

She would hate me, but it was the only wise thing to do. I had to return her home. She didn't belong in this world. She didn't belong with me.

Though her ex was a moron for not seeing how incredible she was, she should be with someone like him. Someone part of the royal world. I was about as far from that as you could get. She deserved someone who wasn't on a death crusade.

I froze, realizing I had just put myself among her suitors. *What the fuck?*

"She should not exist." A deep voice jerked my head to the side. The tall African Druid stood a short distance down the path, the shadows hiding him in the shrubs.

I pushed off the wall, staring at him, anger building up my spine.

"You are a tree fairy." His African accent was more noticeable. "You know this to be true. Black magic goes against nature. It is evil and should be cut out like a disease."

"Is that a threat?" Stepping closer to him, I kept my tone even, but every muscle in me tightened, ready to fight. "You lay one finger on her, and you will find out who the evil one really is."

His dark eyes went to me, his face expressionless, but I could feel the surprise. Tree fairies were known to be pacifists, to love all—literally and figuratively. We were peace-not-war types.

I wasn't normal either.

He stepped back, his gaze still intently on mine.

"She will not only be your downfall, but *ours*," he clipped. "Leave now." At his last words, he barreled away, leaving me vibrating with fury.

My emotions were already wrenched high. I felt like crawling out of my skin, ready to combust. There were only two ways I could relieve energy like this.

Sex and/or drugs.

The thought of the first one had me struggling to breathe, imagining taking every one of my fears and stresses out on someone so fucking ruthlessly they begged me to stop.

Not someone.

Her.

"Fuck." I squeezed my lids shut, my cock becoming stone as I pictured walking back in and what I would do to her over every countertop, every surface.

She's a princess, Ash! And like a little sister…

My depravity laughed right back in my face, shoving the vision of her fucking that kid into my head. Her tits bouncing, her head back, groaning, while he bellowed under her, his hands kneading her naked flesh. The high they must have felt right before. Raven riding him so hard he probably already felt like he died in utter bliss.

My body shook with need, craving it more than air. The intensity, that thrill. It was why I usually had more than one person. What I desired was *a lot*.

I forced the memory of meeting the dark dwellers, her father, out of my mind, trying to remind myself she wasn't some girl I met in a bar, a random fae who got tangled up in my life. She was the daughter of someone important.

A royal princess.

Producing a strangled grunt, I forced myself away from the tent, not trusting myself if I walked in. I needed something to bleed me of all this magic building inside.

"Looks like you could use some of this," a sensual voice purred in my ear.

I turned to see Celeste lounging on a bench by the main fire, her see-through t-shirt doing nothing to hide her hard nipples or the fact she wore nothing else underneath. Her half-lidded eyes were hungry on me, a rolled joint between her fingers. "Think it will ease the tension." She took a hit, then held it up, offering it to me.

Oddly, my first instinct was to say no, to go back to Raven, but I stopped myself. *Why?* I wasn't with Raven, nor did either of us want me to be. We were just stuck together until I could get her safely back home. Celeste was exactly what I needed. Uncomplicated sex. A release of energy, and it would help me heal. Win-win.

Except I still hesitated.

"Come on..." She jumped up, strolling toward me with a suggestive grin on her face. She tapped the end of the joint between my lips. "It will make you feel so much better." She rose on her toes, her teeth grazing my neck. "And I can make you feel better too."

I took a hit off the roll, the herbs instantly billowing a cloud in my head, easing my shoulders.

"See?" Celeste grinned, encouraging me to take two more drags. Stress slid off my back, my head feeling wobbly, and I identified the sensation. Mushrooms.

A snort huffed from me. Mushrooms always made me laugh now; Bitzy and Opie would be forever linked to them. That cranky imp would love this one—it was strong and smooth, and she'd get high as fuck off a hit.

"What?" Celeste took a hit before handing it back again.

"Nothing." *Just miss my friends.* "It's good."

"We have two gardens dedicated to mushrooms and herbs."

Bitzy's heaven.

"I might not leave now."

A hungry smile curved her mouth, and she slipped her hand to the waist of my pants, tugging me through a curtain into a room off the main one. It was a small, dark meditation room.

Celeste pushed me against the wall. The powerful herbs were starting to mess with my mind, my body disconnecting, though I could feel this need to push back. To fight the fall. To stop this.

"Celeste—"

"Shhh." Her finger brushed over my mouth. "Let me make you feel good." She lowered herself to her knees, light escaping through the curtain glinting off her blonde hair.

Blonde... It's supposed to be brown.

She unbuckled my trousers, the sound of the zipper scraping through my head like a warning.

You're not doing anything wrong. You need this.

Next she tugged down my pants and briefs.

"Gods…" She breathed out in a groan, her hand wrapping around my cock. *"Den är enorm!"* It's huge!

My head hit the back wall, my eyes closing. I wanted so badly to let go. To lose myself in the bliss for a moment.

Her tongue slid up my vein before her mouth covered me.

My body jerked as visions of Raven walking in and seeing Celeste sucking me off sprang to my mind. They were so real, I knew I muttered out her name.

Celeste groaned, taking me deeper.

"No." The drugs befuddled my mind, and instead of feeling good, I felt agitated. "Stop."

"What?" Celeste gasped when I pushed away, my head wagging. "What is wrong?"

"I-I can't." The statement came out before my brain had any clue what I was saying.

"You're a tree fairy, no?" Confusion wrinkled her expression. "I don't understand."

Tree fairies weren't at all monogamous, nor did they turn down sex. It was who we were.

"I don't either." I pulled my pants back up, buckled them, and left the room. The world around me morphed into sharp sounds and colors, everything making me more anxiety-ridden, needing to get back to the tent. Like it was my safety. A place I could breathe again.

Stumbling down the path, I burst into the healing tent, and my chest eased seeing Raven curled up, still sound asleep. Guilt for leaving her washed over me, spinning my head.

Discarding all my clothes, I crawled down onto the bed. I climbed in behind Raven and snuggled up to her back, wrapping my arms around her frame and pulling her into me.

I heard a heavy sigh escape me, and for a moment, I felt like I was out of my body, looking down at us.

The man lying there, his eyes closed, nose snuggled into her neck, looked content. At peace.

Peering down at the guy in the bed, I knew he was doomed in so many ways.

The truth was plain to see.

Light drifted between my lids, pulling me from a deep sleep. The rumble of my stomach, crying out for food, forced my eyes open to a cloudy day. I could tell by the sky above it had to be midday. My system shut down for over twelve hours. I hadn't slept so long in years.

Cocooned in blankets and warmth, I woke up alone. Again. I popped my head up in search of Raven, a frown tugging at my lips. An irritated sense of déjà vu rushed over me when I noticed her vacant spot, rumpled blanket, and my empty arms.

Pushing myself up, I ran a hand through my hair, a vexed grunt rolling up my throat. *Did she not remember what I told her last time about being on her own here?*

Somewhere in my brain, I knew she'd be okay. The people in this place weren't the fighting type. Even Dubthach wouldn't hurt her outright; it went against his creed. Yet annoyance rocked me up to my feet, accompanied by my anger at her for leaving this room without me.

Like you did last night?

A hazy memory of Celeste down on her knees flashed in my memory, her tongue exploring my cock. And I had walked away before it went any further.

I pinched my nose with a groan, examining my clothes strewn over the floor, trailing up to the bed, recalling how easily I had stripped and crawled into bed with Raven.

Even after everything that had happened, all my claims, my fears, in my drug-induced state, I ran back here. To her.

Dread kicked like a stubborn mule, knocking air from my lungs. Caring just led to pain. The last time I let myself go down that road, I barely made it through, and some part of me didn't.

I died with them. I would not do it again.

She didn't belong here. Not in my fight. She needed to go back home, where they could deal with who was after her. The king and queen were a lot more capable than I was. She should've returned home the moment her bodyguard was murdered in that pub.

Why didn't she? Why did she follow me instead? Drawing me into a situation I never needed to be in? I doubted her family would believe I didn't know who she was, dragging her to Romania and getting the princess involved in life-and-death circumstances.

They'd hang me.

My emotions turned to ire, pointing at her.

I took the quickest shower ever, needing to get the feel of Celeste's mouth off me. I dressed quickly and left, moving through the camp, searching for the thorn in my side.

As if I knew where she would be, I headed toward the food tent but came to a halt at the gardens, my lungs hitching. Hair pulled back in a messy ponytail, her cheeks rosy and healthy, Raven crawled on her hands and knees through dirt in the plant bed, hands caked in damp soil.

I stood there enjoying the view of her surrounded by nature, smiling as she conversed with an older human woman with graying hair next to her. They chatted away while they picked herbs. Every inch of me got hard, reacting to a kink I didn't know I had.

Rejuvenated energy and magic thrummed off her. Without the bracelet, I could feel it hum in my bones, making something in my gut flare, then instantly turn to rage.

I was perfectly content before she came into my life. Satisfied to avenge my lovers and be done with it all. Join them in death. It was what I wanted.

She had no right to come along and flip everything upside down, especially because of who she was. Something I could never have. Being here with me was only temporary until she moved on from her ex.

There was no way I would love again, but even if I did, it could *never* be her... for so many reasons.

I started out wanting her to go home, but now it was my mission. For her safety and for my sanity, I would force her.

"Raven." I stomped over to the garden, cutting through their chatter like a cleaver. Their heads popped up. Raven's smile wilted off her face, her eyes taking in my tense attitude. "What in the hell are you doing?"

Her lids constricted. "Gardening." She returned to digging up mushrooms, her tone combative. "As a nature fairy, I thought it'd be pretty obvious."

A huff streamed through my nose, her insolence driving a nail through the back of my neck, generating even more exasperation.

I used to be calm and cool. Centuries of living with Warwick set the bar high to invoke turmoil. Pretty much nothing ruffled my feathers anymore. Except her. She had me losing my shit faster than anyone.

"Yes," I gritted. "I see that."

"Then why did you ask?" She dropped the fungi into the satchel, brushing back a loose strand of hair with the back of her hand. "Helping Maria make mushroom soup." She nodded at the woman next to her. The lady smiled nervously at me, her eyes darting between us like she knew she should leave, the tension straining like an out-of-tune violin.

"Raven," I muttered her name, my jaw tight. "Can I speak with you for a moment?"

"No."

"No?" I sputtered in surprise.

"No," she stated again, glancing up at me with defiance. "Think we said all we needed to."

"The fuck we did." I reached over and grabbed her arm, tugging her to her feet and out of the garden bed. "Excuse us," I said to the woman, pulling Raven with me.

"Hey!" she protested as I dragged her behind the shed out of earshot. "Let me go!"

"Please." I pushed her up against the wall, catching a flare of red taint her eyes, but I knew it wasn't from fear or anger. "Like you couldn't just gut me where I stand if you wanted."

Her nose flared, a bloom of heat rising off her, seeping under my skin and wrapping around every nerve. My hands curled, my molars grinding, the sensation of her emotions making my eyes water with pain.

The pain I usually enjoyed.

"I've asked you this before, but I will ask again." I leaned closer to her, the satchel full of herbs and mushrooms she still wore padded between us. "Why are you here?"

Her brows furrowed, her head wagging. "What do you mean, why am I here?"

"You know what I mean."

"No, clearly I don't."

"Why did you follow me instead of just going home?"

"Because—"

"Don't lie to me." I stopped her. "If you were some ordinary rich girl, afraid for her family, fearing the retribution of the Mafia, I could almost see that. But you are one of the most protected people in the world. If anyone could handle the Russian Mafia and Dimitri, it would be your mother and your uncle!"

Her lips pinched, looking away.

I grabbed her chin, yanking it back to me. "Your bodyguard was murdered in front of you. Your other bodyguard was found to be a traitor tied to the Mafia. The leader of Russia wants you dead. You should've gone straight home. Been protected by your family. Yet you chose to drag me into the mix. Why?"

"Drag?" she spit back. "Sorry I have been such a terrible nuisance. Guess sleeping with your hand gripping my pussy all night is such an inconvenience."

I sucked in, my head rearing back, chagrin shooting up my neck into my face. I had no memory of doing that last night. My brain was addled by drugs and deep in healing slumber. Though, I recalled with perfect clarity waking up the morning before with her in the hut and being in the same position.

I had touched her again? Unconsciously reaching for her in my sleep, like I was guarding what was mine.

"I'm sor—"

"Whatever." She cut me off, her cheeks pinking, adjusting the satchel across her chest. "I know it's not a big deal. Tree fairies are touchy-feely." Except I had *never* done that to anyone else before, never woken up with any of my lovers with my fingers inside them. And I had awakened next to *a lot* of people in my life.

"You're evading my question." I turned it back on her, not waiting to analyze any of my actions last night. Like why I had turned down Celeste and returned to the very person I was trying to get away from. "Why did you follow me that first night when you should've been on the first plane back to your parents?"

She stayed silent.

"Raven?" My hands went to either side of her head, and I fought to keep my temper in check. "Tell. Me."

"I don't know," she exclaimed.

"You don't know?" I repeated. "Bullshit. Try again, *dziubuś*."

Her eyes flickered to me at the pet name *little beak*, and I realized what I had said, but I kept my expression locked.

"I don't know!" She pushed at my chest, moving away from me like she needed air. "In all practicality, I should have. I get it. But something had me following you instead. I don't know why, I can't explain it… I just felt this…" She tapered off, her hand flattening over her stomach. "I have been accused many times of being pampered and spoiled, hiding behind my mommy and daddy, behind the sea of my extremely powerful uncles and aunts." She took a heavy, centering breath. "Since I was a little girl, I was trained to fight by the best instructors *in the world*, but I've never once had to protect myself. I've been surrounded by bodyguards, babied by family, and protected by the royal house.

"For once, I didn't want to hide behind my parents or have Uncle Lars start an international war because of me. I murdered the guy. Me. Neither my brother nor anyone in my family was going to suffer because of me."

"Instead you disappear? Come on a suicide mission with me?" I barked, my head shaking. "You think you're being selfless? That your family is better off not knowing where you are?"

"No," she shouted back. "But is yours?"

I stepped back as if she hit me, her words slapping my face when I realized the hypocrisy of my own censure. Was I any different?

"I had no other choice," I muttered low. "You do."

"No other choice?" She swung her arms out. "Everything is a choice. And you *chose* to be here. To pick revenge over your friends."

"Don't make this about me!" I dug my index finger into my chest, then turned it on her. "I told you what I was doing, what my plan was. I never lied to you. If anything, I tried to deter you at every turn. You still decided to follow me. Lie to me!"

She folded her arms, her ponytail whipping over her arm as she turned her head away from me, drawing my attention to the band around her finger. Dirt clumped the red stone ring, the same color as her eyes when she shifted. I suddenly had a flashback, seeing the same stone ring on all the dark dwellers when I met them.

A family emblem, stating exactly who she was the whole time. All it did was remind me where she really belonged.

"We are heading to Brașov tomorrow." I copied her stance, firmly stating my decision.

"What?" Her head snapped back. "Why?"

"It's the best place to find a phone. Contact your family and have someone come get you."

"No!" she yelled. "You can't just force me—"

"I should've forced you the first time around!"

"No!"

"You're going home. End of discuss—"

A squawk impaled the sky, a dark form gliding overhead, catching my complete attention. Intuition walked over my chest like death, the brown-winged bird of prey circling the sky right above me and Raven.

"Fuck." Horror cascaded on me like a tsunami when my gaze fully caught on the bird above, recognizing it as more than the average hawk. "Nyx," I whispered.

"Who? What?" Raven reacted to my fear, her head snapping up to the bird.

"We need to find Iacob now!" I belted, turning for the main area.
"Ash!" Raven grabbed for my arm. "What's going on?"
I looked at her, a lump forming in my throat.
"They've found us."

Chapter 4

Raven

They've found us.

The phrase rebounded in my head as I watched him speed toward the main dome. Instinct had me tearing after him, the cry of the bird from above seeming to tell the world where we were. It looked just like the one at the fortress, the one circling the marketplace. Prince Iain's pet.

Alarm bells clanged through the encampment while the spells shouting of the intruders entered the sacred space. Dozens of inhabitants spewed from the food tent and more peeked out of their homes, confusion and fear streaking their expressions.

"Iacob!" Ash's voice howled, sprinting for the man who stood in the middle of the camp, frantically addressing Vlad, Dubthach, and a handful of others who stood around him. "Iacob!"

Catching up to Ash, we came to a stop next to the leader, Iacob's hands flying out as he spoke. Residents were running around us in chaos. Parents screamed for their kids, elders collected provisions and items, while anyone over the age of fifteen headed to Iacob for direction.

"Vlad, get your team to the border of the spell. Find out who it is and what—"

"I know who it is," Ash inserted, snapping every head to us. "It's the Romanian army."

"What?" The color drained from Iacob's face.

Ash nodded above to the hawk circling. "She led them here."

Realization dawned on Vlad, his eyes widening as he noted the bird above, probably recalling it from the fortress. "You." Vlad's shock turned into fury. "She tracked *you* here! This is your fault!" He lunged for Ash, his chest puffed out. "And you are the reason I had to run from the fortress and leave all the weapons I purchased behind!"

"Whoa, whoa!" Iacob put up his arms, stepping in between. Codrin grabbed his friend, pulling him back. "We don't need this right now!" Iacob shouted at Vlad. "We deal with the enemy at hand before we start pointing fingers and fighting amongst ourselves. Now go," he ordered Vlad.

Vlad stared Ash down but took his order, peeling away from Codrin. A dozen other men and women waited for instruction, leaving Dubthach to glower hate and resentment at us both.

"I'm sorry," Ash spoke to Iacob. "We brought this to your door."

"You may have brought it earlier than expected, but this danger was eventually going to come." Iacob squinted in the distance as if he had any chance of seeing what was arriving. "At least with the Druid protection, we should be able to keep them off for a bit." Fae magic couldn't break Druid magic, which was why they feared and hated us so much. It was why my mother was beloved, but at the same time, some would never accept her as their queen—an impostor standing in until a real fae queen could be crowned.

"Go reinforce the spells. Maybe she can help you?" Iacob turned to me.

Deep shame boiled down through my body. Embarrassment and sorrow blinking my lashes. "I-I can't," I muttered. *I was* an impostor to both Druids and fae.

I couldn't help Dubthach reinforce the boundaries like a normal Druid could. His spell was white magic. Protection. An obscurer was only black magic. Mine was to kill and harm, coming up short of anything good.

I grew up knowing I was "special" or, as some might say, defective or unnatural. Many times as a child, when my temper flared or I was going through fae/Druid puberty, I had to go into a time-out because my powers could hurt people. My parents, wanting to keep me safe, taught me how to mask my powers and keep myself calm, especially when my dark dweller was invoked as well. The combination was deadly and depleted me for days.

The embarrassment was all-consuming when I learned I could never fully shift like my brother, leaving me on the sidelines when my whole dark dweller family did a forest run. Though they never treated me differently, I was an outsider even to them. The only one who understood was my uncle West, who, after extensive trauma, couldn't shift anymore either. But my Aunt Ember was the one who understood me the most. As a Dae and half dark dweller because of Uncle Eli, she also was considered a monster by many, her kind hunted down and obliterated.

"Go." Iacob nodded at Dubthach, confusion lining his forehead at why I couldn't help. A disgusted noise came from Dubthach, sneering at me before he took off.

A shriek impaled my ears from above as the hawk-shifter Ash called Nyx flew closer to where we stood. I swear I could feel the hate coming off her. This was more than a tracker carrying out her master's orders—this was personal.

The alarms wailed from another section of the property, screaming of intruders, turning us toward the south.

"They are surrounding us." Ash's tone seemed calm, but I could pick up the anxiety in his inflection, the tightness in his muscles. "What do you need us to do?"

"Leave."

"What?" Ash and I both spun back to Iacob.

"If it's you they are after, then you need to get as far from here as you can. We can hold them off with spells, but we have no other means of fighting an army." The few guns Vlad collected would not hold up against a throng of royal soldiers.

"We can't just leave you!" Ash countered.

"Two people will not hold back a troop." Iacob shook his head at us. Louder squeals from the spell plucked at the sky, coming from the north side of camp.

My powers were coming back, but I knew they weren't at the levels I needed to fight for long. The battle in my body, trying to fully shift when I never would, drained me as much as when my obscurer invoked its magic. It took me days to recuperate. Another painful reminder I was fucked up.

It was like when my brother and I were in the womb, he fully developed while I came out stunted and "undercooked."

Iacob struggled to stand still, his attention fluttering around to his panicking inhabitants. "I hope you understand, but my people come first."

A ripple of energy broke against my skin, my ears crackling like they had just un-popped, flooding in sound from outside the spell.

"Iacob," a voice shouted, the sheer panic gripping my lungs. I somehow knew before Viorica came running up that the army had gotten in. "They have broken through!"

"What?" Iacob went still, his head trying to negate what she just uttered. "No, it's impossible! They can't just walk through a Druid spell!"

"They can if they aren't either fae or human," Ash muttered more to himself, staring off toward the commotion. Gunfire and screams ballooned in the air, the voices growing closer, coming for the encampment.

"We need to get everyone to safety! Now! Do you have an escape plan?" Ash shouted at Iacob. His need to protect, to make sure everyone was out of harm's way, took over.

"Y-Yes." It took another beat for the human to snap out of his shock, his attention finally going to his people, the pandemonium bustling at the seams, whipping up more terror.

"Go!" Ash pushed Iacob, invoking him to act. The flip switched on the stunned leader as more gunfire and cries progressed toward the center.

"Retragere!" Retreat. Iacob ordered his people, rounding up the terrified parents with their kids, rushing them for the west side of the encampment. "Get yourself to the caves!"

There were a thousand caves in this area, so I knew he wasn't talking about the ones Ash and I came from. Probably one they had secured with provisions, a hideout in case of this very event.

"Go with them!" Ash demanded me, heading for the first line.

"No!" I sprinted after him, furious he was trying to sideline me.

"Raven…" His expression twisted up. "Please go!"

"I'm not leaving you," I volleyed, the sounds of war thrumming into every fiber. "When will you get it through your head? I am not a child!"

"No, you're a fucking princess," he snapped back. "And if anything happened to you…"

"I am your greatest weapon here."

"You aren't strong enough yet."

My mouth parted in surprise. How did he know that?

"Please." His eyes pleaded with me right as the piercing shriek of a hawk, no longer muffled by the barrier, rang out at us.

Ash's head jerked up and the hawk swooped in for the ground, her body appearing like it was morphing back into a human form. This time, I saw a weapon strapped to her breastbone.

A gun.

Not far behind her, Codrin and others were retreating, a swell of soldiers on their tail.

There was no chance to fight. They outnumbered us by dozens, all loaded down with armor. Everything Vlad had feared.

A strangled noise rose from Ash, his hand grabbing mine as he swung us around and started running. The satchel knocked against my thighs, my pulse beating in my ears as we tore through the encampment. A loud squawk chilled my blood, and I twisted my head to see Nyx swooping down at me, her talons scraping over my scalp.

"Ow!" I screamed, my arms trying to cover my head as she swooped in again.

Land of Monsters

"Get the hell off her!" Ash batted at her, yet she returned for me over and over, her claws cutting into my skin. Why was she coming after me?

Nyx's wings fluttered as she dove toward me. Her talons pierced my shoulder, digging in, pain exploding down my arm.

"Ahhh!" I wailed, curling over, spots dotting my vision, the pain swishing my stomach. The dweller growled; the pain was a trigger to attack. To kill. I could feel my claws pushing from my hands, my teeth digging sharply into my lip. A whisper of the obscurer rode the dweller's back like a horseman of the apocalypse. A symbol of death.

A rush of fear slammed the cage on them. It was a knee-jerk reaction to the power they conjured, the terror of having no control.

"Get. Off!" Ash bellowed, trees cracking overhead, limbs bending to his energy, raining snow on us. He grabbed one of her wings. "How many times do I have to kill you before you die?" I heard a pop of cartilage, then a long shriek of pain rang through the skies before her body fluttered to the ground with a broken wing.

"Go!" Ash grabbed me, hurrying me on.

Clenching my teeth, I hurried my steps, feeling blood leak from my shoulder. The trees this time of year were twisted webs of empty branches, making us easy to see. The snow marked out our path. There was no way to not leave footprints in the snow, so our only escape was to outrun them.

We were their target, and though staying and fighting was the honorable thing to do, I understood we'd merely bring them more suffering.

While gunfire echoed behind us and the troop searched for Ash, we slipped away over the rocky terrain, heading to the one place we could disappear.

The sun had long set by the time we reached Brașov, frozen and stumbling down dimly lit streets clouded with the stench of urine. Returning here was dangerous, but it was the only town nearby we could get lost in, hiding among the mass populace and debauchery.

Crowds mulled outside busy pubs and brothels, conversing and drinking around barrels crackling with fires, drunks spilling in and out of the establishments. A dozen off-duty soldiers mixed in, yelling and falling down into the dirty slush.

"Like we never left," I muttered into Ash's back while we weaved through the dark alleys.

His bright green eyes flickered back to me, his head deep in his hood.

I could see the strain on his expression, but even more unsettling was how much I could feel it. Without the bracelet, everything about him was sharper to me, thrumming under my skin.

His mouth parted, and I could hear him silently tell me to "stay close" and "keep my head down," but he closed his mouth as if he didn't need to remind me. I understood.

His hand reached back, linking with mine, pulling me tighter into him. I sucked in from the pain, my shoulder throbbing where the hawk-shifter dug her nails into me.

Concern wrinkled Ash's mouth as he turned us down a familiar passage.

Women and men were already hanging out of the windows, displaying to anyone who could afford it that they were open and ready for business.

"We're going back here?" I glanced up at the brothel sign. We had stayed here just over a week ago, but it felt like a lifetime. Two different people walked in now, changed by what had happened... or not happened here last time.

"We have no money." Ash shrugged. "We have to bank on pity and hotness." He tried to play it off cheeky, but it didn't quite hit.

The warmth of the overcrowded room slapped my face, burning my cheeks and tickling my nose. "Wow." I blinked around at the overflowing room, patrons and prostitutes heaving in every direction, the commotion jarring me after hours of the quiet forest.

"Oh my gods!" A dramatic pitch turned us to the foyer. Dressed in a glossy gold robe and wearing a blonde wig with sparklers sitting on it like a crown and thick, glittery gold makeup, Maestro Silk strutted up to us, his red-painted mouth open in shock. "My beauties have returned!"

"Good to see you." Ash dipped his head.

"Oh, we are past formalities, my kittens." He came up, air-kissing our cheeks. "I am so happy to have you back." His nose wrinkled when he peered down at our dirty, torn, and definitely smelly clothes. "A little worse for wear, but nothing a bath and some clean clothes can't change!" He waved off what we were wearing and returned to look at us. "My goodness, I forgot how unbelievably stunning you both are. And so beautiful *together*." He winked with a little shoulder wiggle. "Are we looking for a room together for a few hours?" His painted eyebrow arched up dramatically, his eyes flaring with insinuation. "A party room?" He was somehow able to speak with this dramatic flair, but also a million miles a second. "It *is* a celebratory night, after all!"

Land of Monsters

Awareness crept in, and I understood his crown of sparklers and the overabundance of customers. "It's New Year's Eve," I muttered, peering around at the alcohol, drugs, and prostitutes flowing through the room, a surreal feeling setting over me.

Last year, right before my world came crumbling down, I had been partying in a nightclub with my friends, drunk on champagne, dancing with the man I loved, thinking life was perfect. I had found my happily ever after. Found my "mate."

Now I could look back with clearer eyes. How distant Wyatt was being, how he watched Piper. The guttural pain in his eyes observing her with her date, wanting to tear the man apart. The excuses he would make to be near her.

It was later that night he declared how he felt to her, and she could no longer deny she was in love with him, seeing him with me.

Star-crossed lovers.

And I was Roseline, not Juliet.

Reid and Eve were there guarding me at the New Year's party, Reid gushing about his daughter learning to walk, and Eve patting my back when I threw up in the toilet later. Not yet a traitor.

That party girl was a stranger to me, as I would have been to her. A one-dimensional character I'd watch on TV and roll my eyes at, while she would have laughed uncontrollably if anyone told her where she'd be in a year.

How young and innocent to the world I was then. Pampered and naive, thinking I had it all. My life set. Rich, powerful, pretty, and with the most desired man around.

And in less than two weeks, I became a murderer.

A monster.

I stared down at my filthy, torn pants and sweater, which still had blood stains from myself, Ash, and the two men I killed. My hair was stringy and dirty, my skin dry and cracked, standing in a brothel with a vengeful tree fairy.

My life had changed so much from the girl I once was.

Tucking hair behind my ear, my eyes prickled with emotion, not knowing if I was mourning that girl or she was mourning me.

"Speaking of a room." Ash retrieved my attention, a flirty grin tipping the side of his face. "You don't have an unused storage room or abandoned basement?"

"Sweet thing, why would you want the basement when you could have—" Maestro stopped, his fake eyelashes fluttering. "Oh. You don't have any money."

"Not technically." Ash grinned more, and I swear the room became hazy, like he was the drug.

"Technically?" Maestro's lids tapered, his lips pinching in skepticism.

"We have mushrooms." He flipped open the top of the bag strapped around me. "Good quality."

Maestro Silk leaned over, peering in at the soil-covered, smooshed mushrooms.

"Those are fresh?" His eyes widened. Farming was difficult nowadays, but in the dark recession of winter, vegetables and plants were almost impossible to get. Unless you were growing them in a hothouse, which no one could afford, but where Iacob's group lived, it was always warm and protected.

"Yes." Ash nodded.

"Where did you get them?"

Ash smiled in response, and Maestro nodded in understanding. He didn't need to know.

"They're a little unprocessed—"

"You think you can find this kind of quality anywhere right now?" Ash lifted a brow, closing the bag. "This is the high-priced stuff you eat, and also smoke without getting a hangover. And people will pay a lot for it." He jerked his chin to the people around us, desperate for an escape, to feel happy.

"One bundle for a room, food, unlimited alcohol, and whatever room we want to play in." Ash laid down the price.

"Unlimited alcohol?" Maestro touched his chest in shock, knowing it hit the hardest out of all of them.

"How serious are you about your patrons forking over money for raw, unrefined fae mushrooms?" Ash taunted. "That's our deal."

"Wow, aren't you just the hottest little dealer."

"Nothing little about me." Ash tilted his head. The insinuation heated my skin under the jacket because my mind pictured it, and he was correct.

An impish smile spanned over Maestro Silk's mouth. "Brains, beauty, and cocky. I think I just fell head over heels in love with you." He slipped his hand into Ash's. "Deal."

Ash shook in agreement, then put his hand on my back, leading me deeper into the room.

"Uh-uh." The procurer tsked. "Payment first."

Ash exhaled and reopened the top of the bag, taking a handful of mushrooms and holding them out.

"You expect me to touch those filthy things?" Maestro exclaimed. "I don't do dirty, darling." He nodded to a door. "Drop them in the kitchen while I take this exquisite thing upstairs and get her into a bath."

Ash gritted his jaw, his expression clear he wasn't comfortable letting me go off without him.

"So possessive," Maestro teased. "I promise, loverboy, she will be perfectly fine in my care."

Ash's eyes met mine before he took off for the kitchen, his hands full of mushrooms. If anyone here was sober and saw what he was carrying, they'd realize the bounty he had in his arms.

"Now for the really important item." Maestro's attention moved down me. *"Dragă."* Sweetheart. "You are severely insulting your beauty in such a disgusting ensemble." He wrinkled his nose at my clothes. "I will find you something far more appropriate to wear."

"Oh, um—"

Maestro had already turned away, his arm waving in the air for me to follow, not allowing me to decline his offer. We wiggled deeper into the throng of people—drugs, alcohol, and sex already freely being distributed throughout.

Maestro took me up two floors, pointing me to a bathroom. "This is your stop. I will not let you in any of my rooms with so much filth."

"Coming from someone whose place is covered in cum and bodily fluid."

Maestro let out a howl of laughter, waving at his eyes so he wouldn't smudge his makeup. "You two are like my medicine cupboard."

"What does that mean?"

"Full of fun surprises." He nudged me into the bathroom. "Go. I'll find both of you some extra clothes." Maestro closed the door.

In the quiet bathroom, the music and chatter far below, I stared numbly at my reflection in the mirror. I almost didn't recognize who was looking back. Void of makeup, bruised, flushed, and exhausted, I no longer had the sheen of wealth, the glow of a girl who thought she was confident and put together.

She was the illusion, while the girl who had survived the last month stared wisely back. I couldn't say what it was, but I appeared older. Grounded. With a confidence my younger self thought I had, but didn't. Though I respected this girl now, part of me longed to go back. To be satisfied with designer clothes, clubbing, and lunching with my friends.

It all sounded so trivial. Like I had lived in a tiny box. I had seen and done too much now. Whatever happened, I could never go back to her.

The door squeaked open, and my eyes flicked up to the mirror, imagining Maestro stepping in with clothes, but mossy green eyes found mine instead, hitching my breath.

"I haven't gotten in yet," I protested, a strange nervousness jumbling my words. "But if you want to go first." Ash closed the door, twisting me around to him. In one hand, he carried a cloth and an unlabeled container. "What are you—"

"Take your jacket off." His low tone was demanding.

"What?"

"Where Nyx got you." He nodded at my shoulder. "I need to clean it."

Fae healed quickly, but we were still susceptible to infections, and the way my shoulder ached, I wouldn't be surprised if she dipped her talons in poison beforehand. She had cut into a nerve, and I could barely move my arm, cradling it most of the trek here.

I bit down on my lip, trying to lift the bag from my body with my good arm.

Ash stepped in, placing the towel and antiseptic down. He grabbed the handle, pulled it over, and set the bag down on a stool. His hands returned to me, curling around the collar of my jacket, his knuckles brushing my neck. With care, he peeled it off my body, letting the torn item drop to the floor in a heap. His fingers reached up, trailing over the holes in my sweater, the dried blood caking the fabric.

"I need your *pulóver* off." He cleared his throat, not looking at me.

"I need help." My voice came out quiet and wobbly, like I was asking for more than him to assist me.

His eyes rose to stare at mine in the mirror. We had been naked around each other before. I knew the sounds he made in pleasure. He knew how I tasted. But something about him undressing me, his eyes locked on mine in the mirror, felt far more intimate.

He coiled his fingers into the hem and slowly pulled off my shirt, my hair falling back down around me. The cheap, see-through sports bra did nothing to cover my breasts. His eyes stayed on me in the reflection, his throat bobbing. Under his scrutiny, my nipples hardened, my skin flushing in places.

He swallowed again, tearing his gaze away, snatching up the antiseptic.

"It's starting to close up. I will need to reopen it and clean it out properly. You can jump in the shower, and then I'll bandage it up after you get out. Okay?"

I nodded.

"It's gonna hurt. You ready?"

I bobbed my head again, my teeth cut into my bottom lip. When Ash pulled my healing skin apart, a whimper-hiss watered my eyes, and fresh blood oozed down my side from the reopened wound. "Fuck!"

"Sorry." He wiped up the blood, dipping the other end of the cloth into the sterilizer and swiping it over the gash.

"Holy shit squared, multiplied, and divided!" I yelped.

"Whaatt?" Ash started laughing, a small snort coming from his nose, making me chuckle.

"It's something my mother always says," I replied, a stab hitting my heart at the thought of my mom. Gods, I missed her. She was busy a lot while Rook and I grew up, but I understood. I was proud my mother was out there trying to make the world better. She was the best mom. Kind, compassionate, and so loving. More the rule follower, while my father broke them all. They were the perfect balance.

"Your mother." His humor died away, and his demeanor shifted instantly at the mention of her. "You mean the queen."

"To me, she's just Mom."

He let out a scoff, continuing to clean my wound. Whatever was there just a moment ago was gone, distance weaving between us. I hated that any mention of my family reminded him of who I was, changing his view of me. I was no longer the girl his tongue had slid through. The person he had treated like an equal. But a princess. Someone untouchable.

"Hey?" I said roughly, regaining his focus back on me in the mirror. "I'm still me, no matter what label I have or who my parents are."

He watched me.

"I don't judge you for your family, so don't judge me for mine."

A crazed sound came from him. "You sound like our families are equal. That yours is some normal, everyday run-of-the-mill family and mine is just eccentric. Mine was a fucking *cult*. Fucked-up people who liked orgies with neighbors and hinted at pedophilia!" He exploded. "We are not even close to being the same!"

I whipped around, confused and angry at why he was so mad at me.

"You have a family who loves you. Who would do anything for you. Take it from someone who didn't have that kind of family as a kid... *go home*."

I didn't want to. It was absolutely crazy, but being here with him made sense. It felt right. I couldn't even explain it to myself. Like against all odds, the girl who partied last New Year with her boyfriend was supposed to be in this bathroom this year with him.

Yet I knew my family had to be freaking out, and I was only bringing more danger to Ash the longer I stayed. My family wasn't the kind you just called and told you were fine and not to worry. They would track me down from one phone call.

Either I stayed silent and remained with Ash, or I called them and knew it meant I would be going home.

Fuck. I didn't want to think about my father's temper once he hugged me and knew I was okay. He would shift into his beast for days, denting the deer population. But really, it was my mother who, when truly provoked, scared the daylights out of me. Her natural obscurer could kick mine's ass. She had that quiet anger where you wished to be screamed at instead. While my brother would probably whack me on the back of the head and say, "Glad you're back, doofus."

Ash brought us back here to send me home. To do what was "right." And it seemed better for everyone if I just made the call. Have someone come get me and jet me back to America, our journey concluding uneventfully.

"You should get in the shower." Ash stepped back, curving for the door. "I'll go find our room."

"Wait." I clutched his hand, stopping him, a desperation to keep him close. What if tonight was our last night? What if I never saw him again?

"I need help getting these off." I indicated my pants and boots.

A nerve jumped in his cheek. Ash took a long moment, and I was ready for him to make an excuse. To walk out the door.

He finally turned to face me, and I didn't move, staring up at him, waiting for him to act.

As if he could read my thoughts, he picked up on what I didn't say. He stepped closer to me, his body barely inches from mine. His hand reached for the waist of my pants, undoing the top button and sliding the zipper down. His fingers slipped along my skin, palms sweeping out over my hips under the material, pushing the material over my ass.

Ash lowered himself to his knees, his mouth only centimeters away from my pussy, the heat of his breath sinking through my underwear, curling into me.

Air moved in and out of my lungs, and I could not control my response to his touch. To him.

He untied my boots, helping me step out of them, and pulled off my socks. His hand wrapped around my thigh, and I leaned into him as he took each pant leg off. Slowly. In complete control. While everything in me wanted to snap.

I could no longer hear moans, beds squeaking, or music and loud voices from below. I existed just in this room. My heart pounded in my ears, desire stirring up my dark dweller.

It needed. Craved.

Leaving me in only paper-thin underwear and bra, his palms glided up my legs to my hips as he stood, his body almost against mine, looming over me. His gaze dropped to my mouth, his fingers digging harder into my hips. "Raven…"

"Knock, knock!" a sing-song voice called out, the door opening, Maestro's head popping in.

Ash jerked away from me, but the procurer's eyes danced from us to my clothes strewn over the floor.

"Oh, I'm so sorry to interrupt." His eyes flared with lust. "I'll just leave these here for you." He dropped the pile of clothes onto the floor. "You can use room 306. But I'll warn you, the bed squeaks really loud." He winked before shutting the door, taking whatever might have happened with him.

Ash was back on defense, his hand running through his dirty hair, and he avoided looking at me.

"Don't use all the hot water," he grumbled before grabbing the satchel and stomping out of the room.

It was a full two minutes that I stood there, confused, wanting to cry, and trying to tell myself he wasn't about to kiss me.

I wanted to kill Maestro, but at the same time, it might have been for the best.

Ash was still in love with this Kek and Lukas.

I wanted him to kiss me because he couldn't think of anything else. Wanted it more than air and not because he was lonely, horny, and lost.

I would never be someone's second choice again.

Chapter 5

Ash

Fuck.

My hand strangled the back of my neck while I paced the small room, trying not to acknowledge my throbbing erection, need rattling through every fiber. The impulse to go back down the hall, barge through the bathroom door, and take what I wanted had me grinding my teeth until my jaw popped.

I squeezed my cock over my pants like I could calm it down, soothe it or something. Get control of myself. Though it seemed this was a losing battle lately.

It was natural for me to get this horny. It was who I was. *What* I was. And it had been a while since I took the edge off. That's all this was—excess magic needing an outlet.

Except you could've had it last night! Instead you walked away from it. What the hell is wrong with you?

Not wanting to answer the question, my gaze flew around the simple chamber, landing on the full bed taking up most of the room. I could hear the squeal of the old metal frame without even sitting on it, knowing how it would squeak and cry with every thrust.

A buzzing started under my skin when I had a flash of Raven under me, groaning, her hands tied to the frame. My hands clasped tighter on my dick, and I drew in heavy, deep breaths.

I couldn't share this bed with her. No doubt my weakness would win out.

You'll probably lose her tomorrow anyway. Her family will take her back home. This might be your last night together. The fiend whispered in my ear, chipping at my fragile will. Another part of me was terrified, knowing that if we crossed the line, everything would change.

My goals. My life. My revenge. *Me*.

The door opened and Raven stepped in, wrapped only in a minuscule, ratty towel, her hair wet, her skin glistening with water, with clothes tucked in her arms.

Any foundation under me dropped away, my body flaring to life. I felt like I was scrambling in the air, not ready to admit that gravity was about to pull me down.

"What are you doing?" I sputtered, my words coming out angry.

"Walking into the room."

"You can't just walk around like that!" I gestured to her wet, barely covered body. "Anyone could be lurking around out there!" I could hear the crazy in my voice, the ridiculous argument I was starting.

"We're in a *brothel*," she scoffed. "I'm wearing more than anyone in this building."

"I don't care!" I couldn't seem to stop. Her presence, in only a towel, shrunk the room to a pinpoint.

"What the fuck is your problem?" She tossed the clothes on the bed, fury flashing her eyes a tint of pink. "You know what? I don't care. I'm sick of you treating me like a child. Haven't I proved enough to you I can handle myself? That *I'm* the one people should be afraid of? That you should bow down to me?"

That was the problem. I had been on my knees before her already, and I wanted to drop to them now.

Her eyes flared at me. "You won, okay, Ash? I will call my parents tomorrow and get out of your way. But tonight, I want to live in the moment. Live like I'm not the fucking princess of the Unified Nations. I'm *just* me!" She grabbed some clothes, turned with a huff, and dropped her towel.

Lightning struck me, the sight of her naked ass and back electrocuting me inside and out as she drew on some lacy panties Maestro had gotten for her, frying my brain.

Right then, loud moans from the room next door crackled through the walls. We could hear the two men pounding into each other, and their energy cut straight into me, making my mind hazy with lust. My willpower evaporated, and I felt myself falling.

Spending time in brothels was practically home to me, with Kitty being one of the top madams in Hungary. The way I grew up, sounds of sex were like white noise.

But right now, if I didn't get out, I would do something very stupid. Every fiber in me wanted to taste her curves, feast on her. Cross the line and double-dip a few times in it.

She was not someone you could use like that. Especially if I was putting her on a plane tomorrow, never to see her again.

"Fuck this." I strode for the door, every muscle locked up. "Don't wait up."

"Where are you going?"

I slammed the door behind me, practically jogging down the corridor to the last room at the end of the hall. I knew what was inside, and I wanted to get as high and as drunk as possible, my specific needs taken care of.

And most of all, I wanted someone to make me forget what I just left in the room. To bleed her from my veins.

Leaning over the table, I sniffed in the line of fairy dust, my system crying with glee at the familiar substance. I had gotten better at ignoring the craving, but it had always been there, waiting under the surface. My shoulders eased just a little, and I took another line right away. I was too keyed up, and my brain wasn't letting me black out images of Raven naked.

Yes, we had been naked before together, but this felt different. In that older man's hotel room, we were his puppets, just acting out his fantasies. Here, we were acting out our own.

I tipped my head back, letting the drugs flood my system. The room buzzed with an abundance of energy and people. A mix of fae and human, everyone here ready to orgasm their way into the new year. The need for even more wickedness and twisted kinks had the room moaning in unison, sex covering almost every open space.

"It's crap, but it gets the job done." A man's sensual voice came up next to me at the table spread with drugs and alcohol, doing a line next to me. I looked over, taking in the tall, built, beautiful naked fae. His long flowing black hair and overly carnal aura suggested a *zburător,* similar to an incubus. I recognized him instantly as the same man who had been touching Raven the last time we were in this room, kicking up a flare of anger.

"Yeah," I replied curtly, tasting the chemicals that made up the cheap drug at the back of my tongue, knowing I had something that could offer me a better high back in the room. And it wasn't the mushrooms I was thinking of.

A sensual smile warmed his features, my tone misunderstood—or ignored. Licking his lips, he looked me up and down without recognition. He clearly had no memory of me or that night.

"You are gorgeous." His hand slid over my ass, though his gaze stayed on my cock. "And fucking massive. Gods, I want to suck you." His hand dipped lower on my ass, and he stepped into me, his light-purple eyes suggesting he had some high fairy blood in him. "What are you looking for? I'm into it all."

A sensation crashed over me, a pull I couldn't describe, but I instantly felt it burn through me, commanding me. Craning my neck to the door, I went still.

Air sucked out of the room while everything in me came alive.

Once again, Raven stood a few feet inside the door, but this time, a confidence radiated within her, a strength I hadn't seen before. As much as she feared her powers, they made her who she was. Authority billowed from her skin, making us all want to bend the knee to her.

Dressed in just those lacy black knickers and a matching see-through bra. Her damp hair tumbled down to her lower back, her chin high and regal. Gone was the nervousness she displayed the last time she came in here.

As she stared at me, she took my breath away, and at that moment, I knew I was done fighting her.

The man followed my gaze, his mouth dropping open.

"Futu-ti." Fuck. The man whispered in awe. *"Ce dracu este ea?" What the hell is she?*

He could feel it too, the unique magic that was only Raven, her signature.

Mine.

My feet moved, logic deserting me as I strode for her. Her chin rose higher, preparing for my confrontation. She held her ground, but I noticed her cheeks turning pink, her eyes straining not to slide down my physique, her throat struggling to swallow.

I loved knowing I affected her too.

"What the hell are you doing?" I stopped about an inch away from her.

"No." She put up her hand, moving around me.

"Wh-what?" I sputtered, moving back in front of her. "What do you mean, no?"

"I mean, we aren't doing this again." She tipped her head, her eyes blazing into mine with determination. "I am a grown adult, whatever you may think, and I make my own decisions. I want to be here, and you can't do anything to change that."

"But why?" I motioned around at the debauchery happening around, a woman moaning from the top of her lungs in the swing over our heads with three other people. "This is what you want?"

"What? Am I too proper for you now? Too high on a pedestal?" she shot back. "Guess what, Ash? I am a flesh and blood person who has experienced tragedy, heartbreak, and death… who also wants to feel, be touched, live in the moment." Her eyes stayed on me. Reaching around, she unhooked her bra, letting it slide down her arms. She was small, but her pert tits would fit perfectly in my hands.

And mouth.

I bit back a moan, my dick so hard tears formed behind my lids.

"I want this night just for me. Tomorrow I can go back to my role as princess, leave you alone on your revenge mission to die." Her lip lifted. "But in here, I want to be more than the title, more than the fucked-up mess I am. I have been so scared to breathe, so scared to live outside my comfort zone because of who I am and what I can do. The world watches me, either putting me on a shelf like a pretty doll or waiting for me to screw up. I become a sum of what headlines say about me." She stepped closer, her hands wrapping around my forearms, her nipples brushing my torso. Short, shallow breaths moved in and out of my lungs, only a hair away from breaking. "So either step up or back off." She walked around me, leaving me reeling over what she had just said.

Step up or back off. An invitation to act. To do something.

I watched her walk away. The *zburător* was already in front of her, lust written all over his face. He moved in close, his hands trailing over her hips, and whispered something in her ear, his lips grazing down her neck.

It made me feral with possessiveness, the foreign emotion switching off logic, muting the voice that kept her at a distance. There was no backing off. Not when it came to her.

Mine.

A growl flared my nostrils, and I moved to her. The man's mouth was dragging down her neck to her breasts, her head falling back as his tongue swiped over her nipple.

I came up behind her and wrapped my palm around her neck, pulling her into me. I tilted her head back, my teeth scraping at her ear. "Is this what you want, Raven?"

She gasped, a shudder going through her, her ass arching into my cock. I gripped her hip, squeezing it. "Want me to eat your pussy again?" I rumbled into her neck. The incubus moved to her other breast, flicking and sucking on it. "Or do you want him to?"

She curved her head, her eyes meeting mine. "I want you to watch him eat my pussy."

Shock and lust poured down on me. Raven took me by surprise, but it was like she knew one of my kinks. I loved watching. I wanted her eyes on me, wishing it was me, while she got off with someone else. I grabbed her chin, turning it more to me. "You want to do this?" I flicked my chin to the other man.

A nervousness flickered over her face, but she nodded. She would go forward with or without me and like hell was I standing to the side.

"If we're going to do this. We're going to do this my way." I jerked her chin harder while the other man licked a trail down her sternum.

The grotesque sounds of sex, of a human puking in a potted plant, of this being too communal, itched at my skin.

I never had a problem with it being too public. I used to fuck Lukas and Kek in the community showers all hours of the day, with people in the next cubicle.

But with her, I didn't want this public, like so much of her life was; I wanted this just for her. Raven being the only focus.

"And not here." I grabbed her hand, nodding to the fae man. "Joining?"

He looked at both of us. "Fuck yes."

I fought back the need to tell him to fuck off, but I didn't, knowing she needed this. To experience a night where she was the complete focus of our desire.

To have us both on our knees for this woman.

Chapter 6
Raven

Ash nakedly directed us down the hallway, back to our room. I was trying to shut down my brain, not think about what was happening, but my nerves were starting to rattle through me. And it wasn't over the stranger following us. It was Ash. I was forcing him to cross this very fragile line. What if I ruined everything?

He's handing you over to your parents tomorrow and not looking back. He doesn't care about you like that. Just use him.

My stubborn nature attached to this thought, and I stepped inside the dark room, ignoring the crazy nerves parading under my skin like a swarm of bees.

Firelamps from outside flickered through the window, giving us just enough of a glow to see, like whatever happened in this room stayed here.

"Rules." Ash turned to the fairy, not caring to know his name. "You can do whatever she wants you to do, except you will not put your dick in her. Understand?"

The man smirked. I could pick up his similarities to Uncle Nik, the same sexual vibes. He was an incubus of some sort.

"Can I put it in you, then?"

Ash exhaled, a frown etching his brow, but he nodded.

A surge of possession shot my dark dweller to the edges of my skin, my teeth baring. "No." A growl curled in my throat, jerking Ash's head to me. Our eyes stayed locked, like we were communicating every thought and feeling without saying a word.

He dipped his head, returning to the man. "Mouth only."

"As long as I can suck the monster there." The man licked his lips. "And eat hers."

Stepping away from the incubus, Ash went to the table and grabbed the bag, taking a mushroom out.

"What's that?" The man stared at the item. "Is it what I think it is?"

"Raw fae mushroom."

"What?" The guy's eyes widened, excitement and need filling them. "You have unrefined mushrooms?"

Ash broke off sections of the fungi, holding out a piece for him.

"It's pure," he warned.

The incubus took it, examining it with shock. "This is real shit." He popped it into his mouth.

Tearing off a tiny piece, Ash strolled up to me, not stopping until we were inches apart, his body practically pressing into mine. "Want to try?"

"I've had mushrooms before," I whispered, not able to ignore his cock standing up between us, my body shaking more from desire than nerves.

"These will hit you a little different." His gaze crawled over me, noticing the nervousness dancing between us. "It will relax you." He leaned into my ear, his breath gliding down my neck. "Make you feel *so* good."

My breath hitched. I had no need for drugs. Ash was my aphrodisiac, but I wanted to lose myself. To have this one night. Tomorrow, everything would change.

I opened my mouth, letting him place it on my tongue. This act felt erotic as he watched me swallow it down. Lifting my gaze to his, I observed him do the same, our eyes never leaving each other.

"Just let me know if you want to stop at any time."

He was giving me an out. A safety net. For once, I didn't want one. I had lived with one all my life. We both understood this was the final moment to stop what was going to happen. The line was about to get eased out of existence.

I was ready to go down in flames.

Reaching over, Ash brushed my long locks over my shoulders, exposing my breasts. His hands slid over them, my nipples immediately going hard, my thighs clenching as his thumbs rolled over them.

"Fuck, they're perfect." He leaned over, his tongue swiping the peaks, sucking them into his mouth. My body instantly reacted, a noise escaping my throat, my head tipping back. It felt even better than I remembered. The one time we had been together before was a haze of fairy powder and alcohol.

The man came behind me, his hands gliding down my sides, his fingers tracing over my skin, making every inch tingle. His mouth skimmed the curve of my neck, licking and nipping, while his hands hooked on the waist of my knickers and slid them down my legs.

Completely naked, I stood between the two men, the murmur of the drugs starting to block any nervousness or insecurity.

The incubus slipped his hand over my waist, skating down, letting out a loud groan when his fingers parted me. His dick hardened against my back, his tongue drawing up my neck as he rubbed through my pussy.

A gasp caught in my throat as I watched precum ooze from Ash's rigid cock, his eyes flaring with intensity. Possession.

"You wanted me to watch him tongue fuck you?" His voice growled in my ear. And with no warning, he flipped me around, my front facing the pretty fae man, my tits still wet from Ash's mouth. "I'll watch from here," he rumbled against my neck, causing me to shiver.

The man's eyes lit up, a weightless feeling buzzing through me, though it made me want to float into the clouds. The incubus went down on his knees, my breath going sharper when Ash pulled me back into his chest, his cock pressing between my ass, while the man drew his hands up my thighs.

"Fuck, you two are hot," the incubus said breathlessly, staring up at us. He kissed up my thigh. Ash gripped my hips in place, opening me wider as the fairy's tongue found my center, licking through me.

"Oh gods." I leaned back into Ash. Every part of my skin was charged, colors weaving through the light in the room, intensifying everything.

The incubus's tongue worked my pussy, but everywhere else, I felt Ash. Like it was only him and me here.

"She tastes amazing, doesn't she?" Ash spoke in a gritty timbre.

The man moaned in ecstasy, nodding his head.

"I've never tasted anything so good." His tongue lapped through me, my eyes hazing until I saw Ash on his knees in front of me instead of the incubus. The mushrooms were taking my imagination, letting me feel everything in abundance, experience everything without limits.

Ash's fingers dug into my skin, spreading my folds open even more so he could see everything the man was doing to me over my shoulder. The feel of Ash's touch, his cock throbbing against me, dominated the room and seized my attention. There was something in the back of my brain, a warning, like he was slipping into my bones like an invader. Though he felt anything but. I wanted to feel him inside and outside of me.

"I want to taste you both." The man clenched my outer thighs, his gaze on us.

Ash reached down, shifting his cock, and sliding it through my folds.

"Oh goddd." My legs almost gave out as he ran himself through me, his grip on me tightening to keep me on my feet. His huge cock slipped through my pussy, nudging past until I could see the tip, covered in my wetness and dripping with precum.

The fairy let out a loud moan as his lips wrapped around Ash's cock, sucking and licking us both with feral abandon. He reached around, cupping Ash's ass, fitting us together against his mouth, wanting us to fuck his face.

"Watch him suck your taste off my cock." Ash rocked into me, the slight friction trembling my muscles. "Look how drenched my dick is from you."

My eyes took in the scene, just becoming wetter. Fuck, it was so hot and dirty to watch, getting me more turned on. I loved the feel of Ash's cock, like it was the only one my pussy craved.

"Now let yourself feel what we are doing to you, *Dziubuś*."

Ash kneaded my tits, his teeth nipping at the sensitive part of my neck, and I tipped my head back, falling into utter bliss. The drugs rushed through my veins, the world around me becoming dream-like and free, where I felt nothing but pleasure and had no fears or inhibitions.

My hips bucked with Ash's, riding his cock as the incubus sucked on us both. Though in my mind, both were Ash. He was everywhere and in everything.

Ash trailed his fingers down from my breasts, his thumb rolling over my clit, making me cry out. The incubus reached between our legs, cupping Ash's balls, fucking my pussy harder with his tongue.

Ash grunted in my ear, driving up my desire.

"Oh gods…" I fluttered against Ash's cock, rocking faster. Reaching my arms to wrap around his neck, I felt an orgasm crawl up my spine.

"No. Not yet." Ash bit at my earlobe, somehow sensing how close I was getting. He stepped back. The sudden loss of him forced a whimper from me. "Lay on the bed," he ordered me.

With no hesitation, I did what he instructed, settling on the bed.

"Open your legs wide."

My hazy eyes took in two of Ash, watching me spread my legs for them. They both stared, my nipples aching, my clit throbbing, feeling so needy. Craving to be filled.

"Play with yourself," Ash growled. Energy weaved a connection between us across the room.

My fingers slipped inside me. Ash moaned under his breath, his eyes never leaving mine. My pussy pulsed, and I swear I could feel his touch, like his fingers were inside me, not mine.

Ash hissed as if he felt the same; the incubus began to rub Ash's cock up and down, taking him into his mouth.

A growl filled the room, and it took me a moment to realize it came from me. The dweller prickled at my skin, tingling at my nails and claws. *Mine.*

"Stop," Ash grunted out, his gaze locked on me, but I knew he was speaking to the fae. He stepped away from the incubus, his green eyes bright as he stalked to me.

"Your dweller is possessive."

I nodded.

"She wants my cock," he smirked.

I couldn't have lied if I tried. The mushrooms made me answer honestly.

"Yes."

Grabbing me, Ash flipped me over him. Laying under me, he settled me over his face. "First I get to her eat her pussy."

A smirk danced over my mouth, and I twisted around before he could act. Nothing felt in my control except need, and the need to taste him consumed me.

My knees were on either side of his head, my mouth sliding down his stomach, grazing his cock.

"*Dziubuś.*" Ash groaned when my tongue slid out to taste him. I barely had the chance that night weeks ago, and I craved him more than anything. Lapping at his precum, the dweller rumbled like a purr. My tongue licked up the vein in his cock before I took him into my mouth.

"Fuck!" Ash's hips jerked, yanking me down, his tongue finding me. I groaned deeply, taking him deeper down my throat.

My hips rocked harder against Ash, his tongue making me lose every ounce of reality. Colors and movement clawed over the room, things scurrying and moving in the shadows. Nothing seemed real, but I felt everything so acutely.

"You two are gonna make me come so hard," the incubus growled. He moved to the bed, stepping up to the headboard and kneeling behind me and over Ash. He pressed his cock between my butt cheeks. Gripping them together, he slid his cock through me with steady friction.

"Fuck!" he barked, moving quicker, his free hand gripping my breast.

I started to shake, my body on overload as everything came to a pinpoint.

Ash's tongue went deeper, his lips sucking hard on my clit.

Then he nipped down.

Everything exploded around me, and I screamed. The men moaned, and cum spilled over my back and down my throat, and then there was the brush of something beyond anything anyone could touch. It was so brief, but I swear I could feel Ash brush against my soul. The intensity caused me to climax again.

My core clenched so tight, pulsing, and I heard more cries bay out in the room.

I floated and soared, but as the saying goes, what goes up must come down...

I came crashing down so hard, met only by darkness.

Chapter 7

Ash

"Stop petting his penis. It's not a pet."

Chirp!

"What? No! I would never!"

Voices tugged me from a deep sleep, something about them making me feel confused and jumbled, and I tucked in tighter, wishing for the blackness to take me back.

"You're the one who stuck your finger in there, not me!"

Chirrrpppp!

"It was a total misunderstanding!"

No.

No. No. No. I felt the refusal groan from me, my lids still shut.

"Stop trying to fly!"

Chhhiirp!

Fuck. I knew those voices. "Please, gods, no…" I groaned, flinching as my eyes opened to the room. Morning light streamed in, my lids pinching together at the brash intrusion.

"Master Ash! Master Ash! You're awake!"

"Please tell me I'm still high," I grumbled, my eyes fully opening, seeing a brownie standing on my chest. Not even a foot tall, his nose dominated his heart-shaped face, thick brown hair spiking up in a mohawk, and a bushy beard plaited with ribbon.

Opie.

"Well, she definitely is." He thumbed back to the tiny imp, her three-prong hands skimming the air like she could feel it, a chunk of mushroom stuck to the side of her head. She was half his size and looked like a bald Aye-Aye.

"Fuuuuuccckkk," I moaned, pinching my nose and taking a deep breath.

"It looks like you did plenty of that last night," Opie replied, wiggling his thick eyebrows—one had a sticker gem attached to it. Opie was a house brownie Brexley met in Halálház. His kind were known to clean, but Opie wasn't like a normal brownie, nor was his best friend, Bitzy. She was a cantankerous, grouchy imp who rode in a backpack on Bitzy's back and flipped everyone off.

Though when she was high, Bitzy turned into this happy, mellow, smiling thing.

Freaked me the fuck out.

Chirrrpppppp! She wiggled her hands around like something was there.

"Lies!" Opie huffed, his disproportionately large foot stomping on my ribs.

Chirp. Chirrrrp!

"I'm telling you it was—"

"A misunderstanding," I finished for him. "Yes, we all know."

"Well, it was!" He pointed his finger at me. "And you shouldn't talk. How good could you be if they didn't even stick around for morning bumpies?" He nodded to the empty spot next to me.

I sat up, tumbling the brownie onto my lap with a cry. A jumble of memories from the night before came back to me. I recalled almost blacking out when I was coming down Raven's throat, our guest leaving while I cleaned her up and put her to bed.

Next to me.

"Why doesn't anyone warn a brownie before they do that?" he grumbled, standing up and straightening his outfit—an outfit made with gold silk.

"Oh gods… tell me you didn't?" I climbed out of bed, reaching for my boxer briefs. The cut-up fabric he weaved through his beard and mohawk looked identical to what Maestro wore last night.

"What?" Opie flounced the golden fabric he had bowed on his spiked hair, a red pleasure feather sticking out of one of them on top. He wore a deck of cards from the gambling table, fanned out in a pleated skirt, and I was pretty sure he used a whip from the party room as a strange halter top. Bitzy had more parts of the whip bound up her arms, her torso wrapped in the gold silk like a one-piece bathing suit. "You don't like?"

I learned to never say no to this question.

"It's great," I groaned. "But what the hell are you doing here?" Yanking on my pants, I couldn't stop looking at the rumpled sheets. The cum stains still streaked the duvet, the spot where her head had lain still imprinted on the pillow. Where was she? Another thought hit me, dropping anxiety into my gut. "Wait." I froze, looking between the two sub-fae, my muscles locking up. "You. Are. Here."

"Good on ya for spotting that one." Opie folded his arms. "And here I thought you were the wise one of the group."

Cccchirp!

"Right?" Opie motioned to me, answering whatever Bitzy said. "Maybe his brain leaked out of his *exceptionally* large dick. Not that I noticed… or saw… or touched."

Chhhirp!

"No, I didn—"

"Is Brexley here?" I interrupted, looking around like she would jump out. If Brexley was here, it meant Warwick was too, and probably the rest of the group.

"Did you not grasp our outfits?" Opie motioned down like it was obvious. "We're spies."

"Spies?" I stared at his gaudy outfit. "How the hell would I get spies from that?"

"We blend in." He pretended to be melding in with the space around him.

"Nothing about either one of you blends in."

Chirppp! Bitzy swayed, a creepy smile on her face, blinking at me with adoration.

"How much did she have?"

Opie shrugged. "You left it open." He nodded at the bag in the corner.

"That shit is pure!" I exclaimed, tugging on my shirt. "She's going to be high for days."

Chirrrrrp! Her smile widened.

"You're complaining, mushroom man?" Opie played with his skirt, spacing the deck of cards out perfectly.

"Answer my question."

"No, Master Fishy isn't here." He put his finger to his lips. "Don't tell, but we are on a secret mission to watch over you. You don't know we're here."

I stared at him.

"Oh. I guess our secret is out."

"You think?" I huffed, shoving my feet into my boots, not even bothering to lace them up. "How long have you been following me?"

"Well, technically, since Master Scorpion told her he saw you in the train station. But really, our first day started more… well… now."

So Scorpion did see me that day. My family could find me no matter how much I tried to hide from them.

"Wait." I yanked on my jacket. "That was a month ago."

"Not my fault!" Opie flung down his arms. "There are a lot of distractions from there to here. It's her fault!" He pointed to Bitzy.

Chrrriiippppp! She flopped on the bed, doing snow angels on the quilt, giggling to herself.

I squeezed the bridge of my nose, my concern going back to the empty spot where Raven had passed out last night. Many times on this journey, Raven had been gone when I woke up, but I couldn't get rid of the odd feeling this time.

Maybe she needed to get away from you. Away from what happened between us.

I recalled everything that transpired last night, what we did, what was said. I wanted to blame the hallucinogenic, but deep down, I knew it would be a lie.

"Stay here!" I pointed at Opie.

"But…"

"Stay, or I will tie you to that bedpost!" I ordered, grabbing my jacket.

"Not really a deterrent there, is it?"

"Opie, I swear," I threatened, hiking for the door. I paused, pivoting and snatching up the mushroom bag. No way I trusted them alone with it.

Banging out the door, I pretended I wasn't racing to the stairs. She was probably downstairs drinking a coffee or something, and I was panicking for nothing.

My boots hit the ground floor, my heart beating faster than normal, my head snapping around the quiet room. Last night's celebration now looked like a crime scene, laid out in empty bottles, confetti, discarded clothing, and passed-out bodies curled over table benches and on the floor. The smells of sex, sweat, and alcohol hung heavy in the air, ghosts of the festivities of last night.

But Raven was nowhere to be found.

Unease formed in my throat, riding my shoulders, a nagging worry scraping up the back of my neck.

She left you.

What if she was already on her way home? Appalled by what happened last night, she called her family and slipped out without a goodbye? Dread fogged my mind, filling my lungs. My legs took off, not thinking past the panic consuming me.

She left you. She left you. It looped in my head as I tore out of the door, feeling out of control.

The cold air smacked my skin, billowing clouds from my mouth. The sun was hazy, denying us any real warmth from its rays.

"Raven?" I called her name, hoping she had stepped outside for air. The cramped street was vacant of the partiers and drunks from last night, but remnants of the debauchery scattered the passage. A mist of cold air blocked some of the putrid smell of vomit and piss. "Raven?"

For once, the silence unsettled me, jarring my nerves. It was like I could feel she wasn't here, an emptiness I could sense.

She left you. She left you. She left you.

Sprinting down the lane, I had no real idea where I was running to, but desperation took hold, steering me toward something.

Every lane I hooked around sat vacant, invoking stronger emotions. They strangled my throat, pounded against my ribs, and hazed my mind.

Weaving through the streets, I came out onto the main square, condensation puffing out like smoke, my nose and ears burning with cold. My pulse pounded in my ears as I scanned the space. Only a handful of people were up, milling around, lingering close to the stands with coffee and baked goods. The plaza was trashed with alcohol bottles, clothes, streamers, and garbage. Remains of the festivities.

Scanning every figure, panic almost choked me when none of them were her.

She left you. She really left you.

It was what I wanted. What I had asked of her over and over since she walked into my life. I was going to make her leave today anyway. Yet, my heart accelerated at the thought that she did, my lungs not able to catch enough air. The sensation of wanting to tear out of my skin had me prancing in place, circling around.

In that moment, everything was stripped down to the raw truth. I didn't want her to go. Along the way, I had grown used to her being next to me. Needed it now.

A cold sweat beaded at the back of my neck, deep panic almost turning me to stone.

Abandonment.

Their choice or not, people continuously left me. My parents, sister, Kek and Lukas, even Warwick when he went to prison for years, and Kitty when our relationship fell apart. It was all I had ever known. But Raven leaving snapped something in me, darkness flooding into my chest, drowning me like I would never see light again.

A strangled noise hissed through my teeth. I struggled with knowing what to do—and understood I'd be too late anyway.

Land of Monsters

"Raven," I grunted out, hearing the desperation, the pleading in my tone.

A petite girl I hadn't seen, hidden by a stocky man in line, stepped away from the stand with two coffees in her hands. My heart stopped in my chest, my eyes going over the figure, hope surging up my throat. Even bundled in clothing, hood up, and far away, I still knew every inch. Recognized her aura like it was my own. My body sprang to life, realizing she was close.

"Gods…" A heaved exhale broke from me, almost curving me over. Relief knotted emotion in my throat, mixing between grief and bliss.

She didn't leave.

Taking in a breath, I tried to calm my heart. My mouth parted, about to call her name across the large square, but her head lifted like I had already spoken, hearing me without saying a word. This far away, I couldn't even make out the details of her face, but I didn't need to. I felt her looking back at me. Sensed her on my skin.

And then the moment shattered.

Squealing tires impaled the quiet morning air. Two army jeeps filled with soldiers came screeching into the square right next to the coffee stand. They leaped out, their shouts booming with authority, startling everyone around like birds.

"Mainile sus!" Hands up! Armed, the eight men quickly surrounded Raven, their weapons pointed at her, their movements twitchy and unpredictable.

Everything happened so fast.

Coffee slipped from her hands as they grabbed her, splashing out onto the cold cobblestone, steam rising around her. Two red flames flashed through the mist, the power of her beast instinctually coming to the surface, ready to attack. It vanished as fast as it came. Raven dropped to her knees before a guard, a manacle around her wrist, the goblin metal ripping the fae magic from her. Raven's mouth started to move, though I knew her obscurer wouldn't be nearly as powerful now. Her magic was intertwined together, not separate. They were half of what they were without the other.

Her name surged up my chest, my legs lurching forward when a guard came from behind her, his baton striking across her head, her body slipping to the ground, unconscious.

"Raven!" Terror knifed through my lungs. I felt a sensation of being out of my body as I ran for her, not caring what happened to me. I needed to protect her.

My untied shoelaces caught underfoot, a cry spitting from my mouth.

My body sailed forward, my palms grating across the rough stone surface. I slammed into the ground, the bag buffering my dick, but my chin, knee and chest hit hard, my clothes and skin tearing. The impact knocked the breath out of me, paralyzing me on the ground, gasping for air.

My muscles locked up, and I watched helplessly as they lifted her, the men rushing back for the jeeps, tossing her in the back, and piling in.

"Noooooo!" The word barely croaked from me, my feet scrambling under me, my lungs spasming. I pushed myself up. My legs stumbled again, oxygen still not reaching my brain.

The jeeps revved, the wheels squealing out with the same momentum they entered.

From a distance, I heard a bird shriek.

"No!" I shouted again, shoving myself up, limping toward the vanishing brake lights, the automobiles disappearing around the corner. I tried to keep up, my knee screaming with pain, hobbling after, but I knew it was pointless. She was out of reach.

Pain shot up my leg, and I came to a stop. I bent over, gasping for air. Fury and grief roared from my gut, anger at my fuck up, for not protecting her, not getting to her fast enough. This was my fault. They came after her because of me.

"Ffffuuuuuuuuuuuuuuuuccckkk!" I bellowed, the pigeons around me flapping and fluttering away as I slammed my fist into a pole. Trees nearby creaked, limbs breaking off in my fury, raining down on the road.

She was gone.

But now, I would've given anything for her to be heading home like I first feared. Safe in her family's embrace, even if I never saw her again.

My gaze flickered to the sky. I couldn't see her, but I had no doubt Nyx had led them here. Searching for us, she must have spotted Raven in the square, because if she knew where I was, the soldiers would have raided the brothel.

Or she knows how to really hurt you. To make you feel the pain of losing someone like she did.

Though it was Warwick and Brexley who killed her girlfriend, it was me who shot Nyx to save them, leaving her for dead. She hated me too and would love to see me grieve, to tear my world apart.

My feral anger shifted into calculating, vengeful energy, my shoulders going back, determination setting my features. If anything happened to her, I would murder them all. Slowly. They thought Warwick, the Wolf, was the legend of death? They had no idea of the pain I would rain down on them.

I just had to find where she was and get her back. In my gut, I knew they wouldn't kill her. Torture and starve? Yes. But they wanted me down on my knees. To hand myself over to them.

She was bait.

My heart thumped with resolve, every nerve zapping under my skin. I would not stop until I found her.

Along the way, Raven got under my skin, and without realizing it, I started to live again, *feel* again. Something I hadn't believed could ever happen. But with the taste of her still on my tongue and the feel of her mouth around my cock, I couldn't fight the hollow feeling from deep in my soul.

Mine.

"Where's Maestro?" I barked, slamming through the door, fury rolling off my shoulders. The few workers who were up, cleaning or drinking coffee at the bar, still looked half asleep and haggard from the night before and jerked their heads to me, staring. "Where is he?" My patience was barely contained.

"Hey, hey…" Maestro entered the room, his hands motioning for me to calm down, his brow furrowed. Dressed in a paisley dressing gown, looking like an old movie star, he sashayed to me. His face was devoid of makeup, his head wrapped in a cap, showing the man underneath the performance. "My beautiful boy, what has you coming in here screaming like you want to wake the dead? Most of us are still suffering, you know."

"Where is the base camp?" I had no time for frivolities.

"What?" Maestro's frown deepened. "I have not had my coffee yet. So please, tell me what is going on?"

"They have her."

"Have who?" His thin eyebrows puckered.

My mouth opened to utter her name and stopped. He already thought she reminded him of someone, her true identity barely a subtle hint away. Her name would only confirm who she was. And I couldn't have that. I needed this to stay quiet. Sonya and Lazar couldn't find out who they really had in their grasp. I couldn't give them that leverage—the power to bring the Unified Nations to their knees.

Getting her was *my* priority.

"My girl." I cleared my throat, the sentiment feeling odd coming off my lips. I had *never* called anyone that before. Ever.

"What? Who took her?" He exploded with shock, no longer speaking quietly. "What happened?"

"Sonya's men." They certainly were no longer Lazar's men. He was a facade. An actor playing a part with no power to speak of anymore.

"The queen's men?" He placed a hand on his chest. "I-I don't understand."

I couldn't stand still, resentful for every minute I wasted. "I don't have time to explain," I grunted. "I need to know exactly where they are based. Where would they take prisoners?"

"Prisoners?!" He gasped. "Why do you think I would know?"

My teeth ground together, my hands balling up at my sides. Maestro gulped, taking in my reaction, feeling the rage billowing off me.

"Yes, okay." His shoulders dropped, and his hand stayed clutching the fabric near his throat like it was a protective barrier. "A lot of soldiers come here." He looked around as if one would burst in the room. "We hear a lot of things."

"I know." When in doubt, always go to a brothel for information. They were the nuclei of everything going on. Men had trouble keeping their mouths closed when someone was milking them dry. They loved to brag, to have some secret which made them more astute. Bigger than their small dick size.

"I know the main base is in Bran." He lowered his voice. "Sonya has taken over the castle there."

The place of legends and horror had also been a fae holdout when humans hunted us, causing us to flee to the Otherworld. The magic was so strong even humans could feel the energy in the air. Though they would conjure vampires and bats, while the real monsters were right in front of them, hiding under beautiful faces with powers to glamour and seduce.

Sonya using it as her hub was almost cliché. The blood-sucking predator taking shelter in a make-believe vampire's lair.

"How do I get in?" The place would be guarded and impossible to break into—Sonya would make sure of it.

"I don't know."

A noise gurgled up my throat.

"I don't!" Maestro held up his hands. "I swear." Another disapproving sound vibrated my vocals. "But I know someone who might."

"Get them here now."

"That's impossible!"

"I. Don't. Care." I never sounded more like Warwick in my life, even more so when it had to do with Brexley.

"Give me the day," Maestro stated with more firmness. "I will do everything I can to get him here by tonight. He's not an easy man to pin down."

I could get supplies and come up with a plan until this man arrived.

"Fine," I rumbled in a deep grunt. "*Tonight*."

"So *demanding*..." Maestro shivered with desire, coyness dancing in his eyes. "She's a lucky girl."

His eyes felt as if they could see right through me, seeing how I felt—that the world would burn to the ground if I didn't get her back.

Huffing, I started to move around him, heading for the stairs.

"Oh, and whatever you did with Mihai..."

"Who?"

"The man you invited into your room last night." Maestro's eyebrow lifted sultrily.

Of course he would know everything that went on here. Nothing was private between the "madam" and what happened inside the brothel walls.

"He's become a patron now." Maestro played with the tie on his robe. "He's a very wealthy man, and I've been trying to convince him to invest in my little business here for a long time now. He always said no." His lips curved. "Whatever you did... he changed his mind. So thank you. You have my complete loyalty." It meant a lot coming from the proprietor of a brothel. If you had their loyalty, you were protected, and if anyone did anything to you, like rob or hurt you, they would find themselves at the bottom of a river.

"Good." I bowed my head. "Then get your informer here by nightfall," I ordered and ran up the stairs.

My stomach squeezed when I reached 306, not knowing what I'd find behind the door.

Were they still there, or did they leave too?

Walking through, my gaze landed on Bitzy curled up on the pillow, her little snores making me instantly let out a breath of relief. Then my attention drifted to the other pillow.

Opie was naked, tied to the bedpost by the straps of the whip, his bare butt facing me, a pleasure feather between his toes.

"What the..." I slammed the door behind me and Opie's head jerked over his shoulder, his cheeks instantly turning bright red.

"It's not what it looks like..."

Chapter 8

Ash

My nerves crackled, the tension around me like an electrical fence. Swirling the țuică in my cup, I kept myself tucked in a dark corner of the bar, my attention prowling the room like a hunting lion. The night brought in a steady stream of customers, already starting off the year with the same vices and sins.

Not even a month and a half ago, I would have been right there with them, blowing my mind out on fairy dust, alcohol, and sex. None of those seemed important to me anymore.

Two scantily dressed prostitutes had entertained the idea I might be up for it again, slinking up to me, trying to sit in my lap. My skin crawled at their touch. Within thirty seconds, they had their tails between their legs, running for safety.

I didn't even recognize myself.

"What can I get you?" The barkeep had come up to me earlier, leaning on the bar, winking at me. "A drink or something *stronger*?" I knew he meant drugs.

Fairy dust.

"Drink. Whatever is cheap."

He nodded, pouring the clear liquor into a tumbler and handing it to me. Sensing my mood, he retreated, staying at the other end of the bar.

I would never lose the initial craving for fairy dust, but I seemed to lose the desire for what it did. I no longer needed to dull my pain and strip myself of reality. I wanted to feel it all.

Because of her.

Downing a sip of the stomach-warming liquor, I shifted on my feet at the reminder that she was gone, and once again, I had failed. With her absence, my body seemed to long for her more, the sounds of her moans still echoing in my ear.

What the fuck was happening to me? I had *never* been this obsessed before. It was unsettling. When did my appetite shift from drugs and easy sex with several people to one girl who seemed to be an all-in-one addiction for me?

The wall to protect myself, to deny I felt anything for her, was there. The knee-jerk reaction to berate myself and flog her from my system because I didn't deserve to be happy. I shouldn't be able to move on.

Especially with her. Not that anything could come of it anyway.

I needed to mourn the two people I thought myself so in love with just a year ago.

There wasn't a question that I loved Kek and Lukas, but I was starting to realize the way I loved them was different. I had known Raven for barely a month, and she knew me better than Lukas and Kek ever did. At that time, it wasn't important to chat about our pasts or really talk much at all. We were in a physical relationship. We didn't snuggle after sex; we passed out. We didn't talk, we fucked, and if we did talk, it wasn't about anything outside of the war and living another day. Going through Věrhǎza together bonded us past words, yet I realized how much of myself I kept from them, kept from everyone I had been seeing steadily. How little I knew about them. Sex was the only language we spoke, which, don't get me wrong, was a fucking unbelievable way to communicate. It was my favorite pastime, but with Raven, there was more, which made me distressed.

Distressed that she could conjure more in me and distressed I hadn't loved Kek and Lucas in the same way. They deserved better from me.

The contradicting emotions set me on edge, invoking impatience and crankiness. Plus, I had two maniacs upstairs sleeping off the mushrooms, giving me a small window before they woke up and wreaked havoc on this place again.

"Will you please stop scaring my workers?" Maestro strolled up, looking elegant in a black silk robe, blond wig, and glamour-style makeup.

"Is he here yet?" I had turned into a Neanderthal, a.k.a. Warwick.

"Not yet." He sighed. "Will you relax? I will tell you when he is." He rubbed his temples. "Today has been a day."

My old nature of caring about people kicked in. "Why?"

"I think we have rats." He motioned for the barkeep to bring him a soda water. Like Kitty, he stayed sober on the job, keeping a keen eye on his workers and business. "I found holes in my favorite robe this morning."

I choked on my drink.

"The little fuckers ate through it, though it was hanging up, so I have no idea how they got to it." Aggravation blew from his red lips. "I have to get Andon to set traps."

"Sorry about that." I coughed, patting my chest, trying not to laugh. "They can be such *pesky* creatures."

Maestro took a drink of his soda, looking around the busy room. "Oh. He's here."

My head jerked, following his gaze to a table in the far corner. Only an outline of a hooded figure could be seen in the dim light.

"I didn't even see him come in." Maestro set down his glass. "Would you like me—"

Pushing off the bar, I didn't even hear anything more Maestro said, my legs striding toward the man. My focus dwelled on him, noting how easily he blended into the surroundings, his deep hood keeping his features hidden. Blink and he would disappear.

Slipping in the chair across from him, I kept my voice low. "I heard you can help me."

He stayed quiet; something about him prickled awareness at the back of my neck.

"Can you or not?" I huffed.

"Still short-tempered and hanging out in brothels, I see."

I went still, his voice pinning me to the chair.

"Though something is vastly different about you." His hands lifted to his hood, pulling the heavy wool down.

"Holy fuck," I whispered, staring at the man before me, taking a moment to sink in. "Dzsinn?"

The moment I uttered his name, the shock of the moment dissipated, and a guffaw coughed up my throat. "Of course it's you." I shook my head with a scoff. "I should've known."

"My business covers a lot of places, especially now Hungary is not as profitable for me."

Because Killian was improving living conditions, jobs, and life. Never good circumstances for swindlers and opportunists.

"Yeah, real torn up about that." I sat back in my chair.

"Yet you keep needing my help." Dzsinn folded his hands on the table.

I shifted in my chair, hating that he was right and what it meant for me. "I need to get into Bran Castle without notice."

His eyebrow lifted at the mention of the fortress.

"They are holding someone prisoner." My throat tightened, her face popping into my head, squeezing my heart. I didn't notice I was rubbing at my chest, like it actually felt pain, until Dzsinn's eyes lowered to my swirling hand. I dropped my arm, clearing my throat as I sat up straight.

"She's someone very *important*." I tried to distance myself from my claim, sounding detached. *This is the truth, not personal*. She was the princess of the Unified Nations, so it made her particularly important. Telling myself it didn't stop the pounding of my heart.

"Someone who, if they realized who they had…" I tapered off, my gaze on him revealing how serious this was. "I *have* to get her out." I could hear the desperation hinting at the edges, the raw truth wanting to knock me on my ass. I had to keep my feelings out of this. Emotions got people killed.

Dzsinn leaned back, rubbing his hands together like he could grant my wish right there. Too bad that wasn't how they worked. Genies weren't trapped in a bottle, ready to grant wishes, but they had the influence to get you what you needed. Power of information, resources, money, and connections to spies. With those three things, you could secretly own the world.

"The Bran Castle was designed to be impregnable," he stated. "And if rumors are true, then she would have made sure it would be impossible to enter."

"Are you saying you can't do it?" I leaned forward on my forearms, the challenge lying between us. "That Sonya bested you."

His lids narrowed. His mouth pursed. "Do not try to provoke me, Ash. I do not fall for little boy games."

I huffed out my nose, shifting in my seat again. "Can you help me or not?"

"I never said I couldn't. I just want you to be aware of the price. You still owe me one favor already. You need to be clear on what you are asking me." His dark eyes peered into mine. It was actually unsettling how common his features were, like you could forget what he looked like while staring right at him. So plain, the chair he sat in had more ornament and interest than him, which made him perfect for what he was. A genie was better off not being found or remembered.

"I don't care what the price is." The statement rushed between my teeth in a hiss before my mind slammed my mouth shut. It was too late.

Dzsinn's eyes sparked with understanding. "Ahhh… I see."

I wanted to deny it, to tell him he didn't see shit, but I didn't.

"Like I said, she's important." Wars will start if Sonya hurts her.

Dzsinn dipped his chin in understanding. "Give me until tomorrow night—"

"Tomorrow night?" I exclaimed. "That's too late!"

Dzsinn slanted his head at me. I moved around in my chair, taking a breath and pinning my mouth together.

"This is not a small ask. And I need to call in some favors, get more information on the fortress." His dark eyes pierced me with the magnitude of what he'd be doing for me. I didn't want to think about the favor I'd owe him later. It didn't matter; Raven was my only concern.

"Tomorrow," I restated.

The genie watched me for a moment, seeing far more than I wanted him to, before he rose from the table. "Talk soon, Ash." He slipped away, the crowd swallowing him up, and I could bet no one took notice of him walking out.

Chirp!

"I told you no."

Chirp! Chirp! Chirp!

I didn't have to look at the tiny imp on the table to know I was getting flipped off. Her curt, angry tone told me how cranky she was. I took away her mushrooms.

Rubbing my head, I paused my constant pacing, feeling like a caged animal. Two dim firebulbs glowed, putting the room in shadows. The moonless sky and the dark and quiet outside reversed the mood from the night before.

A noise worked up my throat, and I sat down on the bed, my head in my hands. Memories from last night wormed into my brain, reminding me of her cries, her moans, her taste, and how she looked at me as I watched her and him.

How her lips felt wrapped around my cock, like she owned me.

"Fuck me." I popped up again, my body agitated, my mind relentless.

"I wasn't! That was a total misunderstanding!" Opie popped out from the drawer, where he had found something of interest.

My gaze slid to him as he peered around, realizing I wasn't speaking to him.

Chirp!

"Nothing. I didn't say anything," he huffed, crawling out of the drawer. "You think with those big ears, you'd hear better." He plonked down on the nightstand, wiggling his big hairy toes, which glistened with a gel-like substance. "Ohhh... my toes are getting warm! They feel all tingly!"

I snorted. Warming lube.

"Wait. What are you wearing?" I hadn't really taken notice when I came back to the room, my mind buzzing over my conversation with Dzsinn. Every moment I sat here, not knowing what they were doing to her, was torture.

"Oh." He swung out his legs, waggling his gel-coated toes even more. "It's just something I *threw* together." Gold tassels hung off his hips, one placed right in front of his crotch, and two were on his nipples. What looked like strips of the bedspread were tied into his beard, and he had more of Maestro's gems decorating his cheeks, torso, and penis. "You like?"

I peered over at the lamp, which *used* to have gold tassels hanging from the shade. "Opie..." I palmed my face again.

"I had very limited material to work with!" he huffed. "You locked us in here! What was I supposed to do?"

"You're sub-fae. You can't be locked up anywhere," I replied, slanting my head.

"Oh, well... I got... stuck."

Chirp!

"I told you both it was a total misunderstanding!"

"Tying yourself to the bedpost naked was a misunderstanding?" I lifted a brow.

Chirp!

"Don't judge me!" he shot at Bitzy. "You were the one who cuddled his penis this morning!"

Chirp! Chirp! Her angry tone retaliated.

"Oh, right... that was me too." He huffed under his breath, then waved his arms. "Again, a total misunderstanding. It was cold."

"You know what? Why don't you both be quiet for a while." I pinched the bridge of my nose. I knew I should be resting, but I couldn't shut down my thoughts. I was about a hair away from losing my shit.

Normally at a time like this, I distracted myself with sex. It took the edge off and let me relax. I was in the perfect place for that, and I could get any person in here within seconds. However, even the vague idea of being with someone else bristled, making me stomp back and forth in the small room. It created an agitation like I needed to climb out of my skin. To run to her tonight, not caring about the consequences, desperate to see her.

What the fuck?

My boots came to a halt, air catching in my lungs. Seriously, what was wrong with me?

Respectful to Lucas and Kek, I wouldn't have slept with anyone else outside of us if that's what we all decided. However, I *never* stopped having fantasies about others when I saw someone attractive. Hell, the memory of kissing Brexley played in many of my daydreams while I was with Kek and Lukas.

There never seemed to be enough for me, whether it was the number of people or the sex. It never fully sated me. Always searching for more, for another person to fill my needs. Another thing Kek and I got along about, we never had enough. Lukas would be passed out, and we'd continue fucking for hours. He'd wake up and join us before conking out again.

A tree fairy never had just one person they loved, nor were they content with sex with just one. We were primal creatures, the energy of the earth and plants keeping us restless and fickle. Love all and love vastly was our motto.

So what the fuck was this?

Anxiety stirred in my lungs, a cold sweat dotting the back of my neck.

"You okay, mushroom man?" Opie leaped down on the bed, his greasy feet marking the quilt as he walked across. "You look like you want to throw up."

I kinda did.

"I'm fine." Lie.

Chirp?

"You are not getting any more mushroom tonight!" I yelled over at Bitzy, somehow comprehending what she had said.

Her lids narrowed to slits.

"Uh-oh." Opie scrambled back to the pillows like something was about to explode.

It did.

Chirp! Chhiiirp! Chirp! Chirpchirpchirp! Her middle fingers waved in the air at me. *Chirpchirpchirpchirp! Chirp!*

"Whoa…" Opie's eyes went big. "I've never heard her call anyone that before."

"Tough, young lady." I pointed my finger at her. "You had enough." Wow. I sounded like the old Ash. The one who used to care.

Technically Bitzy should still be high as a kite off the raw mushrooms, but their tiny bodies burned it off ten times faster than us, like little hummingbirds.

She snarled, snapping her mouth at my finger, flipping me off. She moved away from me, sulking like a teenager.

"I need you coherent tomorrow." I plopped back down on the bed, laying back, my arms under my head.

"For what?" Opie padded up onto my chest and I frowned at the oily stains he left on my t-shirt.

"I need your magic fingers." I cleared my throat. "Let me clarify that. I need your sub-fae talents of breaking locks and getting through tight places."

"Oh, I love plugging myself into tight places."

"I'm *not* going to think about that." I closed my lids briefly, exhaustion beginning to burn my eyes. "We are going to break into a fortified castle."

"It sounds exactly like the thing Master Fishy told us to stop you from doing." Opie sat down, folding his legs.

I plopped my head onto the pillow, looking at him.

"I'm asking for you to not go back to Brex or tell any of them," I said sincerely. "I need your help, Opie. As a friend."

His eyes went big, his long lashes fluttering like he was going to cry. "A friend?"

Sub-fae were always treated as less than in fae society. It was even in their name, putting them beneath us. To offer friendship or see them as equals was a great honor to them. And I did see them as that, but I won't say I wasn't laying it on a little thick.

"And a partner in crime," I added.

"Ohhhh, Master Ash." He leaped up, his cheeks turning a deep pink, his eyes blinking with happy tears. "It is such an honor."

"Will you help me?"

"These magic fingers are yours!" He put his hands in the air in excitement. "Whatever tight, dark places you want me to stick them!"

The next day lasted a week. After taking only an hour to get supplies, I had the rest of the afternoon to sit around and think. Think about what could be happening to her.

It was impossible to fully plan until I had details—the layout of the castle, the weaknesses and possible ways I could get in.

I had to wait for Dzsinn.

Trapped inside the building, inside my own head, and confined with two bored sub-fae, I was about to lose my shit by the time the sun lowered beyond the horizon. I ended up giving Bitzy a bite of mushroom after I woke up with her perched over my face, watching me, an evil smile on her lips like she'd done something horrible while I slept. The little sleep I got. I had dozed on and off all night, leaping awake with a strangled cry. I kept looking at the spot next to me like she would suddenly be there, and all of this had been a bad trip.

"Stay quiet, both of you," I muttered, coming down the stairs into the busy lounge later that evening, hitching my new backpack over my shoulder, filled with supplies and my friends. I didn't trust them alone. Not with the mushrooms, and certainly not after Opie came back tangled in a rat trap this morning.

"What the fuck?" I was barely awake when Opie stood on my chest, a guilty expression on his face, a trap snarled in his beard. "What happened?"

"It wasn't my fault," he whined. "I was minding my own business..."

"And where were you *minding* your own business?" I rubbed my eyes, blinking against the sun coming through the window.

"I couldn't help it! His closet has so many pretty things!" Bitzy sighed dreamily. "So many silky, pretty things. They demand to be touched, to slide over my skin. And his sparkly gems... so, so shiny. I just wanted to look closer at them."

"You mean steal." I pried the trap off him.

"That's not what I would call it."

"What would you call it, then?" I motioned to what he wore. His eyes were layered with fake sticky jewels, and he had a black silk robe tie wrapped around his figure like a complicated bikini, with a dozen condom packages taped together over his shoulders like a cape.

He crinkled every time he moved.

"Ummm... borrowing. But with no intention of giving back."

Now both were tucked inside my pack, heading down to the lounge. My eyes scanned the dark, sultry room. The gambling area was boisterous, while a man was already getting his dick sucked at the bar and a male prostitute pumped into a man in a dark corner, his hand over his mouth while they watched the other couple silently. The room was bristling with sex and drugs.

It scared me how little it seemed to affect me, my cock staying mostly flaccid as the man being sucked off moaned louder, his hips pushing harder down her throat.

Something was wrong with me. I was broken. I had to be.

Marching over to the table where Dzsinn met me yesterday, I nodded at the server to bring me a drink. Slipping into the chair, my knee bounced with anxiety, restless to go.

What was happening to her? Was she okay? Beaten? Already dead?

The last thought hit my gut like a sinking ship, the wreckage smashing into the bottom and shattering into pieces.

No. I breathed out. *She's alive.*

I had no understanding of how I knew. I just knew. As if I could feel her in the world, sense her reaching for me. I would feel her death. Know it in my bones. Plus, why take her if it wasn't meant to draw me in?

They took her on purpose. To get to me.

The chair across from me was suddenly occupied. Dzsinn lowered his hood, his movements imperceptible.

"Do you have what I need?" I didn't bother with small talk.

Dzsinn watched me like he was studying me, a strange expression flittering over his face.

"I couldn't."

"What?" My mouth dropped open, my eyes widening at Dzsinn. There wasn't anything he couldn't do or get.

"My informants." He paused. "Are no longer accessible to me."

"What does that mean?"

I recognized his expression now. It was uncomfortable. Unease, like this had never happened to him before.

"I do not know what is going on there, but the men *owe* me a favor?" Human or fae, you couldn't go back on your word to a genie. They were their own Mafia. "They both ignored my summons."

"Maybe they're dead?"

He didn't answer, probably didn't know.

"So you got nothing?"

"I didn't say that." He frowned, pulling something out of his cloak. "I have the blueprints of the castle." He laid the map out on the table. "It's old, but nothing should have changed." His finger tapped at the layout. "This is the main entrance, and of course, it is heavily guarded. This castle is high on a hill, cramped and confusing. Not many ways to get in or out besides the entrance."

"But you know a way?"

His chin dipped, his finger sliding to another area that had strange markings on it. "I know a way."

"What's that?" I pointed to the designs. His silence drove up my irritation. Every second, I was wasting time. "Are you going to tell me?"

"No," he replied.

"What?" I barked. "Why not? I told you I would pay your price."

"That's not it."

"Then what is?"

"Something is going on there. I need to find out what it is." He rolled up the map. "I will be going with you."

I stared at him like the world just went topsy turvy.

"Going with me?"

"When humans are able to ignore my magic. Disregard *my* summons." A nerve in his jaw popped. "It's something I have to investigate. When you owe a djinn, there are no second wishes."

Chapter 9

Ash

The moon slipped through the heavy woodlands. The craggy terrain, coated with ice, snow, and mud, made the trek strenuous. Smoke billowed from the chimneys of the homes scattered around the land, the soil heavy with magic.

There was no escaping the sensation that the land felt haunted, the result of centuries of war, death, and pain. Tragedy soaked into the earth, wrapping itself with fae magic, which pulsed like a vein in the neck.

Bram Stoker's fairy tale, though he never stepped foot in this country, lured people from all over the world with his words. As if the story he made up was what really happened inside these walls, when the truth was far more salacious and luring. This history wasn't recorded in human history books but were stories that simply echoed in the land if you listened closely enough.

"There." Dzsinn pointed through a break in the trees, speaking for the first time since we departed Brașov.

My gaze went up to the stone castle perched on a hill between two valleys. Firebulbs glowed around the base of the fortress, making it look like it floated in the sky. Snow coated the reddish-brown peaked roofs and tipped the branches of the trees like frosting.

Sitting at the Eastern border of Transylvania, the fortress was once used in an attempt to stop the Ottoman Empire's expansion. Vlad the Impaler passed through here, burning villages and murdering hundreds of people. After the fae abandoned this land and went into hiding, it had seen many human leaders come and go and witnessed many wars and famines.

The place spoken in lore, truth or not, became the bones of the castle. It sat high, casting a dominance on the village below. It wasn't the biggest or prettiest castle in this area by far, but it held a power. A past that clung to the stone, a memoir of its complicated tale.

In my gut, I knew Raven was here, as if I could hear her calling for me. Feel her power drawing me to her like a spell more commanding than any lore.

"There are at least a dozen guards based around the entrance." Dzsinn held binoculars to his face, his head scanning over the property. "A dozen guards are at the front gate, a few in the forest behind, and a handful down at this back gate." He handed them over to me.

Taking them from him, I peered through the night-vision lens. The distance and clarity were so sharp I could make out every feature of the men through the dense night, even the smallest details of the old gas jeep sitting at the back gate.

These weren't cheap. "Nice."

"My connections allow me the best of the best."

"Someone is pretty high up in the Unified Nations to get top-grade stuff like this." I shifted my pack on my shoulders, feeling the warmth from two tiny forms sleeping in there.

Dzsinn didn't respond, and I didn't expect him to; his connections were what kept him in business. He would protect them at all costs.

"I have no doubt they will have Druid spells around the walls." I handed him back his binoculars.

"And I told you it wouldn't be a problem." He stuffed them back into his bag, his attention still on the castle.

I stared at him, recalling our chat from the night before, the intimate information he shared with me about himself earlier.

"There are all sorts of Djinns, and each type holds unique powers. My type, which is very rare ...I am immune to Druid magic."

"What?" My head jerked to him.

"It's where we got the reputation for being all-powerful. When Druids couldn't hurt or stop us, some believed we held the ultimate supremacy." He folded his hands. *"And unless my moles are dead, no one, except another genie, can break our summons."*

That's why he reacted the way he did when his spies didn't respond. "So either they're dead, or Sonya has another Genie hidden away in there?"

His attention went to the room, not answering my question.

"If you are touching me, I can get us both through any Druid spell

Land of Monsters

without notice." Dzsinn looked uncomfortable sharing this knowledge. "I can get us in, and I have connections to get a fae lock pick. Though they are getting less reliable, the spells to guard them are getting tougher."

"Won't be necessary." I grinned, sipping my brandy. "I have my own."

Sitting back now, my gaze darted to the pack hanging off my chair, then returned to him. "Now tell me how we are getting into the castle."

"The tunnel location is near that back gate." He pointed down the road to a handful of guards and two jeeps. "Getting through the spell will be easy enough, but getting past them and through fae locks won't be."

I smirked, my elbow tapping into my pack. "Wake up, menaces. Time to rise and wreak havoc."

Dzsinn's lids narrowed, not understanding who I was talking to until a muffled noise came from the bag.

"Keep your super-packin' briefs on, mushroom man," Opie grumbled, climbing out of the pack and onto my shoulder, the imp in the backpack behind him looking pissed off at the world. "This level of art takes time."

Dzsinn tried not to react, but it wasn't every day you saw a brownie and an imp dressed in strips of rope, parchment, bits of t-shirt, and duct tape.

"Opie, did you destroy the rope?" I groaned, nodding at the bag I kept the supplies in.

"It's really your fault, isn't it?"

Yeah, I should've known better.

"That shirt was to find Raven's scent." I motioned to the fabric around his ass.

"You know how bored I get! And we were in there for years!"

"It was two hours."

"Close enough," he exclaimed, touching Raven's shirt that he cut up like a fringe miniskirt, strands of rope bunching the fabric up around his waist. Duct tape circled his chest and biceps like a tube top, and he added a paper fan, made from the castle blueprints, on top of his head like a crown. Bitzy had a mini crown, which was held down with duct tape, t-shirt diapers, and a rope as a tie. "I thought you left supplies for me to fashion amazing outfits like this."

Dzsinn stared. "A brownie?" Brownies were known to be exclusive creatures, only venturing out at night to clean and pinch tiny, shiny things in payment. They *usually* preferred very little contact with people, but Opie was anything but ordinary.

"This is Opie and Bitzy." I gestured to them and nodded to him. "Dzsinn."

Chirp! Bitzy flipped him off with both hands, slumping down further into her little seat. She was still pouting because I left the mushrooms back in the room.

"Ohh, you're a genie?" Opie clasped his hands. "I'll bet you love when they rub you off!"

"Oh gods," I muttered, trying not to groan or laugh.

Dzsinn just blinked more. Opie was a lot to take.

"You have sub-fae with you?" Dzsinn's gaze went over them.

"Fortunately or unfortunately. Not quite sure which one."

Chirp! Chirp! Basically, *fuck you, asshole.*

"Yes, Bitz, you think I'm the worst right now." I rolled my eyes, muttering. "Cranky imp."

"An imp?" His attention snapped to her, really taking her in like he hadn't quite noticed her before. They were almost non-existent anymore; the population was nearly annihilated because their bodily fluids were known to have great healing properties for fae.

Shock flickered to a hungry glow in the genie's plain brown eyes, like he could see her worth. The price of such a rare species. What someone would pay for her.

A blast of fury cracked a tree branch over his head, dropping a heavy limb next to his feet, his focus jumping back to me. I didn't have to say a word for him to understand what I was saying.

You touch her. You die.

His eyes narrowed in confusion at my response. It was rare, even in today's world, for sub-fae to be treated as equals. To be protected. I never liked the behavior toward them before, but even more now because these two were family. Against our refutes and denials, especially Warwick's, they had wiggled into our lives and become part of us. And every one of us would kill for these two.

"Do you like it when they rub your lantern hard or soft? Or maybe spank it?"

"Opie…"

"What? He might be into that! Who are we to judge?"

I sighed. "Remember I said if you came along, you'd stay quiet?"

"No, but I remember when you begged for these fingers, which can spread magic in the tiniest of holes and crevices, to assist your needs." He wiggled his hands.

"I'm regretting all my life choices right now," I grumbled, slipping the backpack off my shoulder. "I also asked for you to find Raven. And since you're *wearing* her shirt, I need you to track her scent so you can locate her once you're inside."

"Wh-what? I'm sorry, did you say track her scent?" Opie exclaimed. "I'm not a dog!"

"Do you find someone by their smell?"

"Well, yeah…" He crossed his arms. "But I'm more like a sommelier!" He whiffed his hand at his nose. "Detecting the subtle hints of their bodily juices."

"Oh gods. Please shut up." I turned my attention to Dzsinn, his eyes still greedily watching the imp. My manner shifted, my voice low. "Just know they belong to Brexley, and if anything happens to them, you do anything to either, it won't just be me you will deal with. *The Wolf* will come for you too."

I saw the most subtle gulp before he nodded.

"I understand." I could see truth in his eyes. "Besides, sub-fae, in my experience, can be some of the best moles."

"Dogs, now moles?" Opie huffed, stomping his foot on my shoulder. "Do I look like a furry animal with a big nose to you?"

"I'm not gonna answer that," I replied, placing Opie on the ground. "Remember what I told you?"

"Yes." Opie nodded with a huff. "Don't be myself."

"That's not what I said." I ground my teeth. "I said don't do anything crazy. We need just a small distraction, nothing that tells the entire castle we are here. Stick to the plan and get back to us. Do not deviate. Got it?"

Another huff.

"Got it?"

"Yes."

Chirp! Bitzy flipped me off. I was gonna take it as a yes too.

I gulped, emotion gripping my chest, realizing everything at stake. "And please stay safe."

Opie peered up at me. "You too, Master Ash. Otherwise, I will have failed Master Fishy, and the big guy will be so mad at me."

Chirp! I translated her middle finger as words of love, but more likely, it was, "Don't die, asshole, because I won't get those mushrooms you promised me!"

Without another word, the brownie and imp disappeared into the darkness, heading for the group of soldiers guarding the back gate. The plan was simple: if they drew the guards' focus enough, we could slip by unnoticed.

"You trust them to pull this off?" Dzsinn asked, gripping a gun in his hand.

"I trust them to cause mayhem." I tucked further into my hood, pulling my weapon from the back of my pants. In my mind, I envisioned the map we had studied the night before, the blueprint of the castle, the markings that noted a tunnel built just under the building in the back entrance where the guards stood now. Most likely designed for the rulers of the castle to escape if they were invaded. "Let's go."

Sonya and Iain would be expecting me; they'd be waiting for me to come for her and be on alert for any sign I was trying to get in. I wanted to make sure that didn't happen. Slip in with the help of a genie without detection.

Jumping across a frozen creek bed, we crept closer to the back gate. The way the men weren't chatting or moving around prickled at my gut. The way they stood seemed unnatural, robotic, and a few of them twitched, as if something under their skin was starting to consume them.

I couldn't deny Sonya had the formula and was changing these human men, following in Istvan's footsteps. I had seen it too many times in Věrhăza: guards losing themselves bit by bit, day by day. As if their systems first went into shock, shutting down, going unemotional, before the fae essence started to change their chromosomes, turning them into beasts. Most humans couldn't adapt to the change, their brains pretty much melting and dying in the most painful way. Human bodies were not meant to encase magic like ours.

My working theory was if you did survive, like Hanna, it was because somewhere in your bloodline, you had fae DNA.

"Where the fuck are they?" Dzsinn muttered to me as time ticked by, every second adding to the tension, the fear this would all fall apart before it even started.

"I don't know."

Right as I spoke, a hissed crackle filled the air. Dread dropped in my stomach. Peering around a tree, my eyes caught a burning rag dangling from the old jeep's gas tank. Even a hint of gasoline or fumes left inside would be enough.

"Oh fuc—"

BOOOOM!

The jeep flew up into the air, a fireball exploding from the belly, twisting the frame as it flipped down the road, the shriek of metal tearing through the quiet sky, scraping the pavement. The guards reacted instantly, running toward the jeep, their hollers mingling with the roaring inferno, creating more chaos.

"That was *not* the plan," Dzsinn hissed next to me.

"No, but it worked."

Taking advantage of their distraction, we slipped out from the woods, darting across the street. The sounds of more men shouting from above, heading for the commotion, drove up my adrenaline.

This pretty much just announced my arrival.

"Grab onto me and don't let go," Dzsinn ordered me, pulling up his cloak and displaying his pale arm. I had to be touching him directly for the spell to let me go through too. I squeezed his forearm as he pulled us through the enchantment, running through the arched stone gate. Normally, going through fae doors or spells was like stepping through jelly. It rubbed at your skin, the energy fizzing around you, but this felt like it recoiled, sucking back, not wanting to touch us. Like we were the ones who had a barrier around us, giving us room to walk through.

The moment we were inside the grounds, we darted for the specific structure. The blueprint showed the tunnel started right under one of the outbuildings.

"It's locked." Dzsinn tried the handle.

I peered around for my two companions. The reverberations of another car rumbled down the hill from us, the shouts of men just feet away. At any moment, they could return and find us here.

"Where the fuck are they?" Dzsinn snapped. The sound of boots hitting the gravel caught my breath. Two figures came around the building, freezing us in place. Deep in our dark wool cloaks, we pinned ourselves into the shadows as two soldiers, leaving their guard posts along the forest behind, ran by. My finger pressed on the trigger, ready to fire, my pulse hammering in my ears. The guards barreled past us toward the commotion.

"Too close," Dzsinn muttered. "We can't stand here. We have to find another way in." The genie twisted for the steps heading up, the dark forest providing more cover.

Right then, my attention caught on something scurrying toward us through the darkness, my chest heaving with relief seeing Opie scamper up the steps to us. "Your saviors are here!"

"Saviors?" I clipped, swiping down and picking him up, Bitzy snug in his backpack, flipping me off. "You practically screamed we were here. I asked for a subtle distraction, not this."

"That *was* subtle." Opie frowned.

"To Warwick, maybe."

"We had to improvise." He shrugged.

"Hey." Dzsinn motioned for the locked door. "Talk later. Unlock this door now."

"So bossy." Opie put his hands on his hips. "Sounds like you might need your lamp rubbed again."

Chirp-chirp.

"I was not volunteering myself!"

"Just unlock the door!" I hissed, peering over my shoulder. The noises from the fire and the men drowned us out, but I could feel their interest in the explosion waning. No longer looking for the how, but looking for the who. "Hurry."

"The broomstick is back up your ass again, fairy." Opie stretched his fingers together, using my hand as a perch. "Relax."

"I'll relax when you get us in."

"How many times have I failed?"

I slanted my head.

"Okay, how many times today?"

"Just get us inside."

He started to fiddle with the lock, his face scrunching up. "Ohhhh, this is old school." He bit his lip. "I thiiinnkk I goottt it…"

"Hurry!" Dzsinn whispered hoarsely. The screech of an army jeep pulled through the archway, the headlights beaming along the back, but it would only be seconds until someone looked over and spotted us in the doorway of the building.

"Opie…"

Click!

The door gave way, and we stumbled into the dark room. I shut it behind us, listening for anyone calling out our location. Seeing us enter.

"Can we stop with the close calls?" Dzsinn huffed. "Brownies aren't usually this loud and annoying."

"And to that I say, you are welcome, sir." Opie bowed, showing the parchment fan on his head was singed at the edges.

"That wasn't a compliment," Dzsinn muttered, moving deeper into the space.

Chirp! Bitzy stuck up her fingers at the genie.

"Everyone be quiet," I muttered, already scoping out the room. The house was probably once the groundkeeper's, left mainly abandoned with just threadbare, dusty curtains and a large rug. I searched for any cuts in the wood panels, uneven sections, or a trap door that could lead to the tunnels.

"Shit." Dzsinn's low voice pulled me to him, following his attention to the far wall.

I blinked.

"Fuck." I stood straight, taking in the top-grade rifles decorating the entire wall. "Sonya's got some connections."

"They're Russian-made." Dzsinn's brown eyes met mine. "Military issued."

"*Kapd be a faszom.*" *Suck my dick.* I muttered, not wanting to think about the implications. The very people pretending to play nice with the Unified Nations, trying to become allies, were giving weapons to Sonya? Was this a one-time transaction, or were they working together?

My stomach knotted at the notion the same people hunting Raven were also tied to Sonya. Did she already know who she had in her prison? Was I too late? Anxiety bubbled up my throat, a desperation to find my girl.

"*Caută pe camp!*" *Search the field!* a voice boomed from outside, whipping us around, drilling more panic into my bones.

"The entrance to the tunnel has to be somewhere here," I spat. The building was old, but not as old as the castle. The tunnels would have come first. "Check the floorboards." I dropped to my knees, Opie leaping down next to me on the ground, searching as my fingers ran over the planks.

Dzsinn kicked at the rug, pulling it away from the floor, but nothing looked different, no hidden trap. "There's nothing here."

The door to the house rattled and my heart stopped, my head lurching up. The door handle twisted, only seconds away from people entering, finding us here.

Dzsinn and I moved at the same time, bolting across the space to a closet near the gun wall. Swinging the door open, I stumbled forward, my foot not finding purchase. A full step down, my boot hit a stone stair, my body slamming into the wall with a thud.

Dzsinn rushed in after me, Opie slipping in right as our door shut and the outside door opened.

Darkness enveloped us, the clunks of boots moving right next to us, squeaking the wood floors. I could hear them grabbing weapons before running out again, the door slamming behind them.

Taking a deep breath, I sought to calm my beating heart, my eyes trying to adjust to the pure darkness, feeling Opie crawl up onto my shoulder.

"Does it smell like rat cum to you guys, too?"

"What?" Dzsinn choked at Opie's words.

Chirp!

"I don't know personally, I was *just* asking!"

Chirp! Chirp!

"Not true! That's a total misunderstanding!"

"Both of you shut up." Digging into my pack, I yanked out a flashlight, the beam defining the small stairwell we were in. Uneven and worn, the steps curved around, taking us to a low basement. The stale air held a timeworn smell of rotting soil, vegetables, and oats, like this was once used to store food. Before refrigerators, most basements were used to keep things cool. They came back in style after the wall between worlds fell twenty-two years ago when electricity frizzled out all human-made appliances, the system not able to bear the magic.

Dzsinn pulled out his own flashlight, moving to the opposite side of me, both of us searching the dingy room. Nothing much was in it except a stack of wooden crates at one end. Trudging to them, I shoved them over, my torch illuminating the ground where they sat, landing on a change in the foundation, a cut in the stone.

"Here!" I dove down, my fingers scraping around the outline of a trap door. Dzsinn rushed over, and we dug out the packed dirt around the edges, pulling the hatch up with a grunt.

Pointing my torch into the hole revealed another set of stairs leading deeper underground to a tunnel that would bring us inside the castle walls.

To her.

Images of her smile, her irritation, her laughter, making me scramble down the steps, desperate to get to her with a frenzy I didn't understand. It robbed me of air. Of any logic.

Pulling out my gun, I kept the flashlight in my other hand as I descended the steps, the air becoming even more stale and musty.

Dragging the crates back overhead, trying to show as little evidence of our existence as possible, Dzsinn followed me down. His own torch bounced shadows off the walls, our feet echoing our steps on the uneven stone. Low, crude ceilings forced my head down, the walls closing in on my shoulders. The tunnel stretched out before me, with nothing but endless darkness in front of my beam. PTSD from my prison time kicked in, heating my veins with anxiety. To be trapped underground, in dark, cramped quarters bubbled up a wail inside my chest. I wanted to turn back, to breathe air, to feel dirt between my toes, but I pushed forward.

Raven. Her name repeated in my head like a chant.

"When was the last time anyone cleaned down here?" Opie fidgeted against my neck. "Not that I would clean it... I mean, I hate to clean... but it's so filthy!"

"So is your mind," I muttered.

Chirp! Chirp! Chirp! Bitzy responded, sounding more like a cackled laugh.

"Really, tree humper, you are going to talk about dirty after what I watched in the room the other night?"

"I thought you didn't arrive until that morning?" My nose wrinkled up.

"Technically it *was* morning…"

"And you watched?"

"No."

Chirp!

"Okay, well, not the *whole* time."

Chirp!

"No, I didn't enjoy it!" Opie exclaimed. "Like you can talk. I know where your middle finger went later!"

"Please, stop talking now." Though I welcomed the distraction, their chatter kept me from losing my shit.

Taking steady breaths and staying calm, I kept my feet moving forward. The path quickly began to climb, taking us up the hill in long switchback sections.

The beam of my torch reflected off something in front of me, my eyes squinting to make sure I wasn't imagining it.

A hiccup bounced in my lungs.

"Look." I pointed my light for Dzsinn to see a ladder stretching up to a manhole overhead, the metal of the cover bouncing back my light. Tucking the flashlight and my gun in my pants, I scaled the creaky wooden ladder. A deep grunt rose from my chest when I pushed at the manhole, my muscles straining as I rammed my strength into it.

A pop of air released with a whistle, the cover sliding over and revealing the night sky.

"Turn off the torch," I ordered Dzsinn below me. Gripping my weapon again, I slowly stuck my head out of the hole, peering around. The castle loomed overhead, the lights from it glowing down on the snowy trees and bushes, a frozen pond a few yards away. Opie hopped off my shoulder and dropped into the powdered snow.

"Good thing I brought the warming toe gel!" He wiggled his feet.

"Yeah, that's what it's used for," I scoffed, cataloging every detail near me.

I slipped out and Dzsinn scaled to the top right after, getting his boots on solid ground.

"There." Dzsinn motioned over, my eye following him to an arched doorway built into the rocky hillside. "One of the last queens here put in an elevator and a direct passage from her tower to her private gardens in her older age. That should be our way in."

Snow crunched underfoot as we made our way to the door. Voices from below could still be heard, but the commotion was no longer a distraction. They were on high alert now.

Reaching the door, I cast my senses out, trying to hear anything on the other side. Met with silence, I put my hand next to the lock, nodding for Opie to climb up to my arm.

Not even a minute later, I lifted the handle, gun pointed forward, opening it gradually so as not to make a sound. I stepped inside, my finger twitching on the trigger, ready to find a troop of guards waiting for us. My gaze and body darted around, scanning the larger corridor we moved into.

Opie, returning to my shoulder, gripped my hair as if he sensed something wrong like I did. A sick, sinking sensation dropped into my gut.

Firebulbs flickered on as we moved deeper into the large underground tunnel. The remains of old tourist displays were scattered around, giving information on the castle and mythical vampire, but they weren't the most recent additions to this ancient place.

"Fuck. Me." The gun almost dropped from my hand. Hot-cold sweat dampened my skin at the memory of seeing this before, knowing exactly what it was.

A factual horror was being written here.

"What the fuck?" Dzsinn's tone shivered up my spine, his eyes wide, not understanding what he was seeing.

The wall was lined with several dozen tanks, each filled with a body suspended in liquid. Humans.

My stomach heaved when my eyes landed on the person inside the first tank.

Iacob.

"Oh gods," I muttered as my gaze drifted down, recognizing a handful more human men from the pagan encampment. There were ones I didn't recognize, and I assumed the rest of the men were from villages around here.

Unconscious and naked, they were submerged in a clear substance, a mouthpiece breathing air into their lungs as they waited.

This was their priming station, the first step in their change to becoming fae-like.

Volunteers or not, most of these people would die in the transition.

"Seriously, what the fuck is this?" Dzsinn asked.

"Frankenstein's lair."

The rumors about what Istvan had been doing leaked out with dime-novel absurdness. Most never got close to the truth of the chilling things he achieved, even worse than the stories. Many did not want to believe it, even when they saw the soldiers he created with their own eyes.

I had seen it all. Experienced the truth of every rumor.

Land of Monsters

Dzsinn would've heard all the tales, his ear close to the ground, but seeing it was different than experiencing it.

"This is the first stage." Air battled in my lungs at the knowledge that soon a fae would be hooked up to them, dumping their essence into the human body, changing their human DNA forever. If they survived it.

Caden was the first successful case done this way. His own father hooked him up to Warwick, ripping the Wolf of his magic and placing it in his son, turning his son from human to fae.

Caden and Warwick now shared characteristics and traits, bonding them like twin brothers, while they continued to resent each other, disliking the link tying them to each other for infinity.

"They are being prepped to be connected to a fae." Sonya was replicating Istvan's work. Taking what he did and making her own mindless drones. To do this, she would need a lot of fae to use as donors, fae that were at her mercy. Like others from the encampment, like Vlad and Codrin.

A growl formed in the back of my throat. My determination to find Raven grew like weeds taking over my body.

"Ash!" Dzsinn hissed as I bolted down the corridor, my fury ready to level everything that got in my way. If one strand of hair on her head had been hurt, I would rain hell on this fortress.

The firebulbs flicked on when I passed, my feet clipping the paved floor, my soles squeaking when I came to the end in front of an out-of-use elevator, cutting off our path to reach the castle.

Every second I wasted, she could be tortured, could already be losing herself to Sonya's mission. Warwick was lucky; death seemed to stay clear of him, but most fae were not. They didn't make it after all their power was drained from them.

"No." I tried to rip open the doors, but the doors were jammed firmly together. "No!" I bashed at the frame, prying and pulling, noises burning the back of my throat.

"Ash?" My name drifted to me, but I couldn't stop, my frustration snapping into pieces. "Ash!"

Dzsinn's voice finally snapped my head to him. He stood just slightly around the curved elevator, waving me on to follow him. Confused, I peered around, thinking it was a dead end, but a small hallway trailed behind the elevator to another section of the underground labyrinth.

The rough cut of the walls, the fresh dirt and rock dusting the unpaved path, suggested it was a newer addition, sending a warning up the back of my neck.

Dzsinn and I held our guns, slipping down the passage, when noises started echoing through the tunnel, booming roars and high-pitched shrieks. Every hair on my body stood on end, my system flooding with alarm. The path turned, becoming a metal walkway with a bridge opening up to a cavern below. The entire ground floor was filled with at least thirty cots with young women chained to them. Wearing almost nothing, some human, some fae, they all appeared beaten, drained, and shut down.

My stomach rolled again when I spotted Celeste, Viorica, Brândușa, and a few others from the camp among the women chained to the beds.

However, the beings watching them, moving through the beds, guarding the women, turned me to stone. My brain struggled to understand what I was seeing, trying to classify it so I would understand.

"What the fuck?" The words barely made it out. Unfathomable fear drove a stake through me, pinning me to the floor. Every ordeal I went through in Věrhăza, every horror I experienced, hadn't prepared me for this.

The stomach-turning beasts were below me.

And right in the middle was Raven.

Chapter 10

Ash

Monsters.

There was no other word for them. They were not biologically from this earth, nothing but atrocities to nature. Their magic even felt off, stronger than it should've been, their genetic makeup making me nauseous, the sensation grating up the back of my throat to my tongue.

One had crocodile skin, with a mouth full of sharp teeth and a thick tail that slid over the ground as he strolled between the beds. Another man on guard had snake skin, fanged teeth, dark beady eyes, and a rattle-like tail, but with a human body. My gaze finally took in a monster rutting into one of the women at the far end, his grunts huffing off the walls. He had a thick, stocky build with a rhino nose and tusks. While the fourth one watched his friend fuck, he rubbed at the tusks at his mouth like it was his cock. With his snout, ears, and coarse black hair running down his spine, he resembled a wild boar.

Bits and pieces of creatures, the things looked like a horror movie, the real monstrosities living in the walls of a castle whose legend was based on fiends and predators.

"What the fuck?" I repeated again. Bile seared my esophagus, my mind still not wanting to accept what my eyes were seeing. I expected more humans in tanks, more Istvan-style experiments. Not this.

Dzsinn stood still, his eyes on them, but he didn't seem as shocked as I was, as confused as to what the hell they were. He peered at them with a sense of knowing.

"Dzsi—"

My words fell off as an enormous figure stepped through a doorway below, his frame barely making it through the wide archway. Shadows glinted off the rocky walls, the firelight flickering over him.

I took in the beast, the oxygen ripping from my lungs. The man's heart-shaped face was scaly, with piercing green eyes. He wore patchwork pants cut to fit him, but nothing else. His arms, shoulders, and legs were like a man's, but were overly muscular. He had no neck and a short torso, making him appear deformed. But that was nothing compared to the thick shell overlaid down his back to a thick, barbed scorpion tail.

"Z." The snake-man dipped his head like this scorpion-man was their leader.

"Show me the new breeder." His strange, scratchy voice reached my ears.

"She's strong. Her magic is nothing I've felt before. I want to request to mate with her."

Dread plunged into my toes, breaking through the floor.

I already knew who they were talking about.

My gaze snapped to Raven. She was unconscious, and both her wrists were cuffed to the bed with goblin metal, her body limp like they had drugged her as well.

"*I* mate with all the strongest females," the man, Z, snarled.

"Of course I meant after you." He motioned for him to follow him. The two creatures traveled through the rows of beds, all the women sleeping or staring blankly at the wall, as if they had disappeared so far into themselves that they were no longer there.

They headed straight for Raven, stopping at her cot.

Z's gaze went over her, his lip curling with lust. "Yes, this one is special. She is exclusively mine to breed with."

My body reacted, everything in me screaming *mine*. The thought of them touching her whipped fury in me like a tempest. Her name stuck in the back of my throat, sweat dripping down my back as I lurched forward.

"No," Dzsinn hissed, ramming his arm into my chest and shoving me back into the wall.

"Get the fuck off me." I pushed him off, my need to get to her taking over every thought.

"Ash." He shoved me back again, stepping in front of me, his tone severe. The noise in the cavern disguised our voices, but he shot a look over his shoulder, making sure we had not been discovered. "You can't go down there. Not yet."

"Fuck off." My nostrils flared. I was ready to toss him over the railing, desperate to get to her.

"You *can't*." He kept me in place. "You will be killed in seconds. And then she really has no hope." His grave expression momentarily paused me. "I know what they are. Where they came from."

My brows rumpled. "What do you mean where they came from?"

He swallowed, his gaze going down to the monsters leaning over Raven.

"I'm assuming you've heard of Dr. Rapava?"

A knot formed in my throat, my head bobbing. He was the scientist Istvan tried to replicate, taking his formula for changing humans into fae. Istvan had advanced it, but Rapava was the man who started it all.

"These are Rapava's first 'successes' at creating a stronger species." He nodded down to them. "Put parts together from animals, fae, and humans. He wanted to build a resilient, more lethal species. They were thought to be all dead by now, or maybe hoped, since they haven't popped up anywhere in a long time. But they should have known these things are almost impossible to kill. As far as I know, you have to cut off their heads to even have a hope."

"How do you know all this?"

Dzsinn swallowed. "Someone I know has been hunting them for over fifteen years. Had me on the lookout if any talk or sightings came up. He was there when they were created. They're not merely the strongest of fae. They also come from a seer."

"*Szar.*" I gritted my teeth. Seers were mainly humans who could see through fae glamour and couldn't be controlled or tricked. Back when the fae were in hiding, they were the only ones who could perceive the creature under the magic and identify the fae hiding amongst humans. Many times the government hired them to become hunters of fae.

Z ran a scabby hand over Raven's face, sliding it down to her hips, as if he was seeing if they were good for birthing. His hand went to his pants, loosening the waist tie. My body jerked in response, wanting to tear every limb from his body and strangle him with his own intestines.

"Stop." Dzsinn pushed his weight into me. "That thing will rip you apart in seconds."

"I'm not going to stand here and let him touch her or…" I couldn't go on with the thought, knowing the way his greedy eyes moved over her, what he would do with her. What they were doing with all the women. It was very clear why these women were drugged and chained to the beds. It made them easy to assault. Most of these women were not even conscious when they did it.

The rhino-man had moved onto another half-conscious woman,

rutting into her with grotesque animal grunts, spilling his seed with a heavy grunt.

"They are using these women to create more of them."

"That's what it looks like," Dzsinn muttered.

At least half of the young women were human. Probably daughters and wives from the villages around. Their husbands, brothers, and fathers were in the tanks we saw at the beginning.

The human women might be able to conceive and carry, but most likely would bleed out and die after giving birth. The rest seemed to be fae and half-fae women, the ones strong enough to carry their abominations for more than one pregnancy.

Being a Druid made Raven a prized possession. Physically, mentally, and magically capable of bearing many fae children. In our dark past, many fae took advantage of Druid women, using them to carry on their line.

The idea of this brute thrusting himself into Raven made my vision blur. No one was going to fucking touch her, not if I still had air in my lungs.

"Z?" Another monster walked in, part man and part what appeared to be a rhino-beetle. He had a round face with dark eyes and hair, normal legs and arms, but had a black shell that protected his chest and back and had a horn for a nose like a beetle. "Queen Sonya wants us to sweep the forest."

A hiss rattled Z's chest, his neck swinging to the beetle. "That bitch is not a queen." He stomped over to the man, retying his pants, stepping up into the beetle's face. "I am your leader. Did you forget that?"

"No, Commander." Beetle dipped his head slightly.

"You take orders from *me*," he threatened. The beetle tipped his head more in response. Z watched him for a while, then spat out, "Fine. We'll go sweep the forest and get something to eat at the same time so I'll have extra energy for this one." Z nodded to Raven, stepping back from the beetle. "T?" He called over to the rhino, who was in the last throes of reaching his orgasm, huffing loudly, the bed squeaking under his quick, short rhythm. "You hit your limit for the day."

T bayed out his release, then quickly climbed off the girl.

"You stay," Z ordered the one with crocodile skin, then nodded to the rest of his men, all of them following him out. The rhino, T, yanked up his trousers, running after them, leaving just one to guard over the drugged women.

My attention went from Crocodile to Raven, assessing the layout and situation. Whatever expression was on my face screamed my intentions.

"Ash, no." Dzsinn shook his head.

"I don't give a fuck what you do." I yanked a blade from my belt. "I am going down there and get her."

"That one is like a dozen well-trained fae fighters. And it only takes one shout from him to warn the rest we are here."

"Then we make sure his mouth never has a chance to open." Flipping the full-tang knife in my hand, I slipped past him. Staying low behind the stone wall, I kept my gaze on the crocodile, inching toward the steps down.

The reptile peered over his shoulder at the door, like he was making sure Z was really gone before moving through the cots. Acid bubbled up in my throat. The power Raven exuded was a magnet; they couldn't stop themselves.

Reaching Raven's bed, he reached out and touched her, a vibrating noise coming up his throat. The sound of a mating call.

Fuck. No.

A growl shot from my mind down into my bones.

Mine.

"Ash…" Dzsinn tried to call my name, but I was already gone. I snuck down the steps, my serrated knife in hand. The gun would call too much attention, and it would take a lot of bullets to penetrate his thick scales.

My boots soundlessly hit the rocky floor, wrath burning through my muscles at seeing him unzip his pants and crawl onto her bed. With no one here, he thought he could get away with rutting her first, sinking his seed in before Z could. Unaware that the real monster in this room was me.

"I'm gonna make you bleed, little girl." He climbed over her, his white, translucent penis pushing out through his scaly skin, already erect.

Burning rage exploded in front of my eyes, the color of blood painting everything I saw, a deep primal voice rumbling out of me like I was possessed.

"No, I'm gonna make you bleed, you piece of shit." I slipped behind him, grabbing his head, my blade slashing across his throat. For anyone else, the blade would have cut so deep into the bone that their head would've been hanging on by only tendons, but his thick scales prevented it from penetrating deep enough.

Croc thrashed into me, stumbling me backward, barely staying on my feet when he lurched for me, his teeth gnashing. Pain blasted through my shoulder as he knocked me fully over. His heavy form landed on mine, my bones cracking under his weight.

His mouth opened, snapping for me again, blood trailing from the wound I inflicted. Rolling to the side, I tipped him off me, his hand reaching for his gun as I sprang to my feet, kicking the weapon from his grip.

"You are dead," he hissed, springing for me, moving quicker than I expected, his mouth snapping down on my thigh.

A scream caught in my throat. My legs folded under me, and I dropped to the ground. A cruel smirk twisted his bloody lips as he scrambled forward, reaching the gun I kicked away and pointing it at me. "Such a soft, pathetic species."

His finger tugged on the trigger when a snapping, squelching sound jolted him in place, a blade pushing through his throat. Croc froze as the blade twisted, digging a deeper hole through his esophagus. The popping of his spine resounded in my ears.

A gurgled cry escaped his throat as I forced myself to stand, getting in his face.

"Who's pathetic and soft now?" Using all my force, I stabbed my blade into the softer part of his belly, flaying him open.

His body dropped, revealing Dzsinn behind him, his face dotted with blood. "You ever make a stupid move like that again. I'll snap *your* vertebra."

I snarled, stepping over the monster still gasping and bleeding on the floor but trying to rise back up, and I rushed to Raven.

Left only in a thin tank top and underwear, she looked so small and vulnerable. Up close, I could see how beaten and drained she was. Her eyes and cheek were bruised, her lip split, her skin ashen, with marks down her legs and arms. A frenzy of rage thickened my throat. They took something so strong, brutal, and deadly and bled it out of her until she was a shell. A victim.

"Raven?" I cupped her head, my thumbs sliding over her cheeks. Her skin was sticky and swollen, increasing my fury. I wanted to murder every single person who caused these marks. Yet a sense of serenity came over me the moment I touched her, a rightness I hadn't ever experienced before. "Hey, wake up." I tried to jostle her, but she didn't stir. *"Dziubuś."* I whispered her pet name, and I swear her lashes fluttered, but she stayed asleep. The goblin metal was draining her dark dweller, and the drugs kept the obscurer weak. Until they were off, she couldn't fight.

"Hurry up," Dzsinn commanded, yanking the long blade from the back of Croc's neck. The man still gagged and sputtered, getting to his feet, showing how hard they were to kill. Dzsinn drove the blade through him again, the bone and cartilage snapping like cracking ice, slicing through it until his head rolled away from his body. "That should do it." He used the man's clothes to wipe off his blade. "We have to go."

"Opie." I tapped on the pack on my back. "Now."

He must have sensed the urgency, the thin thread my emotions were riding on. He quickly slipped out of the pack, Bitzy on his back, crawling down onto the bed to the cuffs on her wrists.

Land of Monsters

"Oh yes, I recognize her juicy smell. Very notable." He sniffed at her. "Strong, rich, sweet notes with a smoky edge."

Or maybe he didn't.

"Opie…" I snarled.

"What? She smells good. Though, the smell of monkey cum is sure strong around here, isn't it?"

"Uncuff her now." I spoke slowly, barely keeping it together.

"Or is that hippo cum?"

"Rhino," I seethed between my lips.

"So close." He snapped his fingers.

Chirp!

"It's called research," he exclaimed.

Voices came from the passage above, the sounds of people moving toward us. Dzsinn bolted to the shadows near the exit Z and his men left from, his gaze meeting mine as both of us realized the way we got in was no longer an option for our own exit.

"*Bazdmeg*," I cursed. "Hurry!"

Opie worked her cuffs. Every second tapped against my shoulder blades, my feet shifting as the voices grew louder and clearer. They would see us soon, but even if we hid, they would see the dead crocodile here.

"Alllmooost…" Opie bit down on his tongue.

Grabbing the body of the crocodile, I heaved him up on the cot next to Raven, his blood oozing out of his thick neck, the bed squeaking under his weight.

"Got one!" Opie darted to the other cuff, my heart slamming in my chest as I dropped his head next to her and covered him with the sheet, hoping they'd think it was a girl and give us a little time.

The click of boots on the metal platform above blasted through my head.

"Opie."

Clank. The manacles hit the ground.

"This way." Dzsinn motioned to the tunnel Z's men took.

I lifted Raven and cradled her to my chest as Opie leaped onto my shoulder. Turning, I sprinted toward Dzsinn, hearing men's voices reach the bridge area overhead. I didn't dare look over at Celeste or the other two, feeling the stabbing guilt of leaving them here, knowing I couldn't get them out. Not now.

Sparing no time to glance back, we took off down the passage, not knowing what was ahead of us. All I knew was I had her in my fucking arms again, and if I was going to die, I would go out protecting her.

We tried to trek quietly over the gravelly ground, the tunnel a steady climb, with only a few firebulbs guiding our way. Raven stirred in my arms, her lashes fluttering, trying to claw out of the cage they forced her mind and magic into. Her powers were there but had been significantly depleted from the goblin poison.

I hitched her higher in my arms, my nose nuzzling into her hair, needing to touch her, appreciate she was alive.

"See?" Opie hung on to my tied-back hair. "Like dark chocolate with smoky caramelized bacon."

"Bacon?" A snort tickled the back of my throat.

"Or maybe it's crocodile sperm."

My molars slammed together, grinding at the understanding that if I wasn't here, he would have raped her. Been inside her. Touched something against her will, hurt her... and experienced something I hadn't.

A rumble drummed in my chest, my dick twitching with the overwhelming need to claim and protect her at the same time.

Mine.

The overpowering possessiveness clubbed me over the head, robbing me of air and making me stumble. I didn't get possessive. It wasn't in my nature. Yet the thought of anyone near her boiled me alive.

A distant shout dropped me back into the moment, shoving out everything else, pushing those thoughts deep inside.

Dzsinn stayed in front of me, his weapon ready, while I held Raven, keeping tight to the narrowing wall. Noises and murmurs of people trickled to us, a chilly breeze sweeping across my face, telling me the exit was getting close.

The clopping of soles hitting stone slowed us to a crawl, my head ducking against the low ceiling, the passage ending inside a small room. Maybe once used for storage or a guard station, the space was empty, the white stone walls aged with time and history. We stood just inside the wooden doorway, peering out to the lowest part of the multi-leveled small courtyard. The taste of strange magic coated my tongue and sparked memories. I already knew what I would find.

Over fifty figures, mainly men, were packed shoulder to shoulder, marching stiffly out of the castle gate, their movements reminiscent of what I'd seen before in Věrhăza. Most would soon turn feral, and almost all would end up dead. Sonya, like Istvan, had echelons of worth. These people were nothing but bodies to throw away in battle. Poor villagers she turned into the first line of defense. Some others would get the transformation, like Caden and Warwick, and some would become the monsters below.

Trepidation weaved in the back of my throat, rotting my gut. There was only one reason she'd be doing this.

"March out!" a deep, snarly voice called out into the frosty night, the man hidden from my view. My pulse accelerated, thumping in my neck, warning me of something. It sounded familiar, but my brain couldn't place it, causing more prickles of alarm to stand my hair on end.

"They are brain dead. Basically sleepwalkers." Dzsinn stared, watching them clomp in unison.

I studied the once-human men, probably innocent villagers, men looking for work, a way to survive. Now they were only weeks away from a brutal death.

Did they have a choice? Get sold a bill of lies? Think they were providing for their families, not realizing they had signed their lives away to the devil? By their dead eyes, they no longer cared about those families they had loved so much.

They were Sonya's minions.

"Think we found why your spies no longer report back to you," I whispered, feeling Raven stir more in my arms.

"No." He shook his head, his voice tight. "Nothing should be able to break it. Unless…" His attention went back out the door. Searching.

A shout suddenly tore up from the tunnel, a cry of alarm.

"Think they found Mr. Crocodile Man," Opie said.

"Fuck." Panic surged through my veins when the echo of boots came up the path. It would be just a matter of seconds before we were found. We had nowhere to go, and both our exits were blocked.

Dzsinn hissed, reaching over for my wrist under Raven's body. "Stay close to me."

His palm wrapped around my skin, then came the tingle of magic, and our forms slipped out the door as the three guards came into view.

I waited for them to call out, to take note of our fleeting figures, but nothing came. We hugged the wall, the dark night and flickering fire torches keeping us against the stone like shadows, while only feet away, the last of the guards marched out, their robotic movements feeling unnatural. Not one looked over. Not one took note of our presence.

Dzsinn could practically vanish and appear before your eyes, like a genie in a cloud of smoke. His magic gave him the ability to be forgotten and unnoticed. In extending that to me, he labored under the weight. He breathed heavily, and a sheen of sweet veneered his skin as he fought to not only keep me undetected but Raven as well.

"Intruders in the castle!" a man barked, coming out of the tunnel way and running into the emptying courtyard. "One of the *Primul* is dead!" *The First.*

I heard a thundering growl, like a savage dog barking, the sound hitting somewhere deep, a terror that froze me in place.

"Go," the deep voice ordered from a walkway above us. "Find them now!"

A handful of figures descended from stairs around the yard, the night keeping them hidden, but one of them moved like a cheetah, his lean, muscular body darting down the passage before I could even see him. Others with animal qualities followed, leaving the quad silent in their wake.

We stayed still, my pulse ticking the time, my legs itchy to move. After several moments, Dzsinn let go, his head leaning out to peer up at the balcony overhead.

"He's gone," he muttered to me.

I surveyed the yard, recalling the map we had studied. "There is an exit through that way." I nodded with my head, readjusting Raven in my arms. "We can escape through the forest. Opie, get in the bag." Not waiting for either of them to respond, I crept for the door leading to the front, holding a gun under Raven's legs, feeling the brownie crawl in the pack.

A groan broke from Raven's lips, her forehead creasing, consciousness starting to pull her from sleep.

"Shhh, *Dziubuś*," I muttered into her hair, bringing her closer to my chest. "Please stay quiet." Snow crunched under my feet as I made my way toward the exit, which took me through another chamber, a layer of defense. I ducked my head through the doorway, the thick, white stone walls ebbing the harsh chill from outside. What used to be a gift shop and museum for the thirteenth-century castle had been pilfered long ago. All the important artifacts and history were stripped for money, leaving the space empty except for creaky wooden floors, painted motifs, and bulky furniture no one could move.

I glanced over my shoulder at the genie, finding no one behind me.

"Dzsinn?"

Silence.

"Dzsinn?" I hissed again, hearing shouts come from both outside and inside the castle, my window of opportunity shrinking.

A whimper came from my arms, drawing me back to her. To why I was here. Getting her to safety was my *only* priority.

Click. Click.

A barrel pressed into the back of my brain.

"You thought it would be so easy, Ash." A low snarl hit the back of my ear, the familiarity of my name confirming my fear. "I've been waiting for this."

The barking noise wasn't from a dog. It was from a gorilla.

Numbness slid over my shoulders.

"Joska." I breathed out, twisting my head to see the former HDF soldier who tortured us as a guard in Věrhăza and then tried to kill us in the pit. Joska was a violent extremist before Istvan experimented on him; afterward, he became a deadly monster.

"You remembered." He had a high, domed forehead and wide nostrils. His body was bulked up, his chest heavy like a gorilla. He was no longer human, but not exactly fae either. He seemed to belong better with the things down in the cave.

"I was told you fled like a coward after the battle in Budapest." Hatred seeped out of me. "I should've figured you'd join another tyrant to hide behind."

A disturbing smile tugged on his face, like I was missing something.

"Joska?" Another man ran into the room, followed by the handful I saw in the quad.

The thin, cheetah-like man stopped, glaring at me, his canine teeth protruding from his lips.

"Samu." Abhorrence oozed from my mouth, staring at the other former HDF soldier. "Not surprised you are still trailing after Joska like a lost puppy... or should I say pussy."

His jaw snapped, his nose wrinkling like he was ready to swat at me with his paw.

My shock at seeing them had melted quickly to animosity, and I was more surprised at myself for not seeing this coming.

"I'd love to catch up, especially to find out how Brexley is doing..." Joska sneered. His hatred of her was deep. To him, no matter how hypocritical it was, she was the ultimate fae traitor. She also killed one of his classmates in self-defense.

He wanted her dead. That girl had an ever-growing list.

"I'm gonna enjoy even more what's in store for you." Joska jabbed the gun into my head harder, turning me back where I came from.

Three other men and a woman I didn't recognize stood behind them, all with animal characteristics. Like others who survived Istvan's first experiments, they found their way to each other. A calling only they could hear.

"Balazs, take her." Joska nodded at Raven, ordering a man who had hyena-like qualities—black and brown spotted hair, pointed ears, and a pronounced jaw and nose, his energy hyper and nervous. The man, Balazs, stepped forward, reaching for my girl.

"Noooo." The guttural word vibrated the room. I twisted away from him, keeping her close. The trees out in the forest snapped with my wrath.

Thunk!

Joska's thick hand and gun hit my skull, the force knocking me to the floor, Raven tumbling out of my arms.

"No!" I cried out, my arm stretching for her.

A boot stomped down on my hand, crunching the bones with sharp pain. Joska grunted down at me, the gun pointed at my face.

"The only reason I haven't torn your limbs from your body and crushed your brain between my fingers is that she wants to see you first."

Grabbing my backpack, he heaved me up to my feet, my head swimming as he stripped me of the bag and all my weapons. My stomach twinged when he peered into the bag, but I knew Opie and Bitzy would be gone. Sub-fae were the best at disappearing.

Though blurry vision, my eyes stayed locked on Raven. The hyena-man picked up her limp frame, a snarl blowing through my nose as his hands slid up her barely dressed body.

"Move." Joska shoved me forward while Samu kept his gun pointed at my head as they escorted me back outside. The clips of our boots pounded in tempo with my heart as they walked me into the small, cramped courtyard. Subtly, I peered for any sign of Dzsinn, though I knew better than to think he'd try to save me. Genies didn't do anything out of the kindness of their hearts. It was all transactional.

Fire torches flickered in the gentle wind, lighting the yard and letting me get a better look at the long-standing castle.

Dark timber beams with white, thick stone walls, cobbled ground, and red slated roofs set the idyllic backdrop for a Gothic fairy-tale castle overlooking the snowy valleys below. A decorative well sat as the focal point on a higher tier. It might look picturesque, but it was built for invasion and war. Various levels and sections of the castle circled the multi-level courtyard, impossible to invade successfully because most of the levels didn't connect. If you found you went up the wrong stairs or they weren't in the right area, you had to go all the way back down and find another way. For those raiding, it made them confused and vulnerable.

"Ash." A beautiful voice glided down to me from a parapet walk above, my head tipping up to the woman. "I expected you here sooner." She wore an elegant, pale rose dress, sleek and fitted to her body, her hair set in an elaborate braid down one side.

A squawk pierced the air, and hawk wings swooped over my head, landing on the railing next to Sonya.

Nyx. That fucking bitch. One of her wings was slightly bent from where I broke it, but healed enough for her to fly again.

Sonya stepped up to the railing, petting the hawk. "I had to put on such a performance for you. Pretend I didn't know you weren't already within my walls." She gave off a smugness at knowing I was here the whole time. Nyx had been watching me, waiting to lure me in. "Though I am curious how you surpassed my spells without setting them off?"

I didn't respond. Sonya loved to look like she was the shrewdest, smartest person in the room.

The burning torches lit around the space, ignited her stunning face, her blonde hair shimmering in the soft glow. Bright eyes so similar to ones I had looked into so many times, had loved, now peered down at me with disgust in someone else's face.

Like Iain, there were too many of Lukas's features I saw in Sonya. The reminder of his absence stabbed the betrayal of what they did deeper into my heart.

"Took you long enough." Her head tipped at Balazs. He moved forward, dumping Raven onto the snowy ground just out of my reach, her almost naked body fragile and weak as she tried to fight back against the poison in her system.

Deep rage strummed through my muscles, licking at my bones like fire as if I were set on a pyre, left to burn. I wanted to put my body over hers, protect her, get her far from here. And I was useless to do any of it.

"I was starting to think she doesn't mean all that much to you. Just as my son clearly doesn't to you anymore." Her voice was calm and beautiful, but her words cut through me like an axe.

"Fuck you!" A growl snapped up my throat, my body moving without my consideration. Joska grabbed me, pulling me back, the muzzle of the gun denting into my temple.

Sonya's head tipped back, her laugh twinkling down like stardust, but cruel and diabolical.

"To have a mother like you…" I spat, my anger shivering the tree near the well, waking it up from its winter slumber. "At least with me, he knew real love."

"Real love?" She placed her hands on the rail, her head slanting in condescension. "Was it? I mean, how quickly you seem to care for another. Took you no time at all to move on."

I felt myself glowering. "See, what you aren't aware of is when you have a soul, you can care for more than one person at a time."

"Yes, I know you seem to like more than one, don't you?" Her words were intended to condemn me, to remind me of both Kek and Lukas.

"Don't let this bitch get to you, pretty boy." I swear I could hear Kek in my ear. *"She wants to provoke you."*

I knew she did, yet it was hard to control my response, the emotions and injustice I carried for them.

"You have me." I spoke evenly. "Let her go."

A fake smile curled her lips. "Did you really think it would be so easy?"

"The fight is between you and me. She has nothing to do with it."

"*You* made her part of it. She's in this now." Sonya gestured to me. "Seems like anyone near you ends up hurt or dead."

"Oh, it's my fault your son murdered your other son? You don't seem to care at all."

For one moment, wrath contorted her face, her hands rolling up before her expression went cold again. "Lukas chose his side and the consequences that came with it."

"Consequences?" I blurted. "It's not like he was kicked out of the house for staying out all night! Iain murdered him in cold blood! Shot him through the head!" My voice volleyed through the courtyard, emotions taking over. "But I guess that's what you do to your own flesh and blood."

"*I* didn't shoot anyone."

"Doesn't make your hands any less bloodstained." My body shook with adrenaline. With abhorrence.

"This world has one less demon in it. That's a good thing."

The darkness of my hate thundered through me, branches from the tree in the yard snapping off, dropping to the ground, the trunk creaking as it swayed under my power.

Her spine straightened, pointing from the guards to me. "Cuff him!"

They responded instantly to her order. Grabbing my arms, they yanked them behind me, locking my arms together. My knees bent as the goblin metal slid over my skin, a hiss driving through my teeth as I pushed through the nausea and pain.

It was like being back in prison, living in that nightmare, the underbelly of hell, day in and out. Dealing with constant weakness and agony. But just like many others, I built up a strong immunity to it. Not that it didn't affect me, it did, but I could stand more than most.

The wave of sickness washed over me. I took several breaths to keep the bile down, getting my legs steady under me. The goblin metal stripped my powers, but it peeled away everything else too. Like all the excuses I had built up to keep Raven out. Denying what was in my face for a while now. Dying had been my plan all along, yet my chest ached at the notion. I no longer wanted to die in vengeance. I wanted to live. For her.

"I thought you were smarter than this." Sonya shook her head. "Did you really believe I would release her just because you gave yourself up?"

"No," I replied. "I figured you wouldn't."

Sonya's eyes narrowed, confused at my response. "But you gave yourself up anyway?" She let out a laugh. "Some deluded notion you could save her?"

"You think I did this for her?" I lifted my brow, keeping my voice cold. "I came here for you."

"You came a long way to be greatly disappointed and then die."

"As long as I take you out as I go."

"I could kill you right now." She leaned on the rail, smirking at me. "Problem solved."

"But you won't."

She stood up fully, curiosity and bewilderment blinking her lids. "And why is that?"

"Because I'm nothing but a nuisance to you, right? Not a true threat."

She folded her arm, invested in my conclusion.

"However, I mean a lot to the leader of Hungary, don't I?" I baited. "This is why you are doing all this? Building an army? To conquer and rule more land?" I gestured around with my chin. "I'm great leverage as a prisoner to provoke Killian," I lied. Killian would do the right thing and chose his people, his country. Not me. He'd make a strategic, rational decision.

Couldn't say the same about the rest of my friends though.

"You know what my family is capable of. The hell they'd rain down on you if you killed me."

"Oh, don't you see?" Her blonde brow lifted. "It is *exactly* what I am hoping for." An arrogant smile curved her mouth.

"Killian is aligned with the Unified Nations. You attack him, you will have the UFN after you too. You think the little monsters you have here will stand against that?" I snorted.

If she only knew the woman lying on the ground would bring the world to a standstill if the UFN found out she was a prisoner.

"Tree fairies should stick to fucking and making healing remedies." Sonya clicked her tongue with a heavy sigh. "It's all your race seems capable of." She wagged her head with condescension, arrogance wafting off her like perfume. "Istvan might have been a little hiccup in my plan, but that didn't change anything in the scheme of things. Czech and Hungary may think they are succeeding, but they will fold just like the rest." Her fingers pressed into the railing. "And I am *far* from alone. Especially not when the ultimate prize just fell into my lap."

"What are you talking about?"

Her lips twisted in mocking grief. "The agony of losing a child can really bond people together. We both know what it's like to lose a son. Especially when they've been murdered in cold blood."

Acid rained down my throat.

"The loss of the *Vozhd's* son, the sweet Alexsei Kozlov… His poor father is beside himself with grief." Her eyes flipped to me. "Wants revenge for his son's murder."

Fuck.

"And Dimitri Kozlov agreed to unite forces in exchange for obtaining his son's killer." She smirked. "Who also happens to be my enemy's greatest weakness. So no, dear Ash, I am not doing this to battle Killian for Hungary. Your country is insignificant to me. I'm going for bigger fish." Her chuckle twinkled in the air at my simple thoughts. "And you are not the one who'd make great leverage as a prisoner…" She peered down at the girl on the ground. "She is."

Chapter 11

Ash

My worst nightmare hung in the air like a ghoul, sucking the energy and life from my marrow.

A vindictive smile twisted Sonya's mouth, arrogance polluting her aura.

She knew.

Throat tight, I tried to swallow, keeping my reaction flat, trying not to display the fear engulfing me.

Sonya recognized Raven was not just someone important to me, but to the entire Unified Nations.

The queen's daughter. The princess.

Sonya had the UFN by the balls, and I didn't see them standing aside for the better of the country. Her father and her uncles alone would shred through this castle to get to Raven. But it wasn't merely these walls imprisoning her, keeping them from reaching her.

Russia had been quietly building their military for decades, manufacturing weapons, expanding trade, and making deals with other countries. By themselves they weren't a huge threat, but rumor was China had associated with them as well, which brought Sonya's threat into reality.

"Did you think I wouldn't know who she is?" Sonya stroked Nyx's head. The hawk glowered at me, enjoying my pain, relishing in the agony of watching someone I care about hurt.

My lips stayed pinned together. Sonya's snappy overconfidence told me she hadn't been aware of Raven's identity, not until recently. Probably when she and Dimitri Kozlov realized they were after the same people. Otherwise why would she think the girl in raggedy, dirty clothes, slumming it with me in whorehouses, was the princess of the UFN? Raven was famous, but social media hadn't existed like it did before the barrier fell. Her likeness was just seen in print magazines and newspapers. Stuff the rich could afford to buy in the Eastern Bloc.

"She is the merely leverage I need." She dropped her hand from Nyx, nodding to Raven, her gaze never leaving mine. "You are useless and will only cause me problems." She clicked her tongue. "So sad you came all this way to seek revenge... for nothing." She nodded at Joska behind me. "Kill him."

"Gladly." A deep growl came from his throat, sounding more animal than human. "Just know before I tear your limbs from your body that I will hunt Brexley down and make sure she and her little wolf are next."

The flare of wrath gritted my teeth, but I forced a chuckle between my lips. "Good luck with that. You'll be dead before you could even get within a mile of Brexley." She could kill him with her eyes closed without even putting effort into it, but she wouldn't have to. Warwick would cut him down before he stepped into town. Anything threatening her was dead on arrival.

"Quickly!" Sonya ordered Joska. "Then take her back to the breeding room. Let the *Primul* mate her until she conceives. To have her power, her bloodline as one of my soldiers... I will so love to see the expression on Her Majesty's face when she sees her *adorable* grandson."

Madness drank me in, embodied me, became the blood in my veins and the beat of my heart. Numbness buzzed in my brain, possessing me, while Samu and another approached her.

"*Kurvára ne nyúlj hozzá!*" *Do not fucking touch her!* I bellowed, the voice not even sounding like mine. Pushing against the goblin metal, I thrashed against Joska's hold, tugging him with me as I tried to move to her curled-up form on the muddy, icy ground.

Sonya's laugh played like a soundtrack in my mind, adding to my craze.

"*Basszon agyon a kénköves istennyila!*" *Get fucked to death by lightning with sulphuric stones!* I screamed at her, pulling against Joska.

Joska dragged me over against a wall, my shouts tearing up my throat, my energy draining from me, which only added to my anger.

I was helpless. I didn't have power like Brexley or Warwick had; my magic was limited to earth and nature. I was born a healer and even though I was raised a fighter, it wasn't in my DNA to fight against goblin metal, no matter how much I tried. The organic makeup and magic were a nature fairy's worst nemesis.

"Raven!" I hollered her name, needing her to know I hadn't left her here all alone. I came for her. But between the two of us, sadly, I was the luckier one. My death would be quick. What was in store for her was unfathomable.

I needed her to wake. To fight. To get out of here and live her life. Fall in love and be happy. *Dziubuś,* I cried in my head. *Wake up. You have to fight...*

For a moment I thought I saw her leg twitch, but it was more likely I hoped I saw it.

Joska pointed his gun at my chest, just slightly off from my heart.

"I'm gonna watch you bleed out while I rip your limbs from your body." A hyper-excited yip came up his throat, his chest puffing out.

Samu couched down to pick up Raven as Joska pushed down on the trigger.

I am so sorry I failed you.

"Seems you're being a bit rash." A voice cut through, swinging everyone's heads to the newest addition. Sucking in, I froze as I watched Dzsinn step into the courtyard, pulling down his hood, his focus on Sonya. "Though you always were. So desperate to be the best, to be recognized and seen, you tended to overlook things..."

Her eyes widened, shock tinting her features while Dzsinn moved to the middle.

"Even as a child."

Fury bloomed in her eyes, her expression turning impassive, her chin lifting in defiance.

"Dzsinn." She uttered his name with intimacy, sinking my stomach into the ground.

"It's been a long time. Glad you still remember me... *cousin.*"

What. The. Actual. Fuck?

Cousin?

This whole time he not only knew of her, but was related to her? What the hell was going on? Was this all a trap for me?

My gaze jumped between them in disbelief, noticing the animosity.

Her lids narrowed. "We share no blood, genie."

"And yet, you wear my family's heirloom like it's yours to have." He flicked his hand to the luminous crystal necklace around her throat. It was nothing I really took notice of before, a woman's trinket. "I was wondering how my people were ignoring my summons." He seethed. "The Cintamani stone is rightfully mine, Sonya. You stole it *from me.*"

The Cintamani stone?

It was a sacred stone to the jinn race, which most believed was more a myth than truth. A symbol with both the Hindu and Buddhist traditions. One of the stories was that it originated in the stars and had fallen to Earth as a meteorite from the gods. It was known as the wish-fulfilling gem. It gave luck and opportunity to whoever wore it, emitting vibrations and assisting in resourceful manifestation with an energy source. Some linked it to the Philosopher's stone—the elixir of life.

"And unless my moles are dead, no one, except another genie, can break our summons."

Holy fuck.

I stared at her, her chest rising and falling under the legendary stone. It made so much sense. Her continuous rise to the top, acquiring so many to follow her without thought, getting away without a scratch, and succeeding in everything she did almost effortlessly.

People died right and left around her, yet she skated by, only becoming more powerful. Because she had the foundation of genie magic around her throat.

Dzsinn glared daggers at her. "You came into my family, were raised and loved like one of our own, and this is how you repay us?"

"Loved?" she spat. "I was treated like an outcast my whole youth."

"Because you were a righteous, conceited bitch even then," Dzsinn jabbed.

"For all I went through... I earned this." She touched the jewel. "Plus, the necklace chose me. I was the worthy one out of all of you and your brothers."

"It belongs to me." Dzsinn's vocals tightened. "And I've come to reclaim it."

A loud laugh sang through the yard, her head tipping back. "And you expect me to hand it over to you?"

"With or without your head attached. I am taking back what is mine."

Her amusement tinkled in the air again, her head shaking, the humor slowly dropping away.

"Kill them both."

The clicks of guns snapped in unison, her soldiers reacting instantly to her order. I held my breath, waiting to hear the shots, feel the bullets burrow into my body.

But instead of a gunshot, a rumble shook the ground, knocking against my skin and diving into my lungs. The entire world seemed to stop on a point.

She rose from the earth like she came out from the depths of hell, her skin and hair bathed in night. Her back curved, sharp blades tearing through her tank, her hands becoming scythes of death. I couldn't see her face, but I knew the fire blazing in her eyes, the dagger teeth ready to rip into flesh.

Fear filled the air, their terror turning on her. Wondering what the hell she was.

The hyena bayed out a cry. A shot went off, the bullet grazing by her. A chant hissed from her directed at the hyena, but he raised his gun again.

Raven's lips peeled back, darting for him, but he was just as fast as her, his own teeth chomping for her neck.

Raven stumbled back, her dark dweller livid with anger, but confusion blinked over her face for a moment.

It was like I could feel her fear, her understanding of what had just happened.

Holy. Fuck.

Her obscurer had no power over them. Their minds were different than fae or humans. They weren't even in-between. An obscurer was rare, despised, and hunted down, but their magic was still based in nature.

These things were not.

"Get her! But don't kill her!" Sonya ordered from high on her perch, Nyx taking flight, squawking overhead. The world became chaos, a frenzied energy of distressed howls and commands aimed at her. From all directions, bullets volleyed for her, her beast roaring with fury.

"Raven!" I belted as Joska turned his gun on her, her head snapping to me.

Bang! Bang! Bang!

Her mouth moved faster, a power shimmering around her body, blood starting to drip from her nose. Every bullet missed her, embedding into the stone behind her. Joska pounded on his chest, his roar matching hers. He leaped for her, their bodies colliding in a thud.

"Raven!" I belted again, lurching for the pair fighting, my weak legs dropping me to the ground, my face smacking hard against the stone. A frustrated cry burned my vocals, and I glared at my cuffed hands behind my back.

"Hmmm... the tree humper looks like he needs us." A tiny figure jumped on my back.

"Opie," I breathed out. "Uncuff me!"

Chirp!

"Bitzy wants unlimited mushrooms."

"What?" I exclaimed. "Are you serious? This is not the time to bargain. Let me go."

Chirp!

"She says this is exactly the time."

"Fine, whatever!" I wiggled my arms, peering back toward Raven, though I couldn't see anything from where I was. "Just uncuff me."

"That was for Bitzy." Opie tapped his fingers on his mouth. "I want unlimited access for my designs. Any fabrics or jewelry, which *includes* a certain fae book. I have a particular design in mind from the seventh century."

My teeth gritted. Fae books were sacred to me.

"Fine!"

Opie smiled, putting his attention to my manacles. I turned my head back in her direction, hearing her dweller roar in pain.

"Hurry!" Panic strangled my voice, the terror of her fighting them all by herself. Every second was years; every moment made me more afraid I'd hear her cries of death. I knew her power could only sustain for a short time.

"I think I got—" The second I felt the cuffs drop away, I pushed up, scrambling across the quad for her. I could see her claws slicing across Joska's chest, stumbling him back.

As if she felt me, knew I was close, her head snapped in my direction, her flaming eyes finding mine. Black blood poured from her eyes and nose, her teeth dripping with blood reflected in the torchlight.

It was only a second, but I felt her sink into my soul, her beast marking me as hers. It was like we didn't even need to speak, a connection between us growing like a network of intricate roots snaring deep into the ground.

Sonya shrieked, snapping reality back into place. "Get her!"

All their attention on Raven, I snuck up behind the guard running for her, slamming my elbow into the back of his skull as I kicked his knee. He dropped to the ground while I yanked the gun from his hands.

Bang!

I didn't hesitate, shooting him through the back of the head before pointing it at anything in my path to get to her.

"Kill him!" Sonya barked, her finger pointed at me.

More of these mixed species came for me, firing their weapons, the bullets skating by my head. It would only take one to stop me.

"NO!" Raven thundered, her eyes completely in flames as she shoved past Joska, her claws slicing across Samu's throat, propelling him into the wall, her deadly frame tearing into everything that stood between us. Blood gushed over the courtyard, which was littered with bodies. It was as if her obscurer was feeding off her anger, off the violence, turning her more savage.

Feral and wild, her teeth bared, black liquid flowing from her nose, her eyes swimming with fire and blood. A darkness encased her in a different plane of existence, slipping from my reach. In my gut, I felt like I was losing her, and if she hit a certain point, she wouldn't make it back to me.

"*Mroczny,*" I called out to her, reaching for her. Her tempestuous gaze snapped to me, her chest heaving, taking a moment for her snarl to abate. "I'm here." I curled my fingers for her to come to me.

Slowly, Raven moved to me, a growl still humming in her gut, her frame caked in carnage, the gore-drenched the castle as a backdrop to the true horror.

"Come here, *mroczny,*" I ordered, standing in challenge against her power. I stretched out, taking her wrist. Her body shifted back to normal when I touched her, as if I was what centered her, brought her back. Her face was pallid, her shoulders sagging, her bones shaking. Magic was draining from her quickly.

"I need you to run." My command was low and determined. I locked my attention on Raven, needing her to push against the exhaustion, to continue to fight for our lives.

She nodded, but we both knew it wouldn't be long until she had nothing left. We had to get as far as we could.

"What is wrong with you freaks!" Sonya screamed, peering down at the bodies groaning and bleeding out. "Get them!" she yelled at Nyx.

"Now!" I took Raven's blood-covered hand in mine as Nyx screeched down for us. Pulling her with me through the gate, I was aware sometime during the frenzy, Dzsinn had once again disappeared.

Swiping up my pack, we took off. With what little energy we had left, we sprinted from the castle.

The night didn't hide us from Nyx. Our figures moving through the forest outside the citadel were like glowing heat sources to her. Her squawks pinpointed our location, directing the soldiers Sonya had coming after us, feeling like déjà vu.

Shooting up at the sky, the hawk dodged the bullets, screeching even louder, staying far enough away to not be a target. She wasn't here to kill us; she was there to keep tabs on our whereabouts.

"I need to kill that bitch once and for all," I snarled, holding on to Raven, the thicker snow causing her to stumble. Her bare feet struggled to push on, her figure barely staying upright. "Please, don't give up on me," I pleaded, propelling her faster. The roars of car engines and motorcycles from the castle scraped the back of my neck.

Everything was against us. The chances of escaping were low, but I knew if the monsters they call the *Primul* came after us, we were dead.

Adrenaline drove my body forward, and I took more and more of Raven's weight. Her strength was declining, her body unable to keep up with the demand.

We couldn't slow down. We couldn't stop. Our only chance was putting enough space between us and them. Images of what would happen if Sonya's men caught us again, what they would do to her, especially now that they knew how powerful she was and what a dangerous weapon she could produce if mated with the *Primul*, ran unbidden through my mind.

She was the ultimate prize, whereas I would be shot and beheaded.

Panic and terror became molten rock in my gut, firing through my nerves and embedding into the earth. A signal of distress stamped into the ground.

The trees answered my call, bending to me, inviting me to take, to procure their energy like a siphon. And I seized it greedily.

The raw, untamed magic burned through my veins, the overload singeing my muscles and igniting me. A grunt escaped my lips, my body shaking as the sudden influx of energy almost dropped me to my knees. There was no real thought, no understanding, except intuition. The need to protect her. To keep her safe.

Tapping into the energy, I turned my focus on her, my hands tight on her face, like I was the conduit. She resisted at first, pain splintering across my forehead, knocking against the barrier. Sweat beaded down my face, and I snarled through the pain, pushing harder. I felt her wall break. My magic poured into her system, flooding her.

Raven jerked at the invasion, a cry breaking from her lips, but I only gripped her harder, forcing her to take more. Magic pumped into her like I was inside her, filling her so deeply it scorched into my soul. I sensed every one of her muscles hungrily gorging on it. Her legs stood firmer under her, her wounds knitting back together. Her cheeks flushed as her green eyes danced with flames again.

I stared down at her in awe of her beauty and power. Our enemies were coming for us, but all I could see, hear, smell, and taste was her. The intimacy of the connection was profound, yet my brain was too numb to understand what I had done. What bond this would create. Sharing magic was one of the most sacred experiences you could share with another. It was opening yourself up for them to see everything.

I groaned in desire, my body shaking like I was on the cusp of an orgasm. I could touch her darkness, feel her beast and obscurer skimming through me. No line was between us anymore, her life melding with mine.

Land of Monsters

Somewhere in the back of my mind, I heard a hawk shriek, the rumble of motorcycles, and bellows underfoot. *Go.* We needed to go.

"Fuck." I ripped my hands from her face, breaking away from her. Though all I wanted to do was stay in the bubble with her, to reach that blissful high, not caring about the world around us.

She bent over the moment I let go, gasping for oxygen. "Wh-what the fuck was that?"

"We have to go." Every second they drew close itched my legs, but the anxiety also came from what I had just done. There was a distinct line fae didn't cross unless it was with their mate. And even then, some didn't do it. And I wiped that line out of existence. Sharing magic was the most intimate thing you could do. "You good to run?"

"Y-yes." She bobbed her head.

"Good, because I need you to run like your life depends on it."

Because it did.

Wild animals roared in the distance, setting us off. Our legs tore across the snowy ground, Raven's slight frame outrunning mine, her skin almost a glow of excess magic. It hummed off her with familiarity, like my smell, my mark, was imprinted on her skin.

Fuck. What the hell did I just do?

With another screech in the sky, I shoved all thoughts out of my head, the trees breaking away to farmland, giving us no place to hide.

"Down!" I pointed to the village below, hoping to get lost among the houses and buildings. Raven and I raced to the country road, turning a corner around an old B&B. Headlights blinded us as the military jeep came to a screeching halt in front of us.

Terror gripped my throat, hearing guards coming down the hill behind us. My pulse drowned out my senses. We had nowhere to go or hide.

We were caught.

"Get in!" A voice barked from the driver's window, a hand motioning us to climb in.

My lids squinted at the man behind the wheel.

"Dzsinn?"

"Get the fuck in now!" he bellowed.

Jogging over, I ripped open the door, pushing Raven into the back seat while I climbed in the front.

"Go! Go!" I yelled as gunfire pinged off the outside of the car.

Wheels spinning, the jeep lurched forward, Dzsinn slamming his foot on the gas pedal. The car skidded over the slush, fishtailing around a corner, while bullets cracked against the back window, shattering it. Raven screamed, covering her head and ducking further into the seat. Dzsinn sped us forward, getting out of range of their shot. Whipping my head around, I watched their figures disappear in the dark, letting out a slip of breath.

"*Squawk!*"

My head jerked to a silhouette in the sky staying in line with us. *That fucking bitch.* Wings spread, Nyx kept us in her sight, gliding with the speed of the car, coasting over to the field on the driver's side. Soon Sonya's men in jeeps and motorcycles would be coming for us, and if we didn't lose her, she would lead them right to us.

"Hold the car steady!" I demanded, the rough country road bouncing us around. Rolling down the window, I slipped my ass out onto the door frame, the icy wind snapping at my face and hair. The roads made it hard for me to hold on to the gun and aim while not falling out of the car.

Raven's hands gripped my thighs, holding me in place. Her heat soaked through my pants, the extra magic she contained humming against my skin, stroking me.

"Fuck." I gritted my teeth, trying to concentrate and not have every brain cell go to my dick. Using the top of the car as purchase, I aimed.

Bang! My shot cracked in the atmosphere, her form swooping, missing the bullet.

"*Szar.*" I snapped, aiming at her again. In the distance behind us, headlights turned onto the road, the guards coming after us.

"We need to lose her, Ash," Dzsinn warned, his eyes flicking to the side mirror, seeing what was coming behind. "Now."

Taking a deep breath, I didn't try to block out Raven's touch, allowing it to seep in, almost like I was using her strength this time. Focused and calm, I squeezed one eye shut, getting Nyx in my view.

Bang!

The gun recoiled, followed by a shrill screech, her form dropping from the air into the dark field.

I let out the breath I was holding, hitting my hand on the top of the roof. "Yes." I hissed through my teeth, sliding back into the car.

"Got her," I announced with satisfaction, turning back to the headlights far behind us, but Raven came into my view instead. "You okay?" My eyes slid over every inch of her barely dressed body. Her tank was in shreds, her hair bloody and knotted, yet her face was flushed with health and vigor. Life brimmed under her skin, which thrummed with *my* magic.

It screamed *mine.* Everything about her affected me, creating a tightness, a deep awareness.

Land of Monsters

I shredded off my jacket, giving it to her to wear, only adding to my possession.

"Yeah," she replied. As she pulled on the coat, our gazes caught, making me feel she could see right through me. Whatever we shared on that mountain went beyond the wall I had tried to keep between us. And I wasn't sure how I felt about it. Or about how close I was to losing her tonight.

Something had changed, and it felt like I was purged back into a world where I was forced to care. To watch those close to me die.

Sitting back in my seat, I rubbed at my forehead. Dzsinn snorted, peering at her through the rearview mirror, then back at me, shaking his head like he could see through us both.

"We need to lay low for a while. She'll have troops searching for us," Dzsinn spoke, pushing harder on the pedal. "This car is too noticeable."

My lids lowered, turning to him. "Why didn't you tell me you not only know Sonya, but you're related?"

"Not really related." His expression didn't change.

"Not the point."

"I don't owe you anything, Ash," he huffed, seeing the motorcycles gaining on us. "And right now is not the time."

"We have to get off these roads before she puts up roadblocks," Raven said, still watching the motorcycles in the distance.

Dzsinn shifted in his seat, a frown on his lips. "I know of a place we can go."

"Another cousin's house?" I quipped.

"A connection. I trust them." Dzsinn pushed the old jeep until it rattled, jarring my already tense nerves. Anger welled at the feeling of helplessness, of what was already lost to me and what could be taken.

I didn't want to feel it again.

I did *not* want to care, yet I was falling down that hole anyway.

The jeep squealed as Dzsinn spun us down another side road, fleeing from the notorious castle whose myths couldn't even come close to the real-life monsters and horrors dwelling inside.

Chapter 12

Raven

Outside the city walls of Brașov, the slums of desolation wore like a badge of honor through the dilapidated buildings. The jeep rolled down the bumpy road, and all those out on the icy streets turned toward us. The military car was an unusual sight.

"Nice place." Ash snorted.

"In my line of work, you make all sorts of connections. Like you have any room to talk, fairy. I've seen the places you've been in the last year." Dzsinn turned us down another lane, rolling the jeep into a place behind an old building. A line of fae-updated motorcycles filled the lot. "This place might hold the worst of the worst, but we have a common enemy. They won't ever snitch on you here."

Ash nodded, his movements stiff. Instead of relief from our escape, I felt his anger multiplying, threading through the car. Pointed at me. It was all so overwhelming.

My body wouldn't stop vibrating, everything feeling like it was too much for me to handle. From the moment I was taken by Sonya, I lived in a warped nightmare, nothing sticking in my mind except wanting him. Dreaming of him. When his voice reached me, his hands touched me, it felt like another dream. One I didn't want to wake from.

I barely recalled the fight inside the castle, my monsters taking over instinctively, fighting for him, stealing the last fragment of me until I was nothing.

What he willingly gave me was so sacred, so intimate, it terrified me.

But when the first drop of it singed my veins, my beast licked it up with hunger, my obscurer absorbing it without reserve, and I dove in with greed. Taking more and more until I swallowed him entirely. That could be the only reason he slid around inside me like he was my prisoner trapped between my ribs. But he was angry, and I couldn't deal with all of these thoughts and emotions now.

Dzsinn cocked his gun and put it in his cloak pocket, bringing me back to reality.

"Thought you said you trusted these guys." I lifted a brow.

"I trust them not to snitch on us." He climbed out of the jeep. "Keep your guard up." He took off for the back door.

Ash helped me out of the car, his hand taking mine, a bolt of energy running up my arm and making me gasp.

He pulled away like I held a disease, his brows furrowing, his eyes avoiding me.

"Stay close," he muttered.

Pulling his jacket tighter around me, the bottom just brushing the tops of my thighs, I padded after him, feeling so powerful and vulnerable at the same time.

Usually, it took me days to recuperate after using my magic, but his energy was a live wire, bringing me to life. On the downside, it opened me up to him and let me feel him, his every mood.

He was livid.

We stepped into the smoky, dark room, my spine stiffening. Men and women, mainly fae, lounged around the seedy bar, smoking and drinking. Violence was a blink away from exploding in the den. The windows were barred and blocked off from the outside, and the inside was crumbling and reeked of stale smoke and alcohol. The place was filled with bikers. A gang.

This should've made me feel at home. My father and uncles were part of a notorious gang back in the day, the RODs (Riders of Darkness). But with them, I was protected. They would murder anyone who looked at me wrong. Here, I was an intruder. And gangs never took to strangers.

"Dzsinn." A stunning, dark-haired woman stood up, prowling to him, her sexuality out on display, her lips a bright red, her eyes a strange navy color.

Demon.

"It's been a while." Her English was heavy with a Romanian accent.

"Daciana." Dzsinn tipped his head to her, but her attention already fluttered back to me and Ash.

"You brought me gifts." Her eyes raked down both of us.

"I'm calling in a favor you owe me." Dzsinn spoke evenly, but I saw his hand slip into his cloak pocket, where his gun was. "We need a place to hide for a few days. Just until things cool down."

"I'm sorry." Her dark eyebrows lifted. "Did you bring trouble to *my* door? To a place I've welcomed you in with open arms?"

"You owe me." Dzsinn's vocals tightened. "I'm here to claim it."

Her navy eyes flashed black, her lip snarling at his command, but it quickly died away, a fake smile forcing her mouth to move. "Of course, Dzsinn, any wish of yours," she jeered, pushing past him to us. "These still better be my gifts. You know me and my boys like new toys to play with. And they came wrapped exactly how I like them. In barely anything."

Oh shit. This was the last thing we needed to deal with right now.

Every head turned our way, most landing on me, my bare legs making me feel completely naked.

A growl rose from Ash, his body stepping in front of mine, his shoulders rolling forward.

"If you fucking touch her—"

"Ash." Dzsinn shook his head, pushing him back into me.

Ash gripped my thighs, shielding me, a snarl on his lips while he scanned the room. A threat. A promise.

"Ash!" Dzsinn warned again to no avail. The room rumbled with aggression, and Ash tipped the scale. Some of the bikers rose from their seats.

"Ash," I whispered in his ear, my hands moving down his arms, tangling my fingers with his at my thighs, squeezing them. "Calm down."

His fingers squeezed mine back, clasping like he needed me to hold on. My thumb brushed the back of his hand, and his shoulders relaxed. He took a deep breath, but he didn't let me go, gripping me even tighter to his body.

"Your present is outside." Dzsinn turned to her, nodding toward the parking lot. "You'll have to get new brakes and strip it of military emblems, but otherwise the jeep should come in handy when doing larger runs across the border."

"You got me a military jeep? It's outside now?" She pointed to the door.

Dzsinn nodded, dropping the keys in her palm. "Strip off the license and the serial number, do a little cosmetic work, and you're good to go."

She nodded at a man closest to the door who jumped up immediately, opening up the back door and peering out. He dipped his head at Daciana, confirming he was telling the truth.

"You know just what I want, genie." She smiled at him, her mood shifting instantly. "My place is your place." She opened her arms to the dingy room. "Make yourself at home."

"Food, bath, and some clothes." Ash stepped away from me. "For her."

Her eyes bore into Ash before she glanced over at a big man with a shaved head sitting on a stool. "Uta?" She flicked her chin to us. "See they get everything they need."

"We don't have extra rooms," he grumbled.

"Then I guess you just volunteered yours, Uta." She turned away, leaving the burly man scowling at us.

Rising from the stool, he didn't reach Ash's height, but his shoulders appeared as if he worked out every day. His heavy steps clunked across the bar toward a stairway, leading us upstairs.

Keeping close to Ash, I followed them up the steps to the hallway. At the third door down, he stopped, shoving the door open and motioning for us to go in.

"You touch anything, I will kill you," he mumbled. His expression twisted with irritation, as if he was about to throw a tantrum. "Bath down the hall, and Tyna will get her clothes."

"Thanks." I barely stepped into the room before he slammed it behind us. "Don't think he's extremely happy about giving up his room." I viewed the small chamber. A double bed took up most of the room, the gray sheets rumpled and unmade, a boarded-up window above the bed. On one side was a dresser and a small closet. The other wall was filled with various weapons: nunchakus, blades, spiked brass knuckles, guns, and a barbed wire whip.

"Think this guy is into some weird S&M stuff." I snorted, glancing over my shoulder at Ash.

His jaw was tight, his attention staying off me.

The quietness of the room and the fact we were safe dissolved all the pretense, urging everything that had happened to the forefront.

I cleared my throat. "So—"

"You probably want to go take a shower. Get the blood off you." He cut me off, his tone snappy.

"Oh." I blinked. "Yeah, I do."

"I'll go track down some food." He turned for the door, opening it.

"Are you mad at me?" I shot at him, confused by his demeanor.

"Mad?" He slammed it back shut, turning to me, his green eyes blazing, his voice rising. "Am I mad at you?"

"Yes." I tossed up my arms, my tone matching his. "I'm sorry if getting kidnapped was an inconvenience for you!"

"You think *I'm mad* because you were kidnapped?" He stomped over to me, wrath practically steaming out of him.

"Clearly!"

"I'm not mad at you! I'm mad because *I* allowed them to kidnap you. Because you were almost raped and used as a breeder to those things!" he seethed, his energy sinking into me. "That I couldn't protect you! That I could've *lost* you!" he snarled, moving me back until my spine hit the wall of weapons, a gasp rising from my throat, wetness soaking between my thighs. "And worst of all… I let you in… so fucking deep…" He gripped my neck, his thumb pushing up my chin. "I can't breathe if you aren't near me."

His mouth crashed down on mine violently. It was the first time he actually kissed me, and the moment our lips touched, a surge of electricity rippled through me, pouring hunger into my bloodstream. A need to devour, to submit, and to own.

Mine. A growl lodged in my throat. I needed more. I needed all of him.

A moan escaped me, and I felt him respond, pressing his body firmer into mine, thumping me harder into the wall.

"Raven." My name came out with agony and anger, like he wanted to punish me for what he felt, reprimand me for the power I had over him. "Fuck." Roughly, his hands knotted into my hair, yanking my head back, deepening our kiss.

Hungry and raw, he destroyed the world around me. I felt the kiss everywhere. Inside and out, he possessed me. Owned me. Licking through my pussy to my soul, reaching so deep inside, he claimed everything I had, leaving nothing but ruins.

He grabbed my chin, tilting it up. "I don't want to stop kissing you."

"Then don't." I breathed. "Ever."

Gripping my chin harder with one hand, he took control, snapping what was left of my sanity. His mouth consumed, his tongue tasting mine with a groan. His hips rolled into me, pushing his erection into my hip. I was barely wearing any clothes, and it would be so easy for him to thrust into me.

Surges of desire swelled through my body, overriding all sense. With every breath, every beat of my heart, I could feel him crawling under my skin, stealing my breath and owning my body. His magic slid around inside me with possessiveness, like he was marking me as his.

Land of Monsters

"Ash." My fingers scraped down his neck, the dark dweller roaring to the edges with need, tearing at his clothes, needing him closer, needing him inside me. He groaned as my nails tore through his clothes, into his skin, trailing blood down his back.

A flash of what I did to Alexsei filled my mind, the shreds of his body left on the floor in a pool of blood. What I could do to Ash. "No. Wait." I pushed him back, trying to summon back the dark dweller, the beast fighting me, wanting to dive into his flesh. "Stop."

Ash jerked back, his eyes tracking mine, probably seeing the flames of my beast flare through them, the animal on the surface. "I-I can't…"

He let out a huff. Grabbing my wrists, he pinned them to the wall, sparking fire through me with a rumble. His nose flared like he could smell my need.

"I'm not afraid of your dark dweller." He leaned in, his mouth brushing mine. "Or your obscurer. I have fought, lived, and almost died among monsters." His hips pushed into me, his cock throbbing against my pussy. A groan caught in my throat, arching me against him. "Let them bite, claw, and tear into me. They won't hurt me. I've already marked you as mine, little beak." His teeth grazed my neck. "All of you. So let them out. I play well with others. Plus, if they bite, I bite back, and I know how to get you to behave." His teeth snapped down on my neck, hitting a particular nerve, a weakness that stilled me. A deep moan hummed from my body, my hips opening wider in submission, my nipples hardening.

In one gesture, he challenged my alpha—and made her bend.

Willingly.

He had done it before in the wagon, when the reverend was trying to help us escape town. In shock, I had brushed it off, explained it away with almost getting caught, my emotions on the surface because no one but my dweller family had power over me like that.

And my dweller barely submitted to them.

Raspy air trickled in and out of my lungs, my pussy throbbing.

"I knew you liked it when I did it last time." His tongue licked around the nerve. "Don't hold back," he rumbled in my ear, his hand sliding down my body, skimming over my underwear, his fingers dipping underneath. A smirk danced over his mouth when he felt how wet I was. "I want *all* of you."

He tore off his jacket I wore and reached over, pulling the thin tank over my head and exposing my breasts. His throat bobbed when his eyes skimmed over my skin, glinting with lust.

"Perfection." Leaning over, he flicked his tongue over my nipple, coaxing a whimper from my throat, before his mouth covered my breast, sucking and nipping.

"Ash…" My hand lanced through his tied-back hair, digging my nails in when he moved to the other, lavishing it with his tongue.

"Dammit, Raven," he rumbled. He pulled back, standing over me. "You are going to make me come so easily." His teeth bit at my bottom lip, tugging it. "And there are way too many things I want to do to your body before we both black out."

His mouth came back over mine. Our kiss was violent and demanding. Prey and predator. We started out wounded, broken bodies filled with pain and lies. Hell had rained down, and we were still standing. Accepted the monsters under the facade, the killers that fed off retribution, the depravity we would bathe in.

Together.

Reaching over, I fumbled with his pants, unzipping them enough to slip my hand in, wrapping my fingers around his girth.

"Fuck." He tipped his head back, and I stroked him. His own fingers slipped under my panties, a hiss snarling from him as he slid through me. "You are so fucking wet."

"Because of you."

His gaze came back to mine, and he slid two fingers inside me. Any barrier I erected to keep myself contained shattered with a cry. My spine curved away from the wall, and my hips pushed back as he pumped deeper into me.

He pulled his fingers from me, dripping with my juices, and sucked them in his mouth. "Fuck. I've been craving your taste again." He groaned. "You know why I'm not addicted to fairy dust anymore?" He lowered himself to the ground, his fingers hooking my underwear. "Because of you. Your taste has become my addiction."

"Ash." I breathed as his lips trailed down my stomach, dragging my panties down my legs.

The cool air slipped through my folds, my form totally bare to him. "Now I can be uninterrupted." His hands skated to the inside of my thighs. "Open your legs," he demanded.

This was Ash's domain. Where he ruled.

Spreading my legs, letting him see how turned on I was, a deep groan came from him.

"I feel like I've been hungry forever and finally have something to fill me." He leaned forward, his tongue slicing through me.

A strangled cry rattled my throat, my head cracking back into the wall.

Groaning, his lips parted me more, licking through me. With every taste, he got greedier, his hands spreading me further, consuming me with abandonment.

"Oh gods!" I belted, my hips bucking forward. This time, there were no drugs or alcohol to escape in. It was us. Raw and uninhibited.

And it felt even more intense.

"Ash!"

Grabbing my calves, he pulled them over his shoulders, pinning my torso to the wall with his hand, taking full control of my body as he fucked my pussy with his tongue, taking my logic and handing me nothing but vicious pleasure.

The dark dweller clawed at the edges, my teeth growing into fangs, the intensity already buzzing the base of my spine. My dweller was usually hard to fully satisfy, our sex drive high and extreme. Ash easily cut through it, hitting every nerve that made me turn feral.

"Eyes on me," he growled against me, a whimper sputtering from me. My eyes dropped to him, locking on the fierceness as he slowly licked through me.

I felt something rub against my ass, pushing against it.

My breath caught at seeing the spiked brass knuckles on his hand, the metal bumps rubbing through me.

"Oh gods…" I choked on my own cry. His eyes stayed on mine as he went harder, the spike digging in. His tongue plunged back into me as he pushed the brass knuckles deeper into the muscles of my ass.

Crying out, my body jerked at the mix of pain and pleasure, everything heightening around me. The feel of his tongue, the heat billowing off my body, and the aching need destroying any shame I had.

"Oh gods!"

"You like that?"

I didn't have to answer. I rode his face harder, my skin growing darker, the dweller snarling up my throat.

"Ash." His name was garbled as he stroked the brass knuckles through my folds. My fingers threaded through his hair, ripping out the tie and tugging harder on his strands. Groaning, I rolled my hips into him, my sharp nails digging into his scalp when his teeth nipped at my clit.

Howls bayed from me, magic crackling over the room.

"Fuck!" Ash dropped my legs back to the ground, his eyes wild, like a kaleidoscope of green, filled with possession.

"I need to fuck you. Now." He yanked me from the wall and tossed me onto the bed. "Get on your hands and knees," he demanded.

I did what he asked, pushing my ass out to him.

"You're killing me," he moaned. I heard him kicking off his boots and unbuckling his pants the rest of the way, fabric hitting the floor.

The anticipation, the need to feel him push inside me, was almost too much, my body shaking, my claws cutting into the sheets. Dark dwellers could keep the beast back during sex, but with Ash, I seemed to have no barrier. The dweller wanted him just as much.

His silence twisted my head around. He stood there, his hair hanging wildly, his cock thick and hard, precum spilling out. His eyes were alight with lust, gaze heated on me, like he needed a moment to fully take me in.

"Ash?" I arched, my body shaking for him. "Please."

"Please what, *dziubuś*?" A smile curled his mouth, his hand moving to his cock to stroke himself.

"Fuck me." I knew my eyes flamed with fire, my need consuming me.

Climbing on the bed, he stayed on one knee, the other leg set by my hip. Grabbing my hips, he yanked me back into him, pushing his cock between my ass. He leaned over, grabbing my chin and twisting it to him, kissing me so deeply my pussy throbbed, dripping down my leg. "Ash." I pleaded.

"I love hearing you cry out my name." I felt the tip of him pressing at my entrance, making me groan. "You're gonna need to hold on." He put my hands on the headboard right as he seized my hips again, then brutally thrust into my pussy.

Black dots skittered across my vision. Overwhelming energy paralyzed me for a moment. I screamed, my claws ripping into the mattress, air retreating from my lungs.

"Holy. Fuck," he cried out hoarsely, followed by a moan. "You're so tight. I'm not even in all the way." A string of curse words came from him as he pulled out almost to the tip. Then drove back in, bowing my back. The fierce pain, his cock stretching me, hitting me already so deep, I lost all understanding, as if he clicked a switch from human to beast. There was no shame or embarrassment. It was only primal hunger for the pain, desperate for the violence, craving brutality. And the way his cock glided along my walls, hitting every nerve, the dweller howling to the surface. It liked being fucked this way.

It wanted more.

"Gods." He wrapped my hair in his hand, his hips rolling, pushing deeper into me. "You feel so fucking good, like nothing I've ever felt before," he choked out as my pussy clenched around him, my teeth snapping in a growl.

"Harder!" I snarled, barely sounding human. Magic sparked in the room, igniting my bones.

Ash growled back, pushing me into a pillow and opening my legs wider. The sound of him pounding into me unforgivingly slapped in the air. His hand came down, spanking my ass.

A wail tore through me, my back arching, my pussy dripping down my thigh.

"You want it harder, Raven?" He rubbed through my pussy, feeling himself fuck me.

"Yes!" I bent over further, sinking him deeper into me, making us both moan.

His hand spanked my pussy then, the spike of pain tearing through me. My body shuddered, my climax climbing higher.

"*Megbasz!*" he gritted, pulling out of me. Grabbing my hips, he laid under me, facing me toward his legs and setting me on his face. "Suck yourself off my cock," he commanded. A surge of desire pebbled my nipples at his order. The other night was the first time I did this. This position always sounded awkward and not sexy to me, but with Ash, I greedily leaned over, my tongue wrapping around the tip of him, sucking myself off his cock.

"Gods." His throat vibrated as I took him deeper down my throat. "Raven…" His hips jerked up, his lips kissing my pussy deeply.

Taking him so deep down my throat that tears spilled from my eyes, I hummed in the back of my throat.

"*Szar!*" He fucked my face as he pushed his fingers into my ass, causing me to cry out, my body starting to orgasm.

"No!" He easily tossed me off, throwing my back on the pillows. "I want to feel you orgasm around my cock." He crawled over me, spreading my legs around his hips. His eyes were wild, his body shaking with need. There was no more teasing.

He gripped his dick and pushed into me, tilting me slightly up into him.

"Fuck!" I barked at the onslaught, my hips snapping up, meeting his with as much intensity.

"This is mine," he gritted through his teeth, his thumb rubbing my clit. "No one else gets to fuck you. Just me. Understand?"

"Right back at you," I growled back, fur spouting along my arms each time he drove deeper into me. I knew this was impossible to ask of a nature fairy. They didn't have mates, nor were they exclusive, but I wouldn't be the kept one if he wasn't.

His jaw locked down, and I was ready for him to deny me. He pounded in harder, his green eyes on me, but I saw no argument in his eyes, each thrust only cementing something in his gaze.

Stretching out as he fucked me, I reached down, grazing his balls and feeling his dick slide in and out of me, sinking my fingers into his ass, knowing what he liked.

His eyes glazed over. His grip on my hips was so hard I knew it would leave bruises. And I loved it. Wanted him to mark me deeper. Ash let out a noise, dropping every barrier he had left, losing control.

Trees outside the window snapped and rattled like a tornado was whipping through, knocking against the boarded-up window.

He railed so hard into me that the wood frame cracked under us, and something inside of me splintered along with it, taking me deeper into oblivion.

"*Szar…*" His cock thrust in harder. "You feel so fucking good."

"Come in my pussy," I demanded.

His lids narrowed on me, his movement quickening. Reality became too much and too little. We clawed at each other with teeth and nails, trying to tear into each other. Savage and sadistic.

Ash stroked into me so deeply my mouth parted. Latin shot from my lips, the obscurer whispering words I didn't even recognize. A chant that scorched through us, sinking us so intensely inside each other we were no longer on this plane.

Everything shattered into a thousand pieces.

I fractured with a scream, my pussy pulsing, milking him, absorbing him into my very DNA like a tattoo.

"FUCK!" Ash roared, his hips slammed against mine. He stilled as his cum surged inside of me, hot and burning, his seed filling me until it pooled down my legs. My head tipped back in a cry, another orgasm shredding through my senses, my pussy crudely taking more as he spilled more into me.

Before everything went black, I felt something knot between us, something I never felt with Wyatt, and I knew exactly what it was. I had no control over it, my obscurer and beast taking with no care. I just doomed myself.

Chapter 13

Ash

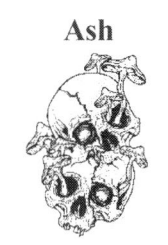

Magic hummed around us, her chant sinking into me. My cum was still pumping into her pussy when I felt her lock around my cock so tightly my vision went black. My mouth opened, but no sound came out.

The sensation went beyond anything I had ever experienced in my very long, long life. Thousands of lovers dissolved away into one. She was all I saw in the past and future, like this whole time, I had been waiting and searching for her.

The base of my cock swelled, pushing against her walls, bracing me even tighter into her until there was no line between pain and bliss. They were one and the same, and I let myself fall into them.

It was a moment, descending into another plane, where I was surrounded by Raven, the dweller, and her obscurer, each one pleasuring me until I felt them sink into my bones. Making me so content, everything before felt subpar.

"Mine."

I could've said it, or she did... I didn't know. Every thought and feeling felt like my own and hers.

"Fuck, yessss." I pushed into her harder, desperate to mark her with my seed, causing us to cry out, my final surge scorching into her as I fell back to Earth. My body collapsed over hers, air knocking from my lungs, and I blacked out for a few seconds.

I gasped for oxygen, my lids flying open to peer down at her, not knowing how long I had been out.

Chests heaving, our bodies trembled at the abundance of magic and sensations rocking through our systems. Her lids lifted to mine, bright green eyes searching mine, her form back to normal, but I could feel her beast rumbling around the perimeter. Still deep inside her, my cock twitched as her pussy started to loosen around me.

"What the fuck?" I croaked out, lifting my weight off her. My cock stirred, not wanting to move from its current location. She swallowed roughly, feeling me harden inside her as if my dick was searching for that high again, not caring about anything else. Grinding my teeth, I took a deep breath, trying to calm myself down. But pulling out of her, seeing my cum spilling down her thighs and my cock covered in our climax, did just the opposite.

Heat scored down my shoulders, a rumble starting in my lungs as I watched my seed leak from her, dampening someone else's sheets.

Another man's bed.

I reached down, scooping some up and pushing it back inside her with a possessive growl. Somewhere in the back of my brain, my response startled me. Kek used to tease me about bringing someone else in, and I never even blinked an eye. I would have been fine with it. With Raven, the idea of merely another man's sheets pissed me off. Like he was getting to share her too. I either wanted to rip them off and burn them or fuck her even more to make sure they were stained with us.

Raven opened her legs, her head curving into the pillow, whimpering as I drove my fingers inside her, rubbing cum over her clit and back in her. Her breathy moans instantly hardened my dick, and a frantic need to take her again, be sure my claim was branded into her bones, overpowered every warning nipping in the back of my head. Deep in my brain, I understood being inside her again would only cement whatever was happening.

"Ash." She rolled into my touch, her teeth nipping into her bottom lip.

"Fuck." My voice was harsh; I was too far gone. I twisted her hips to me, my mouth covering hers, as I pushed into her again at an angle. A shuddered breath escaped her lungs as I broke away from her soft lips, driving in and out in long, slow strokes. I huffed out my nose, my weakened arms doing their best to hold me up as I gripped her thigh and tilted into her. With every stroke, her eyes flickered back, a low, carnal groan vibrating the air, only pushing me to go deeper. "Why can't I stop?" I grunted. "And why does this feel so fucking different?"

Her breasts jiggled as I drove her deeper into the pillows, keeping the steady pace, watching her claw at the already destroyed bed. Her lids squeezing shut like an even bigger orgasm was taking hold of her.

"Eyes on me." I snapped my hips, my back teeth grinding, already feeling her clench around me. "Watch me fuck you."

She lowered her gaze to where we connected, observing my engorged dick, covered in her, thrusting in and out of her heat. Lust brightened her green eyes, flames starting to dance in them. Her nipples hardened, her pussy fluttering, getting even more turned on watching us. Obscene sounds echoed in the room as I pushed her leg higher. "Watch me fuck deeper into you."

She gasped, her hips snapping up to meet mine with the same intensity, our pace increasing. "Gods... Ash!"

I was so hungry for her I couldn't see straight. I knew I was going down. Something was shifting again between us, magic thick in the air.

Leaning over, I took her breast into my mouth, flicking her nipple with my tongue before my lips moved up, nipping at the sensitive part of her neck. "*We* are the monsters, *dziubuś*. The only thing you need to bow to is *me*." I bit down on the nerve in her neck in dominance, jerking her body. Her pussy clamped around me, a howl penetrating the air, bleeding far out into the night. Tree limbs cracked and hit the window outside, and dogs howled down the street. Everything came to a pinpoint.

Latin burst from her again, wrapping around my cock like a leash, tugging. It felt like she was everywhere. Not an inch of my skin wasn't roaring in pleasure, my dick swelling, her pussy strangling me. Grunting, I rutted into her until I bottomed out. Not able to move, she knotted around my swollen cock as I released inside of her.

Holy. Fuck.

This time, our orgasm arrived like a bomb, exploding us into particles, scattering us into the ether. We existed everywhere and nowhere, floating in some other plane.

This isn't possible. This isn't possible...

Yet I felt her embedding into my soul as I succumbed to the darkness.

"I don't think licking his skin for mushroom remnants is gonna work."

Chirp!

"I am not judging you!"

Chirp! Chirp!

"Don't turn this around on me! I did *not* lick his fungi earlier!"

Voices came in, disrupting my sleep, pulling me from the peace I'd surrendered to.

My lids flickered open, threads of slumber clinging to me, wanting to pull me back down. Sleep had so wholly claimed me that it took a moment to recall where I was. The glow of morning light slipped through the boards across the window, giving the room some definition. Although I didn't need to see to know who my body was wrapped around.

I could feel her in every fiber, every pump of my heart.

Raven's dark hair was spread out over the pillow we shared, her back pressed to my chest, our legs tangled, and my hard cock pressing into her entrance like it was trying to sneak back in without anyone knowing. Stay in her tight heat.

Sound asleep, her muscles relaxed into me as if she was home. Safe.

Even with Kek and Lukas, I didn't stick around in the mornings. It was my time to stroll through nature, absorb the quiet peace, and regain whatever energy I had depleted the night before. Except this morning, I vibrated with energy. My dick was sore, my muscles ached, but I felt anything but depleted.

Like she filled me with energy instead of taking it.

Chirp!

"How dare you bring it up again!" The sharp exclamation drew me fully to consciousness. "That was an experimental time."

Chirp! Chirp!

"And that next time was a *total* misunderstanding."

Rubbing my eyes, I exhaled, fully opening my eyes, my brain slow to register the brownie and imp sitting on my thigh, a thin sheet barely covering us. Bruises and scruff burns swathed Raven's skin, while mine was covered in nail and bite marks.

We looked like we had been through battle.

With a grunt, I grabbed the sheet, covering Raven's naked body, frowning at the two.

Chirp! The imp flipped me off.

"Right? Like we haven't been up close and personal with his giant wild mushroom before." Opie rolled his eyes. "And when I say giant... I mean the titan... the king Trumpet—"

"What the fuck are you wearing?" I cut him off, my voice raw and croaky, my vocals strained from last night.

"Do you like?" Opie's attention was instantly taken to his outfit as he twirled around. His ass cheeks peeked out of two small circles in the short shorts.

I forced my lids shut with a groan, hoping I was seeing wrong, but when I reopened my eyes, he was still in the cut-up leather.

"Fuck." I massaged my temples.

His nipples and belly button were circled in red lipstick, the same color as Daciana's. He wore black leathers, most likely from a member's jacket, in the style of crotchless lederhosen, with a biker patch covering up his crotch. Barbed wire twirled through his red-tipped mohawk. My eyes instantly darted to the wall where the weapons were on display.

"Opie…" I groaned, noting the barbed wire whip was gone.

"Like you can talk, tree fairy," he huffed, motioning back to the ground. "I know what you did with those brass knuckles."

"I used them, I didn't destroy property."

"D-destroy property?" He gasped, his hands patting down over the biker patch. "I made these average items a work of art! I mean, it's not my best work, granted, but it is a huge improvement!"

"I don't even want to know whose member jacket you destroyed, but if anyone catches you, you're dead."

"Catches me?" He laughed, his hands going to his hips, wiggling them back and forth. "I'm like lightning! In and out with high-velocity perfection."

Chirp!

"I was told so."

Chirp. Chirp!

"It doesn't matter by who. I have more friends than just you, you know."

Chiiiiiiiiiiiirrrp! What sounded like a crackled laugh came from Bitzy, her fingers flying in the air.

Raven stirred next to me, our voices drawing her from the rest she needed. What she had been through the last week had to be a nightmare, plus what I put her through last night.

Putting my finger to my lips, I slowly inched away from her.

"She won't wake." Opie hopped off my leg to the end of the bed as Bitzy climbed up his back to her backpack. "Bitzy has been licking the residue of drugs coming off her skin for a long time, and she didn't even budge."

Chirp!

"You asked me to try it!" Opie shot back at her.

Chirp! Chirp! Chirp!

"You did too!"

"Stop licking her." I put my feet on the ground, rubbing my face and running my fingers through my hair. I needed a shower badly.

"Look who's talking!" Opie poked at my hip. "Someone is getting all possessive. Never thought I'd see that with you, fairy."

His tease hit harder than I was expecting, the awareness that others saw what I wanted to deny. It was not possible. My kind didn't have just one person.

We. Did. Not. Get. Possessive.

I had flashes of Kek and Lukas's faces, the memory of waking up next to them, leaving them asleep, tangled in sheets, drenched in cum and sweat. My face was full of smiles, my chest warm, but not once could I say I felt possessive.

If I had walked back to them fucking, or adding someone, I would have grinned and joined in. The thought of walking in and seeing Raven with someone else hummed an incensed noise up my throat.

Fear reared through my chest like a toddler running with a knife. Cutting and slicing without consideration of the damage.

Seeing the brass knuckles left on the floor where I dropped them, still coated in her, awareness prickled over my skin, like I could feel her heartbeat within me, sense her clinging to my soul. *It's not possible.* Taking in a breath, I peered over my shoulder at her. Her stunning face was at peace, surrounded by the wreckage we inflicted. The bedframe splintered, the mattress and sheets shredded from her claws. Magic still oozed, the bedding no longer smelling like the man who lived here, but of sex. Of us.

My lungs seized and my stomach knotted because all I wanted to do was curl back around her, push inside her, and wake her up with an orgasm.

Stay inside her all day.

Just her.

A rush of adrenaline shot me to my feet. The need to flee, to breathe, hurried me to the door. Swinging it open, I found clothes folded at the threshold. Grabbing my boots, pants, and a shirt, I tossed the girl's clothes inside before rushing down the hall to the shower, not caring I was naked.

Emotion waited on the cusp, wanting to soak into my bones along with the water. I never let my mind settle as I showered and got dressed, ignoring every mark on my body, every claim of her teeth and nails.

Because her claim went much deeper.

It rattled me, scared the fuck out of me, because I felt calmness deep inside. Peace. And I wanted to tear it out of my soul. I shouldn't feel anything but pain and anger. I couldn't give up on them, couldn't forget why I was here.

Dressed in camo pants and a t-shirt, my wet hair slicked back, I hightailed it out of the clubhouse, the downstairs bar lively with people chatting and eating. Cutting out the side door, I heaved in air, smelling the stench of city life. A park across the street drew me, crossing over rail tracks, the morning gloom making the graffiti area even more depressing and worn.

Cold air stabbed at my lungs, prodding my skin. My jacket was back in the room… where she slept. Where she would wake up. Alone.

Gritting my teeth, I grabbed the nearest tree, trying to pull energy I didn't need from it, like it would heal whatever I was feeling, take away the confusion.

The problem was I knew the truth; I just couldn't accept it.

A wail came from my throat, and I bashed my knuckles into the trunk, needing to cause both of us pain. I was on the last step before the cliff crumbled underfoot, before I dropped into the void, lost forever. And I clung to the ground, clung to Kek and Lukas…

Blood spurted from my hands, my cries burning up my sore throat.

"Stop that, pretty boy." Kek's voice felt like it was right in my ear. *"Those hands are way too skilled to be damaging them like that."*

"I can't," I whispered hoarsely. "I feel like I'm losing you guys."

"You can't ever lose us," Kek retorted. *"We were way too remarkable in bed to ever be forgotten."*

I scoffed at the comment, which sounded so much like Kek.

"You like her." It was as if Lukas was standing on my other side, his soothing, low voice in my ear, hiccupping grief in my heart. *"She's different from anyone you've ever met before. That doesn't make us any less. And all we want is for you to be happy."*

"Though, I'm still hotter," Kek teased, bubbling up another crazed laugh from my chest.

"We don't want your revenge, Ash. It's not who you are," Lukas said. *"Kill for love, kill to protect your family, but never revenge."*

"Speak for yourself. I say kill those assholes." Kek grinned, playing with her blue braid.

"I failed you both." My head dropped, finally saying it aloud. Owning it. "I am so sorry."

"Don't think so highly of yourself." Kek snickered, crossing her arms. *"Like I would've let your pretty fairy ass fight for me. I am a demon. I fight my own battles."*

"There was nothing you could've done." Lukas picked up after her. *"There is no blame to take, Ash. It was not something you could've stopped. You don't have a say in our ends, but you have a say in the life you want to live after our deaths."*

"Always the responsible, kumbaya one. So annoying." Kek rolled her eyes. *"But what he said."*

"It's why we needed him." I grinned at Kek. "You and I were too fucked up and dark."

"Why you need her." Luca's voice was quiet and serious, speaking about Raven. And I felt him drifting away once again.

"So don't fuck this up, fairy boy. We're rooting for you two." Kek's image dimmed, but I could still see her snarky smile. *"And we are rooting for more sex like last night, so we can voyeuristically watch. You guys were so fucking hot."*

A sob huffed through my nose as I felt them dissipate, easing a slight weight off my chest. Their permission was something I didn't know I needed. Their forgiveness and approval. Even if it was in my own head.

I only wished I could do the same for myself.

Chapter 14

Raven

"Master Ash said to stop licking her."

Chirp!

Voices dragged me from sleep, a strange sensation, like sandpaper, running over my hip.

"Don't yell at me. I didn't order you. Master tree fairy, with golden hair and a dick the size of a tree trunk, did."

Chirp! Chirp!

My eyes jolted open when I felt the same sensation again, expecting to see Ash teasing my skin. Instead, I saw a tiny bald creature with big bat ears, its long tongue flicking over my naked hip.

"What the fuck?" I bolted up, two tiny figures tumbling as I yanked the torn sheet up to my chest.

"How many times do we have to ask you to warn us before you do that!" What I knew to be a house brownie huffed, climbing onto his feet, straightening out his bizarre outfit of leather lederhosen with a biker emblem on the front. An even tinier creature was next to him, in a leather diaper and a choker.

Chirp! The thing put its three-pronged fingers in the air, and I swear it was flipping me off, its expression narrowed with anger.

"What the hell is that?" I blinked down at it.

"Have you never seen an imp before?" The brownie motioned to it.

"I guess not." Imps were exceedingly rare. The queen before my mother had let them be hunted almost into extinction for their healing body fluids.

"This is Bitzy." He motioned to the imp, who made a chirping sound, flipping me off again. "And I'm Opie."

"You live and clean here?" Uncle Lars had a brownie in his house, Sinnie, but she barely showed her face to people, always cleaning and dressed in a traditional brown dress.

"Clean?" Opie screeched, his hand going to his chest. "Does it look like I clean in this outfit?" He motioned down to himself. "This is a work of art. Not rags to clean in! Stereotype much? Just because I'm a brownie doesn't mean I clean. I mean… I did when I was living in the prison. But I hated it! Though… I also hate mess… but I'm not going to clean it or anything. Especially this place."

My eyes flickered to the neatly piled clothes at the end of the bed he was straightening.

"Well, I folded those because Master Mushroom just flung them on the bed all willy-nilly. And the pillow was flat and wrinkled, screaming to be fluffed."

My stomach twisted, noticing the empty spot next to me. He was gone, his side of the bed cold. Did he regret it? Would it be awkward now? Did we just ruin everything?

Chirp!

"Not that kind of fluffed!"

Chirp! Chirp! Chirp!

"That is a lie!" The brownie huffed.

"Master Mushroom?" I interrupted, sitting up.

"Master Ash," Opie responded to me. "He ran out of here about thirty minutes ago, probably having to deal with the mess you guys made."

"He ran out?"

Clearly, he regretted it, not wanting to be here when I woke up. While I ached with disappointment and hurt, I craved him even more.

I still buzzed with the connection, the magic that made me feel I could reach out and find him wherever he was. My mind couldn't rectify the unbelievable pleasure he pulled from my body the moment he sank into me, destroying me for everyone else.

We knotted…

No. Impossible, especially with a tree fairy. Only dark dwellers had that type of connection with other dark dwellers. And it was a rarity. Something like one in a thousand ever experienced it.

The idea was ridiculous.

Nonetheless, I couldn't let the thought go. All the feelings I thought I had for Wyatt when we had sex paled in comparison. And it not only scared me but had me choking on guilt.

I had *murdered* someone over my heartache, been so devastated by the loss of Wyatt, I had to be sent away. I hadn't returned home in a year because I couldn't face him and Piper together. Yet in one night, Ash leveled me, flipped me so completely sideways, I doubted everything I ever felt for the boy I grew up loving.

I always thought Wyatt was my mate, my future, but nothing made sense anymore.

What would happen if Ash rejected me… or someone hurt him? What was I capable of then?

Needing to see him, to at least know what he felt, I slipped out of the bed, yanking the sheet with me.

"Damn…" Opie let out a whistle, his attention on the space I just vacated. Looking over my shoulder, my eyes widened at the deep claw marks puncturing the bed. "Which one of you was the beauty and which one was the beast?"

"We are the monsters, dziubuś. The only thing you need to bow to is me."

My beast struggled to listen to my father, and he was my alpha, the leader of our pack. Yet she bowed to Ash with glee, like she finally found a worthy adversary.

Snatching the clothes off the bed, I headed out the door, my heart pounding in my chest. The truth floated at the edges of my mind, but I tuned out all thoughts of last night as I climbed into the shower. Everything we said and experienced, I blamed on the heat of the moment. Ignoring even more the fact my beast could still pick up his scent in the shower. My mind pictured him in here, almost like I could taste his emotions, feel him.

Mine.

No. I shook the thought from my head. I had loved Wyatt all my life. That was real love, not this. This was lust set in intense circumstances.

Dressing, I left my hair wet and ran downstairs, needing air.

Voices came from the bar area, but I turned out a side door, following an instinct I didn't even second guess… until I opened the door.

Ash stood on the other side, his hand reaching for the handle to come in.

"Oh." Air sucked in sharply, my stomach jumping like a rabbit. "Hey."

Awkward. Yet, I still felt myself exhale, like I could breathe again, though I felt anything but relaxed.

"Hey." His throat bobbed, swallowing.

Oh gods, he totally regretted it. He was going to tell me any moment that this had all been a mistake, while every inch of me could feel him, alive under my skin, making himself at home, marking me forever.

Locking my expression down, I pushed up my chin. An ingrained response when I had to disguise my feelings in front of a crowd or heads of state.

"I was coming in to check on you." He shifted on his feet, not quite looking at me.

"Oh." I clenched my teeth, trying not to show the heartbreak I was feeling. My dweller growled at my thoughts, the obscurer brushing up my throat. I swallowed them down, forcing all the training I had to take over and become the princess I was raised to be. I cleared my throat. "About last night—"

"Yeah, I was gonna—"

"I think we can chalk last night up to high emotions." My tone sounded formal. "Let's just forget it. Like it never happened."

"Forget it?" he repeated, his brows creasing. "Like it never happened?" His mouth parted. "Are you fucking serious?"

"You two are finally up." Dzsinn came from around the corner, jerking us to him. "Good." He brushed by me on his way into the clubhouse, giving no notice he interrupted our conversation. "We need to talk. Now."

Ash's expression lost all emotion, his jaw twitching, his head nodding in acknowledgment. Turning me back inside, he pressed his hand to my lower back, making my lids shut as sparks danced down my spine. Seemingly unaffected, he prodded me into the bar area, following Dzsinn to an empty table in the corner.

Dzsinn sat facing the door, forcing Ash and me to sit next to each other, though we made a point not to touch.

Dzsinn's gaze went over us, and I suspected he saw much more than he ever let on.

"Let's get to the point." Ash leaned on the table, accusatory eyes on the genie. "Why didn't you tell me you knew Sonya?"

"Wait, you know her?" I asked.

"My past with her makes no difference."

"Seriously?" Ash's palms pressed on the table. "I think being related to her is *very important* information."

"Related?" I sputtered.

"We're not blood related." Dzsinn's lip lifted.

"How do I know you aren't somehow working with her now?" Ash continued on.

"Believe me, I want her dead as much as you do. And I'm sure she feels the same about me." He scoffed. "She stole what is rightfully mine."

"The necklace?" Ash wasn't really asking a question.

"The stone in the necklace."

"Start explaining," Ash barked.

Dzsinn let out a long sigh. "Sonya and I were raised together, along with my brothers. Her mother, Anastasia, had attached herself to my uncle." He cupped his hands on the table. "Anastasia was the local beauty. Stunning, charming. She had that thing that made men, fae or human, fall to their knees and give her anything she wanted. Which worked in her favor. Anastasia was a gold-digger, and my uncle was kind and giving with his money, a perfect mark for a widowed mother who was looking for someone to take care of her and her daughter. He pampered and adored them, not seeing the manipulative bitch she was, totally taken in with her fake charm and beauty. Anastasia made Sonya in her exact image. When Anastasia died, Sonya stole our family heirloom and disappeared, knowing its worth and power." He rolled his shoulders back with irritation. "I have been hunting her for a long time but could never get close enough. You provided the opportunity. If I had told you of our past, you wouldn't have trusted me."

"The stone she took was the Cintamani stone," Ash noted.

"The Cintamani stone?" I peered between them. "Wait. That's the jewel known as the 'wish-fulfilling' gem." I recalled reading about it in one of my fae history classes. "You can get almost anything you wish for."

"It has limits, like genies do, but it gives you the luck and opportunity to achieve anything," Dzsinn said. "A source of nature's energy, it also prolongs your life, heals any ailments."

"It's why Sonya has gotten so far, and become so powerful with very average fae magic." Ash sat back in his chair. "How she's been able to attach herself to very powerful leaders—climb in power, escape unscathed in war, and probably why President Lazar folded to her so easily."

"And she will continue to grow and conquer, as we've seen." Dzsinn's eyes darted to me. I shifted in my seat. I hadn't let myself think about what had happened in that cave or what could've happened if Ash hadn't come for me. "Unless we stop her."

They assumed I'd be a viable breeder, my Druid body popping out monsters like them, but it would've been a huge disappointment.

My brother came out ideal. I came out fucked up, a glitch in my makeup, which left me barren. I found that out when I went through fae puberty—I would never be a mother.

As if Ash could sense my dark thoughts, his hand reached for mine, then stopped. Pulling it back, he sat up in his chair, keeping his focus on Dzsinn.

"She will hold all the power until we get the stone back," Dzsinn said. "You get it back for me…" He took a breath. "And your favors are paid in full."

Ash's head jerked, his spine going rigid, staring at the genie as if to make sure he was in earnest.

"Okay." Ash swallowed, his head bowing. "How do we get it back from her?" He clasped his hands, like he wanted to keep them far from me. "Cut off her head?"

"Not as easy as it looks." Dzsinn sighed. "She has all the luck and magic on her side." He tilted his head. "I have a connection I think can give us an in, plus others I'd like to contact. I will need a week or so to reach them." Dzsinn stood up from the table. "Daciana said you can stay here until I return." He tapped at the table, lifting an eyebrow. "Though she asked you to stop drawing attention to this place."

"Drawing attention?" Ash shifted, peering up at him, perplexed.

A rare smile hinted on his mouth. "And tone down the sex. Stay out of trouble until I get back."

The man walked away, his figure slipping in with the bikers and disappearing as if he never existed.

Ash rubbed the back of his neck, his eyes still staying off me, the tension growing like weeds between us the moment Dzsinn left us alone.

"You owe him favors?" My voice came out more unsteadily than I wanted. "What for?"

He let out a dark laugh, his head wagging, bitter amusement crossing his face. "The price of revenge." The chair screeched back as he stood up. "And you." His tone was contemptuous and annoyed. He turned away, stomping out of the bar, not able to get away from me fast enough.

I stared after him, anger simmering inside my chest, hating that his dismissal dredged up my deepest insecurities.

A failure in who I was born to be, not loved enough by the one boy I loved more than anything. My brother was the one everyone adored, his talents easily praised while mine were hidden away. My parents were too scared of how the world would react if they knew the princess was a dark dweller and obscurer in one, not able to control her powers. Druids were hated enough, but an obscurer, even in the Druid world, was a detestation.

Something that shouldn't exist.

My parents raised me to be strong; their love and support were never the problem. It was outside the family bubble that was all pretend. The media bought into the image of me, the reserved, pampered princess. And after a while I bought into it as well. Shopping, lunches, parties—but having Wyatt by my side kept me grounded, reminded me of who I really was.

Until he was no longer there, and the ground vanished from under my feet. For so long I'd felt I was falling, with nothing to hold on to. Scared of what I was capable of, not trusting or believing in myself, hiding behind the bracelet on my wrist.

Somewhere along the way, I found solid ground under my feet. This journey changed me. I was no longer the spoiled, naïve girl who would put up with shit. And I would not put up with Ash's.

When I made to stand up to go after him, Daciana slipped into the seat across from me, her hand grasping my wrist.

"Don't go." Her demon eyes locked on mine. "I wanted to get to know my guest a bit better."

Alarms instantly rattled in the back of my neck.

"I mean, it's strange. I allow you with open arms into my place, and I don't even know your name." She patted my hand, letting go, but an underlying threat sat me up straighter, my gaze sliding to the door where both Ash and Dzsinn had disappeared.

My mouth stayed closed, taking notice of the other people in the bar, all at her beck and call.

"No?" Her red lips parted in a heartless smile. "Then let's cut to the chase, shall we?" She dropped a newspaper in front of me. My attention lowered to the headline of the international paper, once again sensing the ground under me breaking into pieces.

Princess Raven Missing! Queen Kennedy and King Lars Launch Worldwide Search for the Lost Princess.

A huge picture of me at one of the last diplomatic events stared back at me. That girl was a far cry from who I am now, her hair done perfectly, make-up precise, lavished in jewels, and wearing an expensive designer dress.

"How coincidental…" Daciana's finger traced over my image, her eyes staying on me. Locking away any expression, I kept hold of her gaze, not letting her see the panic simmering under the surface. "There is a missing princess out there, who can I say is the spitting image of you, while a mysterious guest arrives, needing the protection of my club."

Silence from me.

"Wondering what kind of reward they are offering for just a tip on their sweet princess's whereabouts?"

In my peripheral, the man whose room we took, Uta, stood up, his massive chest flexing under his muscle, inching closer.

"Though, I've also heard the Russian mafia has been looking for this same girl. Wonder who will pay the most for her?"

"And I wonder the consequences for going back on your word with a genie?" I replied, my voice even.

"I said I would give you two a place to hide out for a few days from those hunting you. I never said anything about not turning you in myself." She smirked. "It's all in the fine print. And when an opportunity drops in my lap like this…" Her hand went back to my picture. "You understand? It's nothing personal." She nodded to Uta, a few others moving with him, coming for me.

"You sure you want to do that?" My nails dug into the chair. "If you know who I am, then you know *what* I am, who my father is."

"A dark dweller?" She shrugged one shoulder. "I think my Uta can handle you." She nodded back at him, my head swinging to the huge-chested man, his shirt ripping as his body shifted, horns growing out of his skull, his head becoming bull-like, teeth elongating and sharpening as he gripped a cleaver in his hand, huffing in violence.

Holy fuck.

A Minotaur. Their population was lessening as our kind was, and they were just as feared.

The chair fell backward as I stood up, my defenses rising, a growl vibrating in my throat. "You kill me, and you lose all the money."

"Oh, I'm not going to kill you, Princess. But I will hurt you if I need to." Her skin turned white, thinning like parchment, her eyes going black. I had seen my uncle lose his temper to the demon plenty of times, and it always scared the hell out of me. *Please, she's a minimal demon. She can die like the rest of them.* My obscurer whispered in my head. "In this world, it's eat or be eaten." She stood up, with both her, a handful of fae, and the Minotaur coming for me.

My teeth snapped together in long daggers, the pressure of the blades in my spine pushing through the clothes, my nails becoming claws.

Let them come, my obscurer replied gleefully, starving for blood. To kill anything trying to hurt me. The dark dweller rumbled in response as more came for me, weapons in their hands. The Minotaur stomped toward me, his axe backward, ready to knock me out, not kill me.

There was no difference to my monsters. A threat was a threat.

Light came through the door. Ash burst into the room, panic on his face as if he had felt the danger from afar, had heard my silent cry just for him.

Our eyes met across the room, one of the fae turning to him with a gun, ramming it to his forehead.

It would only take one shot, and he would be lost to me.

I saw red. It smeared my vision, bled into my bones, and dripped in my veins. The dark dweller thundered with fury, moving across the room with a roar.

Mine.

Words hissed from my mouth as I tossed men out of my way. With a lash of my tongue, the Minotaur stopped in his tracks. Pain burst through my head, his size and strength fighting against my powers.

Warm liquid dripped from my nose. Grunting, I spat out the spell and watched Uta's eyes inside the beast widen, his hands bringing his cleaver back to himself.

My legs dipped as he fought and wrestled against my magic, a bellow breaking from him. Gritting down, I struggled to force out every word.

The blade sliced across his thick throat with a gurgled cry. A scream filled my ears, blood spraying the room, drenching me. His head hit the floor with a thwack, his dark eyes wide, his mouth open in a cry.

"Raven! Stop!"

The name no longer meant anything to me, though the voice tugged at something deep in my core. It drew me in like a tide, breaking me across rocks to get to it.

Bodies dropped as my teeth ripped through them. The flick of my tongue gushed blood from their mouths until nothing more came at me, my body heaving, searching for more blood to spill.

One by one, they fell at my feet, blood garnishing the walls and soaking the floor.

"Raven!" Hands cupped my face, green eyes finding mine. "Look at me."

I fixed on his gaze, which held no fear—not of me, anyway.

Those eyes were my ground. My air. What made me burn with life, and what calmed the monsters like cool water.

"Ash," I croaked, my body shaking as I returned to myself, dots impeding my vision.

"I'm here, *mroczny*." His voice made me feel safe. He was the rock I could cling to. So I was no longer falling.

A moan pulled my gaze from him. Daciana's throat was slashed, but her chest moved up and down. Some were still alive, their shallow breaths wheezing in the room, but so many were dead. A bloody trail leading right to me.

"Ash…" Emotion clogged my throat.

"No. Look at me." He kept his hands on my face, making my attention return to him. "Keep your eyes only on me."

"I killed them…" Darkness took more of my vision, blood dripping from my nose and eyes. Terror fizzed up, a core fear of what Ash would do when he found out what I truly was. What I was capable of without thought. "Please, don't leave me," I begged, clinging harder to him.

"Never, *mroczny*." His words were barely a whisper before everything went black.

Chapter 15

Ash

Deep in my hood, a cloak covering the bloodstained figure in my arms, I kept to the shadows. The cloudy afternoon dusted the narrow cobble streets with what little light was left in the day.

Getting Raven out was my only thought, her safety my first concern before anyone regained consciousness. My backpack was abandoned upstairs, so we had no money, no food, and no place to go. So many were after us, so many more willing to turn us in.

Especially now that the world was looking for the missing princess.

When Raven passed out in my arms, I noticed the newspaper on the table, her face in all her finery staring back, the headline dropping my stomach. Nowhere would be safe now. Headhunters, opportunists, and her own family were out searching for her.

They would take her away from me.

A fierce noise had worked up my throat. Picking her up and holding her to my chest, I carried her out. *Mine.*

My muscles shook after two hours of carting her across town, but I didn't relent. Readjusting her in my arms, I pressed on. My body craved energy, needing nature, but snow clouds bristled overhead, dropping the temperature, shaking her bones. She needed warmth and shelter.

She needed a safe space to heal.

Glancing over my shoulder, I made sure we weren't being followed as the trek took us back to the old town. Not that anyone was coherent enough to follow us from the club. If they did survive, they would be healing for weeks after what she did to them.

Raven was magnificent in the most terrifying way. Her devastation was felt in the atmosphere, watering the earth with blood, which even nature bowed to. I stood in the middle of her chaos with no fear of her wrath. Death fell around me like dominoes, a whirlwind of blood and screams, and I was the one she bowed to. As if I was the rock she had to smash against to find herself in the madness.

Wind whipped at my face and nose, the storm rolling in fast, the taste of snow in the air. I rushed to the only place I could think of. When we turned the corner, music rose in the air, and people milled in and out of the door, debauchery already eliciting customers in to escape life.

There was nowhere else to go, not when Raven needed to heal. With my own energy dragging, I required a place I could think. Come up with a plan.

I ducked inside. The dark lounge was sprinkled with only a few patrons at the gambling tables, hoping their luck would strike early.

The director of the house spotted our covered heads and vagabond clothes and came storming toward me, a cheery yellow robe fluttering behind him, contradicting the dark mood I carted through the door.

"What do we look like? A halfway house? Get out! We don't allow—" He came to stop in front of me, his mouth parting when I lifted my head under the hood. He let out a gasp, his eyes widening at Raven's limp, bloody figure in my arms. "Oh my gods…"

"We have nowhere else to go," I rumbled, my gaze darting around, assessing everyone in the brothel.

Maestro Silk swallowed, his gaze running over Raven and the dried blood she was bathed in.

"Of course. Come." Maestro motioned me to follow, instantly reacting, knowing this wasn't the time to talk. "Let's get her upstairs. Zabel?" He clicked his fingers at one of the workers. "Get brandy, some towels, clothes, and warm soup," he ordered, taking the steps up to the second floor, down the hallway, to the last bedroom. He bumped the door open, motioning to the full bed, the room almost identical to the one we stayed in last time.

I carefully placed Raven down on the creaky bed, and she let out a small whimper, her muscles trembling violently. Wrapping the comforter over her, I peered around the room for more covers.

"Do you have a hot water bottle and more blankets?" I could hear the strain in my voice, the discomfort of watching her suffer at all.

"Yes." Maestro nodded, darting out of the room, not even questioning my demands.

"*Dziubuś.*" I brushed hair off her forehead, strands stuck to the dried gore around her nose and eyes. "You're safe." I tightened the blanket around her.

"Here." Maestro returned, dumping two more comforters onto the bed. "Zabel will bring up the heated water bottle and whatever else you need."

I wrapped them around her, nodding back at him. My stress eased a little now that she could get warm. Start to heal.

"Thank you." I turned to him, my deepest gratitude conveyed in my face and tone, my eyes making full contact with his. "I'm indebted to you."

"Oh. Don't even think of it. Plus, I am the one indebted to you, remember?" Maestro swished his hand with a half laugh. "And really, I like pretending I'm some grand hero, saving all the beautiful people so I have something delicious to stare at."

I dipped my head with a smile, getting the feeling sentiment made him uncomfortable.

"Let me know if you need anything else." He headed for the door and stopped. "She'll be okay?"

"Yes. With rest."

He touched his breastbone in relief before taking one more look at Raven, then slipped out.

I stared down at Raven, her body still shivering and convulsing. Crawling into bed next to her, I wrapped my body around hers.

My eyes shutting, I breathed her in, willing my energy into Raven as I drifted off to sleep along with her.

When I woke, night colored the windows. A single firelight flickered on the table, the room glowing softly. A tray of food and supplies was left for us, and a hot water bottle was tucked at Raven's feet. Muffled sounds of people congregating in the lounge below, spilling into the street, laid like a soundtrack to the brothel. I could tell by the quietness upstairs that it was still a little too early for activity to be rampant in the bedrooms.

My attention turned to the woman next to me. Blood caked her skin, but she slept soundlessly in my arms, her skin flushed with color, her breathing steady. Her magic hadn't returned yet, but she seemed to be healing faster than before, as if I somehow let her use some of my energy to restore her own.

Was it even possible to share my magic with her? What we did on that mountain in the middle of the forest was impossible. It shouldn't be feasible between two different fae races.

Yet, we did.

The question of why roused me from the bed. I extracted myself from Raven's body without waking her. Quietly, I moved to the table, grabbing the brandy bottle and taking a swig. Letting the liquor burn down my throat, I exhaled, trying to keep centered.

It shouldn't be possible… nor did I even want it to be. I came here with a simple plan. Revenge. To take the lives of the two people who took from me. My plan derailed the moment she walked into the bar. I didn't even notice it creep in. When did everything change? How did it go from wanting her gone from my life to now clinging to her with desperation? Wanting to keep her next to me at all costs, even when I knew I couldn't. We could fight a lot of things, but her family, who she was, was not one of them. She was a true princess. Her role was there.

The queen and king of the Unified Nations were not a force I could battle.

Of course they were scared and wanted her home safe with them. I wanted it for her as well.

She shouldn't be in this mess. This was all my doing. What might have happened to her in the castle would haunt me for the rest of my days. The mere thought of Raven being raped and brutalized had me gasping for air, taking another swig of alcohol.

I couldn't leave the rest of those women there, like Celeste, Viorica, and Brândușa, to suffer that hell any longer. Nor Iacob or the innocent villagers. They were all there because of me. Because Sonya came hunting for me, and they got caught in the crosshairs.

My design to kill Sonya and Iain was only stronger, though it led to the same outcome. I probably wouldn't make it out of this country alive. Not with what I had to do.

Whatever connection was between Raven and me didn't matter. She was never meant to be part of my world. And I couldn't handle it if anything happened to her.

"No."

The voice whipped me around. Raven was sitting up, her eyes burning into me.

"You're awake." I moved to her, sitting on the bed. "How are you feeling?"

"I'm not leaving you." Her gaze burrowed in, not allowing me to deter the subject.

My mouth parted, baffled at the directness, the fact she responded to something I was simply thinking when my back was to her. "What?"

"I said, I'm not leaving. I know what you were thinking. And we've been here before. Several times. Stop thinking you know what is best for me."

"How did you know I was thinking that?" I frowned, anxiousness rolling in my lungs.

Her throat bobbed as she swallowed, her hands twisting together, her voice low. "I just did."

Scrubbing my face, I let out an aggravated groan. "Raven—"

"No." She shook her head. "I'm in this fight too."

"But you shouldn't be!" I stood up from the bed.

"Too late. I am."

"The world is searching for you." I paced in a line, aggravated and restless. "You're famous. Everyone will be out searching for you, wanting to cash in, like Daciana. I don't even know how truly safe we are here."

"I'll cut and dye my hair." She climbed out of the layers of comforters, standing up, far stronger than she should've been. "I don't care. But I'm not leaving you to this fight alone. I was there. I not only witnessed what they were doing to those women, but *I* experienced it."

My muscles locked up at her words. The need to level the castle and destroy everything in it clenched my fists into balls.

"You have no right to take away *my* revenge."

"If it saves your life, I fucking do!"

"So you can sacrifice, but I can't?" She came up to me, shoving at my chest. Her legs were still wobbly, but fierce indignation flickered in her eyes. "No," she challenged. "I forbid it."

"You *forbid* it?" I scoffed.

"Yep. I demand you go back to Budapest, where you belong." She folded her arms, searching my face. "See? Don't like when someone tells you what to do, huh?"

"Raven." Aggravation pinched my brow.

"No." She wagged her head. "You don't get to order me to do something, then not do the same when I ask you. Not how this works."

"How this works?" I widened my legs, crossing my arms, mimicking her. "And how *does* this work, exactly?"

Her gaze went to the window, picking absently at the dried blood on her hands, her lips pressing together.

Since we escaped the castle, the elephant we ignored had grown from giant to colossal, weighing down the room and thickening the air with strain.

Between what happened on that mountain and the *unbelievable* sex, like *I think she broke me* sex, tension clouded the space between us, signaling something far deeper than I wanted to go.

My cock hardened painfully at the idea of being inside her again, but fear made me step back, pushing me toward the brandy.

"Please." I took a huge swallow of țuică, keeping my back to her. "There are too many against us. Do this for me."

"Exactly why you need me more!"

"No!" I whirled around. "It's why I can't protect you! And if anything happened to you—" I cut myself off, anger bristling off me, staring to the side. *You will destroy what is left of me.*

"Look at me, Ash," she demanded.

I shifted on my feet but didn't trust myself to do what she said.

"Look. At. Me!" Her dominance yanked my gaze to her green eyes, bright with emotion. "Do I *look* like I need your protection?" She opened her arms, displaying torn clothes, her skin caked with other people's lives. "All my life, I've worn pretty dresses and put on a smile for the most dangerous people in the world, including my own family, knowing *I* was the thing they should dread the most. All my life I have tried to control it, to keep myself in check. My obscurer desires death, while my dweller craves their blood. *I am* the monster they fear. And I bow to no one."

"You bow to me." The statement came out of my mouth before I could stop it.

"What?"

"You. Bow. To. Me." I stated firmer. Setting my glass down, I sauntered back to her until my boots hit hers, my body looming, my lips about an inch from hers. "*They* bow to me."

Her cheeks flushed while her lids tapered. She looked ready to fight me.

"You can't lie to me," I whispered hoarsely. "I am the *only* one they succumb to." I felt it in my soul, could sense them. Read her like she could read me.

Slowly her head dipped in agreement, our breaths starting to labor, the tension circling the room like prey. "I'm scared I'll go too far."

"I'm not. I don't fear them." My voice dragged across the ground. "They want to unleash their fury… they unleash on *me*. They crave blood… they taste *mine*." My thumb slid over a bit of dried gore on her cheek. "You need to bring yourself back from the brink? I am what you anchor to. They need to fight, fuck, or kill?" My hand slid to the base of her skull, knotting my fingers through her hair, yanking hard on the strands. She let out a gasp, which my dick felt down to the veins, throbbing with need. "They take it out on me, understand?"

"Yes, but—"

"There are no buts." I pulled her head back more, my mouth ghosting over hers.

"There are always buts." A fierce growl rumbled in the back of her throat. "We're in this together, okay? I am not leaving. Discussion over. Understand?"

Staring down at her, I realized how truly fucked I was. I would never win a fight ever again. She owned me in ways I had never understood before.

"You're not cutting your hair," I mumbled, tightening my grip on her stands, Minotaur blood soaking it.

"Should we talk about what happened?"

"Do you want to talk about what happened?" I slid my thumb over her bottom lip.

"Not especially." She sounded breathy. "I need a shower."

"Do you?" I cocked up an eyebrow.

"I'm still pretty weak and unsteady." She peered at me through her lashes. "I might need help."

"Well, you're in luck." I leaned closer. "Tree fairies are exceptional at assisting people in need." I gripped her chin. "Especially those hard-to-reach places."

"Good." She went on her toes, her lips grazing mine in a taunt. "Because my pussy is a place I can't seem to reach."

"*Szar, dziubuś.*" A sputtered cough moaned out of my throat. "You are killing me."

"I'm the only one who gets to."

My mouth slammed down on hers, our hunger already forgoing all the things we needed to discuss, my mind on one thought. I needed to be inside her more than I needed to breathe.

"Let's get you clean so I can get you dirty all over again." I picked her up, her legs wrapping around my waist as I took us down the hall to the bathroom, stripping her clothes along the way, not caring who might be walking by.

My mouth never leaving hers, I stumbled into the bathroom, ramming her spine into the wall as I reached back for the door.

"Leave it open." She pulled away, her hands fumbling on my zipper.

"What?"

"I want everyone to watch. To hear us." She pushed my pants down, a mischievous smile on her lips. "To experience and envy every time you push deeper inside me, making me scream."

Air caught in my chest, my cock becoming so hard my eyes watered.

I was very much into being both a voyeur and an exhibitionist. Before, I would be fine with whoever was watching or joining in. Now, a rage ignited in my chest at the thought of anyone else touching her, being the reason she cried out.

Fuck. No.

But them watching me touch her, hear her scream my name… fuck yes.

A groan worked up the back of my throat. I set her down, and we frantically kicked out of our boots, tearing at our clothes. My cock throbbed as I turned on the water, both of us unable to stop touching each other as we stepped under the cold spray, not waiting for it to heat up.

I could hear people coming down the hall as I slammed her back into the tile, my mouth covering hers, the curtain wide open.

A small gasp sounded from someone in the hall, their feet stopping as they came upon us. Adrenaline sang in my veins, my fingers sliding down her torso, parting her legs, and sliding into her pussy.

"Ash…" She tipped her head back.

"Put your leg onto the side of the tub. Let them see what I get to have," I ordered. Heat danced in her eyes as she did what I said, opening wide and putting herself on full display for our viewers.

Dropping to my knees, I dragged my lips down her stomach to her inner thighs, feeling the extra attention turn me on even more. Except the moment my tongue slid into her pussy, all I could think of was her.

When the fuck did this happen? I couldn't even recall exactly when things flipped on me. When I no longer yearned for death, but for life with her.

Her nails raked through my hair, her hips fucking my face, the taste of her smearing over my tongue. When did she become home?

I learned young that home did not mean blood ties, nor did it insinuate a place. It was where I found family. Only a handful of people actually were at that level, a place where I let down my guard. To be myself.

Somewhere along the way, Raven found her way under my skin, burrowing into my bones. Making me feel something I thought myself incapable of. It pissed me off that I couldn't fight it, especially knowing this couldn't go anywhere. I couldn't live in her world, nor could she stay in mine.

"Ash!" Raven's moans were mixed with others, the hallway sounding slightly more crowded, our energy luring them to us. "I need you inside me." She yanked my head back, pulling at my hair. "Now."

I licked at the wetness covering my mouth, and when I saw the red flicker in her eyes, I knew she was on the cusp. I climbed to my feet, gripping her hips.

"Watch them respond to the way I fuck you." I huskily spoke in her ear before twisting her to face the open door. "Grab onto the rim."

She leaned over, her grip wrapping around the lip of the tub. My hands slid over her ass, spanking it.

She jerked, a sound puffing from her lips, her excitement sliding down her leg.

I spanked her again, her back bowing, her groans louder. "Please…"

My need was so desperate I couldn't even pretend to torture her any longer. Widening her legs, I bent her over further. Clutching her throat, I held her in place, thrusting deep into her.

Raven's howls echoed in the room as I pushed in all the way, her legs dipping as I bottomed out.

"Fuuuuck!" My body tingled, dots forming in my vision, and I pulled out enough to plunge back in. This time, no actual words came out, just belligerent sounds choking out of my throat. The sensation of being inside her hit even harder than before, as if each time she sank deeper into me, intensifying the pleasure until she was so much a part of me, I would never come back. The fear of her power over me, of the damage we were lying down in front of us, burned in my lungs.

But my desire to let go, to fully jump in, had me railing Raven harder.

The room disappeared. We were only semi-aware of our audience joining in. Two women prostitutes got each other off near the sink while a well-dressed man fucked a whore right against the opposite wall. Another prostitute, barely half-dressed, her legs wide open, fingered herself as she watched us in the doorway.

"You like this?" I grunted, not easing a bit. "Like them watching us? Getting off to how wet I make you?" I pressed my thumb harder into her throat, feeling her strangle my cock.

"Yessss." She spat out each word. "I want them to know it's my pussy you're fucking. That's making you lose your mind. Your cock will only be fucking *me*!"

Oh. Holy. Fuck. Something in me snapped.

Her claim made me as feral as her. A noise snarled from me, like her beast crawled into me and took over. I wasn't just fucking her… I was *mating* her.

"Oh gods!!" Raven's entire body shook. My hips pounded into her so hard tears poured from her eyes. "More!" Our sounds were so obscene I knew they could hear us downstairs and up the street. "Ash!" Her pussy tightened around me, squeezing, flickering my eyes back in my head.

"*Megbasz…*" I hissed through my teeth, trying to keep my legs under me. I could feel how near she was. Her beast growled at the surface, her magic forming on her tongue.

Pulling out, I twisted her around and lifted her up. Her legs wrapped around me as I sank into her again. "I need to watch you come." I gripped her chin, my teeth bared. "Do not take your eyes off me."

Her gaze locked on mine, flickering with flames as I pumped in harder, my balls slapping her pussy. Water cascaded down our bodies as we moved together. I let go, feeling myself not just sink inside her but sink inside her soul.

Fire took over her eyes, and I saw her mouth part, but she bit down on her lip, stopping herself.

"Do it," I snarled, egging her on, craving the pain it would later cause. To put the final nail in my coffin. Her core started to flutter, and I knew we were both close. My thumb hooked over her bottom teeth, tugging at her jaw. "Do. It!"

Latin hissed from her mouth, the spell slipping off her tongue and wrapping around us.

Throttling my cock.

I heard myself bellow, the magic strangling her around me so tightly I could no longer move. The base of my cock swelled as she locked around me, my seed spurting out in hot waves, stuffing her pussy to the point she could no longer take more.

"ASH!"

We were no longer on this earth, transported to a plane where sight, smell, and taste didn't mean anything in the normal sense, though she was everywhere and in everything.

Where reality was a faraway dream, and the dream was sharp and real.

Her eyes never left mine as I continuously came inside her. The barriers between us disappeared to the point I could read her thoughts, steal her knowledge, and truly understand what was happening. What I tried to ignore the night before.

It shouldn't have been possible. A tree fairy shouldn't be capable of it for many reasons, but nature didn't seem to give a fuck.

I bellowed out as she knotted around me, tying me to her with no hope of escape.

"Just because it looks like a *massive* mushroom doesn't mean you should lick it."

Chirp!
"Trying to give you some friendly advice.
Chirp! Chirp!
"I licked it first, only to be sure it was safe... *for you.*"
Chirp!
"Noooo," I groaned, rolling my head into the pillow. "Go away." Wanting to ignore the voices pulling me from my deep slumber, my arms automatically pulled Raven into me, digging my head into her neck.

After what we did in the bathroom, she was barely conscious. I cleaned her up and brought her back here, passing out next to her. In the middle of the night, I woke up enough to slide inside her, slowly fucking her until we conked out again.

"Don't touch or lick *any* part of me or her," I muttered.

"That's not what you were saying last night."

I opened one lid, peering at the figure standing on Raven's hip, his arms crossed.

Another moan sank my head deeper into the pillow. "What the fuck are you wearing?"

"Don't you like it?" Opie's expression filled with hope. Just one critical word would make him cry.

"Um... sure."

Dice from the gambling tables dangled on a fringe around his waist, barely covering him. Gold silk draped off him in a cape, and pleasure beads wrapped around his beard, connecting to the clip-on nipple rings he wore on his chest.

"What do you expect?" he exclaimed. "You drag us to these places, which have nothing for me to work with. I do the best I can."

Chirp!

My eyes dragged to the imp, climbing up next to Opie. Bitzy wore a gold silk diaper, nipple rings in her giant bat-like ears, and pleasure beads around her neck.

"Right." Opie nodded. "You still owe us, Mushroom Man. I get a whole section of the Byzantine era to make into a work of art. And Bitzy wants a dozen mushrooms."

I exhaled with irritation, though I couldn't find it in me to be. My system was still blissed out and buzzing with energy, my dick sore, but in the way it wanted to be inside her again.

Fear hovered on the edges, knowing reality was ahead of us once we stepped out of this bubble. What I pushed her to do last night scared me to face in the light of day. The connection I doubled down on. I wanted to pretend it was some strange dream. Not something plausible that could happen between us, though I had seen my friends fall to their significant others in the same way.

Tree fairies did not mate. Period. The end.

"Look at you." Opie's bushy eyebrows went up and down. "The smitten kitten."

"Don't ever call me that again."

Chirp!

"Oh yeah… you guys need to stop leaving your mark everywhere you go. It's like a calling card."

"What are you talking about?" I lifted my head.

"The trees outside." Opie motioned over his shoulder to the window. "You did the same at the last place."

"What?" I flicked the back covers, climbing out of bed.

"Whoa, whoa! Warn a brownie before you swing your wild mushroom about!" Opie ducked. "You could hurt someone with it… like hurt in the *do it again* way."

Chirp!

"I wasn't implying I wanted to be that someone!"

Ignoring them, I traveled to the window, pushing the thin curtain to the side. The hazy sun barely broke through the clouds, fresh snow covering the ground and sill, but my attention caught on something else.

"Holy shit," I whispered.

The trees planted along the pavement were all bent into each other, their limbs tangled and tied together.

A lump formed in the back of my throat, and I struggled to swallow, knowing we did this. It came from the magic Raven and I produced—we had *knotted* them together.

Like we were.

Chapter 16

Raven

Voices dragged me from sleep, my lashes lifting to reveal a figure standing by the window. My body instantly reacted at seeing Ash's naked physique, his gorgeous profile. The man's plump, firm ass was on display, demanding to be bitten into like a juicy apple. Bruises, bites, and claw marks from last night's pursuits decorated his skin, showcasing my endless hunger for him.

Standing there, he stole my breath and caused a kaleidoscope of sensations to flutter in my stomach. It curved through me, the connection I felt to him, the blooming in my chest I had never felt before, not even remotely with Wyatt. I stopped breathing at the intensity of emotion, at what it all meant.

Last night, when he demanded words from my obscurer, pulled forth my beast, and saw only me, there was a final line I walked right over and fell.

"Look, Master Mushroom, your fun-girl is awake." A small voice popped my attention to the figure standing on the bed next to me. The same brownie and imp I saw at the bike club. "Get it?" The brownie snickered, the dice skirt around his hips swaying under his large belly clicking together. "*Fungirl*, instead of fung—"

"Opie, shut up," Ash replied, his voice monotone, not even looking back.

Chirp!

"Right? You'd think he'd be in a much better mood with all the gardening he did last night, planting his seed until all hours of the night!"

Chirp!

"I wasn't watching! I just assumed."

Chirp! Chirp! The imp's fingers flew in the air.

"Well, I didn't purposely watch!"

Chirp!

"That is a total misunderstanding!"

"I don't understand." I pulled the sheet up to my chest, sitting up. "Why are you guys here? I thought you lived at the biker club."

"Live in a biker club?" The brownie sucked in, his hand going to his chest, his voice rising. "Do I look like someone who lives in a biker club?!"

Chirpchirpchirp! I had no doubt the imp was definitely flipping me off.

"They belong to my friend," Ash inserted. "I have to babysit sometimes."

"Babysit!" Opie exclaimed. His dice skirt swung and showed off all his bits and pieces. "How many times have we saved your behind, tree fairy?" He put his hands on his hips. "If anyone is babysitting, it is us! Why do you think we are even here?"

Chip! Chirp!

"You are free to go back to Budapest anytime," Ash muttered, his mood pensive, but it only called to me. Climbing out of bed, I grabbed a shirt left for me. I tugged it on, padding to where he stood.

"You okay?" I couldn't fully disguise my nerves, terrified he would say this was all a mistake. Or maybe I was scared he wouldn't. We both had been hurt so much before, and to feel this deep connection terrified me. Yet I couldn't stop the need to be near him. Touch him.

"See for yourself." He flicked his chin out the window, taking my focus with it. It took me a moment to understand what I was looking at. The branches from the trees reached for each other, tangling, twining together almost seductively.

"Are they…?"

"Knotted together?" He glanced over at me. "Yes."

"Holy shit… did we…" I swallowed. "Did we do that?"

"Yes."

"You should see what you did to the trees outside the window of the last place." Opie chuckled, strolling to the end of the bed. "You guys are just knotting limbs everywhere you go."

"What?" My mouth hung open, a panic speeding up my pulse. "We did this before?"

"Taking the being knotty to a whole new level." Opie tipped back his head, his hand on his belly as he laughed. "Get it?"

"Unfortunately." Ash sighed. Turning to face me, he noticed the worry on my face. "Hey." He sat his bare ass on the windowsill and pulled me between his legs, completely comfortable with being naked. "It's okay."

"Did we hurt them?" I lifted my gaze back to the gnarled limbs together.

"No." A slight smile hinted on his face. "It didn't hurt them *at all*."

"What do you mean?"

He took another deep breath, his head lowering.

"They feel what I do." He peered back up at me. "I can share energy with trees, and they can feel my emotions. They could feel both of us… so more than anything, they are pollinating very early this year."

"What?" Heat traveled up my neck to my face.

"The entire floor watched us fuck in the shower last night, and this gets you blushing?" His thumb swept over my cheek. I melted at his touch, his tease causing me to redden more at the memory. With Ash, I felt comfortable to explore, to see what I liked. Wyatt had been great, but we were young, and he wasn't really in love with me, so something was always slightly off.

This was…

My attention went back outside, taking in the power we created together, feeling the fear creep back in.

"Ash…" I nipped my lip. "What happened last night between us—"

"And the night before last and all of last night and this morning." He lifted a brow. "Yeah, I know what it means."

"I shouldn't be able to… We shouldn't be able to do any of this." I swallowed, not able to say the word, motioning to the trees, indicating what it symbolized. "It shouldn't be possible." There weren't a lot of women dark dwellers anymore, my aunt Gabby being the only full-bred one left. And she told me knotting between mates should only happen when dark dweller women mated with another dark dweller. I was just half dweller, so I shouldn't experience it at all. I couldn't even link mentally to my alpha or family, so I sure as hell shouldn't be able to do this. "I don't understand. It is so rare and should only happen with another of my kind." I stepped back, wanting to run. "This is bad." I swore under my breath, the burden of what this meant sagging on my shoulders, knowing of all people, a tree fairy was not the mating or knotting type. "This is the last thing you want. Plus, I'm a freak! I shouldn't even be capable of it."

"You are not a freak." He yanked me back into him, his face going serious.

"How many obscurers, dark dwellers do you know? And one who can't fully turn into either? I can't link with my family like other dark dwellers. I can't use my powers without either killing others or myself! I am a freak and a monster!"

"Makes you rare, not a freak and definitely *not* a monster." He threaded his fingers with mine. "And who said it was the last thing I wanted?"

"Ash." I slanted my head. "You came here to avenge your lovers, not find me, or…" I cleared my throat, not looking at him. "Knot with some girl."

"Hey." He tilted my chin up until I was looking into his eyes. "You are not *some* girl." Annoyance flashed in his eyes. "Not even close. You think I could share my magic with some girl?" I sucked in at his declaration. We hadn't spoken about what happened between us when we fled the castle. The raw intimacy of sharing his magic with me. Once again, it shouldn't have been possible.

"You're right, I didn't come here looking for you or *anyone*. I was supposed to get the information on Sonya and Iain that night and walk out of the bar, none the wiser. I'd come here to kill them—and probably die in the process. But the plan went to shit the moment you stepped into that pub. I didn't prepare for you, and I tried like hell to get rid of you."

I tried to step back again, but he didn't let me move.

"Before Sonya's men took you to the castle, I thought you left me. Went back home without saying goodbye." His throat bobbed. "And I realized it was the last thing I wanted. You have burrowed under my skin, *dziubuś*." His head wagged with astonishment. "All my life, the notion of being with one person forever bored the fuck out of me, made me feel restless and agitated. And I was fine with that because it's who I am. Nature fairies don't have mates. You understand, right?" His throat bobbed, fear twitching his cheek. "So, I don't know what the fuck is happening here."

He didn't want this. And I felt it was my fault. He had no say when my body decided he was the one.

My father told us the story of when my mom first rejected him. The year he lived in agony. What happened to dwellers when their mate refused the connection. They would grow weaker and weaker, and some eventually died.

Panic fizzled in my chest at the notion of Ash walking away from me. I not only had the bond, but my body knotted with him. Him, of all people. A tree fairy whose very nature went against being mated.

I could see no way out for me, but I couldn't do that to him.

Land of Monsters

"This isn't your fault." I stepped out of his hold. "It's on me. And don't worry, I'm not asking you for anything."

His lids narrowed. "What are you talking about?"

"This." I motioned between us. "It's my problem. I'm the one who glitched—"

"Raven." He cut me off. "You're not hearing me." He spread his legs wider, pulling me back in, his cock erect against his stomach. "I don't know what the fuck you did to me, *dziubuś*." His voice scraped between my legs. "I never had a problem sharing before. *Never*. But the thought of someone else touching you, being with you… Just know. I will *not* share you." His hand grazed up my thigh under my shirt, forcing me to bite my lip. "This is mine." He trailed over my pussy. "I have lived a *long* fucking time, fucked *a lot* of people, some I even loved. But I've never felt like this." His fingers parted me, making me gasp. "I won't pretend it doesn't freak me out. But I can't walk away from you now." His free hand laced through my hair, gripping the back of my head. "Even when I know this can't go anywhere."

"What?" His words contradicted what his hands were doing to my body.

"You are a fucking princess."

"So?"

"So?" He scoffed. The hand in my hair slid to my lips, his thumb hooking my mouth. "You belong in that world with your family. In America. I don't…"

"Don't tell me where I belong." I bit down on his thumb, my breath stumbling as he slipped deeper inside me. "What if I belong here? With you?"

"Raven." He tilted his head, giving me a look, both of us understanding. I didn't have a say. My birthright was chosen for me.

"Think of it this way… I most likely won't make it out of this country alive, so it won't be a problem anyway."

"Don't say that." Fury and fear roped off my lungs.

He paused his movement, his thumb tugging my chin down to look at him.

"I'm not leaving until Sonya and Iain are dead. Whatever that takes."

"I can help you."

"Let's enjoy the time we do have left." His voice went low, his fingers picking back up as he towed my face to his. The moment our lips met, I ceased to remember anything else, only aware of his naked body against mine. His hand trailed down, cupping my breasts, rubbing at my hard nipples.

"Ash," I moaned, desire claiming all my thoughts, our kiss deepening as I straddled him on the windowsill. I was starving for him, like it had been years instead of a few hours since I had him inside me. Wrapping my hand around his thick girth, I rubbed my thumb over his tip, spreading the precum down his shaft.

"*Megbasz*," he hissed.

Breaking the kiss, I stared into his eyes as I gripped him firmer, angling him into my entrance and sliding him through my slick folds. Playing and taunting him.

"Raven," he growled, ripping off my shirt.

The energy between us, the need, was so thick it smothered the room.

"Choke me as I slide down your cock," I whispered. He gripped my throat as I slowly sank down on him, the lack of air causing me to feel everything in abundance. My mouth parted, a guttural groan vibrating my chest. The feel of him stretching me to the point of pain. "Oh gods, you feel so good," I croaked out.

"Oh fuck." His hips lifted, pushing deeper. He let go of my throat and gripped my ass, pulling me into his thrust, causing me to already see stars. "What the hell are you doing to me?"

"Ash!" My nails clawed at him, rolling into him, our pace picking up. "I don't want this to ever stop." I leaned back, achieving a deeper angle, pressing him into the window. I loved that anyone could look up from the street and see us. Watch him fuck me.

"Get out," Ash snarled.

"What?"

"I know you're still in here," he breathed, the trees starting to sway outside. "Watching." He flicked his chin toward the empty bed. "Two dozen mushrooms if you leave."

I realized he wasn't talking to me.

There was a long silence before I heard a chirping sound.

"Two dozen for Bitzy and all the clothing supplies I want!" A small voice came from the other side of the room.

Ash grunted as I rolled harder into him, his grasp on me leaving a mark.

"Whatever the fuck you want," he agreed, holding me as he stood up, continuing to fuck me. "And leave some dice."

"You want me to ruin my masterpiece? No way!"

"If Bitzy wants the bag of mushrooms I left here, you will leave now." *Chhhhhhhhhhhiiiirrp!*

"Fine!" Opie huffed, though I couldn't find them in the room. "But just know you are ruining a work of art!"

Ash smirked as he carried me across the room, dropping me on the bed. The moment he slid out of me, I whimpered, but he grabbed my thighs. "Spread your legs. I want to see your dripping pussy." He opened me wide, his eyes brightening with lust. He leaned over, swiping up something off the bed. Three dice rolling in his hand. "A game I know I can win." He took the die, placed it on my clit, and started to rub into me.

My back arched as he added another one.

"Oh gods!"

"Like that, little beak?"

"Yes," I croaked.

"You'll like this even more." He went down on his knees, his hands spreading me even more. His tongue slid through me, before his mouth swiped up the die and covered my pussy in a deep kiss. My hands gripped the bedding as he used his tongue to slide them through my clit and up into me.

"Oh fuck!" I heard myself bark, my skin flushing hot as he worked me, the dice adding a bit of pain to the unbelievable pleasure. My body jolted as he pushed one into my ass. The others he licked through me, hitting every nerve that made me lose my mind.

"Ash!" The beast howled, my nails cutting into the mattress.

"Come on my tongue, mroczny." Dark one.

I knew he didn't speak out loud, his tongue busy fucking my pussy, but I swear I heard him ordering me to comply.

His fingers twisted the die deeper into me, touching something I never felt before, detonating an explosion in me.

I bowed off the bed in a scream as I violently came. He groaned into me, lapping every drop of my release until my body sagged into the bed.

"Holy fuck." I gulped for air, my head spinning.

"Those are my lucky dice from now on." He lifted his head with a confident grin. Standing up, he rubbed his erection, the tip almost purple. "I'm nowhere near done with you." He pulled me up, my legs barely able to stand. "I want you to watch those trees respond to us, watch them knot while I feel you do the same around my cock."

"I'm starving." My voice vibrated against Ash's chest as I watched the late morning light spill into the room, my nails tracing over his abs.

"I know. I can hear your stomach growling." He chuckled, stretching out his arms and legs underneath me. "We burned a lot of calories earlier.

And last night. Well, most of the night." His hands slid through my hair, stroking down my back.

After he fucked me against the window, observing the trees twine and quiver with our force, we were barely able to crawl into bed before passing out. It felt purposeful this time. Like we both accepted the connection, jumped into it, and bent it to our will. Yet, deep down, neither of us wanted to think about the outcome down the road, the consequences of what we were doing.

The devastation it would cause.

His sentiment earlier about this having no future hurt. It hurt because it was true. I was destined for a world no one should be forced into. For good or bad, I was my mother's daughter. A princess. It meant being under a microscope every minute of my life. Judged and critiqued, praised and condemned. I never felt comfortable in it, too much like my father, but I played the part I was born into. I didn't realize until I was out of the spotlight how much I hated always being in it. How fake and shallow I had been. However, it was still my future.

That life wasn't Ash. He was wild and free, living in the woods, growing herbs, while I was in an expensive gown, meeting leaders of the world.

I was too aware of how my mom's "job" tormented my father. He was the opposite of all the pomp and court, prowling the edges of the party, forcing a smile at some jackass senate member because he loved my mother beyond this world. He kept from tearing their heads off *for her*.

No way I would want it for Ash. His family and life were in Budapest.

I listened to his heartbeat against my ear, my throat closing up at the idea of saying goodbye to him. Or even worse, his life being taken from me.

Agony watered my eyes, the notion of him not in this world pulling bile up my throat.

"You can't die."

"What?" His hand stopped skating through my hair.

"I think I can survive if I know you are still in this world somewhere." I lifted my head, twisting to look at him, my brows furrowing. "Promise me. Don't die."

His mouth parted to speak, but I rushed in.

"It's the only thing I ask." I pushed up on my arms, peering down at him. "I'm made differently than you. And I'm not saying this because I'm a girl or anything. I'm saying it as a dark dweller." I swallowed, hating how vulnerable this made me. "It's not only the idea of you not existing." I shook my head, wanting to throw up. "But I won't stay alive either…" I looked away. "And again, that isn't a platitude. Dark dwellers don't survive long without their ma—" I cut off my own sentence. Saying it out loud felt like flaying myself wide open for him to peck at, like a dead corpse. "It's not your fault or on you. I know you aren't designed the same way I am. And I know you said this can't go anywhere." I rushed out, hating how young and clingy I sounded. Exactly what he accused me of when we first met. "All I ask is for you not to die. Please." I bit my lower lip to stop babbling. "For me," I interjected before snapping down again.

"Did you just say please?" Ash's brow curved up, a hint of a smirk on his face.

"Shut up."

"There's my girl." In a blink, he had me flipped over on my back, his body nestling between my thighs. With no warning, he pushed one knee up, then entered me with a slow thrust.

"Ash!" I grunted, my head going back into the pillow. I was so sore, but him being inside me felt so fucking good. I became greedy for more each time.

"You're right. We aren't created the same, and as I've told you, nature fairies don't have mates." His nose flared, his eyes brightening as he sank into me, his hips rolling, pushing in again. "But I guess I've never been good at being a nature fairy." He spoke low, our eyes locking as our bodies moved together. "You say you're a freak? I am too. I've *never* been normal. Even as a child. Where tree fairies strive for harmony and nature, I've always lived in violence and conflict. I pretended for a moment I was happy living in peace, but the moment chaos stepped back onto my doorstep, I welcomed it. Eagerly. I realize now I was bored without it.

"And it's taken me until you to accept that I *thrive* in discord. I feel alive in battle. I enjoy variance." Ash moved so unhurriedly, hitting every nerve, each strike of his hips causing me to gasp and moan, my nails digging into his back. His mouth brushed over mine, fucking me so steadily, my vision blurred at the edges. "You are my chaos, *mroczny,* my battle, my variance. It's like I was waiting for you this whole time." He pushed my one leg higher, hooking it over his shoulder.

"Ash…" My pussy gripped around him.

"Yeah. Keep your eyes on me." A muscle in his jaw clenched. "You feel that?"

He wasn't talking about his size, though fuck, I felt that too, but the magic snaking around us, the undeniable bond winding tighter.

"Use whatever term you want for us. It doesn't matter to me because what this is?" He rocked harder into me. "Goes way beyond labels." He grabbed my arms, pulling them over my head, his tempo picking up. "Just know, you have me at your will, little beak. And whatever is in my power to do for you... I will do it."

"Don't die." The obscurer would annihilate this world if he was lost. "And never cheat on me. I *don't* share either." The dweller would murder anyone who touched him.

"I will try. And not a fucking problem. You own my cock now." He leaned over, his tongue sliding over my lips before claiming them, pushing in deeper. "Though I will always be up for people watching me fuck you." He let go of my wrists, gripping the frame and using it as leverage, sliding in and out of me, the sound of us slapping the walls.

"Oh gods!" I rasped out, feeling the burn of my orgasm, my tongue blistering with possession, the spell to knot him swelling up inside me.

"Fuuuuck," he hissed, slamming into me, feeling the magic gripping him. "You have me so fucked. I *need* to fill you with my semen, put my seed in you," he growled. The bedframe struck the wall with loud bangs, my cries no longer contained. "For everyone to know this pussy is mine. You are mine."

His words pushed me over, my cry sprouting with the spell, my obscurer taking over, swelling me around him.

Ash roared, and I felt his hot cum like a brand. Air was ripped from my lungs, yet it was like I could finally breathe. For a moment, no line was between us, no separation of souls. I felt his desire, his feelings, his thoughts like he could mine.

But in that moment, my barriers down, I felt something else. A familiar tug humming in the back of my brain, reaching for me. Calling my name. It was a whisper of something I knew, something I recognized but didn't want to believe. A connection that had nothing to do with the man coming inside me. Then it was gone. Disappearing as fast as it came, it evaporated from my mind as my orgasm shook through me.

"*Raven.*" Ash pulled my attention back to him, my body hungrily milking every drop before we crashed down, his body sagging over mine.

Gasping and heaving together, he stared down at me in awe until he was able to speak.

"I know how dangerous this is with a Druid, even if you are protected with the tree fairy potion." His finger traced my lip. "I don't care."

Tree fairies were known for concocting iron-clad birth control potions, and they would stay in place until you went back and took a counter potion. This seemed to work for everyone except Druids. Me and my brother were a result of the potion failing. Though my parents were glad it did, we were still a surprise.

"You don't have to worry about that," I said quietly, my voice hoarse.

"That's the thing. I'm not worried." He wagged his head. "*That's* what worries me."

"No, I mean… I can't." I blinked with the shame that something was wrong with me. "I told you I was a freak. Whatever turned me out like this left me barren." I looked away. Ash still knotted inside me, made this conversation even more intimate and raw.

"Hey." He tugged my chin back, forcing my gaze on his. "Do not ever be ashamed of that. Never. It is such bullshit that having kids makes you complete or something. You are whole just how you are, *dziubuś*. I want nothing more. You understand me?" He waited for me to nod before kissing me. "I told you I didn't want kids."

"You'd make a good father."

He lifted a shoulder, a smile pulling his lips. "Kids are a pain in the ass and will get in the way of me fucking you whenever and wherever I want."

"You promise?" I clung to the thread of hope this had a future.

"To fuck you whenever and wherever I want?" He smirked against my mouth. "Yes. Fae don't make promises, but for that, I will."

Wrapping my arms around him, I sucked at his bottom lip, taking his mouth. My pussy squeezed even more around him, creating a moan in the back of his throat, deepening our kiss.

Right then, my stomach chose to speak out again, grumbling loudly, breaking the escalating desire in the room.

Ash laughed against my lips. "I'm not scared of your dark dweller or obscurer, but your stomach? That I am terrified of." He whispered to me softly, rubbing my side. "I need to get you fed."

"Oh I want *bulz*… no maybe *plăcintă*. And all of the ham." I licked at my lips, my stomach taking over. "Oh, and definitely some *gogoși*! And a huge coffee."

"You're gonna have to release me," he teased, my body still secured around him. "If you want me to go get you something to eat."

"What do you mean? I'm going with you."

"You can't. Everyone is out looking for you."

"I'll wear a hood. I need food *now*. I need meat." My dweller was famished.

"Is it why your pussy is swallowing me whole and won't let go?" His mouth dragged up my neck.

"Shut up." I playfully shoved at his chest, pulling a deeper laugh from him. The sound was like music, easing my body, allowing him to adjust and slowly ease out of me, pooling ropes of his cum down my legs.

"Fuck." He sat back on his knees, staring at me, biting down. "If you want to eat anytime today, better get up quickly before I change both of our minds."

I almost let him, but with another grumble of my stomach, he let out an exhale, pulling me to sit up with him.

"I need to take a shower."

"Nope." He leaned over, his lips sliding over mine. "I want to know the whole time we are out, my cum is dripping from you, pooling in your panties."

"You are dirty," I muttered against his mouth.

"You will continue to learn how right you are." He kissed me quickly. "Now get dressed."

"Oh finally! We're *starving*!" A voice came from somewhere in the room. "And bored!"

Chirp!

"Lies! I was totally bored!"

Chirp!

"I was *not* watching!"

Chirp! Chirp!

"Like you can talk!" Opie's voice pitched. "Don't tell me you weren't observing that colossal mushroom bury itself in the garden over and over!"

"*Mi a fasz van veled?!*" Ash palmed his face with a sigh. "I can see why Warwick wants to kill you two all the time." Ash stood up, striding over to where someone put our cleaned clothes on the table. He tossed me my items and boots, and I quickly dressed, not thinking about how the clothes were still bloodstained in some places, the spots reminding me what I did the day before. The pile of bodies I was leaving was growing.

After what I did, I should've been comatose for a week, but just a few hours after, I was screwing Ash in the shower for all to watch, feeling even more alive.

No doubt after what happened on the mountain, we were sharing energy.

Peering over at Ash, I watched him dress, my heart lurching in my chest.

To think I didn't even want to go to the bar that night. It was Eve and the others dragging me there. Now I understood why Eve wanted me to be there, but I couldn't help but feel strangely grateful she betrayed me.

Land of Monsters

Otherwise, I never would've met Ash. And that hurt more than the idea that Eve had wanted me dead.

"Ready?" Ash held out his hand for me to take, yanking me up to my feet. He draped a cloak around me, pulling up my hood. Grinning, he stepped into me, cupping my face and kissing me like he also couldn't stop touching me. "Let's get you some food."

"It's about time! Bitzy wants double the mushrooms on everything." A tiny body dressed in a skintight, white silk jumpsuit, with his chest exposed and clamps on his nipples, darted up Ash's leg, climbing up to his shoulder, a backpack, holding the imp on his back.

"I'm sorry, but is that a... *buttplug* on her head?" I sputtered.

"Yes." Ash scoffed.

"No." Opie glared at Ash. "It's called a *fascinator fastener*," he corrected. "A sophisticated headpiece. She likes how she looks in them."

"And I like how *she* looks when one's in her." Ash winked at me, my cheeks blushing. Lacing his hand in mine, we strolled out of the door. The downstairs was quiet, and we slipped out into the streets, heading toward the square.

Keeping deep in my hood, my hand in his, I couldn't stop the smile plastered on my face. I was giddy. Happy. Like, deliriously happy.

It should've been enough to warn me not to ignore the prickling feeling I sensed earlier. But I had been blinded by Ash, too absorbed in our little bubble to understand what was coming.

That was always when everything came crashing down.

Chapter 17

Raven

"Here." Ash plopped a bag of warm *bulz* in my hand. The scent of ham and cheese grilled inside the polenta had my dweller clawing at the surface, desperate for protein. "Eat. I can hear your stomach from here." He winked.

While Ash waited for the rest of our order, I attacked the food, scarfing down several at a time. My tongue barely tasted the delicious flavors before I shoved another one in my mouth, forgoing all etiquette and manners.

Mid-bite, a hum crawled up the back of my neck, tugging in my chest, slowing my chewing as my attention went to the large square. I knew the sensation better than my own heartbeat, but my brain did not want to accept it.

No. It can't be.

Swallowing, I struggled to get the polenta down my throat, my pulse rising in my ears, my gaze darting around, scanning every face.

He can't be here.

"What's wrong?" Ash stood in front of me, holding two coffees, his attention darting out, trying to find what was upsetting me.

"Nothing." I turned back to him, putting a smile on my face.

"You know that won't work on me," he replied. "You can lie to everyone else, but not me. I feel you, little beak."

"It's just—"

Raven?

It was barely a whisper in my mind, but it sounded like a shout, whipping my head to the side. Everything blurred around me except the

Land of Monsters

lone figure far across the square, which was sharp, the black of his cloak vivid against the snowy ground.

The bag of *bulz* slipped from my fingers, dropping onto the cobbled ground, a harsh inhale piercing the back of my throat.

"What?" Ash went into defense mode. "What is it?"

The hooded form lifted his head, his identical eyes landing on mine across the distance, locating each other as if we were magnets.

He was here. He found me.

My twin.

"Rook..." I whispered his name, knowing he would hear me when no others could. The familiarity of him, the feeling of being whole, made my eyes tear up.

Rook and I were close, but we never had that deep twin thing—probably because I was messed up—though we still shared more than I did with anyone else. In proximity to each other, he was the only one I could sort of link to, unlike the rest of the dark dwellers, who could all communicate with each other through a network without talking out loud.

I didn't have to hear or feel him to sense his anger, his confusion... his hurt. But none of it mattered in the moment. My heart let out a small cry and I took off running toward Rook.

"Raven?" I heard Ash call me, but I didn't stop, my brother jogging for me too. He was such a mix of mom and dad. Dark hair, green eyes, and the stature of our father, but he had mom's fine bones and high cheeks. He was a blend of rugged and refined prince, and he could flip the switch on either in a blink. He was just as comfortable in a tux, shmoozing with elites, as he was in jeans hunting with our uncles. Charming, funny, and slightly arrogant, my brother had been fawned over his whole life by girls and guys alike.

"Roo," I muttered the pet name I gave him when I was a baby, his arms wrapping around me, his tall build towering over me, lifting me off the ground.

"Ravy." His voice croaked, pulling me in tight, squeezing me with a heavy exhale. "You're all right," he whispered over and over, like he needed to reassure himself. "You're alive."

"I'm sorry," I hiccuped, my guard coming down with my brother, my heart realizing how homesick I was for my family. "I'm so sorry."

My apology triggered him. Pulling back, he dropped me back down, his gaze rolling over me, his lids narrowing.

"What the actual fuck, Raven?" His head wagged, anger washing out the worry now that he knew I was okay. "We have been losing our minds thinking you were kidnapped or killed! You have mom and dad so sick with worry. She hasn't slept in a month!" His voice rose. "She is having episodes again, thinking she sees you running for your life! That bull-like monsters are holding you hostage!"

Mom was a powerful seer Druid and occasionally would have dreams of the future, outcomes that could possibly happen. They usually struck when she was stressed or something horrible was about to happen. When she got them, it took her a while to get out of them. Dad was the only one who could bring her back and settle her. Their bond and love were something I always wished to have. I thought I did with Wyatt, but now I see I was forcing it to be that when it never was.

"I'm so sorry." I swallowed. Guilt over what I had been putting everyone through finally hit me.

"Sorry? Are you kidding me? Sorry is not enough." He threw out his hands. "What the hell happened? We got intel about Reid being killed and you possibly being taken! But Uncle Lars and mom never received any ransom messages. I've been out searching for you this whole time!" He peered around, seeing I was perfectly free and didn't even have the cuff on my arm. "Why didn't you contact anyone… call me?" He motioned to himself. "*Me* of all people, Rav."

"I know. I should have—"

"But you didn't!"

"Hey." Ash's deep voice cut between us, stepping close to me, his head scanning around. "This is not the place for this."

"Who the hell are you?" Rook's attention snapped to Ash, a flash of red flickering in Rook's eyes, his chest puffing at the intruder.

"Rook." I said his name in warning. Rook's eyes snapped back to mine, then darted between me and Ash, taking in the way his body touched mine, his nearness, reading me like no one else could. "This is Ash. Ash, this is my brother Rook."

"Seriously, Rav?" Rook nose wrinkled, his forehead furrowing, his expression reminding me so much of dad when he was furious. His anger and disappointment curled his lip, and I knew what he smelled on me. Sex.

"I can't believe you…" He wagged his head. "Here we've all been worried sick. Uncle Lars and mom have spies scouring the earth. Dad, Uncle Eli, and Aunt Ember are out searching. Wyatt has been jumping every place we could think of around Switzerland to find a shred of where you might have gone, and here you are—" He motioned to Ash. "In Romania, the most dangerous country to be in right now… getting laid?"

"Hey. Enough." Ash stepped between us, his shoulders rolling back.

Rook's eyes flashed red, his teeth snapping as he silently stepped into Ash. Ash was still about an inch taller, but my brother could shift into a dweller on a dime, slaughter the entire piazza in minutes.

"You do not get to tell me what is enough. She is *my* sister. Who the fuck are you?"

"Rook. Stop." I wiggled between them, pushing them both back. "Ash, can you give us a moment?" My eyes pleaded with him.

"I don't think—"

"Please. I just need a moment."

Ash jaw clenched, but he nodded, "I'll get you something more to eat," he mumbled, not happy to leave me, but strolled off for the food wagon.

"Rook." I faced my brother.

"Who the hell is that?" He jerked his arm toward Ash's retreating figure. "He's acting all possessive, like he needs to protect you from me?"

"No, he's just trying to keep me safe, period, which isn't easy to do."

"Don't I know it." Rook folded his arms.

"I know you are mad at me. You have every right to be, but this is not the place to discuss it." I glanced around at the people milling about the plaza. Any of them could be a spy, and we were bringing too much attention to ourselves. Even hooded, it wouldn't be long before someone spotted the prince and princess of the Unified Nations right in front of them. "I have a lot to tell you. You don't know everything. The reasons I ran off. Why I couldn't contact you."

Hurt twitched Rook's cheek. I knew I was such a soft spot for him, someone he grew up wanting to protect, to shield from the world, afraid the press or people outside our bubble would find out about me. Discover I was fucked up and wrong. A monster. It was why he always stepped up and took the lead on the royal duties, pulling focus to him. He loved it, but he also did it to keep the press from looking too hard at me.

"Rook." I took his hand in mine, peering up at him. "I am so sorry. And I swear I will tell you everything, but not here, okay? It's too dangerous."

He huffed, but dipped his head. "You are such a pain in the ass."

"You too, *little* brother."

"Three minutes, Ravy… by three fucking minutes." It was a point of contention our whole lives and I loved teasing him about it.

Starting to turn toward Ash to get his attention, I paused. "*How did you find me, anyway?*"

"Oh—" Rook glanced over his shoulder, right as someone stepped up beside him.

My world stopped.

"Me." My body went still as a blonde moved in next to him, her smile curving up her face. "So good to see you, Raven. We've been so worried about you since you disappeared. Since the night we were attacked, and I lost you."

Rook nodded to her. "Eve's been a real help—"

"Get the fuck away from him." My teeth gnashed together, and I grabbed for my brother's arm.

"Missed you too." Eve tilted her head, her smile turning more malicious.

"Raven, what the hell?" He stumbled as I yanked him closer to me, keeping Eve in my sight, but at the same time scouring the plaza for Nikolay.

"You can't trust her, Rook. She's one of them."

"One of who? What are you talking about? This is Eve." He shook his head in confusion, pulling away, almost madder at me. Because this was the Eve he knew as my bodyguard, someone who had been in our lives since we were twelve. A friend. Someone we trusted.

I was stupid to think she wouldn't have the gumption to go straight back to them and play the worried bodyguard, using my brother to get close to me. To find me.

"Rook, she's not who—"

"You've been such a help, gorgeous." Eve winked at Rook, cutting me off. "Not only bringing me right to her, but now I have two royals instead of one."

"What?" He barely got the word out before Eve clutched his arm, slapping a goblin cuff over his wrists.

"Nooo!" I heard myself scream as my brother dropped to the ground, agony and shock twisting his features as the goblin metal tore magic from his body. She quickly gagged him, knowing his Druid powers needed to be spoken out loud to work.

Though my magic was not fully back, it buzzed under my skin, my fear calling it up to the surface. I lurched toward Eve.

"Don't!" In a blink, a gun was pointed at my brother's head, cementing my feet to the ground, stopping dead in my tracks. "I wouldn't test me, Raven," she sneered. "You have no idea the lengths I will go to."

My gaze dropped to my brother. Torment and confusion swam in his eyes, the pain from the metal almost doubling him over.

He was my twin. My everything. And in one moment, she could take him from me. The notion bowed my legs, my throat closing up.

"Eve, don't do this." I pleaded, my frame vibrating against the need to shift to protect my family. "Please."

"Then don't make me." She pushed the barrel deeper into my brother's temple. "You come with me, and I won't hurt him."

Figures encroached around me, and out of the corner of my eye, I noticed Nikolay. The feel of being circled around like prey had a deep growl rumbling up.

"You make one move, Raven, and I will shoot him. Make no mistake. And no one here will even blink an eye."

They wouldn't. When you lived under a suppressive government, you learned to keep your head down to survive.

"You understand?"

I nodded my acceptance, my body shaking with savagery.

"No," my brother muffled around his gag, his eyes going to me. I could read them so clearly, knew what he was thinking.

Fucking fight, Raven.

But I couldn't. Not when his life was on the line.

"Just kill me." He struggled to speak over the cloth, sneering at Eve. She knew us, knew how our powers worked.

"Aww… so sweet." Eve rolled her eyes. "So easy to be a martyr when you have no idea what true sacrifice is. I have watched you two grow up in privilege and wealth. So fucking pampered and bubble-wrapped in your little world. You imagine yourself so strong when you wouldn't survive a single day in the life I grew up in."

"Is that what this is about?" I snapped. "We happened to be born into our family and had parents who loved us? Is this all about jealousy?"

"Americans." She snorted derisively. "Your arrogance will always be your failing." She grabbed the back of my brother's neck, trying to pull him up. "Now move."

It was a split second, but my twin's gaze shifted to me, his intention clear. I opened my mouth to stop him. He had no idea of the brutal lengths Eve would go to. She was not fibbing. She would shoot him without a thought.

His elbow rammed into Eve as hard as his limited energy would allow him, stumbling her back with a cry. Her shriek was like a bell through the plaza, triggering her faithful dogs.

"Raven!" I spun toward Ash's cry, seeing him run for me just as Nikolay and the other men came upon me, carrying goblin cuffs, their guns held high, pointed at me and Rook.

POP!

A single bullet fired, the shrill sound tearing away any reservations. My mind blurred as instinct kicked in, driving my predator. I had no say, no control. Only the need to protect my family and kill everything that stood in my way.

With a savage roar, my dweller sprang to the surface, blades shredding through my clothes. My fingers twisted into claws, my teeth gnashing together.

"Raven!" Ash yelled again, but I was no longer listening. The obscurer gurgled in the back of my throat, yet I couldn't seem to get any spell off my tongue. Trails of blood already dripped from my eyes and nose, energy draining quickly from me. My teeth snapped out for a man in front of me, nails cutting through his chest, dropping him to the ground. His scream bounced off the cobblestones as I stepped over him.

I tried to keep my sight on Eve, her blood a craving on my tongue, but more of the mafia moved in for me, blocking both her and my brother from view.

"Muzzle her!" Nikolay barked at his men, pointing at me, pulling my attention to him. Setting him as my target to hunt. His eyes widened when he felt my attention on him, his gun pointing at me.

My eyes flared with death, pitching for him, craving his blood.

Bang! Bang!

"Raven!" Ash's voice was the blast in my ears, ringing with warning and fear.

Warmth trailed down my legs, blood oozing from my stomach where two bullets went through.

"Nooooooooo!" Ash bellowed, firing at Nikolay, the plaza turning into a war zone.

Everything hazed around me and I took a step, my body crumbling to the ground. A symphony of violence was performing in the air, a sonata of screams and bellows between the spray of bullets. Locals hid behind anything they could find nearby, children crying.

"Rook…" His name clawed up my throat, my head lifting enough to see Eve yanking him with her. He tried to fight, but his body was too weak, his vocals cut off by the gag. The men covered her as she and another man got Rook into a jeep. I tried to push myself up, but my arms collapsed under me, and the jeep peeled away. "Noooo!" The scream of terror barely made it through my lips as I tried to pull myself across the cobbles, still denying my brother was gone.

Blackness filled my mind and sight like a swamp.

"Raven?" Ash was suddenly next to me, rolling me over onto my back, his expression pinched with terror. "Stay awake, *dziubuś*." Panic reverberated in every word, his eyes wild. "You will be fine."

I blinked, wondering why he sounded so frantic. I felt no pain.

"Rook," I croaked out.

Ash crushed his jaw together, not answering me. He shoved his arms underneath me, picking me up.

"Stay with me, *dziubuś*. Please," he muttered, more to himself. He rushed us out of the square, leaving families cowering and my victim's dead body bleeding out, his final breath long over.

Once again, my mark stained the ground, leaving debris of violence in my wake.

"Stay awake, little beak." His timbre weaved along the outskirts of my consciousness, pinning me back down, when all I wanted was to let go, fall into the peaceful darkness. "Please, Raven. Open your eyes."

I tried, but my body wouldn't respond, exhaustion pulling me down deeper, trying to keep me numb to the pain.

As if I floated just outside my body, I could smell the snow he had laid me in, the tang of the trees, and the sharp dampness of the earth.

It was a quiet, peaceful place to die.

"*Szar*," Ash hissed. "Raven. Don't you dare leave me. Wake up!"

I wanted to, for him, but I could feel nothing left inside to fight, my energy and blood almost completely drained.

"No!" he shouted.

I felt the faraway sensation of pressure on my mouth, the understanding that his lips were on mine.

In one moment, it went from peace to the most excruciating agony. A scream exploded inside my body, shaking through each bone as he shoved his magic into my body. Energy lashed through me like barbed wire, the pain robbing me of breath, ramming me back into the brutality of life. I tried to scream again, move away from the onslaught of magic burning from the inside out, but his mouth only poured more fuel into the fire, creating so much agony, I finally bowed to it, letting it inside me.

The pain was my tormentor, my solace, my anchor, dragging me back across glass, bleeding and shredded. The inferno of magic charred my vocals, melted my muscles, and seared my veins, and he only urged more into my body, reminding me I was alive. Like dripping water on your tongue when you were perishing in the desert.

Every fiber of my being reacted, consuming him in return with an unrelenting hunger.

Ash's groan hit me like a spiked whip as his invading magic forced each bullet from my gut, reopening the wounds that had tried to heal, more blood spilling out of me in sacrifice like we were part of a ritual, calling upon the gods and goddess.

My blood trailed down my stomach, slipping between my folds, my eyes bursting open with a different cry.

The magic and blood summoned the demented gods, and they demanded our sacrifice. Magic crackled at the edges, overpowering my system and shaking me violently. It was too much.

"Ash…" I whimpered, knowing he would understand. He knew what I needed. What they required of us.

"I got you." There was no fanfare before he pushed his cock inside me, coating himself in the blood dripping from my wound. Acting as a conduit, it sparked the magic already blistering around us. "What the fuck?" he barked, slamming inside me again. My lips parted as he thrust again into me. Pain shook my muscles, but I no longer was the victim of it.

I was the fire.

And even though I felt every lick of the flames, I welcomed it, my hips meeting his as he fucked me deeper into the snow.

"*Mroczny.*" He groaned against my mouth, moving inside me, his magic settling in, scorching my soul as it branded his name inside.

"Oh gods!" The air was ripped from my lungs, bowing my back. His magic had healed me before, but not like this. This time, he was imprinting it on me, making it part of me.

My dweller and obscurer eagerly welcomed him in, feeling him go further than just the physical, penetrating so deeply that a torrent of Latin flew from my lips. Spells I couldn't even identify.

"ASH!" I think I screamed. I didn't know.

Using the energy he was pumping into me, I flipped him under me, riding him with everything I had, branding my magic inside him as well.

"FUCCCKK!!!" His hips bucked up, his hands clasping my hips, pumping me harder up and down his shaft, watching my blood cover his cock, seeping into his skin. Sweeping up a bit of snow, he rubbed at my clit, his other hand wrapping around my neck, pushing another surge of magic into me.

I couldn't cry out or breathe, my vision going black as the magic finally broke into pieces, raining down on us. My body twitched and convulsed as he filled me with his cum. Knotting so tightly around him, he convulsed under me.

"Raven…" he choked out.

My muscles went limp, and I fell over him with a whimper.

"Fuck the gods," he heaved out, his arms wrapping around me, both of us gulping for air.

"I think we just did."

He snorted, kissing my head. We didn't move or speak for a long time, reality melting in like the snow we laid on. An awareness filled me that something had shifted between us once more, and we shared magic… we shared blood.

His heart pounded against my ear, sounding like home. A million threads strung between us, linking us in a way that was no longer refutable.

My dark dweller growled at the idea he was anything but hers, still knotted, like she was making sure he knew who owned him.

I knew no one else was for me. Ever. Even if he walked away, I would follow, and that terrified me. I fell for a man who I thought was my forever, and he broke my heart. Ash wouldn't just break my heart; he would demolish it. I did not like giving anyone that sort of power over me.

"Are you cold?" He rubbed my shivering back, drawing me back to the present. The cold was not why I was shaking.

Looking up, I realized he had taken us to a wooded area close to the square, with paved trails and an out-of-order gondola nearby that went up the mountain. A public park. Anyone could have walked by. Not that it would have stopped us. I seemed to forget everything when I was near Ash.

Like my brother being kidnapped.

"Fuck." I sat up with a jolt, and Ash bit down on his lip, his cock still inside me, a grunt huffing from his nose from my abrupt movement.

Reality barreled into me without slowing down.

We just fucked in the middle of the park after my brother was taken prisoner by the Russian Mafia.

"Oh my gods," I gritted through my teeth, trying to move off him.

Ash hissed, his cum oozing from me as I stood up, yanking up my pants. "I can't believe this."

"Can't believe what?" He followed me up, pulling his own pants up.

"This!" I motioned between us. "Eve just took my brother!" I stressed. "The Russian Mafia has him and they will probably hand him over to Dimitri Kozlov! Or even worse, to Sonya! He's being held prisoner while I'm fucking you in the woods not ten minutes later."

"Raven." He finished buckling his pants. "Ten minutes ago, you were bleeding out and about to die." He nodded at my stomach, which was healing back up, the two shells on the ground in the snow. "Fucking me saved your life."

"Seriously?" I popped an eyebrow with a huff. "You think you're that fucking good?"

"I know I am." He grabbed my arm, pulling me to him. "But that's not what I am saying and you know it, little beak."

I rolled my jaw.

"You're scared and angry."

"Don't—"

"Don't what, Raven? Act like I know you?" He let go of my arm, but only moved closer. "Because I do. You can get as mad as you want, but it doesn't change the fact I probably know you better than anyone else." He leaned over me. "To watch Nikolay shoot you, to not be able to get to you in time…" He rolled his hands into balls, his expression deadly. "I almost lost you. So I don't give a fuck if you're scared or mad. Lash out at me, but I am going nowhere. You understand me?" He waited until I nodded. "What is between us"—he motioned between us—"is fucking terrifying. It scares me too, but there is no running from it. Not ever." He slid his hand through my hair, curling his hand around the back of my neck. "I know you felt what I did, and there is no backing away unscathed now."

"I know." I swallowed, my eyes watering. "I'm sorry."

"Don't ever be sorry." He exhaled, his shoulders lowering at my admission.

"What if something happens to Rook? It will be my fault."

"Coming here was his own choice."

"But he did it for me! And Eve must have my family still believing she's on their side." I wiped quickly at my eyes, anxiety dancing my feet. "I have to find him. We must track him down!"

"Raven." He clutched my arm before I could move. "You can't. They are long gone by now."

"My dweller can track him." I wasn't as good at tracking as my family, especially since he was in a car, the goblin metal cutting him off from me, but I knew the bond to my brother would lead me to him like he'd found me.

"Raven, stop. You are still weak. We need a moment to regroup."

"No! Every moment I waste, he gets further from me. They will hurt him, Ash."

Ash gripped my face, trying to talk reason into me. "There is no way I'm letting *you* get hurt again. We need to come up with a plan."

"This is all my fault. I can't lose my brother…" My voice broke. "If this was your sister? What would you do to keep her alive?"

His spine went straight, and he sucked in sharply, his head bowing in acquiescence. "Okay." He curled his fingers into my head, pulling me into him. "Then we go after him."

"Try to keep up," I told him. "When the beast finds the scent to lock on, nothing else matters."

"You can't lose me." He cupped my cheek. "No matter where you go on this earth. I will follow."

Chapter 18

Ash

The heavy army jeep left deep tracks on the road. My boots barely imprinted over them while running behind Raven, taking us farther out of town. The snow clouds tumbled overhead, snatching away any bit of warmth from the afternoon sun.

She sniffed the air, tracking her brother, moving faster than I could, but I pushed harder to keep up. I didn't like being out of reach. I had watched her almost die. The necessity to protect her was always high before, but now it bordered on obsession.

With every step, I could feel her release coating my cock, knowing my cum pooled in her knickers, and it only increased my volatile emotions. It charged fire through me, a deep, fearful rage I could no longer control. Her blood was inside me, a tattoo under my skin. She *literally* marked my cock as hers.

Watching her being attacked from across the square, not able to reach her, was my worst nightmare, the epitome of hell. It snapped me back to Lukas and Kek, watching their lives being taken, and I was not able to reach them in time. Save them. Experiencing that with Raven had me losing my mind, ready to gut everyone there, whether innocent or guilty, I didn't care. I was ready to litter the streets with bodies.

It made everything very clear. She was mine. And nothing would take her from me.

If they did… Well, for those who thought I had lost my way before, they would find me the embodiment of destruction. The image of death and ruin.

Warwick would have a rival in bending death to its knees.

I was there to watch Warwick and Brexley fall in love, the connection everyone could hear and feel from miles away. To undergo most of my friends finding their mate in the last year, to see the protectiveness coming out when their partner was in danger. I thought I understood, or could at least correlate to Lukas and Kek. Because I loved them. I loved them with everything I was capable of.

At that time.

I got it now. What mate really meant. What it felt like in your bones. It flipped me on my ass and called me its bitch. This level of connection was something I never could have imagined before it happened to me. My feelings for Raven weren't even in my control. They were embedded in my DNA, wound in my very being.

I had doubled down, making sure of it, not even giving her a choice when I sensed what was coming earlier.

I had loved pushing inside her, drenching my dick in her blood, using nature's response to us to heal her, but when I felt something shift, the blood acting as a conduit, I didn't even want to stop it.

Blood rituals were not for the faint of heart. The gods and goddesses were a twisted, perverse bunch. This shouldn't have been on their radar, yet they accepted it anyway. When her blood mixed with my seed, it burrowed our connection into the foundation of the earth.

If there was a second when I thought I could walk away and leave her to her life, that was over.

About twenty minutes out of town, a low rumble came from Raven. Her back curled, blades peeking from her already torn clothes.

"What?" My gaze darted around as we climbed a snowy incline, noting a sign to the First Romanian School Museum. Slowing my footsteps, I peered around, trying to sense any threat.

Why did they bring him here?

Fresh tire tracks drew us up the cobbled lane through an arched stone gate, taking us to an Orthodox church and school. Thick, white stone walls blended into the dwindling hazy daylight. Two army jeeps were parked in front of the school. A single guard stood at the doorway, his rifle set in his hands.

A noise coiled in her throat, a vibrating threat that sounded like death. Her nails extended into claws, her eyes flashing red.

The man was already dead.

A murmur of words rose in a chant, a spell pushing out toward the man. Immediately, I could feel the connection between us, sensing her body being drained. I knew I could have denied it, ignored the tug, but my response was embedded in me now. She needed me. My magic rushed up to help, letting her take whatever she needed from me.

The man dropped his gun, his eyes bugging as he clawed at his head. Raven stepped closer, Latin sliding through her canine teeth.

Red veins in his eyes started to pop, trails of blood dripping from his eyes. His mouth was wrenched open, but no sound could escape.

Her energy weighed heavier on me, a trickle of blood leaking from her nose as she pushed forward. I felt the link between us straining.

"Raven?" I muttered, but she continued, ignoring me, her obscurer locked on its target. "Raven," I said louder, but once again, she did not recede.

The man's mouth opened and closed like a guppy fish, while she spat out more guttural words. The obscurer took claim of its prey, while the dweller snapped at the fence like a feral, starving dog.

My head started to spin, energy being pulled from me and pouring into her, but it wasn't enough. She still grew weaker. "Raven…"

I heard a pop and a snap before his body crumbled to the ground. Gore gushed from his ears, eyes, and nose, his brain melting out of his skull and into the murky snow.

Fuck.

Lethargy washed over me, but I dug my boots deeper into the earth, asking nature for more. Raven's legs bowed, but she didn't fall, her hand gripping my arm for support until she pulled her shoulders back. *"Thank you."* She didn't say it out loud, but I felt it even stronger than if she had. Similar to how roots talk to the rest of the tree, we no longer needed words to communicate.

"Remind me not to piss you off," I whispered. Both of us stepped over the dead body, and I kept my firearm ready while Raven peered inside the open doors of the school. I wanted to give her the only gun we had, but she was her own weapon. I just needed to be her bodyguard, protect her until she could unleash her rage like she just had.

"He's here." She sniffed the air, mumbling more to herself. Anxiety fizzed in my gut, the energy around us feeling off.

Voices lured us past rooms with naked mannequins, frames empty of artwork, and empty book shelves. Anything that could be sold or used had already been taken.

"We are risking everything." Eve's voice came from the back room.

"We made a deal for *her*, not him."

Ice grew up my throat, the man's timbre tapping at the back of my mind.

"Things didn't quite go as planned."

"Clearly," he clipped. "She is not going to be very happy."

"Neither is *Vozhd*." *Supreme leader*. Eve snipped back.

"How do I know this is not a trick? You give me him, while you take her to Dimitri Kozlov."

"It's not a trick," Eve replied. "And I assure you, he is just as powerful."

What the fuck was going on? The mafia worked for Kozlov. Why did it sound like they were plotting behind his back?

"Can he mate with the *Primul*? Carry their offspring? She wanted a breeder. A Druid breeder."

She was Sonya.

"We're not having a problem here, are we?" Nikolay's tone threatened, the sound of guns clicking, other figures moving around the room. "You promised us a lot of money to get you a royal offspring. We did. Now pay up."

"Such a simple task and you can't even do that right." The unknown man's accent hit my ear, pumping my pulse higher.

"Pay or you won't be walking out of here," Nikolay spat.

A cold laugh barely hit the air before it was gone. "You think you scare me? You are nothing, Nikolay. I was trained to hunt and kill before you were sperm. There isn't a time I am not a dozen steps ahead of everyone."

"Really?" Nikolay sounded like a thug compared to the coolness of the other man's voice. "Looks like you are surrounded with five guns pointed at your head. You're the one who is behind."

"You think so?" The man's voice went low.

Hair rose on the back of my neck, an unnatural smell invading my nose, but one I recognized. Terror soaked into my muscles, feeling a presence come upon us, whipping me around.

A fist slammed into my gut before I could even react, the sheer force taking me off guard and dropping me to the floor.

Raven's muffled cry filled my ears when someone else came behind her, knowing enough to cover her mouth with a cloth while cuffing her. I sensed the moment her energy was cut off, our connection muffled through the poison.

"Get up." The man who hit me clutched my jacket, hiking me up to my feet with one arm, jabbing his face into mine. It took me a moment to get my bearings, my mind rattled by the impact. When my sight cleared, my stomach sank.

"Joska."

He huffed, his face taking on more and more of a gorilla-like appearance each time I saw him, the human side disappearing, like he finally understood being human had been his weakness the whole time.

Balazs, the one with hyena qualities, held Raven, her wide eyes locked on me, the barrel of the gun pressing into her temple. Samu stood behind them both, his cat teeth bared at me.

"Your girlfriend's brains will be on the floor if you try anything, fairy." Joska sneered at me.

"It isn't me you should be afraid of."

Huffing, he dragged me into the room, where Rook sat in one of the pews. Eve, Nikolay, and other mafia cronies were scattered around the mock classroom, their weapons swinging to us with surprise.

My focus centered on the man in front of the room.

"Baszd meg…" Air caught in my throat. My pulse thrummed in my ears. An ache in my shoulder sprang up as if it still felt the fae bullet he put there over a year and a half ago. My throat bobbed, the shock dissipating quickly to realization.

"Kalaraja." I addressed the Lord of Death, spitting onto the floor. "I should've known."

His pitiless dark eyes stared into mine without an ounce of feeling. So many fae enjoyed the kill, usually someone who deserved it or to save someone they loved. Kalaraja was different. He thrived off torture and torment. He felt no difference in murdering a guilty man or an innocent child. They were the same to him. Cold-blooded and relentless, he worked for the highest bidder. As far as I knew, he had no family, no weakness to pull at. If he did have a mother, he'd probably watch her die without blinking an eye. And he was another one who escaped when Sonya and Iain had.

"Too bad my bullet didn't take you out the first time." He folded his hands in front of him, nonplussed by all the weapons pointing at him. "I will make sure to remedy that today."

Raven thrashed next to me, drawing his attention to her, twisting my gut in knots.

"The princess." Kalaraja's soulless stare made me shiver. "So you are what the fuss is all about?"

Rook grunted behind his gag, his head shaking. He tried to stand, but Nikolay shoved him back down, putting a gun to Rook's head, forcing a cry from his twin.

Kalaraja gave him no heed, his attention completely on Raven. When he took a step, the entire room turned on each other. A stand-off between groups. Yet the Lord of Death did not stop, methodically moving towards Raven. Everything he did felt empty of emotion, of any empathy. He stopped in front of her, his gaze moving over her. I felt Raven's fear, tasted it on my tongue, but she held her chin high under his scrutiny.

"Take them." Kalaraja nodded to Balazs and Samu. The hyena pulled Raven back, while Samu headed for Rook.

"Wait. What is going on?" Nikolay's head bounced between the twins. "The deal was only for one!" He stepped in front of Rook, his gun pointing at Samu.

"That was your mistake." Kalaraja calmly turned to him. "I don't make deals."

I heard the click of Nikolay's pistol.

It was a breath, a millisecond, and Kalaraja yanked a gun from the heavy black cloak he was wearing.

POP! A bullet drove through Nikolay's head, blood and brains bursting out in a spray, dusting Rook and Eve in a red mist. Nikolay's eyes went wide, taking a moment to register he was dead before his body crumbled to the ground.

Eve let out a scream, about to go to her lover, but stopped when Kalaraja's aim focused on her. The other Mafia members weren't so smart, firing at Kalaraja.

POP! POP! POP!

The three men left dropped in sequence, their lives already forgotten by the Lord of Death.

"I told you," Kalaraja said evenly to Eve, like he was enjoying coffee instead of murdering mafia members. "I am always ahead."

Eve gulped, her face staying neutral, but I could see the fear in her eyes. If Nikolay the Bloody, the notorious mafia leader, and his men could be taken out so quickly, so could she.

"Now it's your turn." He turned back to us, leaning into Raven. "Say goodbye, princess."

"NOOOO!" My reaction was explosive, hitting so hard that the trees outside whipped into a frenzy, their branches beating against the roof as I thrashed against Joska. "Don't fucking touch her!"

"You mistake me." Kalaraja smirked. "It's you she's saying goodbye to." My mind hadn't even registered the modification before Joska swiped my feet out from under me, my knees hitting the stone, a gun shoved into the base of my neck.

Raven's garbled cry howled through the room, her dark dweller and obscurer beating at the cage that kept them back. Balazs struggled to keep hold of her. I sensed the push of our bond trying to connect, but it was like looking through glass, her touch just outside my reach.

"I won't miss this time." Kalaraja pressed the hot barrel of his gun between my eyes. Joska's bullet waited to enter the back of my head just in case that one didn't kill me.

"Nooooooo!" A muffled wail sounded against her gag. Raven strained against the metal keeping her crippled, her body bowing as she tried to push beyond it, only draining her powers more.

"*Dziubuś.*" My eyes lifted to hers, my eyes watering. I knew she could read my expression, the apology for not being strong enough, for leaving her like this, the plea for her to live.

"Don't stop fighting. Ever. You live, you hear me? Live a beautiful full life for me," I whispered to her. Her head wagged, tears spilling down her cheeks, a sob racking her chest. "*Kocham cię.*" *I love you.* I said in Polish, switching to Hungarian. "*Ön a lelkem.*" *You are my soul.*

Raven howled, trying to reach for me, her legs giving out on her, forcing Balazs to hold her up.

I grit my teeth, not wanting to leave her, understanding something deep in my core. I had always felt like I let Kek and Lukas down, that I failed them. I deserved to live in hell, to punish myself.

Being on the other side, my life about to end, I realized I was wrong. Love didn't make you want the other to suffer. I didn't want the burden of revenge and anger to hang on Raven like it had me. I wanted her to be happy, even if it meant falling in love with someone else someday.

Keeping my eyes on Raven, telling her all I could without words, I watched her wither and wail, shoving at her captor, trying to get to me. Sound felt far away, but she was what I held on to, her beauty… as I prepared for the darkness to come.

I sensed the bullet leave the chamber.

BOOOOOOOOOM!!

My body went flying into the air, my brain spiraling, trying to understand what was happening. The explosion shook the school's foundation, flipping and rolling everyone like we were dice in a cup. I hit the ground in a brutal roll, slamming into a pew with a choked groan. My head swam with confusion, understanding one thing—I was still alive.

"Raven…" Pain sliced through me, but I pushed myself up, the room still spinning. Dust and debris choked the air, my ears ringing from the blast. "Raven?" I called her name out stronger, crawling through the rubble. Only a few feet away, I saw her body against the wall, blood oozing from her forehead. "Raven!" Glass from the windows cut through my knees, but I felt nothing. I gripped her face, turning her to me, her body limp. "Baby…" I ripped down the gag, wiping the glass and plaster off her skin. "Please, wake up." Relief exhaled through me when her lids blinked open, her blurry eyes staring up at me.

"Ash," she croaked, tears filling her eyes, her hands trying to reach up to touch my face, but her heavy cuffs dropped them back down again. "You're alive."

"Yeah." I pressed my forehead to hers, needing a moment to feel her warmth, bask in her life. "I'm here."

Voices and commotion shuffled around us in the hazy chamber; it wouldn't be long before they came for us again.

Booooommm!

Another explosion shook the ground like an aftershock, sounding like a car exploding in front of the school, pulling the focus outside. Sonya's men rushed for the door.

It seemed like it was meant to lure them out. To get them outside.

"Oh. Holy. Fuck," I muttered. There was no way. Yet the nagging sensation tugged at me. "A distraction," I whispered to myself.

"What?"

"We need to get out of here." I stood up. "Can you stand?"

"I think so." She nodded. "Where's my brother?" She gripped my arm as I pulled her to her feet, the feel of the goblin metal cuffing her soaking into my skin. "We need to find him!"

I squinted through the haze, trying to find the prince, tripping over a dead body.

Nikolay the Bloody lay under my boot. Half human/half Vampir, a feared top solider of the Russian mafia, and he was taken out in seconds by the Lord of Death.

I stopped short. Bloody locks of blonde hair spilled from under debris next to Nikolay.

Eve.

Raven paused, seeing Eve's noticeable hair, her jaw locking.

"Raven." I said her name softly, not sure what I was going to say beyond that. *I'm sorry* felt strange after all Eve had done, but no matter what, Eve had once been her friend, someone in her life who she trusted.

Raven quickly hid the pain, swallowing back the hurt and betrayal, and turned away from her.

"Rook?" Raven called out for her brother. "Rook?" We scoured through the remains, not finding her twin among the deceased on the floor.

POP! POP!

Gunfire went off outside, voices barking and yelling, reconfirming someone new had joined the discord. My gut sparked with understanding, an instinct drawing me out the front doors.

The back end of the museum was crumbling, and one of the jeeps was on fire, the heat of the flames scorching my cheeks, the smell of gas watering my nose. A jumble of forms made their way toward the surviving jeep, shooting toward the back of the museum at the new assailants.

Joska and Samu shoved Rook into the back of the army truck, his body limp and unconscious, as Balazs climbed into the driver's seat, Kalaraja slipping into the passenger side.

"No!" Raven hobbled down the steps, the jeep tearing away. "Nooo!" She tried to run after them.

"Raven!" I grabbed her, pulling her back into my arms as steady gunfire came from behind me, pinging off the bumper. The jeep squealed around the corner, disappearing.

A whimper cracked her chest, devastation sinking her into my embrace. The jeep engine drifted farther away, giving over to the sound of crackling fire and melting snow.

The back of my neck prickled with awareness, sensing people behind me.

"This reminds me of our time in Belarus." A deep voice jarred my head to the side. A massive figure stepped around the burning car. "So once again, you're welcome, motherfucker."

I stared, my brain registering the two figures moving in closer, yet my mind still felt like it was hallucinating.

"Fuck the gods," I whispered hoarsely, my gaze jumping from the man and woman, Opie and Bitzy perched on the woman's shoulder.

"Funny, that's what he wants me to call him at night." The dark-haired woman lowered her weapon.

"I don't need you to call me a god, princess," he responded, his arms folding. "You're already fucking a legend."

They were not a mirage.

The Wolf and the Grey were here.

Warwick and Brexley had found me.

Chapter 19

Ash

We raced through the chilly late morning air, the roar of engines filling the space between the two motorcycles. We ventured back to Brașov on the bikes Warwick and Brexley had stolen on their journey here.

The shock of them being here had me staring over at them every few minutes, but we did not dare to stop and chat until we were safe.

After hiding the motorcycles in an alley, my hand went to Raven's lower back, navigating her into the brothel. Warwick and Brexley's heavy presence behind us bristled my spine as we jogged up the stairs, the tension crackling like electricity.

Workers were stirring people awake, getting them up to repeat the night they had before, an endless stream of gambling, drug, and sex with as many clients as they could. All things I used to indulge in on a daily basis.

Now, I didn't care to gamble, I no longer craved drugs, and the only thing I wanted was to screw all night was Raven. When did that change? I don't know, though I felt like I got steamrolled by something I saw coming for miles, never getting out of the way, and now wondering how I got run over.

"Go get cleaned up. I'll find you food and some clothes," I muttered in Raven's ear, leading her into the bathroom. She was still weak from the goblin metal, covered in blood, guts, dirt, and my semen.

Opie was able to get the cuffs off her, but her energy was low, and the guilt and fear she felt for losing her brother again screamed silently inside her. I could feel it, her emotion ripping through her, dragging her legs with every step.

"I don't want to leave you." She flicked her eyes back to the pair waiting for me in the hallway with concern.

"I'll be fine." My lips brushed her temple. "Go." I nudged her further into the washroom.

She dipped her head, reaching for her torn, bloody sweater. Clearing my throat, I quickly exited before I could say fuck it and join her, trying to postpone the inevitable.

"In there." I nodded to the room, Brexley and Warwick following me in.

Rubbing my head, I closed the door to the room, turning to my best friends. "Leave it to you to always have explosives."

A rumble from Warwick was my only warning before his fist slammed into my face. Pain exploded behind my eye, fire rushing into my cheekbone and mouth. I dropped to the ground with a thud.

Groaning, I reached up for my face. "What the fuck?" I wiped at my lip, red coating my hand.

"Lófasz a seggedbe!" Fuck you! A horse dick into your ass! He stood over me, fury snarling his face. "You disappeared! You left us without a fucking word, not caring how we felt, to be some moron with a hero complex? You deserve far worse!" He looked ready to punch me again, instead he grabbed my arm, yanking me to my feet again, and pulled me into a hug.

Warwick did not show emotion except to the few he allowed in his circle. He was my brother, and no matter how mad we were, he was my family.

Breathing out, I blinked back emotion.

"Fuck you too." I patted his back. My mouth throbbed, but I deserved his wrath.

"Menj a halál faszára!" Go to hell! Go onto Death's dick, he rumbled.

I pulled back, turning to see Brexley glaring at Warwick.

"What?" His brow furrowed.

"I was supposed to hit him!" She threw out her arms, only making Warwick smirk.

"You want to hit me too?" I wiped the blood from the corner of my lip.

"Yes!" she exclaimed. "Fuck! I am so mad at you. Do you know how worried we were about you?"

"Worried?" I snorted, motioning to the menaces on her shoulder. "You sent your little minions to spy on me!"

"Minions?!" Opie exclaimed from her shoulder, but nobody took heed. "How dare you, tree—"

"Because you cut us off," she exclaimed.

"I-I couldn't be around… anyone." I swallowed roughly. "It was too much."

"I get that, Ash." She stepped up to me, taking my hand. "But we love you and the thought of anything happening to you?" She punched at my arm with more strength than I'd expected.

"Ow." I rubbed my bicep.

Her mouth wobbled, her eyes filling with tears. "Don't you *ever* do it to me again."

"I won't." I cupped her face, suffering the pangs of hurting her. "I am so sorry." I stared into her eyes, making sure she saw the truth in them.

I *was* sorry. I had been selfish and insensitive, but it was the only way I knew how to deal with my pain.

Brexley was in my arms, squeezing me so tight my bones cracked, as if she wanted to make sure I was real. "You're here. You're all right," she whispered, reconfirming it to herself. "Please don't leave us like that, Ash. We need you. *I* need you."

My throat tightened. The familiarity of her voice, her smell, the feel of her in my arms, cracked something in my chest. I had stayed away because I wasn't strong enough to face them, to see the disappointment in their eyes, but now that my family was here, I realized how much I missed them. Needed them.

I held her for another moment before I pulled away to look at her face. Brexley's onyx hair and black eyes against her pale skin always took me back for a moment. A mix of Russian and Irish, her features were unique and so stunning it could almost make her appear cold and fragile. Until you met her and realized she had the warmest heart and could take down a legion of warriors, resurrect men from the dead, and beckon spirits to her will, all without breaking a sweat.

My gaze went to the figure on her shoulder, my lids lowering. "Snitch."

"They were already here! I just pointed them in the direction they needed." Opie held up his hands while Bitzy flipped me off.

"What do you mean already here?" I stepped away from her.

"Dzsinn contacted Scorpion." Warwick leaned on the windowsill. "Told us where you were."

"Dzsinn." I huffed out his name. "What? Tired of babysitting me and handed me off to you guys?" Now I knew where the genie was headed after he disappeared on us. "Like I can't take care of myself."

"Is he wrong?" Warwick lifted his brow.

"I'm doing just fine." I gritted my teeth.

"Really?" Brexley crackled a dry laugh. "You were about to be killed!"

"Different than any other time, really?" Warwick replied.

"And come to find out, Kalaraja is still alive, along with Joska and Samu," Brexley exclaimed.

They weren't even the worst of it.

"Why didn't you come to us?" She placed her hand on her chest like it hurt.

"I…" I swallowed roughly. "I didn't want to involve you guys."

"Involve us?" Brexley snipped at my words like they offended her. "We are your *family*, Ash. Did you hesitate when *I* needed you last year? Why would you think we wouldn't want to be by your side for this?"

My nose burned with unshed emotion.

"Ash?"

"Because I knew you would!" I yelled, louder than I expected. "That was the problem!"

Brexley's head jarred back, while an icy expression slipped over Warwick's face.

"You came here to die," he said evenly, but I sensed his rage fostering under his skin again. I had known Warwick way too long not to pick up on his every signal.

My silence was their answer.

"Ash…" Brexley deflated, tears welling in her eyes.

"Well, don't worry." I lifted a shoulder, switching my weight, knowing what I needed to confess next. "I don't feel like that anymore." My gaze moved to the door, feeling Raven not too far away.

As if Raven was summoned, sensing the tug on the binds connecting us, the door opened. Her petite frame stepped in, a towel wrapped around her. She came to a halt, her gaze darting to the enormous man with a claw-scythe on his back, to Brexley, then to my freshly bleeding lip, putting the pieces together. I saw the fire flare in her eyes.

"No. Rav—" I reached out, but I was too late. Her teeth snapped, blades pushing out through the towel from her spine as she lunged for Warwick.

"Raven, no!" I grabbed for her as Brexley hopped between her and Warwick. The energy in the space hissed. This would go bad fast. "EVERYONE STOP!" I bellowed, jerking Raven back, putting myself in the middle of the three. I gripped Raven's face, forcing her eyes on me, my voice commanding the dweller to submit. "Back down. They are not our enemy."

Land of Monsters

A growl summoned from her throat, her teeth gnashing at me. "They hurt you."

"Back down," I ordered the dweller. "*Now*."

Her nose wrinkled, but slowly her pupils merged back into green. Her skin shifted back to normal, but her attention continued darting to them, still on guard.

"Calm down, *mroczny*." I leaned my forehead onto hers. "They are my friends. The family I told you about."

She exhaled, her fingers clinging to what was left of her towel. Nudity was not a big deal to any of us, but I still didn't like her feeling vulnerable. Snatching a man's sweatshirt off the table, one of the items Silk left out for us, I pushed it over her head, getting her arms through. The fabric slipped down to the tops of her thighs, at least covering most of her.

"You good?" I muttered to her.

She nodded, her eyebrows furrowing at my split lip.

"I deserved it." I linked my hand with hers, tuning back to my friends.

Brexley and Warwick both stood dumbfounded, their eyes intently watching us.

"What?"

"Holy. Fuck…" Brexley's mouth parted, her gaze locking on Raven. "You've got to be kidding me?" She gaped at me.

I bristled as a sense of shame clenched my chest. Were they thinking I moved on too quickly from Kek and Lukas? Insulting their memory?

"This wasn't… planned. It just…" I kept a hold of her hand.

"Which part?" Warwick's deathly voice rumbled the floor. "Fucking… or *mating* with the princess of the Unified Nations?"

Raven and I went still.

"How do you know?" The urge to put her behind me, even protect her from my family, stepped me forward.

"Which part?" Warwick lifted his chin. "Both are pretty obvious."

"We're not blind, Ash. First, her image is *everywhere*. The entire UFN is looking for her!" Brexley motioned to her. "And second, I've known what the princess looks like since I was eleven. At one time, I knew everything about the royal families. I was tested on it." It was easy to forget that Brexley was once a sort of princess herself. An adopted daughter of the leader of HDF, she grew up in the world of elites and leaders. Schooled in the art of corruption and power.

"Have we met?" Raven stepped even with me, her gaze going over Brexley.

"No." Brexley shook her head. "Istvan was a human leader, a puritan.

But he was never on the level to be visited by the king and queen." She shrugged. "But we have met your father. Your family helped us in our fight against Istvan last year, after the king sent Eli and Ember to kill me."

"What? They tried to kill you?" Raven's mouth dropped open.

"Clearly they didn't."

"Aunt Ember and Uncle Eli don't miss a target. Ever."

"It's a long story."

"And you would've had two fewer relatives if they had fucking touched her," Warwick grumbled to himself.

"Not helping, Farkas."

"Not trying to, Kovacs."

"Ohh, Master Fishy. We've missed you guys." Opie sighed into Brexley, petting her neck.

Chirp!

"You did too!"

Chiiiirrpp!

"What?? Total untruth! I did not miss his weapon of mass destruction!"

Chirp! Chirp!

"And I did not cheat on a grenade launcher with a tree trunk!"

Chirp! Chirp! Chirp!

"You're the one bringing it up! I think it's you who missed the wolf stick!"

Chirpchirpchirpchirp! Middle fingers whirled in the air like lassos.

"Fuck." Warwick rubbed his forehead. "I didn't miss this at all."

"Oh, come on, big bad wolfy. You know you missed us." Opie leaped from Brexley's shoulder to the bed, talking to the big man. "I'll bet your sausage club member got so cold and lonely without us."

"How about you shut the fuck up?" Warwick pinched his nose. "Before I snap your bodies in half."

ChirpChirpChirp! Bitzy flipped him off, her chirps sounding a lot like *fuck you, asshole.*

"I wish everyone would stop promising me a good time and not delivering on it." Opie folded his arms in a huff.

"Sorry to be rude, but can we get back to what's important?" Raven's voice raised. "Like getting my brother back."

"Your brother?" Brexley's eyes widened. "Hold on, the guy they put into the jeep was your brother? Prince Rook Dragen?"

"Yes" Raven nodded her head.

"Holy shit." Brexley started to pace. "Let me get this straight. One of the scariest hired assassins has the prince of the UFN right now?"

"Yes. And all I'm doing is standing here uselessly, while he might be beaten or worse!" Raven moved, as if she was heading for the door.

"*Dziubuś.*" I grabbed her arm. "You can't run in blind. Sonya and Iain are bad, but you don't know how ruthless Kalaraja is. We need a plan."

"I can't just sit here!"

"Then stand!" I countered back. "But you're not going anywhere right now."

"They won't kill him," Brexley interjected. "He's worth too much alive."

"You think it makes this better?" Raven tugged from my grip but didn't move, tears filling her eyes. "Death is the *lucky* option at that place. What they could be doing to him…"

"We will find him. I give you my word." I looked deep into her eyes. "We need to come up with a plan, and we can't do it alone." I ran my knuckles over her cheek. I realized how much I needed my family. They were right, I couldn't do this single-handedly. "Do you trust me?"

She inhaled, nodding.

"We will get him out." I brushed my thumb over her bottom lip.

"The Russian mafia might be off our backs for a moment." She swallowed. "But you know he will send more for me."

"*Basszameg.*" Warwick scrubbed his face, leaning on the windowsill. "You have the Russian mafia after you too?"

"Technically, her." I winked at Raven. "And to be more precise, it's the president of Russia who wants her dead."

Warwick's jaw ground together. "Seriously?"

"He is not our concern right now. Kalaraja just killed Nikolay and his men this morning. It will take President Kozlov time to regroup. We really need to focus on the most pressing issue, and that is *where* they took Rook." I asserted, licking my swollen lip.

"What are you talking about?" Brexley's arms folded, like she was guarding herself from what was coming.

"Kalaraja, Joska, and Samu aren't the only dangerous things she acquired. There are other things she has at the castle that are far scarier." I ran my hand anxiously through my dirty hair. "What did Dzsinn tell you?"

"He only spoke to Scorpion," Brexley answered. "He said he knew where you were. You had found Sonya and Iain and were going to get yourself killed. Scorpion said he gave him very little information. It was more a courtesy thing."

I couldn't even be mad that Dzsinn considered my life only a courtesy warning. He didn't find anything outside of his deals worth his time. No doubt he was hoping I would get his family's stone back from Sonya, so he needed me alive.

"You probably need to sit down." I tipped my head at Brexley and Warwick. My stomach rolled, knowing the horrors they had been through, and I was about to tell them it was far worse than they ever imagined. "We have a lot to catch up on."

Chirp! Chirp!

Opie nodded. "Bitzy says we're gonna need *a lot of* mushrooms for this."

Brexley wandered the small space in front of where Warwick sat, her head in her hands, trying to process what I had told them. The sun was far below the horizon, firebulbs dimly lighting the room, the music from below becoming louder, along with the voices in the brothel.

I slumped on the edge of the bed, my adrenaline long worn off, the craziness of the day bearing weight on my bones. I craved food, a shower, and to fuck Raven until we passed out.

"You're telling me the *Primul* are Dr. Rapava's old experiments?" Brexley exclaimed, her head shaking in rebuttal. "As in the man Istvan modeled everything after. The original test subjects?" She opened her arms. "How is that possible?"

"Weren't they all destroyed when he was killed decades ago?" Warwick hitched off the sill, running his hand over his head.

"No." Raven twitched around in my peripheral, antsy to get out of this room, her beast prowling the wall. The more anxiety I could feel pumping off her, the calmer I tried to be, letting her absorb my tranquility. "It was kept hush-hush, but some of them escaped."

"And you know this how?" Warwick's voice cut like a knife.

"Because Aunt Zoey is the seer some of them were created from when she worked for Rapava. He stole her eggs to produce these things. Zoey was the one who killed Rapava."

The entire room stared at Raven.

"I'm sorry... what?" Brexley stared at Raven.

"Long story short, Aunt Zoey was one of his first lab experiments. A baby created in the laboratory. A generated seer. He wanted to create humans who could see through fae glamour and hunt them. She was manipulated and tricked, working for him until she discovered the truth. Then they hunted her. She became even more unique when she took on

Uncle Ryker's powers. So Rapava harvested her eggs and used them to create a superhuman-fae type."

"Gods." A pained expression traveled over Brexley.

"Not far off what Markos was trying to do." Warwick moved next to his mate.

"Before I was born, there was a battle for Uncle Lars's throne. These creatures were brought in to fight my family. It was found if they bred with women, it was easier than trying to recreate them in a lab. But only a few of the children made it, and almost all the women died. They realized they needed to use a lot of human women to dispose of, or Druid women."

My lids closed, bile coming up my throat, realizing how important they thought Raven would be to them. She would survive, produce children from them and not die in childbirth, becoming the perfect birther of monsters. Except she wouldn't end up conceiving their spawn and would be killed for it.

"The *Primul*, or whatever they call themselves, have been living unnoticed for almost thirty years?" Brexley flicked back her black hair. "How?"

"Think how long fae were hiding in plain sight." I shrugged, listened to clients below entering the brothel, the night creeping in quickly.

"They are highly intelligent, adaptable, and almost impossible to kill," Raven said.

"Same with Istvan's experiments." Brexley leaned back into Warwick, like she needed to feel him. "And now Sonya is making more," she whispered. "I thought we destroyed it. Thought it was over. What was the point of all that loss and pain if Sonya is just going to do the same?"

"Even if the formula was destroyed, too many have survived to use as a baseline." The images of all those people in the tubes, like Iacob, or being forced to mate, like Celeste, Viorica, and her cousin. I would not leave them there to die.

"Wait." I paused, a thorn in my thoughts. "It wasn't just human women down there they were mating with. They are using fae women too." I peered at everyone in confusion. "Why would they be using fae women if most are protected by a birth control potion"

The room went quiet, the question buffering through us all with no response.

"I don't know." Raven bit down on her lip. "Maybe they have the counter remedy or maybe their sperm is superstrength or something?"

"If it was, wouldn't there be a lot more of them running around by now?" Brexley replied, falling further into Warwick, her hand going to her face. "I can't go through this again."

I felt guilty, knowing I wasn't there for her after the battle. She and Warwick endured so much psychological damage, being subjected to Istvan's sick experiments themselves, including those linking Caden and Warwick. Imagine having to take the life of a man who, at one time, had been a father figure to you. Brexley was the one to step up and kill him so Caden wouldn't have to.

I was too busy with my own trauma to be there for her or any of them.

"Kovacs." Warwick's tone was deep and intimate, gaining her attention. He gripped her chin, turning her to look at him. "We'll handle this. Just like we did last time." Energy prickled around me like magic channeling between tree roots, the auras slinking against my skin. Their connection went beyond mates, forged in the bones of blood and death, cementing their souls together on another plane. Their spirits could talk and touch without them even being in the same place.

Being a nature fairy, I could always sense their connection throbbing the earth, their orgasms singing through the ether, but I had never felt it so acutely. It vibrated the threads between me and Raven, dancing along my cock.

A growl rumbled from Raven and I knew she could feel it too.

"Could you guys stop?" I gritted my teeth, adjusting myself.

"You really have room to talk?" Brexley gestured between us and then motioned out the window. "Thinking the twisted-up trees right outside aren't a coincidence."

"No." I held my chin high, waiting for their disappointment or disapproval. Brex and Warwick were the first to know about us, and it felt like I was dragging a rake over Kek and Lukas's graves. But the judgment didn't come.

A smile hitched Brexley's mouth as she peered between us. "Never thought I'd see the day." *You and me both.* "So, mates, huh?" Her grin widened.

"Yeah." I swallowed but kept my voice strong and sure.

"I may call mine princess, but yours actually is." Warwick smirked. "You are so fucked."

"Tell me about it," I grumbled, shooting a look at Raven, whose mouth was pursed with impatience.

"Every moment we waste here, my brother is in hell," she reminded us.

"Okay." Brexley nodded, clasping her hands together. "We need a plan to find where they're keeping the prince."

"We already know that," I broke in. "Sonya's base is Castle Bran."

"Bran Castle?" Brexley lifted her brows. "As in Dracula's castle? She's creating monsters in a castle infamous for its monsters?"

"The irony is not lost." I huffed. "She's not one for subtlety."

"What she had there... what they are doing." My attention went back to Raven, the hot sickness recalling what those monsters were doing to the women. What they almost did to Raven.

Raw fear and anger shot me to my feet, and I imagined if I'd been there just a few minutes later. Raven sensed my thoughts, her hand reaching for mine, gripping it with assurance she was okay.

"So, what's our plan to get the prince out safely?" Brexley asked. "While taking out Sonya, Iain, Kalaraja, Joska, Samu, and the impossible-to-kill *Primul*, plus saving everyone inside, and trying not to make this an international declaration of war."

"Yes, and..." I cringed, already knowing the response. "You can't forget killing Nyx as well."

"Nyx?" Brexley did not fail, her shriek filling the room. "She's with them?"

"That bitch is still alive?" Warwick snarled.

"And really hates all of us."

"Fuck." Warwick pinched his nose. "She's like a fucking cat with nine lives. She won't fucking die. You really thought you could do this on your own?" He glared at the door like it insulted him, like he sensed something coming.

"Good thing we brought back up." Brex winked.

The door cracked open, and figures spilled into the room. My instinct to protect Raven had me stepping in front, ready to fight, until I noted their faces. My fear turned to disbelief.

Five people squeezed into the space, turning to me.

"*Ó, hogy baszd meg egy talicska apró majom!*" *Oh, may a wheelbarrow of small monkeys fuck it.* A petite woman pushed through the tall physiques, her white-blonde hair pulled back in her signature ponytail. "Either I punch you or hug you. Pick one, fairy."

"Birdie." I opened my arms, and she barreled into me, her tiny frame deceivingly strong.

My heart clenched as I peered over at the rest of my friends: Scorpion, Hanna, Caden, and Wesley.

I should've known.

I shot a grin at Raven to let her know this was good. My family would never let me do this alone.

Chapter 20

Raven

Nails dug into my palms, my nose twitching and spine burning as blades prickled inside the bones. It wasn't only the need to pull the white-blonde girl away from Ash, my dweller growling with protectiveness. It was the other darker blonde woman standing towards the back who had my dweller ready to attack.

Her scent was wrong. Unnatural. Not fae or human. She smelled like Joska and Samu.

Her eyes shifted to me as if she sensed my predatory thoughts, her pupils slivering. Wild cat-like features shifted over her pretty face, her teeth showing as a low hiss pushed through her lips, drawing the attention of the gorgeous, heavily tattooed man next to her. His gaze bounced between us as another snarl showed off her pointed teeth.

I stepped forward, bearing mine. Ash's arm was instantly tugging me back as she lurched.

"Whoa, little viper." The tattooed man pulled her into his arms, whispering something in her ear. She instantly quietened, but her glare stayed on me.

"Calm down, *mroczny*," Ash muttered into mine, tugging me further into his warm body.

"She's one of them," I snarled.

"I am *not* one of *them*." Her lips curled, spitting out *them* as an insult, forcing the man to hold her tighter.

"Istvan gave Hanna drugs, which changed her without her knowledge," Ash spoke in my ear. "She is family. One of us. So back down."

Grief flickered so quickly over the woman's face I almost missed it, but it was enough to make me realize what she had become was painful to her. It was not her choice. Taking a breath, I eased into Ash, the dweller subsiding, which was not easy for me to do normally. No one else seemed to fire up and subdue the beast like him.

With the threat of a fight abating, the room's silence altered, growing increasingly thicker, eyes no longer going between Hanna and me, but between me and Ash.

Surprise. Curiosity. Then shock.

"Holy shit." The tiny blonde he called Birdie slapped a hand over her mouth. Dressed in all black, her eyes heavily lined, her lips red, she was a cross between an angel and some badass ninja. She stood in front of a tall, well-built man with brown hair and eyes. He looked nothing like Warwick visually, but there was something about them which made them seem related. "I'm in utter shock. And that *never* happens to me."

Ash shifted on his feet under their scrutiny, his grip dropping from me, stepping away. Hurt instantly rose to my cheeks, like he might be embarrassed or ashamed of me. I understood this was probably hard for him. He left his friends, mourning his lovers. Devastated over their deaths, full of revenge and hate, and now only a month later…

There was me.

Struggling to swallow, I drew up my walls, my chin rising, used to being aloof and composed under all circumstances.

Ash stepped to my side, his fingers lancing with mine, jerking my head to him.

"This is Raven." He squeezed my hand, his green eyes catching mine for a moment. "My mate."

I inhaled sharply along with the room, their eyes widening, eyebrows lifting.

"Raven, this is my family." He nodded to them. "Birdie, Caden, Scorpion, Hanna, Wesley, and you've already met Warwick and Brexley."

"Hi," I greeted, my gaze shifting over all of them.

"Ummm… hello? Didn't you forget someone?" Opie protested from the table where he had been busy pretending not to organize everything.

"Oh, right." Ash dipped his head. "I can't forget Kitty, Rosie, and Killian."

Chirpchirpchirpchirp! Bitzy waved her middle finger in the air. *Chirrrrp!* She added the other, sticking it high up.

Brexley snorted. "I'm not sure how deep you should sleep tonight."

A name on his list finally triggered in my mind.

"Wait. Killian?" I repeated the name. "You mean former fae leader, now President Killian?"

Ash coyly grinned. "I have friends in high places."

"So do I, fairy boy." I grinned back at him, getting lost in his heated gaze.

"Yeah, you probably win."

"You're fucking kidding me." Caden peered around, wondering why no one else was freaking out. "Do you not know who she is?"

"No. Am I supposed to?" Wesley's gaze went over me, trying to figure it out.

"Caden," Ash warned.

"She's the princess of the Unified Nations!" Caden's hand wiggled at me, and he glanced over at Brexley for backup.

"What?" Hanna stopped, her head snapping to me, really taking me in. "Oh my gods, you are."

"Shut the fuck up." Birdie scanned the faces of everyone, realizing it was not a joke. "Wait. You're really the princess?" She paused, seeing my head bow and my cheeks redden. "*Megbasz*... should I bow or curtsy or some shit?"

"No." A small laugh sprouted from me.

"Good, because there is only one I go that low for." She elbowed Caden. He shook his head with a sigh, but a smile hinted at his lips.

I instantly liked Birdie. She was so angelic looking but gave off "I will fuck you up and not give a fuck" vibes. All my life I was treated with kid gloves, being so formal, afraid to step out of line. It's why I kept my friend circle close, only letting a few in. It was nice just being treated like an ordinary girl.

"*Te geci*," Scorpion scoffed, stepping up to Ash first, holding out his hand. The man was intimidating, covered in tattoos and piercings, but had a sexy bad-boy thing about him. He dipped his head between us, like he approved. "They'd be happy for you," he said quietly. Ash took his hand, bobbing his head, his throat swallowing.

"And welcome to the club." Scorpion snickered, his gaze sliding back to Hanna. "Expect to never win an argument again."

"Yeah, Warwick already warned me." Ash's shoulders eased, letting go of Scorpion's palm.

"Sorry, this is exciting and all, but we have bigger issues to deal with." Brexley took hold of the room, all attention going to her. She held a power I had never felt before, something you couldn't help but be drawn to, a magic that overflowed the room.

"Bigger than the missing UFN princess being here mated to Ash? Do you know the power of her mother and uncle?" Caden stressed. "What they'd do to us if anything happened to her?"

"Yes, but they'll be even more pissed if we let anything happen to her and the *prince* of the UFN."

"What?" Wesley sputtered.

"Kalaraja captured him earlier today. Well, the Russian mafia took him first, but traded him to Kalaraja," Ash explained.

"Kalaraja is still alive?" Hanna gaped.

"Yes, and working for Sonya."

"What?" Scorpion's gaze went to Brexley. "You didn't share that little nugget with me?"

"We found out a little before you guys walked in, and you were blocking me," Brexley shot back.

"I had to concentrate." Scorpion frowned. "This place is crawling with military. And I have a history here."

"Like we don't?" Birdie motioned between her and Wesley. "Remember, I was the one you sent in to infiltrate the army and steal the general's top-secret codes. After I fucked him and his son... in the wife's bed." Birdie laughed, looking wistfully in the distance. "Good times."

"Excuse me?" Caden folded his arms.

"What? Oh, don't worry, babe. I didn't fuck them together in her bed." She coughed. "That night."

Caden placed his head in his hand, breathing slowly, like he was trying to regain his patience.

"Can we focus?" My own impatience snapped in the air. "Time is ticking. Every moment we stand here, she could be hurting my brother." I tucked my hair behind my ear, the room turning to me. I was used to leading, having all eyes on me, giving grand speeches and boxed quotes to reporters, but this was different.

This was for life and death.

"And it's not just the prince," Ash said. "Sonya has villagers, human, fae... innocent people who only want a safe life for themselves and their children." He stood strong next to me. "She is using them as test subjects and vessels. What she has down there—"

"You will never get past them." A monotone voice came from the doorway, jolting us with a crack. We all reacted instantly to the three hooded figures. Most grabbed for their weapons while blades shot from my back, a growl on my lips, my legs ready to spring into an attack.

"Stop." One of them lowered his hood, his blank face having no reaction to the forces that bounced in the room.

"Dzsinn," Ash huffed out, shoulders sagging, realizing why none of us heard him creep up on us and enter the room. "Fuck. You want to get shot?"

"None of you are fast enough," he responded blandly.

"Fuckin' genies," Scorpion muttered, lowering his gun, though my spine still prickled with warning. There was a smell I recognized, a warning tugging in my gut.

"Sonya's army, the monsters she has hidden in the depths of that castle. You cannot win against them," Dzsinn stated.

"So you brought us here to tell us we have no chance?" Scorpion's forehead lined with irritation.

"She also has ten times the soldiers you have here."

"I'll take those odds," Warwick growled, his chest puffing up.

"Me too." Caden's tone almost mimicked Warwick's, their mannerisms so alike.

"Then you'll all die," the genie replied with no emotion. "Unless you have help."

"Help from who?" Brexley stood beside Warwick, her arms crossed over her chest. "Killian can't assist us, or it's a declaration of war."

"But I can." A familiar accented voice came from behind Dzsinn, the two other covered figures veiled in Dzsinn's energy. They stepped forward, lowering their hoods.

Terror cut through the room and daggered into my lungs. Fear burned fire into my veins, springing the dweller's defense. A growl rose from my throat, my teeth snapping at the man standing only feet from me.

The man whose vengeance was to bury me in pieces—like his son.

Dimitri Kozlov. The leader of Russia.

Everyone responded to the threat, pointing their guns at the new additions, their confusion and surprise filling the air after realizing who he was.

And next to him was… Eve.

The turncoat I thought we left dead back in the museum. But here she stood, next to her *Vozhd*. Healed, healthy, and the reason my brother was in Sonya's hands.

"Bitch." My dweller pitched forward, Latin spilling from my lips.

"Raven!" Ash grabbed for me, my body flinging toward her.

"Stop!" Dzsinn held up his hand. "That is not necessary."

"That's where you are wrong," I growled. "It's a necessity." I tried to push out of Ash's arms.

"*Mroczny*," he snapped in my ear, turning to Dzsinn. "Why the fuck did you bring them here?" None of us bothered to ask how he knew Kozlov; Dzsinn had connections everywhere in the world. But to have the actual leader and not his proxy was jarring.

"He is not here to hurt you." He looked between me and the two behind him. "Nor will she."

"Bullshit," Ash spat, still holding me tight. "He's been after Raven from the start. He's the reason she had to go on the run. He wants her dead. And Eve is why Sonya has Rook. She may be his proxy, but it's personal to her."

Eve lifted her chin, glowering back, but stayed silent.

"True," Kozlov's cool voice replied. "I do want vengeance for my son." He narrowed his gaze at me. "Alexsei was my only son. My heir." His dark brown eyes pierced mine with deep hatred. It swirled inside his pupils, coating his skin, but his expression stayed impassive. "And she took him from me. Brutally. And what did the queen and king do? Sent her off to university." His teeth clenched. "So yes, I wanted her dead. Wanted Queen Kennedy to feel the pain like I did."

Images of Alexsei's face sprang to mind, bits and pieces of that hazy night before I woke up covered in blood, bone, and flesh. His glossed-over eyes stared blankly at the ceiling, his throat torn out.

Could I blame him for hating me? Wanting me to pay the price of his pain?

My dweller faded back, the grief and guilt of what I did making my molars clench together. Holding a sob in my chest, I stayed on guard, my disdain narrowing on the woman behind him.

"But for my country and my people, my son's revenge will have to wait." Dimitri returned his attention to the room. "My country has always come first."

"What are you talking about?" Ash demanded. "You're in bed with Sonya. We're the ones who need to protect our country from you."

Kozlov shifted on his feet. "Sonya has gotten some of my government officials to turn on me."

"That is a *you* problem." Warwick held his clawed war hammer in his hand, the only one who didn't bother with a gun.

"She's promised them money and higher positions under her."

"Ah…" Scorpion huffed. "They start going against you and you lose your position as leader."

"I lose my country." He held his chin up high.

"I've been to your country. That might not be a bad thing." Warwick tucked his weapon back into its halter, clearly not worried about Kozlov.

"Didn't you see what she tried to do to *our* country not too long ago?" Ash nodded to his fellow family. "Don't you realize the snake you worked with to get more power would eventually turn on you? Isn't there a name for that game? Oh, right… Russian Roulette. You lost at your own game." Ash still hadn't lowered his weapon, his glare steady on Dimitri and Eve. "Not sure why you thought coming to us was a good idea. We will gladly let you drown."

Kozlov raised his chin. "Our common interest is that we all need Sonya dead, including the UFN and Hungary. Working together is the only way to do that. I have the troops, the numbers with which to fight her." His attention drifted to me again. "And you owe me. You owe me everything."

"The hell she doe—"

"Yes." I cut Ash off.

"What?" His head swung to me, the middle of his forehead lined. "No. He'll kill you the first chance he gets. He's no better than Sonya."

"Ash." I touched his arm, lowering it. My feelings were right there for him to experience, to understand why I had to do this. It would never take away what happened that night. I stole his son's life. I could never be forgiven, nor could I bring him back, but at least this was in my power.

"*Dziubuś,*" he murmured, agony crossing his expression, yet he lowered his gun with an exhale. "Fine, but if he or she touches you." He pointed from Kozlov to Eve, flipping his attention to them. "You make any move toward her, and I will gut you where you stand. Not even Brexley will be able to bring your ghost back from the dead. Do you both understand me?"

"Fuck you," Eve snapped, stepping forward, but Dimitri's arm blocked her. Abhorrence flashed in Kozlov's eyes, his body vibrating with sheer loathing of me, wanting nothing more than to slay me right here, but he dipped his head in agreement.

"Yes."

"Does she?" Ash flicked his chin to Eve.

"She will not touch her. I give you my word."

The room was silent with the palpable paper-thin deal.

"Am I the only one still wanting to know why the fuck the president of Russia is here?" Birdie finally spoke, her long blonde ponytail flipping around as she bluntly asked. "Is this the twilight zone?"

"I have no one I can trust in my government." Kozlov's jaw clenched like it was a struggle to admit this.

"And you trust her?" Ash retaliated. "She turned on you and was working with Sonya! Sonya's men may have killed the rest of them, but she turned against you too. Cut a deal for themselves with her instead."

Kozlov had no response to the one who betrayed him, his expression perfectly even. But then a glint of something passed over his lips.

"You think Sonya had them killed?" His tone was subtle, but it held a derisiveness. Barely a ghost of a response humored Kozlov lips, so subtle you'd have to know him to see it. It was the exact expression Uncle Lars got when he held all the cards, his opponent having no idea they were the mouse, not the cat.

"Yes. Kalaraja killed them. I saw it happen." Ash's conviction started to ebb, his mind probably going the same direction as mine. He watched Kozlov and Eve, how relaxed they were. "Fuck," he expelled. "Kalaraja works for you."

"I doubt Kalaraja works for anyone," he responded.

"He owed me a favor," Dzsinn said. "I needed him in a position to help us."

"I sensed Nikolay's allegiance was waning." Kozlov clasped his hands. "But Eve confirmed what I already detected. I do not let disloyalty slide."

"It sounds on par for Russia," Warwick muttered.

"You'd be a fool to think Kalaraja is on your side," Brexley snarled, her muscles tense, like she knew this Kalaraja personally. "That he won't turn on you if he has the chance."

"Ms. Kovacs," Kozlov said her name with full authority, knowing exactly who she was, which startled me. "Istvan may have dealt more with the human Russian ambassador than me." His snotty tone suggested he thought far less of humans. "Nevertheless, I knew everything that went on. I know Kalaraja was employed by your ward. Markos's greed and hunger for more power were always going to be his downfall."

"Funny to be saying that while standing here, asking us for help because you are losing hold of your country because of your need for power," Brexley replied contemptuously, her sharp energy even making me shift on my feet. I was a lethal killer, but I suspected she'd give me a run for my money.

"Putting all our personal issues to the side," I intervened. The need to reach my brother glittered with a slight hope. "Is this Kalaraja on the inside? Can you trust him?"

"I never trust anyone fully," Dzsinn answered. "But yes. He owes me."

"Owes you?" Warwick asked.

"We have a past. And he used a favor from me."

"Who doesn't?" Brexley scoffed. "I have a past with him too. Doesn't mean I trust him or I won't gut him the first chance I get."

"Let me ask again. Do you trust him enough to get us in?" I asked.

"Yes."

"Wait." Brexley jolted, her head already wagging. "You want to align with someone who's been trying to kill us?"

"To be fair, Kovacs. A lot of people have tried to kill us." Warwick leaned into her, his eyes glinting with mischief. "And really, he's been trying to kill *you*. We just got in the way."

"Makes it so much better."

"I don't like this either." Ash shook his head, his eyes meeting mine for a moment, understanding how badly I needed this. "But if Raven is willing to overlook these two trying to kill her, I think we can put Kalaraja to the side right now. Not like we have a lot of options. Guaranteed, Sonya has doubled her security since I got in last time."

"She has doubled the men and spells and has the *Primul* hunting the forest for intruders." Dzsinn confirmed Ash's theory. "There is no way in anymore unless you have someone on the inside."

"You have the insider now. Why don't you just go in with your army?" Scorpion frowned.

"Because." Kozlov leaned back on his heels. "The soldiers might be good in numbers for a battle, but I understand I need more than that. She can't be killed easily, and the *Primul* are even harder. Nothing normal soldiers can go up against. I need power like yours." His focus went around the group, singling Brexley and Warwick out more than others. "Need to get close to her to get her out."

"Then that makes *you* the perfect Trojan horse." Brexley's mouth curved. "And we are the surprise inside."

My mouth parted at the understanding of Brexley's idea.

"She still believes you are an ally, right?" I addressed Kozlov.

"Yes."

"Then you are the perfect person to get us to the gates."

Dimitri's mouth pinched, his head dipping in understanding.

"I will let her know I am visiting." Kozlov looked around. "What is your plan after that? Her security will check the car I come in for weapons and any threats to her. You won't be able to hide in the trunk."

"She'd never expect you to come without personal guards." Caden folded his arms. "Father didn't go anywhere without a handful."

"And if they figure out you are not my normal guards?" Kozlov eyed him. "You don't exactly blend."

"We kill them." Warwick shrugged.

Ash rolled his eyes. "We need a better strategy than that."

"I will spell them." I licked my lips. "I can control them."

"Control them?" Hanna blinked at me. "Like mind control? Can a Druid do that sort of magic?"

"I'm not a normal Druid." I swallowed, fear bubbling up at exposing what I was. I had been hiding it from people for so long, it felt wrong to tell people who I didn't really know. I pushed through the terror, straightening my spine. "I am an obscurer."

The silence clouded the room, reeking of dread and shock.

"What?" Caden's mouth parted. "Obscurer? I heard you were half dark dweller and half Druid?"

"My brother is." I swallowed nervously. "I am not normal…" Only three people in this room knew I was not right. And one had lost his son because of me.

Dimitri's hands balled up, and I could tell it was taking everything in him not to come for me. My eyes lowered, knowing I'd deserve it.

"My brother turned out the typical Druid/dark dweller. I did not."

"I love that you think *it's* normal," Birdie sputtered.

"Compared to me, he is." I cleared my throat. "I will handle the soldiers if something happens." I owed Kozlov that much.

"No." Ash turned me to him. "Using those powers hurts you."

"Like you said, we don't have a lot of options." I curled my finger around his. "I can do it. I have you to keep me in check."

I am doing it. You're either with me or you're not, I said in my head.

His head bowed, and I knew somehow he heard me.

"*I am* fucked," he muttered under his breath and turned back to his friends. "I want you all to understand what you are getting into. What is truly ahead. This is my fight, my vengeance, that has led you here. I don't want to see anything happen to any of you because of me. So as much as I appreciate you coming…"

"Who the fuck are you talking to?" Scorpion peered around like there were other people in the room. "Because it certainly can't be us."

"Right?" Wesley snorted. "It's like he doesn't know us at all."

"Ash." Brexley tilted her head. "We're family. It's why we were so upset when you left. Your fight is *our* fight."

"Plus, I'll get cranky if I don't get to hurt someone soon." Birdie folded her arms.

"By the noises you were making last night, it sure sounded like one of you was being hurt." Wesley nodded at Caden and Birdie.

"That's fun pain." She winked back at Wes.

"I don't think you realize what you're getting into." Ash rubbed the back of his neck. "This is different than last time."

"You're not doing this without us," Brexley stated. "We're a package deal. Can't get rid of us."

"Now we sound like chlamydia," Hanna snorted.

"Same difference." Birdie shrugged.

Ash took a breath, pressing his arm into me, a calmness soothing over him with his family around. "First we need to get Kozlov's troops here without being noticed by border crossing."

"Leave it to me." Dzsinn dipped his head. "I know some people. Give me two days."

"All right, then we need more weapons, and a concept besides a Trojan horse."

"Why?" Caden muttered. "Like any of our plans don't go to shit in the first five minutes anyway."

"He has a point," Brexley replied dryly.

"I need new friends." Ash palmed his face, chuckling under his breath.

"Ummm… excuse me, tree trunk." A huffed voice came from the table. Opie stood with his hands on his hips. Bitzy swayed next to him, her little fingers waving happily into the air, high as a kite. She somehow found the stash of mushrooms Ash was trying to hide from her. "You forgot the most crucial people in the plan!"

"Let me guess, you think that's you?" Warwick rolled his eyes.

"Of course!" Opie held up his hands. "It's why we train these so much." He wiggled his fingers, Bitzy copying him, but then got distracted by the air. "So we can stick them in the tightest, darkest holes and create ecstasy magic!"

"You mean exemplary?" Brex's brow lifted.

"I said what I said."

Chapter 21

Ash

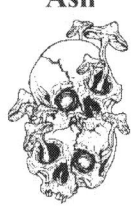

The stolen cars rolled up the potholed lane, the moon glinting down on the castle, which loomed over the land. Wisps of fog clung to the base in the cold, cloudless night, causing the small fortress to dominate the skyline and draw you to the castle. Even though Stoker never set foot in Romania, the castle's magic trapped him in its lure, where myth and truth were so convoluted, there was no separating one from the other. His story was as much a part of magic as the fae, or the blood thirsty monsters who truly lay inside the walls.

I shifted in my seat, the Russian officer's uniform I wore was tight around my muscular thighs, pinching my ass. Whomever wore these last was tall and stick thin. I might be lean compared to Warwick, but I was all muscle, with thicker thighs and ass.

I hated tight clothes, and these felt like a costume, not something I'd wear into battle.

Not something I might die in.

The genie said he would have Kozlov's troops here in time, but heading toward the castle with the night quiet around us, a nerve in my stomach twitched.

What if he didn't and this whole plan fell apart?

The last couple of days were a haze of planning after Dzsinn took off. Kozlov and Eve stayed mostly away after the first day when Raven almost gutted her ex-bodyguard. We thought it was wise to keep them separated unless heavily supervised.

Maestro Silk allowed us to use our room as headquarters and a bunker for gathering weapons and supplies. While others stole necessities, Warwick and I tracked down two working automobiles, those a leader of Russia would use. Not an easy feat when you're in a poverty-stricken country with very few fae converted cars.

It was tense and stressful and during the time we weren't stealing or scamming; the couples were slipping out to use empty rooms where they could fuck their aggressions out. The number of times we were doing it suggested we were all tense as shit. I took all the energy out on Raven—with the door open, in the bathroom, the hallway, against the window. Anywhere and with whomever was watching.

Though, when Brexley and Warwick fucked, the entire building felt it. Those two caused such a disturbance in the atmosphere they woke the dead. Literally. Ghosts had been haunting the building since they arrived. And then there were Birdie and Caden, who fucked so loud they outdid the party room, while Scorpion and Hanna seemed to be competing with them. Maestro Silk's brothel had never been fuller or more popular. Especially the night before the attack.

Bellows came from the room over, spirits crashing into the room as I plunged my cock deeper into Raven, driving into her pussy. My teeth gritted, my hands gripping her hips so hard I knew I was bruising her.

"Ash!" A snarled howl came from her, the blades peeking out of her spine. I didn't care that she cut me, that I bled over her. It was like another mark on her, another blood bond which tied us together. No matter how deep I went, I couldn't get close enough. I wanted to crawl under her skin and own it all. "Fuck... Ash!" On all fours, her claws dug into the covers. I could feel a man watching us from the open doorway and I knew it was Wesley, his hand rubbing up and down his cock as he watched us.

It made me fuck her harder.

"Let me fuck the dweller, *mroczny*." I bit the tendon in her neck. Her beast snapped and snarled, fire flashing in her eyes, claws carving into the mattress, her back hitching up. "I want to sink into the beast's pussy," I whispered in her ear, the hint of her dark fur tickling against my skin.

A shiver ran through Raven's body, her cunt fluttering at my words. A deep growl came up her throat, her body turning red hot. She started to shift as much as she could, the dweller's tightness enclosing around my cock, feeling different than being inside her other form. Not better or worse, just different. And I loved different.

Polish words I didn't even practice anymore hissed from my lips, a groan so guttural I felt it from my soul, and I pulled her into me, going so hard she started to yowl, the bed squealing under the intensity.

"Own my cock, dweller. Claim it... knot around it." I gritted between my teeth. Sweat dripped off my body, blood from the blades smearing over my skin. She bent further over, pushing her ass even higher into me. Her tail glided over my hip, coming around between my legs from behind until it curled firmly around my balls, tickling them.

Everything snapped.

I was no longer present in my body. I became my own beast, a fiend to her monster. Perverse and wicked, I relished the depravity. The sound of her wetness slapped the walls and dripped down our legs. We could hear Wesley moan loudly, stroking himself harder, turning us on more as he came.

It was twisted, but it was us.

My thumb pushed into her ass, pressing down on the nerves. Her body jerked. A garbled howl bayed from her, the feel of her magic locking my dick inside her, the metal bedframe bowing under us as I railed her to the point of intense pain.

But my gods, it felt so fucking good.

Releasing inside her, my vision went, my muscles limp. I felt her shift back into her human form before my body landed on hers, instinctively keeping me from impaling on her daggers.

Still inside her, my chest heaved against her spine, skin sticky, muscles limp. We laid there together in shock. How did each time get better and more addicting than the last?

There was a reason I had so many lovers and usually multiple ones. I got bored easily. As much as I loved Kek and Lucas, and I imagined myself with them longer than anyone, it still would not have been forever. Not with our lifespans. With Raven, I didn't think I could ever get bored.

And on a fundamental level, I understood I couldn't walk away from her. Ever. Even if we lived apart, there'd be no one else.

"*Mroczny.*" *Dark one,* I rumbled into her ear, my lips brushing her temple. "You are going to be the death of me."

"Don't say that," she whispered hoarsely. Neither one of us had addressed the topic of what was coming tomorrow, or what was after if we made it. "Promise me nothing will happen to you."

"I can't promise that." Reluctantly, I moved my weight off her, rolling to my side next to her. Wesley had disappeared, leaving the hallway empty, which I was grateful for.

Her lids squeezed as I slid out of her, her teeth biting into her bottom lip, her nose flaring.

"Did I hurt you?" I knew I went rougher than normal, and we had *never* been gentle in bed... or out of it.

"I liked it." She lifted her head, turning to me. "That's the problem. I like it all. I don't want it to stop."

"And you think it will?" I tucked my arm under my head, my legs still hooked over hers.

"Won't it?" She went up on her elbows, her hair trailing down her bare back where patches of my blood smeared over her skin. "Let's say this all goes off according to plan. What then? Will you go back to Budapest? Come with me to the States?" She frowned. "I can't see you living at court, surrounded by rules and traditions, going to events, wearing suits and ties, small talking with elites at boring parties."

"You don't think I can dress up and charm the elite?"

"Oh, you can charm *anyone*, usually out of their clothes. I know for a fact you'd have the most pretentious ladies dropping their knickers for you by the time hors d'oeuvres were served."

"Not the pretentious men?" I lifted a brow.

She rolled her eyes. "They'd be no challenge. Their underwear would already be flung at you when you walked in."

"Sounds about right." I curled more into her, my hand running over her ass. "So, what's the problem?"

"You wouldn't be happy there." Her emerald eyes pierced mine with truth.

"Yeah, so you'll have to have sex with me more to balance it out."

"Ash…" She nipped on her bottom lip, which was already bitten into, her tone desolate. "I've seen that exact situation between my mother and father daily. Your family is here, your life is here."

"Yours could be too." I ran my finger through the ends of her hair. "Are you happy at those events and parties?"

"No, but it was the life I was born into." She exhaled, looking off. "I can't walk away from it."

"Because you are the next in line." My throat suddenly went dry at the thought of our paths being too different. Even if we were mated, it still was out of reach. She was a real-life princess. I was a tree fairy who'd dabbled in crime and debauchery most of his life. "And they wouldn't allow you to be with me?"

"That's not it at all. My family would never tell me who to be with. My mother mated with a dark dweller, after all. He's still looked down on in some parts of court."

"And I would be too."

"I don't care." She shook her head. "But I see my father and I wouldn't want to do that to you. He hates it, every part. He's there for my mother and I know it puts a lot of stress on both of them." She touched my cheek. "And I don't want you to settle. Not for me. I don't have a choice. You do."

Though being mated to her wasn't a choice either. It simply was.

"Well." I struggled to swallow back the lump forming in my throat. "After tomorrow, we might not have to worry about this dilemma at all."

Liquid watered her eyes, and she curled into me, burrowing her head into my chest.

"Whatever happens tomorrow, just know," she whispered. "I love you, Ash Hemlock Rowan."

My teeth clamped together, my eyes squeezed shut, and I pulled her into my body. Her words burned through my veins like venom, seizing my chest until my heart pounded in my ears and everything hurt.

I had told people I loved them before; I had even believed those words were true at various times in my life. But until I heard *her* utter them, the meaning slipping into my bones, I didn't understand what they truly meant, and what the loss of that could be if taken away. And there was a good chance I'd lose her, whether it be by death or life paths. I couldn't see how I could hold on to her.

She fell asleep in my arms.

"Rabul ejtetted a szívemet," I whispered. *You have imprisoned my heart.* "It is completely yours, little beak."

The car dipped, knocking Raven's shoulder into mine, bringing me back to the present. The two cars moved closer to the looming castle, the fog thick across the grounds giving off an ethereal ness.

A shiver coursed down my spine.

The barrier of magic crackled, licking out and tasting the threat coming, whispering words of dissuasion in our ears. *Turn around.* It sang into every vein, the spell discouraging intruders. It was far stronger than last time, the pressure cracking my knuckles over the steering wheel, all of us in the car going silent.

Wesley drove the first car carrying Caden, Birdie, Scorpion, and Hanna. I drove the second. Raven and Brexley were up front with me and sandwiched in the back were Warwick, Eve, and Kozlov. And of course, a Brownie and an imp were smuggled away in Brexley's bag someplace.

Raven's hand slid over my thigh, our uniform caps blocking our eyes. Reaching for her hand, my fingers curled around hers, our eyes staring straight ahead. I didn't need to see her to hear her heart, feel her anxiety, and taste her fear. And this time, I couldn't do anything to really calm her emotions, as mine were just as turbulent.

The Trojan horse would only take us so far until Sonya recognized us. It wasn't like Warwick was someone you could hide. We needed to get on the other side of the barrier before she did.

"Soldiers are coming up." Raven's vision pierced the darkness, her grip tightening on mine. "Six of them."

Right as she spoke, the brake lights from the front car glowed red, Wesley slowing down.

"Here we go." Brexley clicked off the safety of her gun under the dash, Warwick and Eve doing the same in the back.

I rolled the car to a stop, and the soldiers moved toward us, ready to shoot us at any moment.

"We ready for this?" Brexley breathed out, dipping her hat lower on her head.

"I fucking hope so," Warwick mumbled from the back seat, flicking my attention to the rearview mirror. Our gazes caught for a moment, his bright aqua eyes telling me he would be beside me until the end.

He and Kitty were my first true family. My teachers, mentors, best friends, and sometimes my rivals, but always my brother and sister. And yes, there was a moment when I thought I had feelings for Kitty, but I realized later that not all soulmates are romantic. Some were your core beliefs, your backbone of strength, your essence of who you were as a person. A part of your soul no one else could touch.

A substance far thicker than blood or DNA.

"As my people like to say, 'A man can die but once.'" Kozlov tugged at his suit cuffs, settling back in his seat, his demeanor unflappable. "Fortune favors the bold."

"Or the one wearing the Cintamani stone," I said under my breath. I gave Raven's hand a final squeeze before letting it go and reached to roll down the window as the guards stepped up to our cars, their expressions stern.

My heart thumped in my ears. Everything came down to this moment, and it could all go wrong in a blink. We would not get this chance again.

"State your business," a man barked in Romanian, his eye twitching, his muscles convulsing like worms under his skin.

Most of us in this car had seen this before, the deteriorating brain of someone who had been given the experimental pills. Istvan had implemented them on the lower-tier soldiers, the grunts. The ones who were trained to die to protect him, while he deployed full transfusions to the upper guards and elite.

Sonya seemed to have the same strategy.

"President Kozlov, the leader of Russia, is here to see Queen Sonya." I struggled to get out the last two words, but I kept my voice steady as three more men moved around the car.

"We were given no notice of this visit," the man snarled, his nose wrinkling, showing canine teeth. "Get out of the car."

The strings that tied me to Raven vibrated with ire; a snarl no one but me could hear came from the dweller, the beast wanting to eliminate the threat.

"I assure you, the queen—"

"I said get out of the car!" the man rumbled, his hand jerking and twitching on his rifle.

Darkness slid over my chest like a cloud, the coldness of the obscurer somehow making the car even darker, her power sitting on my skin. Waiting.

"Let us pass, soldier! I am the leader of Russia! I will not be held here by the likes of you." Kozlov barked from the back seat, his condescending authority dripping with disdain. "If you do not let us pass in the next thirty seconds, I will see to it that you are the *Primul's* next meal… or maybe they can do other things to you."

I held my breath. It was risky for Kozlov to bring up the *Primul*. Sonya had never told him anything about the monsters she kept, but would this guard know that?

The man sucked in, taking in Kozlov, recognizing his stature, yet I sensed his real fear was what the *Primul* could do. Most of those on the pills thought themselves invincible, held no concern, yet they still feared these beasts.

A year could have been lived in that single second, a moment suspended in the air like a balloon. My pulse ticked against my throat, my muscles spring-loaded to attack.

The guard's lids narrowed on us, but he dipped his chin, waving his arm to the other sentries to move off the road.

The car in front rolled forward as they gestured us through. None of us reacted, our heads forward as we passed the troop, the tension in the car pounding like a drum.

The pressure driving through the spell stabbed into my head like a migraine, then washed away instantly, granting us passage to the castle grounds.

We made it in.

"Did it feel too easy?" Brexley uttered the same thought pecking at the back of my head.

Thick fog lapped at the car, an unsettled feeling locking up in my chest the further we moved. The lights from the castle above cast heavy shadows over the mist, playing tricks on my eyes. The sensation of stepping into a horror story clipped my breath.

"Of course they would let me through," Dimitri arrogantly huffed in back, his ego shoving back what he had to feel as well. "*I am* the ruler of Russia."

None of us responded.

"There are a lot of dead through here," Brexley spoke again, her eyes glazing over the land. "So much death here."

"You would know," I retorted, trying to keep things light, but my voice held no humor.

"Something's wrong…" Raven's chest pushed in and out, her body rigid, her eyes squinting into the thick mist.

"What?"

A squeal of tires in front of us yanked my head to the car in front. I slammed on the brakes, coming within a hair of the bumper of the other vehicle.

The fog, as if it was pure illusion, dissipated, revealing what was hidden within it.

"Holy fuck," Brexley breathed out in alarm.

Terror constricted my esophagus. I gasped in a small intake of air, but it never reached my lungs.

Lines and lines of soldiers stood perfectly still, covering the grounds. The glow of hundreds of torches reflected off the window, shadowing their outlines in a diabolical scene. As if they were washed in blood and death.

My gaze drew up to the castle, taking in the silhouette of a woman and man perched on the high wall, looking down, their troops ready for an order.

Sonya and Iain.

Dressed in matching red outfits, like they were already mocking the blood that would spill across this ground, their blonde hair reflecting with the firelight.

"She knew," Raven muttered. "She knew we were coming."

"How did she know we were coming?" Brexley asked, her gaze moving around, seeing the guards move around the car, blocking us in. We were trapped.

It was clear. She was waiting for us. This was a setup.

"Are you too afraid to face me, Dimitri?" Sonya's voice boomed over the gardens, full of condescension. "Fae or human, all male leaders are alike. All puffed-up chests and preening. But when it comes down to it, you're insecure little boys who need a woman to do all the real work." Sonya's red lips peeled into a vindictive smile. "Like your wife. She seems to know more than you. A better ruler, I'd say as well."

Kozlov's muscles constricted, his expression turning to murderous rage. He was known to have an ego and a temper. Human or fae, unchecked power was corrupting. They could no longer take criticism, nor see beyond their own narcissism. But the mention of his wife made him scramble for the door handle.

"Stop." I reached back to stop him. "She's trying to provoke you. Don't let her."

Kozlov's lips lifted in a snarl, but he let go of the handgrip.

"Is that a no, Dimitri? Rather save your own skin? See, you are proving my point." Sonya *tsked*, her hand going to her belly. "But let me see if this works." Sonya peered behind her as a guard drew up a tall, thin woman. The twist in her hair sagged to one side, her nice dress dirty and ruffled.

Raven gasped in recognition, her hand going to her mouth as the barefoot woman was pushed onto the ledge.

"Polina!" Dimitri shoved out of the door, screaming his wife's name. Eve followed him.

"Dimitri," his wife whimpered, tears streaking her face.

"Do not hurt her!"

"You should have thought of that before you decided to betray me. You think I wouldn't know?" Sonya clasped her hands, speaking down from her perch above us. "Though I should know better than to ever trust a man. You all are so predictable, especially when your power is dwindling before your eyes. You become desperate. Foolish.

"Next time you send cryptic messages to your wife about your movements concerning the troops coming through the border, you might want to make them harder to decipher."

My gut bottomed out, understanding the predicament we were in.

We had no help coming, and it was only us against hundreds. Plus the monsters she kept hidden below.

"Do you know what I do to those who go against me?" I swear I could feel her eyes find mine in the car, knowing I was here. Her hand rubbed at her stomach again, a smirk like she knew something none of us did.

Iain's sneer became more prominent, his arms locked behind the cape draping from his shoulders, so comfortable in their power.

"I take away what they love the most." Her chin barely moved before the guard shoved Polina off the ledge. Polin's screams pierced the night, her body flailing before hitting the rocky ground far below their perch. Only yards away from where we were parked.

"Oh my gods!" Raven screamed out.

"Noooo!" Dimitri bellowed, trying to run to her, the guards holding him back. "Polina!" He thrashed, trying to reach the mangled corpse of his wife behind the lines of soldiers at the base of the castle. Blood splashed over the rocks and snow like someone spilled red paint.

"I warned you not to deceive me." Sonya tilted her head.

"I will kill you!" Dimitri screamed back, saliva spitting from his mouth. "I will fucking kill you! I will take everything from you! I will rip his heart out in front of you!" He gestured to Iain.

"And how do you plan on doing that?" Both Sonya and Iain laughed. "You are nothing now, Dimitri. You have no family, no mafia working for you, your cabinet has turned against you, and soon you will be banished as leader of Russia. You have no power," she sneered. "You are weak and pathetic."

The insult surely hit his pride like a knife, his body tensing before he yanked away from the guards. Reaching over, he grabbed the gun from Eve's hand, pointing it up at Sonya.

Bullets exploded into the night air.

Guards lunged for Dimitri while I saw Iain reach for something under his cape. In a second, he brandished a bow and released an arrow.

Dimitri moved, but the arrow still found a target, sinking into flesh and bone.

Eve's scream sliced through my nerves, puncturing my eardrum. The blonde stumbled, falling to the ground, the arrow sticking out of her sternum.

"Eve!" Raven cried out. It was automatic, ingrained in her to respond to her friend since she was young, no matter what had happened between them.

Eve gasped and gaped, the arrow affecting her more than I expected, but she was no longer my concern. Neither was Kozlov.

I would protect my family.

A squawk chilled the already frozen air, a dark wingspan gliding over Sonya's head.

"Kill them all," Sonya ordered Nyx.

"That fucking bitch," Brexley snarled as the hawk swooped down for us at the same time the troops took her order, marching for us.

"Fuck." I clenched my teeth, making a hasty decision. Slamming on

Land of Monsters

the gas, I yanked the wheel, spinning the car in reverse. The tires whirled in a circle over the icy ground, tearing through the grass as I punched the car forward. Wesley peeled away, flipping around and following us while hordes of men with fae-like strength leaped for the cars, shooting at our tires.

"Come on, come on!" I begged the car to move faster. We were vastly outnumbered, with no hope of assistance. We had to get the hell out of here.

Inches away from the barrier, magic flared and crackled up the invisible wall, the Druid barrier sparking with power. Spells like this were to keep people out, not in, yet I could feel us being sealed in. The spell sizzled with power, barricading us from going through it like a wall. Tugging the wheel to the left, the car squealed with effort, the right headlight and side smashing and scraping against the barrier, taking the brunt, while I flipped us around.

"What the fuck?" Raven physically jerked, sucking in sharply, black fur prickling her arms and face. I felt it through her, the signature of the spell maker.

Dubthach.

"It's a Druid spell!" Brexley also could feel the difference.

"What? She has a fucking Druid working for her?" Warwick barked from the backseat.

"Dubthach can't be working for her." Raven shook her head like she couldn't fathom the concept. "She must be forcing him."

That meant he was here, close by.

"The bitch locked us in." Brexley's fury was rising, the air crackling with energy. "She really wants to piss me off? Did she not see how Istvan fared against me?"

Warwick might have legend status, but it was really Brex who held the power of death. She wasn't as lethal as she used to be without the nectar, but the girl was still half necromancer and half everything else she absorbed the night of the fae war.

And Raven was just as frightening.

But they could die like the rest of us, and we had too many against us.

Nyx's screech rang out again, close this time, followed by the sound of her talons dragging over the roof, the metal splitting under her claws right over Brexley's head.

"She *really* hates you." I wrenched the wheel, plowing through a horde of guards, their frames tumbling over the hood.

"We have to suppress the Druid's power to drop the barrier." Brexley rolled down her window enough to shoot at the mindless guards coming after us, making me feel we were in some end-of-world dystopia. "Can you do that?" she asked Raven.

"No." She shook her head. "It takes more than one to counter another Druid's magic."

"But you and your brother could?"

"Maybe." She shrugged. "Like I said, I'm not a normal Druid."

"It's worth a try." Brexley shot out one side while Warwick shot out the other from the back.

Raven peered over at me. "I can't leave him here."

"Looks like we're going in." I pointed the car towards the garden entrance of the castle, the one Dzsinn and I had entered. But too many would follow us. "We need a distraction."

"Allow me," Brexley spoke before Warwick did. In seconds Wesley's car broke away from us, twisting in the opposite direction, tossing hand grenades out the windows and creating mayhem, steering most guards toward them.

"What are they doing?"

"I told Scorpion to go the opposite way," Brexley stated. "Take attention off us."

I sometimes forgot she and Scorpion had a spirit-like connection too. Saving his life that fateful night had linked them forever, as well as her and Warwick.

"Okay." I gripped the steering wheel tight, pressing the gas, curving the car around a pond. "Get in the back seat!"

Brexley and Raven crawled over with Warwick, slipping down low and bracing themselves. I pushed the gas pedal to the floor, and the car barreled toward the wooden door of the entrance barricaded with a dozen soldiers, their bullets cracking into the windshield. "Hold on!" I squeezed my eyes shut, the car plowing into the men, chopping them down until the bonnet crashed into the door.

CRACK!

The force punched into me like a whip. The door splintered into pieces, breaking open, but the thickness jolted the automobile to an abrupt stop.

My forehead slammed into the steering wheel, spinning my mind, pooling bile in my throat.

"Raven?" I forced myself to move, turning to peer in the backseat. "Are you guys okay?"

"Yeah, I think." She groaned. Blood trickled out of Warwick's nose and forehead, his body curled over the two girls, taking the worst of the impact.

A hawk's cry sounded from the sky, rushing urgency through me.

"We've got to move." Kicking open the car door, the hinges balked, blood and guts covering the car like icing, dead bodies lying under the wheels.

Nyx soared above, more soldiers rushing our way.

Warwick grunted, drawing his clawed wolf's blade from his back. "Go," he growled at us, his attention on the enemy, his frame widening in attack stance, moving towards the men.

"There's too many!" Raven countered.

"No such thing," he rumbled, swinging his weapon.

"Here." Brexley threw her small backpack at me. "We'll hold them off."

"Brex…" I caught it. My chest ached at the idea of losing either one of them.

"Can't let my man have all the fun." She lifted her gun with a wink. "Plus, I have backup."

The hair on the back of my neck rose, the sensation of ghosts swirling around Brexley as she called them to her. Her invisible warriors rose from the blood-stained fields of the past.

The pair charged the enemy. They had made their decision, and standing here would only waste what they were doing for me.

"Come on." I swung the pack over my shoulder, nodding for Raven to follow me.

We both slipped into the tunnel of the castle where Frankenstein's sleeping monsters waited.

Chapter 22

Raven

Firebulbs flickered on in the tunnel, sensing our presence, the light giving way to what the darkness was hiding. My boots came to a halt, the air stuck in my lungs. Ice cold heat burned through me like blue fire, and bile rose up to my throat like a tidal wave as my eyes took in what my brain was slow to process.

A string of vertical tanks lined the wall. Light exposed floating figures inside, their bodies hooked up to tubes, while gurneys sat at the base of them. Each one filled with a fae, wires and cords attached to their brains and bodies, connecting them to the machines.

I could smell death, traces of magic limping in the air. Agony and sorrow hummed in the emptiness, like their souls had been shredded and ripped out, leaving nothing but particles of what was once there.

"Ash?" My voice barely made it out of my throat. He had explained to us what was down here, but my mind had no understanding of the truth. The reality of seeing it. The horrors.

When I was brought in here before, I had been so drugged that I only remembered bits and pieces of the lair below, a kaleidoscope of monsters made-up from nightmares. This was even scarier.

A flame stoked in my belly at the idea my brother might be used like this. Becoming a desiccated shell. His humor, his cheekiness, his laughter and kindness… hollowed out and destroyed to make Sonya another compliant soldier.

Some of my shock wore off, allowing me to make out individuals among the victims. "Oh gods..." My gaze landed on the faces inside, a cry coming from my lips. "Iacob." My hand flew to my mouth, vomit stinging the back of my throat.

Codrin lay below Iacob, cords connecting them. Codrin's eyes were wide open, his carcass drained of his magic, his life sucked from him. Life Iacob now held.

My eyes stung with tears. Vlad, the older woman I gardened with, the hot guy who asked to sleep with me... they were all dead. Used up and shucked away.

"Gods..." Tears blurred my vision, vomit moving up to my tongue.

"I know." Ash cupped the side of my face, his green eyes locking on mine. "This is not going to be easy, but we can't think about the ones we lost. We can only try to save those who still live." The sounds of battle leaked through the foundation. "Focus on getting your brother."

He was right, it was not the time to mourn them. We had to save who we could.

The possibility of anything like this happening to Rook drove down my spine like a rod. I nodded in agreement, my chin rising.

"Can you sense him?"

My brows furrowed. I had always been able to reach out for my twin, but now we were surrounded by too much magic to pinpoint just his, though something in my gut pulled me forward.

"Down there." I flicked my chin.

He turned around, rushing us down the long row of tubes. I purposely didn't look, keeping my focus ahead, feeling as if each one was reaching out for me, crying for my help.

Ash curved us around a corner and behind an outdated elevator, the smooth edges of stone giving way to crude rock and dirt. The stench of newly soiled earth stung my nose, though something else already wafted in. It coiled over my tongue the further we descended, whisking my lungs in and out at a faster rate. My pulse beat against my neck, the grip on my gun cracking my knuckles. Memories flickered so quickly in my mind I couldn't grab onto anything but the sensation.

The dread and horror.

Black fur sprouted over my arms, and a rumble formed in my chest.

Dziubuś. I felt him speak straight into my body, his calming tone hushing my beating heart, like his hands were stroking through my soul. Ash kept his attention forward, but I sensed him inside me, invading my space, taking over and soothing the beast, shushing the obscurer. And they allowed him in, kneeling to him. It was comforting and frightening at once.

Because if anything happened to him, neither would find serenity again. And what I did to Alexsei Kozlov would be trivial to the chaos I would cause. There was no becoming a better person because I was loved by him. I would cover myself in blood until I was hunted down and destroyed.

The pull I felt gripped me harder, pointing me down another tunnel, when the hums of noise separated and became clearer. Muttering voices, metal clanking, and deep grunts.

Acid dripped down my throat, perspiration dampening my forehead as if I knew what was coming, yet still wrapped myself in the blurred darkness of those triggers.

The cave opened, the dirt path switching to a steel walkway, bridging the open space and inclining into stairs toward the lair below.

I stilled, my lungs attacking oxygen as if it were the enemy. My nightmare had come to life in rich, vivid colors and details, instead of hazy tendrils I couldn't quite grasp. This time, instead of being in my body, I was watching from above, taking in the true hideousness of what was happening.

Rattling from the snake-man filled the cavern as he bred a human woman. I recalled her serving me coffee at the camp. She had a child and a husband, who were probably upstairs being used as research.

Her eyes were barely open, her body moving up and down, but she was not inside, the drugs taking her far away. Thankfully.

But the loudest was coming from a warped looking man with a scorpion tail, on the other side of the room rutting so hard the bed slid across the floor, his final hissing moans scraping my ears like thousands of bugs.

My insides went cold. The flash of his body over mine, his grotesque sneer, his stench still haunting my nostrils. Immobilizing fear crashed over me.

Z.

I knew his name and that he was the leader, but most of all, I recalled his hot breath on my face and the feel of his scaley hands on my skin.

He immediately got up afterward, tucking himself back into his pants, and moved away. The girl underneath lay there as he left her, her darker blonde hair matted, her skin covered in marks and bruises.

This time bile made it all the way up my throat and filled my mouth.

Celeste.

Z zipped up his pants, strolling to a tied-up figure on a bed against the wall.

"You better hope that worked." The arachnid kicked at the figure. "Or maybe I'll try you next with this." Z's stinger scraped over the bed, his laugh sounding like chirping hisses.

My attention lowered to the person he was talking to.

Everything fell away. My body wrenched up, reacting purely on instinct.

My brother was gagged, blindfolded, and cuffed to a bed leg, his face bruised, yet I could still make out an expression of disgust and devastation.

"Rook." His name stuck in my throat, my need to get to him, save him, tingled the daggers in my back.

"No," Ash barked without actually speaking out loud. He grabbed my arm, pulling me back down behind the wall, his head shaking.

I felt the retort on my lips, the *Fuck you, I'm getting my brother* response, but I knew Ash was right. We couldn't run down there with no strategy.

"If it does. I'm next." A man with boar tusks and rough, brown skin stood at the entrance like he was on guard.

"No," Z snarled. "You breed with the humans. *I* get the fae women." He nodded from Celeste to two other figures near her.

My eyes widened seeing Viorica and her cousin, Brândușa, in beds next to Celeste.

Why was he mating with them? They couldn't produce unless somehow they could get around the protective birth control potion almost all faes took around puberty, which was impossible unless you were a Druid…

My thought tapered off, my gaze darting back to my brother, an awareness slithering over me like slime.

Oh. Fuck.

Druid magic could screw with the potion messing with its performance, as my mother found out. Some might think this a weakness, while others might use this to their advantage.

My eyes squeezed for a moment, and I fought to regain my breath. "They're using my brother's magic to undo the spell."

"Undo what spell?" Ash swallowed, though he already knew.

"Reversing any birth protection the fae women have. Making it far easier for them to get pregnant."

"*Szar*," Ash muttered, his head dropping in understanding. These offspring would be even more powerful, shedding the part that might have come out human.

"I will bet you she is carrying my kin now. She took me so deep." Z's voice hissed against the walls, and he nodded to Celeste with a leer. "I'll make sure again later."

"After you've helped Sonya with her little problem upstairs?" The snake-man had finished, moving over to the others.

"Fuck her," Z snarled.

"Yeah, we heard. You did. Several times." The rhino guy who stood at the wall chuckled. "And sounded like you really enjoyed it."

"She may be the first fae impregnated with my child." A sneer moved over his lips. "But she will soon learn her place. I am the king."

What. The. Fuck.

Sonya might be pregnant? She had sex with Z? I might actually throw up.

Now every time she touched her belly earlier, a smugness riding her lips, I understood.

This was her way of striving for even more power and control. With her necklace, she was safe from Z's retaliation if he dared, at the same time making her bloodline the most feared in the world. She wasn't keeping the monsters in the basement; she was adding them to the throne. To become her heirs, her legacy. Making herself the queen of the *Primul* as well. Who would go against her if she could unleash these things into the world? She would encroach on every land, declaring herself and her family the rulers.

This woman really played the long game.

"Why not keep her happy while putting more seed in her belly?" Beetle added. "Only makes *us* stronger. Until she learns she birthed her own worst nightmares."

Z nodded his head, motioning for his men to follow. "Won't hurt to blow off a little steam. Kill a few people for her."

All of them grunted with agreement at his comment, following him up the passage towards the castle level.

My pulse beat like a drum in my ears, my legs itching to move. Ash kept a tight hold on my arm until silence surrounded us for several minutes, their footsteps long gone.

"Let's go," he whispered in my ear. Keeping low, we moved silently down the steps, my eyes sharp, straining to hear anyone coming. Ash couldn't, but I could hear the guns firing and screaming from far above, the castle property alight with battle.

I just hoped everyone we loved was all right.

When our boots hit the ground, my brother's spine went straight, his nose flaring. He smelled me. Sensed me nearby.

The goblin metal blocked us from communicating between our link, but we didn't need one. Our bond was tight, my twin knowing me as well as he knew himself.

"Raven," he muffled out my name. I squatted down next to him, ripping his blindfold off. His crystal green eyes flinched at the dim light, blinking as I yanked down his gag, exposing his badly bruised face. "What the hell are you doing here?" Worry and fear jerked his head around, like he expected the *Primul* to jump out.

"What do you think I'm doing here, little brother?" I replied as Ash came down on his other side. "I'm here to rescue your ass."

"But th-those things." He searched the room for them. "She is with them… Sonya… she forced me to unspell the women here."

"I know." I nodded.

He shook his head as if he couldn't get the bad thoughts from his mind, what he silently had to listen to, hearing the women around and he couldn't do a thing. It went against everything my brother stood for.

"Rav." He licked his dry lips. "There is another Druid here. I can feel his magic."

"Dubthach," I said. I didn't think she could get pregnant in the time Rook had been here, so it made sense Dubthach is how she was able to conceive prior. How did they figure out fae women could carry these monsters?

"These things…" Rook's eyes met mine, his voice wobbly. "They're Aunt Zoey's, aren't they? Her offspring?" He was raised with the same stories, the same terrifying legends of these creatures.

"Yes." I dipped my head. "It's why we need to get you out of here."

"How?" He jerked at his cuffs against the bedframe, the goblin metal trapping him not just physically, but magically too.

Ash made a noise, taking off the pack from his back and opening the top.

"You're up, *utrapienie*." *Pain in ass*. Ash nudged the bag.

Silence.

"Hey?" Ash prodded the bag harder. "Now!"

Two middle fingers pushed out of the top of the bag, sticking up at him.

"Very mature," Ash countered.

Chirp!

"We don't have time for this." Ash dumped the bag over on the bed. Two creatures and some extra bullets and knives came tumbling out.

"What the fuck?" My brother retorted as a string of noises came from the tiniest one dressed in what looked like the wrist band of a black glove around his middle.

"Someone's coming down from her high."

Chirpchirrrpchirppppchirpchirpchiiiiiirrrrppppchirpchirp! Bitzy didn't even take a breath, her fingers high in the air, whirring her sentiment at Ash, her lids narrowed.

"Oh, tree fairy." Opie stood up, brushing down his outfit, which was the rest of the fingered glove. He used the fabric fingers for his legs and arms, the middle finger used to hold his *other* appendage, but it was knotted up in a bow. "You are going to be on her naughty list for a very long time."

"I'll get her a bucket of mushrooms," Ash huffed.

Chirp! Bitzy replied.

"Fine, two buckets!" Ash countered.

Chirp! Chirp!

"Three. That is my final offer." He sensed me and Rook staring at him. "What?"

I grinned, looking between him and the minuscule imp. She had all these huge alpha guys wrapped around her long, prongy fingers.

"Oh, she gets whatever she wants?" Opie waved his arms.

"You are already destroying history—"

"*Boring* history," Opie huffed. "Doing everyone a favor."

"Can you guys release him?" Ash stood up, grabbing one of the knives that fell on the bed. "I'm gonna go help them." Ash moved to a bed nearby. Many of the human women were only tied to the beds with rope, so drugged up and weak they didn't have the strength to fight. Though fae, like Celeste and the cousins, were cuffed.

"Easy peasy." Opie wiggled his fingers, strolling up to my brother's arms. "Watch out, sir, the power of these things makes grown men fall to their knees in reverence."

Chirp!

"Lies!"

Chirp!

"Don't listen to her." Opie shook his head.

Chirp!

"That was a misunderstanding!"

"What is going on?" My brother's expression was pure confusion. "Why is there a brownie dressed in a glove and... I don't know what the fuck that is?"

"This is not just a glove! It's top fashion, sir." Opie frowned. "Okay, I didn't have much to work with!"

Chirp! Bitzy flipped him off.

"This is Opie, and the imp is Bitzy." I nodded to them. "Don't piss her off," I whispered, flicking my chin at the imp. "And tell him his outfits are amazing."

My brother stared at me like I had gone insane.

"My gods, these hands are so talented!" Opie sang after a few moments, the cuff falling from my brother's wrists.

"Fuck, Ravy." Rook's arms instantly went around me, hugging me so hard to his chest. "Thank you."

"Like I could ever leave you." I stuck out my pinky. He hooked his over mine with a smile. Our gesture that we were always there for each other. No matter what. "Now let's get the fuck out of here."

I helped him up as Ash called Opie and Bitzy over to Celeste's bed to uncuff her.

"I heard him with her." Pain flickered over Rook's face as he gazed at Celeste, like putting her face to her cries broke something in him. "She tried to fight. Even after they drugged her." He couldn't break his eyes from her face.

"Ta-da!" Opie threw up his hands when the cuffs dropped away from Celeste's arms. Ash scooped her up the moment she was free.

"Go do Viorica nex—"

BOOOOM!

An explosion shook the ground, dropping debris on us like raindrops.

Ash's form went stiff, his attention toward the passage out. Then I smelled it too.

The burning wick of dynamite.

"Ash!"

"Raven—" My name barely made it out of his lips before another explosion detonated through the room, crumpling the ceiling like a dry pastry, the crust folding on itself. "Raven!"

I heard him before I was hit with force, and everything around me went dark.

※ ※ ※

Hacking, my lungs filled with soot, my body was curled up on its side. A heavy weight lay over my legs and torso like a giant dog guarding its owner.

A giant *deadly* dog.

"Rook." I coughed, the ceiling showering down chunks of dirt, thickening the air. "Rook?" I nudged at the dweller, my fingers running over the familiar fur caked with dirt. His body could instantly shift, fully becoming a dark dweller, while mine strained to be anything more than a twisted version. Like a child drawing a picture from a vague memory of a monster.

A rumble broke from my brother's throat, his eyes opening. Red fire glowed before they turned back to green. Inching off me, he shook his back, the metal blades clinking, tossing more tiny debris off him.

"Ash?" I scrambled up, looking in the direction I last saw him, my eyes adjusting to the pitch darkness. "Ash!" I screamed, clambering over to where I could make out his form.

"*Dziubuś...*" His voice was barely audible before he started coughing. He blindly reached for me, his vision not as adept as mine.

"You okay?" I guided his hand to my face, letting him feel me next to him.

"Yeah." He groaned as I helped him sit up. "That wasn't a Warwick distraction."

"What?"

"Nothing." He shook his head.

Both Rook and I heard the tear; our heads jerked up as the ceiling ripped away from itself, dropping clumps of dirt down harder.

Rook snarled, ramming me with his head to move.

"Ash!" Desperation bled from my voice. I yanked him to his feet, the earth above us groaning with the weight, having nothing to keep it up. "Move!" I pulled him with me toward the exit.

"Wait! Celeste!" Ash yanked from my grip, turning back around.

"No!" My heart stopped beating, and time stopped moving as Ash darted back, feeling around until he found her.

More of the ceiling tore away, plunging down.

"Ash!" His name was a siren song, calling him home, like my voice could shield him from harm, protect him from death. The obscurer ripped from my throat, spouting words of threat to anything wanting to harm my mate. Except there was no mind to control, nobody to bend to my will.

And then Ash tripped, Celeste tumbling from his hold.

Horror and agony exploded in my chest, my own body twisting and warping into the dweller, about to run to Ash. Movement flickered in the corner of my eye, a dark shape zipping out, leaping out for the pair.

"Rook!"

Using his body as a shield, my brother shoved Ash forward to me, where I was shielded by the doorjamb. He moved over Celeste, cocooning her under his bulk, taking the brunt of the downpour. His blades tinged as rocks bounced off, his roars singing along with the earth, his legs bowing, but he didn't move.

"Rook!" I cried out as it tapered off.

Rook heaved out a heavy sigh, his coat slick with blood, his eyes burning red. As he slowly unrolled his body, I could see Celeste perfectly protected under him. Her eyes opened, peering up at the raging beast over her. I was ready for her to scream, to panic at the sight, but she just blinked, staring up at him. He rumbled, shaking off the dirt as she got to her feet.

"Everyone okay?" Ash asked, then turned to me. "Are you okay?"

"You're asking me? Are you kidding me?" I growled, the dweller pacing my skin. "You almost died!"

"*But* I didn't." He pulled me in close, a smirk on his face.

"I'm gonna kill you myself."

"That I don't doubt." He kissed me hard, then stepped back, his cheekiness quickly dying off. "Now lead us out of here. I really hate being underground. Especially in the dark." He took my hand while I escorted us up the tunnel, dodging the fallen boulders. Rook allowed Celeste to thread her fingers into his fur, guiding her forward. She was shell-shocked and heavily drugged, leaning fully into him, using him as a crutch.

Rook's body was tense, and I knew it was partially due to the intimacy of her gripping onto his fur like she was, but also because the dweller was ready to attack and kill if anything came at us.

I didn't want to think about the horrors in that room, what had happened, and who we left behind.

A torture chamber was now a graveyard.

We had no time to mourn or think. We had to keep going.

We were only four to make it out of there alive.

Chapter 23

Ash

The cold air blissfully licked against my skin, my lungs filling with freedom, with life. Earth balanced on a fine line between existence and the void. Either you went too far up in the atmosphere or too far down into the core, and life ceased to exist. The hollowness was like a vacuum, leaving an emptiness in my body.

My toes curled in my boots when I spotted the night sky, giving my eyes focus. I craved the feel of my feet in the soil, the buzz of nature sinking into my bones, whisking away the panic still thumping in my chest.

Raven's hand squeezed mine, calming the chaos in my chest. The thrum of her pulse centered me, like she was the soil my roots needed to embed themselves in.

Stepping inside the courtyard of the castle, she let go, her gun raised as she searched the area, but her weapon was for show. Her dweller lingered underneath; the obscurer sat impatiently on her tongue.

Rook's large dweller shape glided in silently, blending in just as well with the night as he did in the pitch black. His eyes glowed hot, his claws cutting into the cobbled ground. He huffed, his nose nudging Celeste to stay next to him.

Her expression was blank, her eyes still slightly unfocused, her body covered with bruises, cuts, and grime. But she clung to him like a terrified child. She wore a loose tank that barely covered the tops of her legs, and I could see the redness between her thighs, the coating left behind from her assault.

My stomach twisted, my gaze flickering to Raven. She had been within seconds of being his victim too, a body to use as he pleased, nothing more than an empty vessel. Guttural rage surged up my throat, the snap of tree branches echoing through the yard.

The sounds of battle raging on the other side of the courtyard wall finally brought me back to what was important in the moment.

Surviving.

"This way." I pointed us towards the exit. We barely got a few feet.

Swish!

Rook's beast roared, and I whipped around to see his back leg dip, an arrow sticking out of it.

Swish! Another arrow drove into his other back leg, dropping him to the ground. My gaze snapped up to where the arrows came from.

Revulsion strangled my throat.

"I knew the bomb would scurry some rats to the surface." Iain stood on the upper balcony, smugness curling his lips, his bow and arrow aimed at us, shooting off another one into Rook's back. The dweller jerked, his body twitching, trying to shake it off, yet his massive frame struggled to rise.

"Rook!" I felt Raven's fear, her confusion at her brother's rapid response to the arrows. Dark dwellers were the killers, the almost indestructible assassins of the old fae world. A few arrows shouldn't be able to take him down.

"I had these custom made." Iain grabbed another arrow, appraising it. "Coated in a lethal dose of *pure* goblin metal. It seeps into your blood system instantaneously, paralyzing you." Fuck. Pure goblin essence was fatal. "Did you not see what happened to your Russian friend earlier?"

My mind scrambled back to how easily Eve went down, her legs not able to get her back up after the arrow hit her.

"She's dead. And soon your brother will be too." Iain sneered.

A rumble of pure fury vibrated up Raven's throat, taking a step towards him.

"I wouldn't." Iain pulled back the bow, pointing at Celeste and letting another go, zipping over her head to the person who stood behind her.

The tip sank into my chest before I could even move.

"NO!" Raven screamed, her eyes wide in horror, instinctively moving to me.

"Uh-uh," Iain toyed, stopping her in her tracks, her body heaving, her fear radiating through me.

I stared numbly down at the arrow piercing my chest, feeling the poison slipping into my tissue. Plucking it out, I dropped the toxic barb to the stone floor with a clank, my sneer rising to Iain.

"I will make sure you go down with me."

"Such meaningless words." Iain rolled his eyes, lowering his bow, his face a portrait of pure conceit and narcissism. "You will do nothing to me." He nodded to something behind us.

A bulked-up figure stepped out from the shadows, chest puffed as he made gorilla noises while another man slinked toward me, his catlike characteristics stalking his prey. The third shifted shadily closer, the hyena-man going for Celeste.

Joska and Samu advanced on Raven and me, causing her to growl, her magic swelling, her claws and teeth budding from her as the blades on her back pierced her clothes, a hiss of words rolling off her tongue.

Iain grabbed his head with a cry.

"What is happening?" Iain's voice rose in panic. "What are you doing?"

Raven snarled, her obscurer blackening the stars above, dimming the firebulbs, its fury like a fog of death.

Iain screamed, blood pooling from his nose, her power squeezing his brain.

"Stop her!"

Joska leaped for her, but her obscurer was too focused on Iain to notice.

"No!" I bellowed, but it was too late. Joska tackled her to the ground, breaking her concentration for a moment.

It was enough time for Iain to pick up his bow. Aiming it at her, his fingers twitched to let go of the poison arrow.

"*Mroczny!* Stop!" I heaved, pleading with her, not able to handle if anything happened to her, the toxin already tingling my fingers. "Please... *dziubuś.*"

She snapped her teeth, her eyes fire, wanting to disobey me.

Dziubuś. I called to her, running invisible fingers over the monsters inside her, whispering for them to back down. *I can't handle anything happening to you.*

"Nor I you," she responded to something I never said aloud.

"Too late for that," I whispered.

Joska latched goblin metal around her wrists, ripping her fae magic from her. Her body went limp for a moment under him.

"Get the fuck up." Joska kicked at her, dragging her up to her feet.

Iain glared at her, wiping the blood leaking from his nose. "Take them to my mother."

Samu grabbed onto me, pushing me to follow Joska and Raven, Balazs yanking Celeste with him.

"Noooooooooo!" The high-pitched cry came from Celeste. She thrashed against Balazs, screaming hysterically. "Don't touch me! Don't fucking touch me!" Her arms flayed and punched. It was as if his touch dissolved her numbness and pushed her into sheer panic. Her trauma was a place where logic was no longer a concept, and distress had taken over. "Let gooooo!" she wailed, twisting out of the hyena's hold. "Nooo! Help!!"

"Get her under control!" Iain ordered, lifting his arrow again, but she wouldn't stop wiggling and squirming, making it impossible to get a lock on her. "Shut her up!" His agitation rose at her frenetic screeches.

"Get off me!" she pitched from her gut. "Don't touch—"

Balazs reared back, his fist striking her face so hard it cracked like a whip across the courtyard. Her neck snapped back, flinging her body to the ground in a heap.

Rook growled, trying to lift himself up, but fell back down, his system trying to fight the poison crippling him.

Celeste didn't move. I couldn't even tell if she was breathing.

"Good." Iain lowered his bow, nodding his chin at Balazs in approval. "Move them out." He indicated to me and Raven. Samu, Joska, and Balazs shoved us forward to a stairway.

Rook growled as we passed, but his physique sagged further into the stone, the handful of arrows still sticking out of his hide, his breath labored.

Energy crackled in the air between Rook and Raven, as if they were communicating. A sob wracked her chest, a hum in his. They held each other's gazes until the last moment. Joska drove us up the stairs, leaving Rook to die.

In the moments of battle, where death and survival were a blink apart, there was no time to think, to consider true loss when peril was a constant. But I could feel Raven lock down, not allowing even a consideration, a splinter of doubt that he would survive this. She couldn't, not if she had to keep functioning.

But we all knew pure goblin essence was fatal. Even if you got a remedy quickly after it hit the bloodstream, it still might not help. I had worked with herbs, which could postpone the fatality until a remedy was found, but I had none of those nearby, even if I had the chance to save him.

To save myself.

Rook and I were dead men walking.

My only design was to somehow get Raven to safety before the poison overtook me, to know she was secure and away from harm. Then I could die peacefully.

I tripped up the stairs leading to the top, numbness shooting down into my legs. The reverberations of battle drummed through the stone and into my bones like a death march.

When we reached the top, my lungs sucked in. Fire torches ignited the land below in a bath of yellowish red, as if we descended into the nine layers of hell, each one a different horror.

Bodies littered the ground, and I was afraid to look too closely to see if I knew any of them. I could see Warwick and Brexley fighting by the pond and Scorpion and Hanna below us, but the rest were lost in the throng of silhouettes dancing the last steps of their demise.

"Perfect timing." Her voice knifed through my chest, convulsing me with rage, wrenching my head to her.

Sonya stood on the higher walkway, her blood-red dress blowing in the wind, her blonde hair twirling around her face. She turned and smiled, the necklace around her throat glinting under the firelight.

"You can come watch as your friends die." She motioned to the commotion below. "It's been quite entertaining to watch them try, though."

"Looks like most of those are yours." I couldn't stop the quip from snipping out, noting Warwick taking another dozen out while Brexley's ghostly army lined them up like lambs to a slaughter.

"Because I allowed them to." She rubbed at her stomach, the fabric hiding any observation of a bump forming there. Fae had different pregnancy times. Some were equivalent to humans, some showed very quickly, some took years. It all depended on what they were carrying.

There was no real precedence of a fae carrying one of those monsters' babies. If there was, I didn't know of it.

"But now I've grown bored. My emotions are so fickle these days," she mused, her smile haughty. She nodded to her guard, who let out a whistle.

The sound churned my blood to ice, the *Primul* darting out of the gate below, each one heading for a separate group of my family.

Fear and anger rebounded in my chest, the goblin metal robbing me of my magic, keeping the trees from responding. I couldn't do anything but stand here, watching the monsters leap towards my family, taking them from me.

"No," I whimpered, hating my feebleness, hating that I wasn't stronger.

"Go join them." Sonya ordered Joska, Samu, and Balazs. "The baby is making me sleepy, and I want to go to bed soon."

Joska's grin hitched the side of his face, his attention going to where Brexley was.

"Gladly." An excited monkey sound hooted from him. His hatred of Brex was thick in the air. His grudge from their past had him taking off down the stairs, pounding his chest. Samu and Balazs trailed after.

"Caden!" I heard Birdie scream out in warning as the rhino barreled for them, hitting Caden with his horn, flinging him to the ground, rolling him.

Caden! My mouth tried to call for my friend, but nothing came out, my body shaking and starting to work against me.

Raven thrashed against her cuffs, her tongue trying to move the gag from her mouth.

"Oh no, sweetheart." Iain grabbed her ponytail, yanking her back into him, his mouth moving against her ear, malicious hatred pointed at her. "After what you just did, you will watch every one of them get their lungs torn from their chests." His eyes shifted to me, his hand sliding down Raven's stomach. "And he will watch me fuck you before *he* dies." He flipped the button on her pants.

I charged at him, my teeth bared. A razor-edged spear came to my throat, a guard slipping from the shadows to stop me from attacking, but when I peered over, I felt the ground break under me again.

Dubthach.

The Druid was dressed in the same dashiki-style shirt and cotton pants, but nothing else felt the same. His body was tense, and he stared down at me with a detached expression, his jaw tense, his eyes flickering with disgust.

What. The. Fuck.

It was obvious… he wasn't being kept prisoner here. He belonged here.

"Holy shit. It was you." I gaped, seeing everything in a different light. "It was you who led the army to the site. You turned on your friends." I always figured it was me, that Nyx had tracked me down, exposing the camp's whereabouts.

"They were never my *friends*." His lip lifted. "Even in a place that pretended to accept everyone, I was treated like an outcast. I belonged less than the humans did."

"So you turned on them because you weren't in the popular group?" I sputtered. "Becoming a slave to her instead?"

"Slave?" He chuckled. "I get freedom here to be who I truly am. Iacob cut us off from our true nature. We couldn't use magic inside the camp walls, besides my protection spell. He limited us, kept us docile and weak. No weapons of any kind, including ourselves."

"Why didn't you just leave, then?"

"Because he saved my life a long time ago." Dubthach's lip curled. "I was bound to him."

"Until you paid him back."

"I have now saved *his* life." Dubthach motioned under us. "He lives… and is even better off. Superior to his human form."

"Not sure he will feel the same."

"Once his transition is done," Sonya spoke up. "He will see the truth."

"And what's your truth, Sonya?" I sneered, but every word was a struggle, slurring and slow, the toxins burning into my veins.

"That the weakest will always be weeded out." A mirthless smile hinted on her lips, her eyebrow cocking at me before she stared back at the carnage below, her hand once again going to her abdomen. "Laws of nature. The strong take out the weak." She stared off, then yawned. "Iain, my love, before you fuck that girl in front of me, like you did to Sergiu before I killed Lazar…"

What? Lazar was dead?

"Oh yes, such fun." Iain chuckled. "He thought himself so tough, so alpha until I fucked it right out of him as his father watched, had him moaning so loud, even after his father was shot right in front of him."

Vomit coated my throat, seeing for the first time how truly sick Iain was. I shouldn't have been surprised—he shot his own brother in the head without hesitation.

"I don't need you to rehash the moment, my dear." She patted his arm, the one still wrapped around Raven. "The *Primul* are having too much fun playing with their toys, and I am desperate for a bath and a snack. Is Kalaraja ready?"

"I think so," Iain responded.

She leaned over the wall. "Kill them all!"

A chattering hiss filled the air. Z stepped further into the field, his tail curled over his head, and wrapped his hand around someone's throat, picking him off the ground. Their short frame struggled in his grip. I recognized him.

Kozlov.

As fast as a bullet, Z's stinger stabbed through his neck, breaking through bone, cartilage, and guts. Dimitri Kozlov's eyes widened, understanding filling them before Z yanked his tail back, almost tearing off the president's head, the body going limp in his arms. Z flung the corpse to the ground with no thought and headed for his next victim.

Not far from his corpse, Eve laid dead, an arrow still sticking out of her chest.

The squeal of a wild boar echoed across the garden, the *Primul* running into a group, his tusks slicing into Wesley's legs.

I tried to scream, to bark out a warning, but my voice got lost, drowning in my weakness. I pleaded with the nature gods, demanded them to rise, to burn the world down. Nothing happened, except darkness prickling at the edges of my vision.

Iain's hands started to move down Raven's body, yanking on her pants. He fixed his gaze on me, making sure to keep my attention on what he was doing.

I fell further into hell, trapped in my body, hearing the screams of my friends dying, watching my mate being touched by a psychopath, and I could do nothing to prevent it.

Dziubuś. Sajnálom. I expressed my sorrow, my soul aching.

Don't you dare give up on me. I could see her glare back at me, but grief and devastation hinted in her emerald eyes. *You are not allowed to leave me. You understand me?*

I wish that was a promise I could make her.

Ash! Please don't give up.

Did she think I wanted to leave her? To go out like this? Once again, I had let her down. She would be the one to watch me die, and I was helpless to stop it.

My legs dropped to the stone, numbness moving into my brain. I had finally found my soul, my heart, and I lost it all before it even started.

CRACK!

Magic popped the air like a cannon, the particles making waves like a lapping pool. Energy rushed over my skin, my head twisting to the side.

I was hallucinating. There could be no other explanation.

A fae door cut out of nothing floated near the property line, a figure walking through the opening.

Dzsinn.

My lids narrowed, blinking again, trying to clear my vision. My mind was playing tricks on me. Almost no one could work the fae doors since the barrier fell between the worlds. And you couldn't show up inside a protected Druid barrier. Fae couldn't counter a Druid spell.

Yet the battlefield went still, and a gasp rose from Sonya.

"How did they get in? What did you do!" she screeched at Dubthach.

"N-nothing." Dubthach back from me, in shock. "It's not possible."

Sonya shoved her disbelief away, schooling her face, turning to the single man who had broken through.

"Is that your great talent, cousin?" She clasped her hands on the wall, trying to hide her confusion, appearing annoyed. "Popping through fae doors?"

"He should not be able to do it." Dubthach shook his head in a hiss. "He is fae."

"Yes, I am fae." Dzsinn smiled, answering the Druid, but looking at Sonya. "But some of my friends are not."

Movement came from behind him, the air fluttering like waves. Figures filed out of the door, and I heard Raven gasp through her gag, my own voice getting lost in the sea of poison.

Faces I recognized from a year ago stepped into the gardens—Ember, Eli, Cooper, West, Gabby, Cole, Dax, Dominic and a few more I didn't recognize.

But when her father, Lorcan, emerged alongside a tiny brunette, looking so much like her daughter, I had to blink again. Her expression was fierce, magic billowing around her, telling me not to take her petite frame for granted.

The Sovereign of the Unified Nations.

Queen Kennedy.

Chapter 24

Raven

"Mom!" My garbled cry got caught behind my gag. I wiggled against Iain's hold. "Dad!"

Seeing my family, my uncles and aunts there, filled my body with warmth and hope. As if actual adults were finally here to handle everything, and I could be the little girl and hide within their protective arms.

But right behind that feeling came fear. Guilt. They were all here for me. I put them in a position to have to protect me. Save me.

Again.

"Stop moving," Iain snarled in my ear. He yanked out a blade, the sharp sting stilling me when he cut into my neck.

A noise came from beside me, darting my gaze down to Ash. Sweat coated his skin, his eyes shiny and glazed, a lip curled at Iain while he swayed on his knees.

Panic gutted out my lungs. True terror like I had never felt before vibrated my bones. The link between us was hazy, a thread still clutching for dear life. Soon it would be gone.

"Release my daughter." My mother's voice came from the garden below. Dressed down in jeans and a sweater, her long dark hair pulled back, she still held the authority of a queen. Torin, my mother's personal guard, was right behind her like he always was, never leaving her side. She was petite like me, with a youthful face and soft voice, but I knew that tone. The strength and ferocity behind her beauty. So many underestimated her, thought her too delicate to really fight. Some fighters didn't need muscles and weapons. Her mind, like mine, could tear through flesh and break people's will to her own.

Standing to her right was Aunt Fionna, King Lars's mate, dressed in similar attire. Where my mother was a natural obscurer, Aunt Fionna had trained herself in the dark arts and became skilled in black magic, though she wasn't a strong seer as my mother. It went all to her daughter, Piper.

Six years older, my stunning cousin was one of the most powerful Druid seers in existence. Power like hers was a double-edged sword. It broke her grasp on reality some days, made her flighty and not always present in this world. Adrift in the multiple visions of the future that could unfold, she had trouble understanding what was real and what wasn't.

"Your *Majesty*." Sonya's timbre was full of mocking. "What an honor it is for you to visit me."

"Let my daughter go now, Sonya," the queen responded.

Sonya let out a trilled laugh. "You think you hold any power here, Druid?" Sonya's humor was quickly dying away. "This is *my* country. Not that you have much power in the UFN. Let's be honest, Lars is the only thing keeping the people from dragging you out and banishing you."

A snarl vibrated from my father's throat, his eyes flashing red, blades popping up from his spine.

"Oh, does your little consort not like that? Better keep your guard dog on a leash, Majesty." Sonya's blonde eyebrow arched. "And if any of your pets shit on my lawn, you'll have to clean up after them."

A wave of growls bounded from my family, shaking the ground.

"Or maybe I'll have them cleaned up." Sonya smirked, her attention flitting to the highest tower and down to the ground where her monsters waited.

My gaze went up to the tower, where I noted an outline within the shadows. Someone was up there, ready to fire on my family. Thrashing against Iain, I looked from my mom's dark brown eyes, fear leaking through them, to my father's, the same bright color as mine. My dweller tried to scream through the link they all shared, including my brother, but my fucked-up ass could not. The oddity among oddities.

Please don't. I shook my head, trying to tell them. *You don't know what you are up against. I can't have anything happen to you.*

Rage simmered under my dad's skin, the dweller showing himself, but I could feel the love, the intensity of what he felt. My father was my alpha. The need to protect me with everything he had dominated his aura.

"Do not challenge me, Sonya." My mother's elegant voice held a deadly cut to it. "You will not like the results."

"I already like the results." She motioned to me, Iain's knife cutting deeper into my neck. "I have both your children." She tipped her head, voice dripping with disdain. "One is my prisoner and the other one... well, he is already dead."

The silence that hit after her announcement was louder than an explosion, striking my chest with the grief I was trying to keep at bay.

Rook...

With the goblin metal blocking me, I couldn't feel any magic or the link between us. Wouldn't I feel my twin's death deep in my bones, like it would rattle through, a cold empty hole, part of myself dying along with him.

"You lie," my mom spat.

My father's head jerked to Cole, my brother's alpha, both of their eyes widening, realizing Rook was probably no longer a thread among their link. My dad ran his own group, but my brother decided to go with Cole. As much as my brother and father love each other, their mutual stubbornness and tempers worked better without Dad being his alpha.

"I don't need to lie." She grinned smugly, the fingers of one hand absently running along her necklace, the other hand at her stomach. "Not when the truth is so much better," Sonya said. "You let your children out into the world as unprepared little lambs. They walked right into slaughter."

A rumble came from Lorcan before his clothes tore to shreds, his bones popping as he shifted completely into his dweller, claws cutting the earth, his roar penetrating the air with anger and grief.

The sound of losing a child.

My legs bowed at the cry, the agony spinning my head, my gaze darting quickly to Ash. Pale and sweaty, he swayed like a brewing storm, ready to be taken down. My brother was already lost to the toxins, and soon it would be my mate. It was too much. My brain shut down my heart and mind. I became numb.

"By coming here, you invoked international war, and my only rebuttal was to fight back." Sonya shrugged. "Just know, when you watch everyone around you die, it was your own doing. You were never supposed to be queen. You had no right to step into queen Aneria's shoes. You are a disgrace. Your death will be cheered by many." Sonya nodded her head to the monsters below. "Kill them."

The *Primul* howled, drawing attention to them. Expressions of horror fluttered over some of my family, not expecting to see the grotesque beings moving toward them.

My family was strong. We were born killers, but these weren't normal fae.

"NO!" I screamed, but only garbled noise made it past my lips. The sound was drowned out by the thunderous roar of the dwellers shifting, magic crackling in the air. The familiar feel of Druid magic from my mother, aunt, and cousin hummed around us.

I heard a *crack* as beasts and monsters slammed into each other, howls penetrating the soil. Druid magic sparked, the familiarity of it dancing over my skin and burning up my nose as my mother and Aunt Fionna battled against the mindless drones surrounding them.

"Dubthach." Sonya turned to him. "Deal with them."

"What?" Dubthach blanched. "She is the queen."

"An impostor." Sonya frowned. "I want her dead."

"They hold dark magic," he rebutted. "I can't counter that. They are more powerful."

"Then maybe I should employ them." Her nose wrinkled. "I mean, what *use* are you to me?" Her threat was clear. "I dispose of things no longer useful to me."

He nodded his head, heading down the steps.

"I want you to watch, Raven," Sonya spoke, not even looking at me, her hand on her belly. "The weak will always be weeded out. Right or wrong, it is the law of nature. And you will be part of creating something even better. I have come too far, planned too long. Sat for decades on the sidelines, letting others rule me, others dictate. But now it's all in my grasp, and I will not stop until I get what I want."

My pulse beat louder in my ears; the screams of death and agony dragged like claws on my spine.

"You will help to create a new breed of fae." She stared off at the battle below. "So powerful, no one can touch us."

"Us?" I spat back.

"Yes." Her attention cut back over to me. "You will produce their heirs until you are no longer of use."

A woman's scream came from below, chilling my veins. My stomach sank when I recognized the voice.

"NO!" Aunt Fionna cried, terror gripping every nuance.

The snake-man seized Piper by the neck, his venomous teeth at her throat, while Latin words flowed from her mother. The snake smiled at her, Druid magic not affecting him.

Sonya's smile curved her face at seeing both my mother and aunt try to use their black magic against the monster, not understanding it was pointless. Unlike the mindless soldiers, these things were neither fae nor human, but their own species, which did not bow to any magic.

Making them more indestructible. Only by beheading did these things seem to die.

Piper stood strong, her chin high as if she was accepting her demise that she would go out with pride. Her stepfather's daughter. A true princess, even if not by blood.

Agony muffled from me, my heart stuttering for my cousin. Wyatt might have splintered us, my heart and ego unable to withstand the pain of them together, but I never stopped loving her. She was my family, my idol growing up. And now, with Ash, I realized I was a fantasist in my thoughts about Wyatt. They always had a deep connection. Where ours was more friendship, theirs was an unfathomable love they tried to fight. And no matter how much I screamed, cried, and pushed her away, she was here, fighting for me.

Where was Wyatt? He never left her side.

"No," I whined, withering in Iain's grip as the snake flicked out his tongue, tasting its prey. His jaw opened wider, venom dripping from his fangs, his jaw about to clamp down.

"NOOOOO!" The scream rattled my soul, but it didn't venture from my lips. The deep bellow broke across the air like a war cry as more people popped out of thin air. Two enormous men with blondish hair, white eyes, and battle-axes came charging in.

Wyatt, followed by his father Ryker, his mother Zoey, Croygen, his mate Kat, and their pirate crew.

The wanderers—Ryker, Wyatt, and Zoey, did not need fae doors to travel. Their magic was something so rare and valuable that they were the only three to have this type of power. As long as they could picture where they wanted to go, they could "jump" to locations, bringing at least one or two people with them.

Expression carved like stone, Wyatt, a furious, stoic Viking like his father, came barreling toward his mate, his axe swinging for the snake.

Their entry took focus for a moment. And a moment was all I needed.

Ramming my arms as hard as I could into Iain's crotch, I slammed my head back, hearing the crack of his nose burst in my eardrums. He doubled over with a howl of pain. I pitched forward, breaking free of Iain's hold, Sonya's shouts a blanketed screech in my ears.

Iain scrambled for me, slamming us both to the ground, his body landing on mine.

Air caught in my throat, a warm sensation buzzing over me. I knew something was wrong.

Lowering my gaze, I took in the handle of the blade sticking out of my stomach, red liquid pooling out and warming me against the cold air.

I didn't feel pain.

My eyes flickered to Ash, his focus slowly moving from the knife in my stomach to my face.

I expected to see sadness. A distant understanding that this was all over. We weren't walking out of here alive. We would die here together.

No such acceptance came from him. His glossy eyes blazed with fever, one word falling from his lips as he looked at me.

"Mine."

Chapter 25

Ash

Mine.

The claim drove into every fiber of my being, the fierce need to protect her wrapped around my DNA as if it could pause the poison bleeding into my system, clearing my mind in a mist of disconnected thoughts.

The knife in her stomach cut through me, hemorrhaging my vision in red. Rage. Fury.

No one touched what was mine. *Hurt* what was mine.

If Raven died, with my last breath, I would turn the soil into rotting black tar, destroying any life from this spot, a mark that polluted this world in darkness for what it took from me.

"What did you do?" Sonya barked. "I need her."

To be a vessel. To be assaulted and abused, forced to carry a monster's baby.

The only baby she will carry is mine.

Something out of the corner of my eye scuttled along the wall, moving toward Raven, but my focus did not waver from Iain. He had already taken so much from me.

A growl came up my throat, Raven's green eyes still on me, her breathing labored, blood pumping out of her wound. Iain snarled, yanking another blade from his belt, moving to her, ready to finish the job.

She called herself a monster, but in truth, I was.

Rage snarled up my throat. Like roots being torn from the soil, my feet pushed me up. Wrath shoved past the toxins, slamming through the ground, ripping the earth's heart out, letting it pump in my hand.

A bellow shredded my throat as I tried to rise. I had no thought or plan, my anger driving me forward.

"Get him!" Sonya screamed at her guards.

"Stay back! He's mine!" Iain pulled out a pistol from his thigh strap, lifting the weapon to my head before I got to my feet. "Guess it's fitting you should die this way. You can tell my brother hello from me."

The gun cocked.

"NO!" I heard the fall of metal to the ground. Raven grunted, yanking the blade from her gut as she shakily stood, the shackles discarded. I could just make out a small silhouette near her, the one who freed her.

Opie.

"Why are you standing there? Get her!" Sonya screeched at the few soldiers around her.

My eyes met Raven's. It was only a second in time, but I could feel her in my head, my soul, my heart. We didn't have to speak to understand each other. She was so much part of me now that I knew when I died, a part of her would be joining me.

She moved first. Fast and quick, her bloody blade sliced the back of Iain's knee, dropping his one leg as he fired the gun. The bullet skimmed over my head, the force of it burning my scalp.

"Ahhh!" Iain screamed when she sliced at him again, his fist smashing down on Raven's temple, her knife tumbling from her hands, skidding it into my boot. Her pained cry harvested the last scraps of my energy.

Crimson.

It scorched through me like flames and marked him for death.

My shoulders bunched, and I swiped up the dagger. With a cry, I barreled for Iain, ramming into him and throwing us to the ground. When I leaped on him, he had to let go of his gun to stop my knife from going through his neck. Iain and I punched and clawed at each other, my energy struggling, making me sloppy and weak, allowing him to grip the handle, twisting it around to me.

"Say hi to your demon slut for me too," he sneered. The tip of the blade nicked my eyebrow, my blood dripping on him.

The knife pushed for the middle of my forehead.

Raven roared, her magic fizzing over my skin.

POP! POP! The bullets fired until the gun chamber clicked.

Red mist sprayed into my face, the body under me jerking from the impact before going limp. Blood gushed from the two holes ripped through Iain's head, his dead eyes staring up, his mouth open in a hollow scream. A cry that would never reach the surface.

The memory of Lukas, seeing the same hole through his head, the same dead eyes, as bile rushed up my throat, taking me back to that night.

"Ash!" Raven's cry was the only thing that broke me out of my numbness, pulling my gaze to her. She stood there with Iain's gun, her eyes red flames, her teeth like daggers, but her wound still gushed with blood. She was too weak to heal quickly enough.

Sonya's scream rattled my nerves, sliding me off her dead son as she ran to him.

"Noooo! My boy!" she wailed, dropping down, her dress soaking in the same color liquid pooling around him.

I tried to rise, but my muscles went limp, taking me back down.

"No, Ash." Raven was at my side, realizing I could no longer get up. The adrenaline I used burned the poison faster through me. "Don't give up."

"Go." I reached up, touching her face.

"No. I won't leave you."

"You have to." My lids felt so heavy. "Save your family. They need you."

"I can't leave you here. Tell me how to save you." I could hear her panic.

"You can't."

Sonya heaved out a chilling growl. Standing up, she surged with fury.

"I will kill you," she sneered.

"Just try." Raven bared her teeth, rising to challenge her, the blades on her back slicing through her shirt. But I could feel her magic was thin, her body trying too hard to heal itself to be a real threat.

The few guards around Sonya pointed their weapons at us. But instead of ordering them, she lifted her attention to the tall tower right next to us, a cruel gleam in her eyes. "Kalaraja," she called out, "Kill her family now!"

The outline up in the tower a story over us stepped out, the moon casting a glow on half of Kalaraja's face, a long scope rifle in his grip.

"Shoot the queen first, then her father, her aunts and uncles," she ordered. "So she can watch her family die before her eyes. Then take out every one of his, starting with Brexley."

He cocked his rifle, peering through the scope down at the garden, right at Queen Kennedy.

"Nooo!" Raven wailed.

Bang! Bang! Bang!

The gun fired, a bullet cracking across the air. Raven screamed, waiting for the mark to find its target, to see her mother drop to the ground.

Every guard around Sonya fell to the ground like dominoes, a bullet in each of their brains.

Confused, stunned silence descended on us as we took in the dead sentries, following the path of the bullets back to the originating spot.

Kalaraja's weapon pointed down at Sonya. The man who had shot me, who had hunted Brexley, was standing on our side. At least for now.

"What? What are you doing?" she squawked, sounding more like Nyx. "How dare you shoot at me! Go against me!" Her jaw twitched, fury blasting in her eyes at him.

Bang!

He fired again, the bullet getting within inches of her before it went off course, skimming by her. Kalaraja never missed. I could see the area around her judder, the layer of magic blocking her from harm. Sonya's protection not only came from the trinket around her neck, but a spell cast around her.

A spell from a Druid.

Those types of spells were very intricate and took a huge toll on the spellcaster because they constantly pulled at the caster's energy, always needing to adapt and change with the body and environment.

"You fool," she hissed. "You think I hadn't planned for something like this?"

Bang!

Another bullet rang out in the air. This time it reached someone near the castle gates, burrowing deep into flesh, bursting through tissue and bone.

Dubthach's body jerked, his blood painting the snow. The instant his heart stopped beating, his living spells sputtered and snapped, dying with their source.

The invocation dissolved around Sonya, and a flicker of genuine fear danced through her eyes, her grip going to the necklace around her throat.

Pop! Pop! Pop!

Gunfire rained down on Sonya. Crying out, she shuffled out of the way, each bullet missing her by a hair. The stone did its job of making her the luckiest woman on Earth.

It was time her luck ran out.

I struggled to my feet, spotting the disregarded knife next to Iain. Staggering for it, I grazed the surface, but right as my fingers touched the cool steel, another hand snatched it from my grip.

Sonya stood over me, her hand holding the blade, a sneer on her lips.

"You and your whore will die, just like your last ones."

"Not before you." Revenge roared through me like a beast, my body swinging, lunging for her and snatching away the dagger. It wasn't revenge giving me strength, it was my love for Raven, love for Lukas and Kek.

"No, wai—" The blade cut through the flesh of her throat, slowing as it serrated bone and muscle. A howl tore from my soul, unleashing the final death cry of my energy.

Sonya's scream was stopped, her vocals severed, her head cut from her neck in a mist of gore. The Cintamani stone necklace flung into the air, hitting the ground.

Her body collapsed, her head rolling a few feet, streaming a shower of carnage between the severed pieces.

I stared at the corpses numbly, my brain trying to understand the significance. Robotically, I leaned over, grabbed the gore-splattered necklace, and stuffed it in my pocket. The gunfire from the tower had ceased, and Kalaraja was gone. The reverberations of shooting and screams from below filtered up to our place on the wall, feeling like another world still stuck in chaos as silence encompassed us.

I heaved out, staring at her corpse. Iain lay only feet from her.

They were dead.

Their demise was a mirror reflection of Kek and Lucas, as if the two of them were with me. Had a say in their end. Okay, this would be totally Kek. The sick, twisted justice would make her smile.

"Good work, fairy." I could hear Kek as if she was next to me. *"Now don't die yourself, otherwise who will tell legendary stories about me in bed?"*

A sobbing laugh bubbled up my throat, the blade falling from my hands, and I staggered until I lay not far from them.

I completed my mission. I could die in peace.

"Ash! Don't you fucking dare." Raven was next to me, pulling me into her lap.

Go! I tried to tell her, but nothing came out.

She knew me too well.

"I won't leave you." Grief streamed down her face, her throat thick with emotion.

My gaze met hers, my eyes conveying deep love.

"Ash, please," she begged. My lids drooped lower as I drifted away.

"ASH! NO!"

Her cries were worse than any wound I ever had, digging so deeply into me, I knew even in death, I wouldn't find peace. She wouldn't allow me to.

Not until we found each other again.

Chapter 26

Raven

Anguish yowled through my chest, my body shaking. I leaned over, putting my ear to his chest, his heartbeat growing softer, his life slipping from my fingers.

"How do I save you?" I tried to dig deep, to find the source that had bonded us before and saved me from death. I could feel nothing, our power draining instead of uniting.

"What do I do?" I wailed. "Help me." He was my rock, my core, the tamer of my monsters, and the source of my strength. I couldn't do this without him.

No, mroczny. You are all those things on your own. His voice was just a whisper through my soul.

"Ash…" My forehead dropped to his, my tears seeping over his skin.

I could hear our friends and family below, fighting for their lives, Sonya's soldiers not knowing their queen was dead, while my soul was being ripped from me. I was dying even if my body continued living.

The story of my mother rebuking my father at first was well known. Their convoluted past and her dedication to his late nephew turned her away from her mate. They both suffered. But to us dwellers, it was equal to a slow, agonizing death sentence, and none of them had knotted to their mates like I had. It didn't matter if I was supposed to be queen, if my role in life wasn't supposed to include a tree fairy, if everyone in the world didn't think we should be together.

Our bindings went beyond labels and titles.

"Ash," I sobbed, rocking into him. "Don't leave me."

Something plunked on the ground next to my knee, my attention going to a stone coiled within a chain that fell from his pocket.

The Cintamani stone. A tick scurried up the back of my neck, rummaging around in my brain, trying to pull at my school teachings, the knowledge stored within its files.

"It gives you the opportunity and luck. And a source of nature's energy." I heard Dzsinn's voice in my head. It was known to be the elixir of life.

My pulse thumped in my ears, my body flushing with adrenaline. Shakily, my hand reached out for the stone, sensing the vibrations brushing against my palm, the power emanating from it.

My lungs tightened, my heart racing. Hope burned like acid in the back of my throat. I plucked up the chain. Vitality sang from the gem on a frequency my dweller could hear and tickled at my bones.

Every wish I had to save Ash whirled in my mind as I clutched the chain and dropped it over my head.

Heal him! The stone fell against my breastbone, rubbing my skin like a genie bottle as my hand slammed over the arrow wound in Ash's chest. The stone reacted instantly to my plea, performing like a lightning rod, pulling energy from everywhere and funneling it through me.

A scream wrenched from my stomach, pain splintering my nerves as nature answered my call. Life exploded behind my eyes, burrowing deep like roots. I gritted my teeth against flashes of us together; the blood we had spilled over this land fused us. It tied us to the earth, our own marrow a sacrifice to the gods.

The echo of tree branches cracked from the forest nearby, sounding like fireworks, popping and exploding across the sky, answering my call. We had pulled from nature before, drenched the earth in our cum and blood, and I could feel our essence pumping back into me, filling his veins with the connection we shared, and pulling the toxins from his blood.

A howl expelled from my lips, and my body shook, feeling the intrusive poison like it was being siphoned from my own body. The infected blood surged from his wound, slipping through my fingers and oozing to the ground, staining his shirt like a tattoo.

No line remained between us, no notion of individualism or pride. The dweller and obscurer wrapped around his soul like it was theirs while I took his pain, his life, his joy, and heartbreak and dragged it across the scorched land of death, yanking him back into life.

A scream belted out of Ash, his body jackknifing up, his green eyes popping open with blistering heat. He sucked in sharply, his chest heaving. Energy and life thrummed off him. His attention went to the pool of dark blood next to him, then his head snapped to me.

"*Dziubuś,*" he whispered hoarsely, his gaze going from the necklace around my throat to my face.

His voice rocked through me, breaking me. I fell into him with relief, the weight of what I almost lost slumping me forward with a wail. He pulled me to him, holding me close.

"You saved me." He leaned back to look at me, his thumbs wiping at my tears. "Again."

"Of course I did," I choked. "You are mine, Ash Hemlock Rowan. Every part, and I can't be the bane of your existence if you aren't around."

He huffed, a smile tugging his mouth as he gripped my face.

"Then I guess I have to live because I want nothing more than for you to drive me insane for the rest of my days, Raven Haley Scarlet Dragen." His mouth captured mine, his kiss claiming and needy.

A loud cry came from the garden below, breaking us apart.

"Kennedy, stop!" My father's cry soared up to us on the castle walk. The fear in his tone rushed me to my feet. We peered over the wall where the battle dotted the landscape, groups fighting with various foes. I spotted my father standing near my mom, reaching for her as blood dripped from my mother's eyes and nose, her body suspended in air as she used her black magic to control the guards coming at them. Piper lay on the ground nearby, Aunt Fionna over her, while Wyatt and Uncle Ryker still battled the snake-man.

They were all killing themselves to protect me.

Before, I had run from the consequences of my actions, pretended they were better off with me gone. Safer.

I had been a coward. That was not who I was. I was my mother and father's daughter. I came from the bloodline of a high Druid, a queen, a beast, and a killer.

I was a Cathbad and a Dragen, and I didn't bow or cower for anyone.

A growl came up my throat, fury setting my shoulders back. I peered over at Ash.

"Keep the necklace on, Your Highness." He grabbed my hand. "We will need all the luck we can get."

With that, we turned and rushed down the stairs into the sea of beasts, fiends, and monsters.

The tales of my family, the battles and wars they had fought, turned them into legends in my eyes growing up. Especially during the holidays, when more drinks were consumed. I was enraptured by their heroic journeys, thrilled at how exciting they sounded. Rook and I were extremely jealous because we were never part of one, like Piper had been, and Wyatt was too young to remember. She never shared our envy and lust, saying she recalled too much, was branded with the memories of the stench of death. While Wyatt, Rook, and I would reenact them with reverence as children.

Now I understood.

War was glamorized by those who had never been immersed in one. Whose boots hadn't slipped over guts, whose ears didn't echo with cries of death, who hadn't experienced the rancid, metallic taste of bullets and blood on their tongue. The horror of it was like a lashing, cutting so deep into my mind the scar would never cede.

While I wanted to vomit, the dweller surged up, the obscurer hissing with fury, craving repentance from anything hurting my family. No matter what, fighting was in my DNA, death as much a part of me as life.

On the field, the throng of mindless soldiers my mother was struggling to pin against each other was waning. Her energy dipped from her like the black blood seeping from her eyes in thick trails. Our obscurers were not gentle in their retaliation; they took from our bodies as greedily as suckling pigs. They had no understanding of weakness, of stopping to protect us from their craving. Black magic had no off switch.

"Mom!" I screamed, but she didn't hear me, too lost in her bubble, the plane she was hovering on locking her in. My father was trying to reach her, to be her anchor against the power.

With a roar, my own obscurer soared up, not wanting to release her from such a burden, but to be the one killing. Controlling those it deemed unworthy.

"Use me!" Ash barked to me, his hand taking mine again, already sensing what I needed.

Latin spilled from my lips, the world around me hazing, my power escalating. I felt the blades in my back, the length of my teeth cut into my lip, while a chant formed on my tongue.

I used to think of the dweller and obscurer being two separate entities, putting up with each other because they had to, learning to use the other to get what they wanted. Two dysfunctional pieces I fought endlessly with. It wasn't until Ash that I started to see them differently. Like he secured my two fragmented pieces together, melding them into one. Something that made me whole. They didn't use each other. They were part of each other, creating a unique monster, not a broken one.

I didn't need to fully shift like the rest of the dark dwellers, and I didn't need to be a high Druid like my mother's side. I would never be light magic. I sought to destroy. I was twisted, dark, ugly, and fucked up inside, and I was okay with that.

I was one of a fucking kind.

With the energy from Ash, my magic tore out of me, ripping through the minds of the guards, dropping the dozen near me like dominoes, my rage leaving nothing in its wake.

Their minds were like mush, easy to shred through. Sonya had already weakened them. Somewhere inside, I felt bad, knowing most were victims. Villagers who had no choice in becoming her prisoner. But they were dead anyway. Their human minds were not capable of mending after that sort of magic. She damned them the moment they stepped on these grounds.

Reaching out further, I heard the piercing cries. The bodies dropping, gripping their heads, feeling their brains burst and then slither out, as if they were trying to escape like drowning rats. A stabbing headache knifed between my eyes, blood dripping down my face to my chin, but I gripped Ash's hand harder, pushing out even further. In the distance, I could see guards around Caden, Birdie, and Wes, my dark fog slithering around the soldiers and gripping them until I could feel their brains squash in my hands. I didn't want to stop, zeroing in on another area near Aunt Ember and Uncle Eli. The feeling was seductive, the power addicting. My dweller huffed with the need to join, to sink its teeth into their flesh and kill its prey.

To roll in their blood, letting it mark my fur.

"*Mroczny.*" Ash's voice nipped at the back of my neck. A warning.

A snarl wrinkled my nose, my chant slaughtering through another group.

And another.

And another.

"*Mroczny!*" Ash's voice charged through me, his tone tugging on my leash. I yanked back, the pain between my eyes almost blinding, but I pushed on.

"Stop, Raven!" my father yelled. I heard my alpha, yet I still couldn't stop. I wanted to destroy them all.

"I order you to stop. Bow. To. Me. *Mroczny.*" Ash's command burrowed so deep I could not tell if he said it out loud or not. "*Now,*" he growled, the demand sinking into me like his teeth in my neck.

My body stilled, my obscurer and dweller slinking back. Obeying.

The plane I was on broke, dropping me to the ground in a heap.

"Raven!" My mother's cry twisted my head as she crawled to me, her own face dripping in black blood, her expression woven with anguish and relief.

"Mom." I hiccuped. She wrapped her arms around me, holding me so tight, I could feel her heart ricocheting in her chest. "Mom… I'm so sorry."

"You're alive. Oh, my baby… you're alive." She wept. "That's all that matters." She cradled me closer as my dad sank down on my other side, enveloping both of us, kissing my head.

Alive. A wail caught in my throat, my mind going to my brother. The pain was so unbearable I couldn't even hold the notion he wasn't okay. *He's fine. He has to be.*

"My baby girl." A sob broke my dad's voice, and I snuggled into his chest like I did so many times growing up. Tears trailed down my face, his familiar scent making me feel safe and protected in my parent's embrace.

But we weren't safe. Not yet.

My attention landed on my cousin a few feet away.

"Piper!" I broke away from my parents, crawling toward her. She was sitting up, Wyatt and Aunt Fionna on either side of her. Wyatt had ripped off his shirt, using it as a bandage to stop Piper's bleeding.

The snake-man's head lay a few feet from us.

I forgot all past resentment I had, any jealousy that used to sting. It all seemed silly and trivial now. "Are you okay?" I looked at where Wyatt held his discarded shirt against her shoulder.

"I told you all I was having visions of a snake biting me."

"We thought you meant a garden snake." Wyatt smiled down at her teasingly, with an expression he never once gave me. Complete adoration and love.

"This is a garden," she replied, flinching when Wyatt pulled his shirt away, checking the wound. "And he bit me in it."

I snorted, shaking my head and gripping her hand in mine, our eyes meeting. No words were needed; my cousin saw everything in my eyes, squeezing my hand back, hearing my apology.

I'm sorry. For everything.

Me too. Her soft smile said back.

I'm happy for you both.

She dipped her chin, her eyes watering.

I looked at both her and Wyatt, his bare chest cut and bleeding. I wasn't dead, his body was insane, but it no longer made me giddy or held the need to touch him.

"*Dziubuś.*" Ash's rough tone sent heat between my legs. I craned my neck to see him come up behind me. His attention was on my ex, noticing I was checking him out, his jaw clenching. Possessiveness curled like a heavy coat around me.

Mine.

I could feel the vibration, the energy Ash was pushing into the ground, like he wanted everyone around to feel it. Perceive his intentions.

Without thinking, I slipped my hand in his, letting him pull me up, my body flush with his.

"Thank you," I whispered.

"For what?"

"For being there." *Saving me back. Being my anchor.*

He wiped the drying blood from my face. "Always."

I kissed him, not even thinking about anyone else, not hiding the chemistry between us, but I could hear my father's growl, everyone's eyes on us, taking in what we couldn't hide.

"Oh, fuck no—" My father was cut off by a squawk splintering the sky, whirling me and Ash toward the sound.

Nyx swooped over the castle, pulling my focus outside our group. Mounds of bodies dotted the terrain, the ruler of Russia and his wife, Dubthach, Sonya and Iain—the castle of monster lore was their graveyard.

Another screech came overhead. Brexley pointed her gun, firing into the sky, but the hawk sailed away, her cries dissipating into the distance.

"Fuck, that bitch *won't* die." She rolled her shoulder, where wounds from bird claws could be seen through her torn shirt.

Ash's family and mine had moved in a protective circle around each other, still on guard. Wounded, hobbling and bloody, but all alive.

Except the threat was still not over.

A deep growl came from Uncle West and Cole, their dweller forms hunching and snarling as figures moved from the dark to us.

Z, Rhino, Beetle, Boar, Joska, Samu, Balazs, and a few other *Primul* I didn't recognize stood yards away.

Aunt Gabby etched her claws into the dirt, baring her teeth while Uncle Dax and Dom moved around me, probably at my father's order.

"No." Aunt Zoey stepped out in front, her petite frame dwarfed by the monsters. "No more fighting." Ryker and Croygen instantly moved in behind her like bodyguards. "There will be no more death here tonight. You will leave my family alone."

Z's chin jerked, his eyes flaming with what I swore was hurt before flickering to anger.

"Family?" His throat rattled. "Am I not your family... *Mother*?"

Zoey's silence tightened his shoulders, though emotion twitched in her jaw.

"Yes, I know. I was never the favorite," Z jeered. "Guess it goes to pretty boy here." He flicked his chin at Wyatt. "Though I still should be above my brother Zeke. I mean, he did murder your sister, rip out her guts in front of you."

Uncle Croygen grunted, stepping closer behind Zoey, his sword ready to swing. Rage narrowed his dark eyes. Kat stayed close next to him, ready to shed blood alongside him.

"You killed one of mine." Z gestured to the head of the snake near him. "What makes you think I won't kill all of you in retaliation?"

"What makes you think we won't just kill you first?" Ryker snarled, his axe twirling in his grip, his white eyes narrowing.

"She won't let you." Z smiled down at Zoey. "Or you would've already, right, *Mom*?"

"Don't underestimate me," she replied coldly. "It never works out well for those who do."

Ryker stepped forward, and I noticed Warwick came around the other side, holding his own battle blade. A harmony of snarls came from the dwellers, most of them still in their beast form. Aunt Fionna, Piper, my mom, and I grouped together, our magic humming between us. Brexley moved closer, and dead bodies started to twitch. An icy feeling different than the cold temperature rose the hair on my neck like a ghost brushed over me.

Z's eyes darted around, his stinger tail dripping with poison, feeling the sensation too, taking it all in, ready to fight. They were strong, but we had the numbers now.

"I think there will be more death here tonight. Am I right, Kovacs?" Warwick smirked, something telling me there was more to those two than I realized. Like they were messengers of death.

The dwellers agreed, rumbling in unison, inching forward, ready to pounce on their prey.

It was so fast, Z's reaction blurring my vision. He lurched out, grabbing the arm of someone close, and bringing her to him, using her as a shield. A hostage.

"Hanna!" Scorpion bellowed as Z clutched the blonde to him, his stinger primed at her neck.

"This is not our war. We couldn't give a fuck about fighting you. You are nothing to me." Z's eyes darted to Zoey.

"You think we're gonna let you walk away after kidnapping and raping women?" Ryker snarled.

Z took a few steps back, Hanna tensing as the stinger skimmed her throat.

"Don't fucking touch her," Scorpion roared.

Z nuzzled into her neck, his eyes on Scorpion, but then paused, as if something caught his noticed about her. His tongue flicked out, looking like a hairy comb, every fiber picking up the taste of her skin, his nose sniffing her. Hanna stiffened under his touch.

"Interesting." He hummed. "You're like them." He indicated Joska and Samu, but his attention stayed solely on Hanna, like she captivated him. "But even stronger." He tasted her again. "Powerful." His eyes glinted with excitement. Lust. "You are extraordinary. A queen hidden among the slaves."

"Don't touch me," she hissed, her cat teeth showing in her mouth.

"You can fight it, but you know the truth, don't you, wildcat? You don't belong with them." He moved her blonde hair away from her neck and whispered something in her ear.

Hanna went still, her nose flaring, her teeth chomping down. A smile twisted Z's face as he placed a kiss to her throat. His stinger moved in a blink, slicing behind her ear.

She screamed.

"Hanna!" Scorpion bellowed, lunging for her.

Z shoved her forward, crashing her into Scorpion, both of them colliding to the ground.

"Someday soon, wildcat. You'll come for me." He winked, then turned and took off, the rest of his crew following, including Joska, Samu, and Balazs.

The dwellers roared in fury, tearing into the ground and chasing after them into the forest. Ryker, Croygen, Kat, his pirate crew, Eli, Ember, Warwick, Wesley, Brexley, Caden, and Birdie followed behind.

"Viper?" Scorpion cupped Hanna's face, tilting her neck to show the wound. It didn't look like a normal stinger wound, but almost a mark on her skin. A P symbol.

Primul.

"I'm fine." She shrugged off the injury like it was nothing.

"He stung you!" Scorpion pushed her hands away, using the sleeve of his shirt to swab the gash.

"*It's fine.*" She tried to reassure him, but her eyes wouldn't meet his. "He didn't inject me with any poison."

"Are you sure about that?" Scorpion huffed, still wiping at her cut.

Hanna looked away, staring back at where the *Primul* escaped.

"Raven?" My mother took my hand, taking my attention from them, panic hinting in her tone. "Where is your brother?"

The soul is infinite in the love it can hold, the parts it stores away and carries at all times. You can hold so many various types within your body, burrowing deep or skimming the surface.

A twin was wound through your DNA, baked in your essence, entrenched in your makeup. A piece no one could reach. It was a bond nobody could truly understand unless they were one.

Rook was as much a part of me as I was of him. There was no me without him. My partner in crime, my best friend, and sometimes my worst rival. But if you touched one of us, hell would rain down. We protected each other, defended each other, and would kill for each other. And there wasn't even a question that we'd lay our lives down for the other.

Every strike of my boot's sole grew louder in my ears. A numbing terror gripped my stomach as I tried to detect Rook's absence. To see if part of me had been ripped out, the pain so deep I no longer understood loss.

Rook? The cry came from the marrow of my bones, black dots sprinkled through my vision, my lungs quivering as I ran up the steps to the castle, my family trailing behind me, their own fear choking the air.

The courtyard came into view, and I stumbled to a stop, my lungs compressing.

Rook's dweller lay in the middle, his enormous mass taking up a section of the small yard, the arrows torn out and scattered over the cobblestones.

Celeste knelt next to him, her hand running over his fur while two tiny figures stood on top of him like kings on a mountain.

"I'm telling you, these are magic fingers, Lake Lady," Opie huffed. "They have healing powers when I stick them in holes!"

Chirp!

"I've gotten them in smaller places!"

My twin's chest rose and lowered in shallow movements.

He was still alive. Barely.

"Rook!" Mom cried, pushing past me, running to her son, my dad right behind her.

My terror and relief had me frozen in place. Both agony and joy tussled through my body; I couldn't breathe, the effects of the battle wanting to drop me to my knees.

Mom landed next to Celeste, her hand going to his bloody fur, her eyes closing, her seer searching through his pain. My father stood over him, calling his name, demanding his boy open his eyes.

"He's trying to fight the poison," Mom uttered, not really speaking to anyone. "But it's too much. We have to do something. He's dying." Her pleading eyes went to her husband as they shared a moment of unfathomable anguish.

"We will not lose him, little bird. I promise," Dad growled with determination, declaring something he might have no control over.

There were so many people with extraordinary powers here—healers, Druids, necromancers, yet none of them could do anything against the pure goblin metal in his veins. It was something none of us could fight. We were powerless to help, knowing it would take a miracle.

A wish.

Holy. Shit.

Rushing for my brother's body, I crashed down next to him, my fingers dragging through his fur, feeling for the wounds. A noise worked up his throat, a familiar rattle, as if he felt me there. That part of each other's soul. The other half of him.

I'm here, little brother.

The sound of him suffering, taking anguishing breaths, his lungs faltering, roared my own beast up. The need to protect him shook through me.

My brother's form shuddered, like his body was losing the battle.

Don't you dare die on me! I forbid you!

I clutched the necklace in my palm. *I wish for you to heal him!* I asked the necklace again, the wish hissing through my mind, directed at another man I loved. *Save him.*

Slamming my hands on one of his wounds, I poured everything I had left into him. The power careened into me, and it felt like I was being sliced in pieces. The pain blanched my mind, crashing my senses. I yanked at every molecule of toxin that mingled in his blood, extracting it from him.

The obscurer hissed from my lips, preying on the poison in his blood.

"Raven!" I felt more than heard Ash calling me. A hand came over mine, his other covering an arrow wound on my brother's, taking on some of the weight, letting it siphon through him as well.

The connection of us together surged through Rook, a blinding light chasing out the darkness. His wound gushed with black tar, magic cleaning out the deadly poison with force. Rook jerked, his roar pelting the sky, calling to the stars as life and death staged their last battle before one side fell.

Rook's back arched, his blades shimmering in the moonlight, his teeth dripping with salvia, eyes fire red. Another howl echoed, then his body went limp, sagging to the stone, half shifting back to his human form, his chest moving up and down with steady intakes.

Silence echoed like a heartbeat. It felt like the earth was holding its breath. Waiting.

A sharp gasp came from him, his body convulsing, his lids springing open.

"Rook!" I called out, but it came out a whisper compared to my mother's cry, her arms pulling him to her as she sobbed over him.

I sagged back with a whimper, relieved. Ash wrapped his arms around me, holding me up and giving me strength.

Dad grabbed Rook's shredded clothes, covering him as Mom held her son, sobbing softly, but this time in joy. Dad grabbed my hand, the other on Rook, our family holding each other.

"I think that belongs to me," a man declared, twisting our attention to the ordinary figure standing in the entry to the courtyard.

Dzsinn nodded at my necklace and took a step forward. "It is not meant to be held by those outside the jinn line," he stated, sticking out his hand.

I understood why. The lure of such power at your fingertips. To know you could escape death, challenge fate, and be granted life and wishes beyond your dreams. It was corrupting and heady, tempting you to lose yourself in it.

Ash reached around my neck, unclasping the chain. The stone fell into his palm.

He stood, turning to Dzsinn.

"We are even. I owe you nothing."

Dzsinn dipped his head.

"You have my word. The favors you owed have been met."

"And Scorpion's too."

Dzsinn's mouth curled, his head shaking.

"That is not how it works. Scorpion understands what he got himself into."

Ash's nose flared, but knew he couldn't change it. He dropped the chain into the genie's hand. The instant the stone touched his skin, blue light blazed behind the genie's eyes, a color so beautiful I heard myself gasp before his irises went back to a muddy brown.

He let his lids close, his shoulders easing as if finally he was whole. Dzsinn pocketed the stone and turned to leave.

"What about Kalaraja?" Ash asked.

"What about him?" Dzsinn stopped at the entry again. "He fulfilled his favor to me. Whatever you have between you is your problem now. Though he is not a dumb man. I would think he'd be long gone from here." *For now,* echoed in my ears. But Kalaraja was a problem for another day.

Dzsinn's form slipped into the shadows and vanished, leaving us to the quiet death after a battle, where blood and bodies soaked the earth, and the legends of a story held nothing to the reality of it.

Chapter 27

Ash

In the shadowy air Dzsinn had just faded away into, my name came hurling through the dark mist.

"Ash!" Warwick's voice kneaded into my bones, a tone I knew better than I knew myself. After centuries of knowing each other, being at his side in every type of fight, I understood the smallest pitch difference.

Blood rushed up to my ears, my chest squeezing with fear as Warwick stomped in, a limp body in his arms.

"Wesley!" I strangled out, my gaze running over the two puncture marks carving through his gut and chest—holes the size of boar tusks or rhino horns.

Wesley gasped for air, sounding like a lung had been punctured, his eyes wide with terror, understanding what was happening. Each breath might be his last.

"Can you help him?" Warwick kneeled down, placing Wesley on the ground, Scorpion and Brexley right at his side as more yells came from behind them.

"We need a healer!" Eli and Cooper hollered. Their alpha, Cole, was draped in their grasp, holes gouged into his side.

"Fuck!" Lorcan dashed over, helping his brother as more injured came limping in. Birdie, Dom, Ryker, Croygen, Cooper, Gabby and some others were cut up and moving slowly.

"He's bleeding out!" Brexley tried to cover Wesley's wound. Her magic hummed around her, though it wasn't as powerful as when she had the nectar. She could no longer yank lives out of death's hands.

Nor could I.

"I can't stop it." I ripped at my shirt, using it to plug one of his wounds. "I don't have any of my herbs."

"Stay with us, Wes!" Brexley demanded. His body struggled to take in air, but I could see the glaze taking over his vibrant eyes, his skin ashen.

"No!" Scorpion ripped off his own shirt, blocking the other hole. "You are going to be fine."

I placed my hands on his chest, pumping them for air, trying to pull from the earth, yet it barely responded. Like it had given enough to me, depleted its source. Tree fairies were healers, but through using nature's herbs. We couldn't just keep someone alive. What Raven and I had, what mates could create, wasn't transferable. Not in the way Wesley needed.

"Cole!" Ember cried out, jerking my head to her, their alpha shaking violently on the ground. Dying.

"Lorcan! Ember!" Kennedy called out, and I could see her taking control, her head held high. "Get them through the doors to my healers! Now!"

Without hesitation, the pirates and dwellers lifted the injured, following Ember as Lorcan picked up his son, racing for the fae door.

"Wes, hold on, okay? We're gonna get you help." Brexley's voice shook while blood soaked into my shirt. Wesley's gaze was no longer fearful, his expression resigned. Death was claiming him.

Warwick leaned over to lift him, but Wesley placed his palm on his arm.

"Let me die here," he struggled to say, wheezing loudly.

"Fuck off. You are not dying," Scorpion snapped. "Not here, not ever, brother."

"Wesley!" Birdie crawled to him, cuts running across her face and chest, akin to pincer wounds from a Stag beetle. "Don't you fucking die on me. Don't leave me alone with these assholes."

He snorted, only making him choke on blood.

They had known each other for a long time. The stories of Scorpion, Maddox, Birdie, and Wesley went back even before they joined Andris's group. Their bond was like Warwick, Kitty, and me. Family.

Wesley reached up, touching her face. "Don't worry, B." He brushed her blonde, bloody hair out of her eyes. "Maddox is waiting with a drink for me."

A sob bucked out of Birdie. Scorpion's nose flared, his eyes filling with liquid.

"Maddox can wait a while longer. We need you here." I could hear the plea in his statement. *I need you here.*

Losing Maddox had ripped Scorpion up. Wesley was unraveling the seams Scorpion had just sewn back together.

"Take care of her," Wesley ordered Scorpion, his chin flicking to Hanna. He dropped his gaze to Birdie. "And you take care of him." He touched Birdie's hand, glancing at Scorpion. "He's gonna take this really hard and turn into an asshole again."

"He's already an asshole." Birdie tried to tease, tears falling down her face. This was a person who never cried.

He threaded his hand into Birdie's, a love so pure in his eyes. She was more than a friend. She was a little sister.

"Wes…" Panic trounced on Scorpion as his friend's eyes shut for the final time.

A sob came from Brexley, her body shivering as if his soul slid through her on his way out, saying a final goodbye.

"NO!" Scorpion bayed, shaking his friend, trying to get him to wake up, but we all knew it was no use.

Brexley grabbed Scorpion, pulling him into her arms, whispering something in his ear, causing his body to slump over in grief. Birdie leaned her head into Wesley's, kissing his cheek, tears falling from her face onto his skin.

I couldn't take it, my heart having enough loss. Enough pain. And as much as I understood I could do nothing, watching another friend die, especially over something I got him into, burned at that wound that might never heal.

Standing up, I turned, my chest raging in agony and helplessness. I could barely breathe as I stumbled away in grief.

Raven's green eyes met mine, her expression pained. She rushed into my arms, holding me, being the strength I needed, though I understood it was only temporary.

The queen stood yards away from us, her expression torn, her body pulled between wanting to follow her son and stay with her daughter.

Brushing her knotted hair back, I held Raven tightly to me. "You need to go."

"What?" She jerked her head up, understanding my meaning. "No."

"You have to."

"No." She furrowed her brow, shaking her head. "I'm not leaving you."

"*Dziubuś,*" I whispered, trying to fight the selfishness in me that wanted to demand she stay with me forever. "Your family needs you right now." I flicked my gaze quickly to her mother. "Your brother *needs* you."

A sound worked up her throat, hitting the very target I knew it would. Her twin was as much a part of her as what we shared.

"I don't want to leave you." Her voice cracked.

"I know you don't." I cupped her face.

"Come with me." She grasped at my torn shirt, but I could see she already knew my response. Knew the reality of our outcome. Our worlds were so different.

My family needed me. And I was not walking away from those people trapped below us, in a hell they might never recover from.

"It won't be forever." My voice skated the ground, my grip on her so tight. "I'll come for you."

She tried to hold back her sob when my mouth claimed hers, feeling like I was ripping my own heart out of my chest. My tongue twined with hers, kissing her so deep, I felt her dweller rumble.

"Go." I broke the kiss. "Go before I change my mind and claim you in front of everyone."

"That's only making me want to stay," she muttered against my mouth.

In all the agony and pain, my lips twitched in a smile. "*Mroczny, kocham cię.*"

"I love you too." She kissed me before turning away and running to her mother.

Their arms went around each other, holding tightly as they strode away. Raven's green eyes found mine before they disappeared down the steps. My heart lurched up my throat, trailing after her like a lost child, wanting to go with her more than it wanted to stay in my chest.

A buzzing itchiness descended on me the moment she was gone, my legs wanting to run after her, my lungs not feeling like they could totally fill with air. I took a step; the pull to her spun my head.

But a soft sob drew my attention back to my friends. Caked blood, deep wounds, and grief covered them all. My revenge had painted a red path from Budapest to here, and my family followed it without question.

They all had been through so much and continued to stand up against corrupted power. Some might say we won, but those in battle learned quickly that there would be no winner in war. Only death and sacrifice.

Later that night, when dawn kissed the horizon, we ventured down into the tunnels, waking those who discovered a profound truth.

Just because you were left standing at the end didn't always mean you were the lucky ones.

Chapter 28

Raven

I stared numbly at the huge family portrait hanging on the wall, at the girl of sixteen, sitting so primly, her ankles crossed, in a gorgeous gown. No one would have known she didn't want to be there, her smile too perfect, but I could see it in her eyes. Her mind was already on the party later that night, where she was hoping to lose her virginity.

To the boy she thought was her future. Her mate.

My hand went to my chest, the ache constant, ceaselessly worming a hole through my heart.

"I'll come for you."

It had been over two months.

Two months of endless TV and magazine interviews I tried to dodge, constant meetings with Lars and my mother over what happened, copious amounts of lectures from my aunts, uncles, and especially my father, and a barrage of engagements and events I had to smile for. But all that I could get through. For Rook. He kept me from fleeing.

While Uncle Cole had recovered quickly, my brother was still recuperating, still not able to get through a full day without resting for a few hours. Some days he struggled to get out of bed. The healers said the pure goblin metal poison had been in his bloodstream too long, but they were hopeful he'd recover fully in time, which didn't ease my guilt. It chewed on me daily, no matter how much my brother told me it wasn't my fault.

Because it was.

Uncle Dax teased that Rook didn't want to heal fast because he had such a hot nurse at his bedside. Celeste, so different than the sultry, dominant girl I met months before, had become quiet and solemn. She had followed Rook back to the castle and didn't leave his side throughout his healing journey. Even when her stomach grew with her attacker's baby. A *Primul* baby, which she grew more protective of daily.

My parents weren't crazy about her being around. Something was off with her behavior, but they didn't say much after Rook blew up over them trying to move Celeste out of his room.

The relationship was odd between them, as I never saw anything intimate happen at all, not even holding hands, whispers, or longing looks. But there was something. Something undefined and tangible. A bond no one could understand, but it was there.

"I'll come for you." Ash's voice repeated in my head for the thousandth time.

But you haven't. I snapped back in my mind. We had talked a few times, but every time, he was helping one of Sonya's victims resettle in their new life or helping Warwick and Scorpion, picking up Wesley's old job.

I knew I was being bratty and selfish, wanting him to forget who he was, to give up his life and come here for me, knowing he'd be miserable.

Like you are? I sighed to myself, strolling past my family's painting and heading toward my room, where another stunning dress was laid out for me for another event that evening. It was with leaders of some country or another. I wanted to tell them all to fuck off while I stayed in my sweats, ate takeout, and wrapped myself in my blankets. Instead of talking about assisting the homeless at a party while eating shrimp tartlets, I wanted to actually be helping them. Like Aunt Zoey did with the orphanage.

The events were necessary, and my mom did all she could, but I felt even more impatient with this life.

Stifled.

Caged.

We all knew the history; it was my Aunt Ember who was supposed to be queen. Who was the rightful heir to the throne. It was her bloodline, her title. But she didn't want it. She chose a different life with Uncle Eli, handing the title and position to my mother instead.

She chose a different life.

"Raven." The familiar voice jerked my head to the speaker.

His six-foot-three frame stood in the hall wearing a tux, his blond hair slicked back, his scruff thicker, his white-blue eyes taking me in with affection but also a touch of caution.

"Wyatt. You look dapper." I smiled, motioning to his suit, strolling to him. A wave of love rolled over me, but this time it was a different love. This was friendship love. "How are you?"

Piper and I were doing better, but we still weren't chummy like we once were. They tried really hard not to shove their love in my face. In the two months back home, I had only seen him at a few events with Piper. I missed my old friend.

"Good." He nodded, a glint in his eyes, telling me he was thinking about Piper. "Really good. Thank you."

"I'm happy for you." I reached up, wrapping my arms around him in a hug. "Really happy for you both."

His shoulders eased, his arms tightening around me. "Thank you, Ravy."

Pulling back, his gaze ran over me, his head tilting. "What about you?"

"I'm good." I put on a smile, forcing a laugh. "A lot better place than I was when I left here last."

Wyatt was not one for bullshit, his mouth flattening at my attempt to fake anything.

"Rav," he grumbled, his grumpiness coming out. He was so like his father. "You can tell me the truth."

Sighing, I looked away. What did he want me to say? That I missed Ash so much it hurt to breathe? That I hated it here, though I loved my family more than anything?

"Just because we don't hang out all the time now doesn't mean I don't still know you." He folded his arms. "I can see you are miserable."

"Aren't we all at these events?" I tossed out my arms.

"Raven." That tone used to make me giddy, thinking the more I pushed him, the more he'd fight for me. It meant he loved me. Except Wyatt usually ended up walking away, irritated, while my brother would shake his head, seeing what I couldn't.

I wasn't the girl Wyatt would stand and fight against. And he wasn't the boy.

I understood it now.

Ash never backed away. He challenged me at every turn.

The thought of him pulled a sob from my throat. "I miss him," I whispered.

"Then why don't *you* go to him?" he countered.

"What?" I laughed. "Just leave? Like it's so easy?"

"I didn't say it was easy, but it's not impossible."

"Oh, I don't know, maybe because I'm the princess!" I exclaimed. "The next in line."

"And you hate it," Wyatt said. "You *always* have. You never wanted to be queen or in the public eye." Even if I had become comfortable with who I was and no longer would hide my traits, it still wasn't something I wanted to flash around. People in general were judgmental and wanted a reason to tear me down. Even more so because I was royal.

"So?" I shrugged. "Doesn't mean I can just walk away from it. I can't do that again to my parents."

"Maybe not completely, but your mother isn't going anywhere, and why do you have to be next in line?" he asked. "Why not Rook?"

Rook was made to pick up the mantle from my mom. He liked this life.

"Have you even told your parents you don't want to be the ruler?"

I blinked. "Not directly."

"They love you, Rav. You know they'd want you happy." He shrugged one shoulder, a device in his pocket beeping. He took it out, peering at the updated mobile phone Lars was testing, his eyes glinting.

"Piper?"

He grinned. Fuck, that boy was in love. How did I not see it before?

"Yeah." He stuffed the cell back into his pocket.

"You better go." I nudged at him.

He nodded, about to turn, but stopped, looking back at me. "You know those stories we used to make up about people at the parties?"

"Yeah."

"Don't wait for someone else to give you a story, Raven. Go write your own." Wyatt strode away, heading for the woman he wanted his fairy tale with.

I just needed the guts to do the same.

Chapter 29

Ash

"Fuck, I'm exhausted." Scorpion slunk down in the seat across from mine, his lids closing briefly. "I need a drink."

"Yeah." I nodded, feeling the train jerk as it pulled out of the Prague station. We had just finished a run from Budapest to Prague for Brexley's uncle, and now were heading back. Besides the supplies, a few newly human-fae went to work with Mykel, looking for a new life.

Getting the victims of Sonya settled was one of the things bringing me solace lately. It felt good to see them thriving with their new powers, learning to adapt, finding a new home to settle into away from the horrors they went through.

However, not everyone in the tunnels survived that night, and a handful did not want our help, running off like they could escape the truth. But for the last three months, for those who did want help, I did everything I could to give them the chance.

I worked hard for Scorpion and Warwick, proving to everyone they could trust me again. Believe in me. I owed my family everything, and I threw myself into work. I picked up every job I could in Warwick and Scorpion's "supply" business, keeping myself so busy I could ignore the ache in my chest. The pull to her that saturated my dreams and consumed the moments I let my mind wander.

Every second, the desire to go to her was outright painful, but the memory of letting Wesley die, knowing every one of those *Primul* had escaped that night, made me put my head down and work harder.

"Fuck, this train better be fast." Scorpion shifted in his seat. "I need to get home to Hanna."

"How is she?" I already knew the answer but felt Scorpion needed to get it out.

He huffed, his eyes going distant, running a hand through his hair. "Like she hasn't been through enough," he muttered, his hand rolling in a fist. "She has nightmares almost every night, though she tries to hide them from me."

The mark on her neck never healed; the engraved *P* etched into her skin was just as red and vibrant as the day she got it.

A darkness fluttered over Scorpion.

"What?"

He exhaled and appeared to be debating whether to tell me.

"She calls out his name sometimes."

"What?" My eyes popped. "Z's?"

"Not in a sexual way. Like he's tormenting her through her dreams." He swallowed. "Like he's calling to her." He shook his head. "Probably just trauma from her past coming up again."

"Yeah." I pressed my lips together. Hanna had been through more than most. "I'll make something to help her sleep. Take away her dreams."

"Thank you." Scorpion dipped his chin. I could see her hurt was breaking him into pieces.

"She'll get through this. She is so fucking strong."

"She is." He nodded. "Okay, I think I'm gonna go get a drink. Want anything, you miserable pain in the ass?" He stood up, already walking toward the refreshment carriage.

I was here and working, but everyone saw how miserable I was without her.

"No." I shook my head. I didn't fully give up drinking, but I still hated how low they'd seen me, picking me up from the gutters. Plus, drinking made me want her more.

The slice of pain at the mere thought of her closed my lids, the train rattling down the tracks lulling me into my thoughts. My fingers rhythmically played with the two plastic objects in my jacket pocket, things I kept with me at all times, reminding me of her.

I told her I would come for her. It was the truth, but I needed to get my shit together. Set things right with my family. I had hurt them a lot. But the agony in my chest was getting too much to bear, and it was showing. If becoming part of her world was how I kept her, then that's what I would do.

No choice existed for me now.

The scent of a flaky apple strudel and coffee filled my nose, and the rustling of someone sitting across from me opened my eyes. "That was fas—" I stopped and went still, but my heart felt like it was tumbling through my chest.

I blinked several times. No fucking way.

"You didn't even shower, did you?" Her nose wrinkled, her gaze going over my jeans and t-shirt, dirty from moving cargo.

Shock dropped my mouth open, a sense of déjà vu rolling through me, but my brain wasn't accepting the beautiful creature my eyes were taking in. She wore casual jeans and a V-neck t-shirt with no expensive earrings or charms this time. Just her. Nothing like the girl I sat across from back in December.

"What—" I sat up straight. "What are you doing here?"

"This time, it better not be because you spent the night in a brothel." She ignored me, taking a bite of the strudel, a cheeky smile growing on her face. "At least not without me."

The ache in my soul throbbed like a heartbeat, my body shaking with the need to touch her. "I better not be dreaming."

"Why don't you find out?"

"Raven," I croaked, scrambling from my chair. I grabbed her, the coffee spilling on the floor as I yanked her from her seat and heaved her into me, my mouth crashing down on hers. Hunger vibrated my body with a growl, something in my soul settling in place. I devoured her, not caring about the young family a few seats away. Nothing else mattered more than having her in my arms again. "Fuck, I can breathe again," I muttered against her lips before claiming them again. Her hands tangled in my hair, matching my intensity with her own. My fingers threaded through her glossy strands, cut a few inches shorter than before, as I reached for her face.

Staring down into her stunning eyes, I shook my head. "Seriously, what are you doing here?"

"I was tired of waiting." She smirked. "So I came for you. My dweller is possessive. She doesn't like not getting what she wants."

I leaned over, my teeth nipping at the tendon in her neck, feeling her jerk under me, her dweller becoming submissive to me.

"Ash," she whispered, and I smelled her wetness, her desire.

"How long do I have before you need to go back?" I muttered in her ear.

"As long as you will have me."

"What?" I pulled back, my eyebrows knitting.

"I realized following in my mother's shoes is not what I want. I want to be in the action, living life on my terms," she said. "I sat down with my parents and told them I no longer want to be an active royal."

"Wh-what?" I sputtered.

"They didn't fight me because they saw I wasn't happy." She wrinkled her nose. "Though there were some compromises."

"Compromises?"

"I finish school," she stated. "But lucky enough, Budapest has a university I am very interested in."

"Oh, really?" I couldn't stop touching her.

"Yes, and I will have to do some international diplomatic things when the king and queen need me to step in, especially in dealing with both Romania and Russia."

Both countries were in upheaval after their presidents were murdered. President Lazar and President Kozlov, along with their wives, were victims of Sonya. Many were trying to stake their claim and seize power, creating an even more unstable environment within the already turbulent countries. It was not going well for the innocent people just trying to live their lives.

"Yes, I hear from Killian there are a lot of issues with both countries. Might take a long time to work out. Like centuries. At least."

"I heard even longer than that."

"So, you are here. To stay?" My hands roamed over her figure. Fuck, she was stunning.

"Yes, but I think my father will be heading here to settle me into school. He mentioned wanting to speak *with that fucking tree fairy trying to steal his daughter*." She nipped at my lips.

"If I can handle his daughter…" I tucked hair behind her ear. "I can surely handle him." I couldn't stop smiling, but I forced myself to, gazing down at her seriously. "You're sure you're okay with this?"

"You have given up and lost so much in your life." She peered up at me. "I thought it was time someone sacrificed for you."

"So going to school in the stunning city of Budapest, with no job, while getting fucked multiple times a day is a sacrifice?"

"A girl's gotta do what a girl's gotta do." She shrugged with a grin. She quickly went serious, her thumb sliding over my bottom lip. "Look, I don't know what I want to do with my life right now. I just know whatever it is, it's with you."

"And what I want to do with my life… is you." I pulled her in, my lips grazing hers. "You know how insatiable nature fairies are? We're relentless."

"Do you know how horny dark dwellers are? Ravenous." She wrapped her arms around my neck.

I yanked out the pair of die from my pocket, the ones I had used on her in the brothel that one night. My lucky dice. Though Opie still was pissed I ruined his costume. He got me back, taking an extra chapter from the fae book to create a dress with a cape.

I twirled the die between my fingers, watching Raven's mouth gape. "Is that…?"

"Yep." I smirked. "Ready to take a gamble?"

"With you? Always." Her mouth brushed mine. "You know, we never did end up fucking on a train."

"We need to remedy that. Now." I lifted her up, her legs wrapping around my waist as I headed for the caboose cart, not caring what thieves, killers, and criminals were among them, watching me fuck her hard in the hay, listening to her scream and cry out my name.

Because we were the baddest monsters there.

THE END!!!

About the Author

USA Today Best-Selling Author Stacey Marie Brown is a lover of hot fictional bad boys and sarcastic heroines who kick butt. She also enjoys books, travel, TV shows, hiking, writing, design, and archery. Stacey is lucky enough to live and travel all over the world.
She grew up in Northern California, where she ran around on her family's farm, raising animals, riding horses, playing flashlight tag, and turning hay bales into cool forts.

When she's not writing, she's out hiking, spending time with friends, and traveling. She also volunteers helping animals and is eco-friendly. She feels all animals, people, and the environment should be treated kindly.

To learn more about Stacey or her books, visit her at:

Author website & Newsletter: www.staceymariebrown.com

Linktree: https://linktr.ee/authorstaceymariebrown

Facebook Author page: www.facebook.com/SMBauthorpage

Pinterest: www.pinterest.com/s.mariebrown

TikTok: @authorstaceymariebrown

Instagram: www.instagram.com/staceymariebrown/

Goodreads:
www.goodreads.com/author/show/6938728.StaceyMarie_Brown

Stacey's Facebook group:
www.facebook.com/groups/1648368945376239/

Bookbub: www.bookbub.com/authors/stacey-marie-brown

Acknowledgments

I couldn't do this alone, so a massive thanks to:

Colleen - Thank you for being the I in "we" and always having my back. Couldn't do this without you.
Mo & Wendy - Thank you for making it readable! So lucky to have you both to make me sound intelligent!
Jay Aheer - So much beauty. I am in love with your work!
Judi Fennell - Always fast and always spot on!

To all the readers who have supported me - My gratitude is for all you do and how much you help indie authors out of the pure love of reading.

To all the indie/hybrid authors out there who inspire, challenge, support, and push me to be better: I love you!

And to anyone who has picked up an indie book and given an unknown author a chance. THANK YOU!

Contemporary Romance

Down for the Count

How the Heart Breaks

Buried Alive

Smug Bastard

The Unlucky Ones

Blinded Love Series
Shattered Love (#1)
Broken Love (#2)
Twisted Love (#3)

Royal Watch Series
Royal Watch (#1)
Royal Command (#2)

Foreign Translations

Italian Editions

L'oscurita Della Luce Serie (Darkness Vol. 1) (Darkness of Light)
Il fuoco nell'oscurità: serie (Darkness Vol. 2)
Gli abitanti dell'oscurità (Darkness Vol. 3)
Il sangue oltre le tenebre (Darkness Vol. 4)
Blood Beyond Darkness (Darkness Vol 5)
West (Darkness Vol 6)
City in Embers (Collectors Vol 1)
The Barrier Between (Collectors Vol 2)
Across the Divide (Collectors Vol 3)
From Burning Ashes (Collectors Vol 4)
The Crown of Light (Lightness Saga #1)
Lightness Falls (Lightness Saga #2)
The Fall of the King (Lightness Saga #3)
Rise from the Embers (Lightness Saga #4)
Savage Lands (Savage Lands Series #1)
Pezzi di me (Shattered Love) (Blinded Love Series #1)
Broken Love (Blinded Love Series #2)
Twisted Love (Blinded Love Series #3)
Descending into Madness (Winterland Series #1)
Ascending from Madness (Winterland Series #2)
Royal Watch (Royal Watch Series #1)
Royal Command (Royal Watch Series #2)
The Unlucky Ones
Buried Alive

Portuguese Editions

Savage Lands (Savage Lands Series #1)
Wild Lands (Savage Lands Series #2)
Dead Lands (Savage Lands Series #3)
Bad Lands (Savage Lands Series #4)
Blood Lands (Savage Lands Series #5)
Shadow Lands (Savage Lands Series #6)
Silver Tongue Devil (Croygen Duet #1)
Devil in Boots (Croygen Duet #2)
Caindo na Loucura (Ascending into Madness) (Winterland Tales Livro 1)
Saindo da Loucura (Ascending into Madness)(Winterland Tales Livro 2)
Beauty in Her Madness (Winterland Tales #3)
Beast in His Madness (Winterland Tales #4)
Má Sorte (The Unlucky Ones)
Sob a Guarda da Realeza (Royal Watch #1)
Royal Command (Royal Watch #2)

Polish Editions

The Boy She Hates (Shattered Love #1)
Broken Love #2
Twisted Love #3

Czech Republic Editions

Divoká říše (Savage Lands #1)
Wild Lands #2
Dead Lands #3
Shattered Love #1

French Editions

Savage Lands #1
Wild Lands #2

Israel (Modern Hebrew) Editions

Savage Lands #1
Wild Lands #2
Dead Lands #3
Bad Lands #4
Blood Lands #5
Shadow Lands #6
How the Heart Breaks

Turkish Editions

Savage Lands #1
Wild Lands #2
Dead Lands #3

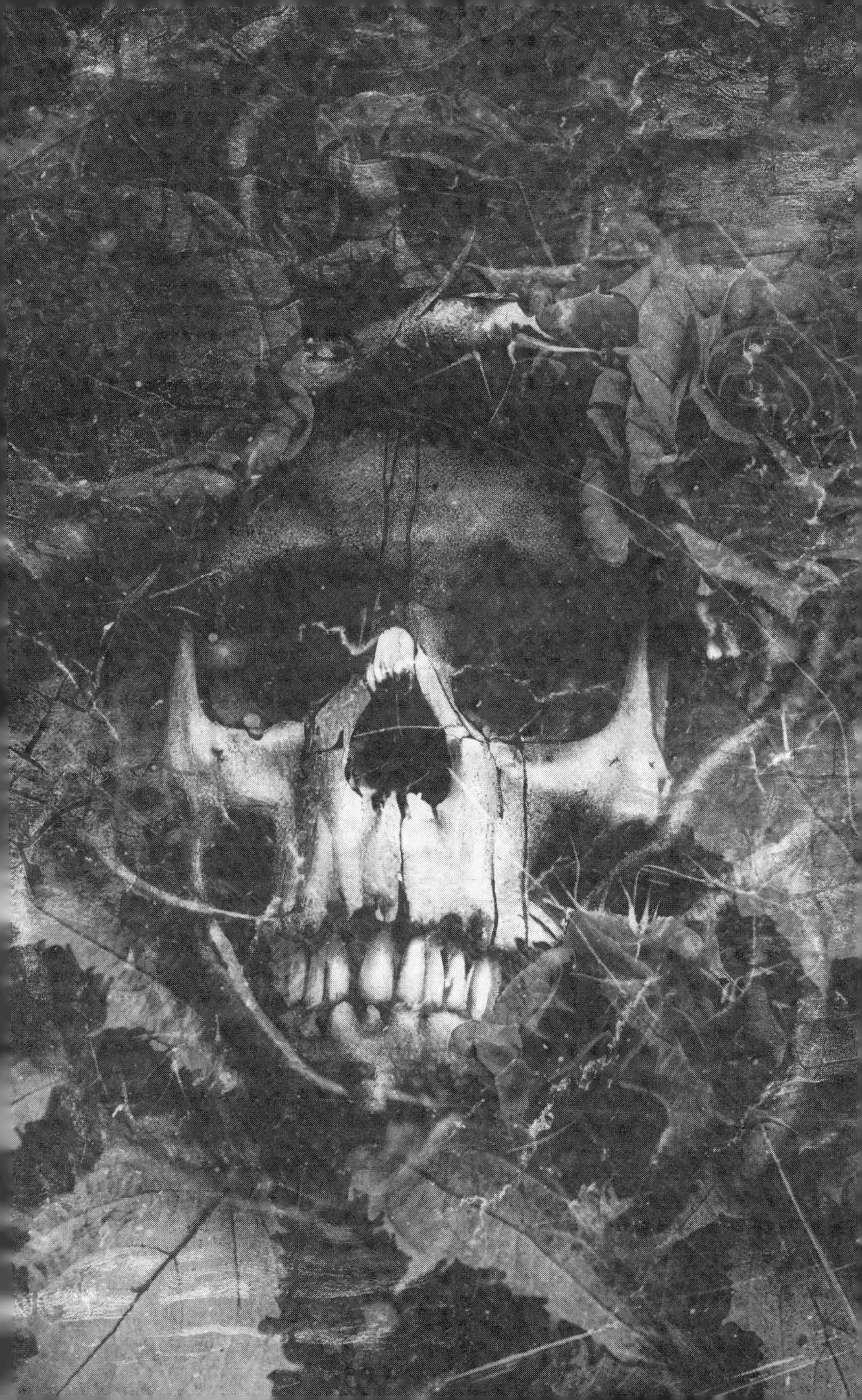

Made in the USA
Columbia, SC
18 January 2025

a0d88532-c92f-473c-9ff1-b952a056b1afR01